A Gekman Investigation

I0589728

By Rowyn Golde

Decided to my real-life Jed,
Alex Swehla

And friends who pushed me through this book:
Robert Silver
Dany Michael
Sophie Lafergola

ISBN 9781087991252
© Rowyn Golde 2021
Published by Team Manticore LLC

CHAPTER 1
Getting to Know You

Michael Crown's body was found half under a knee-high, round, snakewood table, clutching a small multi-tool. The handle had a mother of pearl inlay in the shape of the letter M. That's how the scene was described to me over the phone by Henry Shicovski, the grief-stricken fiancé. His voice quaked as he meandered through the details of the gruesome sight, including described the multi-tool as a gift he had given the victim not long ago.

The body had already been carted off by the time I got to the scene. Officer Hudson was still hanging around and finishing up some paperwork when I arrived. He took his hat off to scratch his pale scalp through thinning, white hair. Straight away, I wished aloud that I'd been there before the forensic team dismantled the place.

"So, he did call you," said Hudson.

"Oh, you were the one Henry spoke to then."

"Sure. He was outside when we showed up. Crying his eyes out, screamin' about the Crowns not letting him inside. He said he saw the body through the window, and the Crowns said he was crazy. I told him to get a lawyer, he didn't want one, two of us questioned him, and we got nothing else. He asked if there was anything more he could do outside us, so I told him you're the only PI in town. I don't want you in police business now, but I figure better you than anybody else." He shrugged and put his hat back on.

Hudson and I went back a few years, and I had left the force for my own practice only a few months prior to the Crown case. Surprised me that there was no bitterness between us, as he had more than once attempted to be an unwarranted father figure. I had rebuffed those attempts and not always graciously.

"Saying I'm the only one is almost an endorsement, I

guess. Well, I'm thankful you led him to me," I said.

"Also, Gekman," here it goes, "We need to talk to Henry again."

"You already questioned him."

Hudson made a face like he'd eaten something sour, "Maybe with you on his side, he'll open up a bit more. He's still a suspect, you know. Fact is that his story didn't make sense. It's not like the Crowns hid the body or lied about it. They're the ones who called us. He's talking about being pushed out, and I don't know about all that."

"Ah. Well, you should call him back then, eh?" Hudson didn't like that.

Sunlight cascaded through the large bay window to catch floating dust motes. That was the nature of such a large old house.

I jumped when the strange digging machines chugged and whirred outside. They were built like enormous capsules with a cockpit, different limbs and wheels depending on the job to be done. I had seen them on the way in, but I hadn't yet heard them in action. Despite the sleekness of their exterior plates, they were not quiet contraptions. They clicked and rattled in a discordant rumble. Tik Tik THONK TikTHUK Tik Tik Tik.

I composed myself to retrieve the small notebook I kept in my jacket pocket.

"What do those things do, anyway? Do you know?" I asked, gesturing loosely to the living room window.

Hudson looked out the window and said, "Yeah. They're for collecting a new energy source. Uh… It's like Lithium…" He had a look on his face that said he knew what he was talking about, and assumed I did not. I lifted an eyebrow and sucked in my cheek, trying not to be offended. He was right that I didn't know, but that wasn't the point. I wanted him to think I knew things.

He continued, "It's called HiEn. The machines have got little metal grabby hands for collecting pieces of it, cause

2

if you puncture some of this stuff, it explodes." It sounded like something out of a comic book. "Turns out there's a stock pile of it under a hunk of the Crown's land. I don't know yet who all knew about it."

I nodded, "Okay, the possible exploding aspect makes the giant drills on some of these guys all the more disturbing. Considering the timing, could there possibly be a connection between this new found Hi... stuff... and the death of Michael Crown?"

Hudson thought for a second, staring off at the peeling, flower print wallpaper lining the wall in front of him. "Maybe someone wanted him out of the way for access to it? I mean, this stuff is worth a lot, I'll grant ya. People wanna use it for everything from batteries to supercomputers."

I was only half-listening about the Hi-En, "If someone were after whatever fortune this is going to be, starting with the kid would be a mistake. I wonder if one of the parents was the real target?"

While jotting down anything I could think of, I wandered over to Michael's father. He had a black stain on his shirt, and reminded me more of a mechanic than a socialite. He was standing with arms folded, leaning against the kitchen door frame.

"Sorry to bother you," I said. "I'm Gabe Gekman. I'm also working this case."

"Fine." He looked me up and down.

"Right, so-" before I could ask a question, he started tugging at his shirt.

He said, "I saw you staring before. The oil all on the front of me is from the machines."

"May I ask why you were so close to them? Was there a problem?"

"No problem. I just like knowing what I'm paying for, so I checked one out. I used to work on cars before getting married." He took in a labored breath, "Ah. What do you want to know?" His left hand started to shake.

Over the din of the machines outside, I asked how old Michael had been.

"He was only twenty-two," said Mr. Crown. That made him over ten years younger than I was. A kid. The word "only" rang through my ears in a heavy sort of way. I had seen young children before, yet someone truly at the beginning of adulthood struck me harder.

At least he was an only child. Kids losing siblings has always been a weak spot of mine, having lost my sister so long ago. I swallowed the thought, consciously straightening up my spine.

This wasn't my trauma. This was Newsburg, a big city looking to revitalize an old shine. There was now mostly empty farm land just off to the side if you drove for an hour, but no one talked about that. My own history was stuck where my house was, in the suburbs of Bellevue. Not far enough away to keep cases like this one from kicking up the murky dust of my childhood.

Michael was a well-off kid visiting his parents on break from Lotgraff University. He had been studying Entomology. "Bugs, basically," as Michael's father so eloquently put it.

When the clamor outside died down enough to ask what was going on, Mr. Crown replied, "It's the machines."

"Yes. I know it's the machines. Do they belong to your company? Do the operators know an investigation is going on in here?"

"Yeah. Well, they're gonna be ours soon." He threw a pointed finger in his wife's direction through a door to a small library, "Ask Mrs. Crown. She knows more about it." His shoulders tightened up.

Looking over to the short, unmoving rocking chair, I saw Michael's mother and her response to her child's demise. She seemed to be in an emotional coma, as she sat in the dim living room corner, hands clenched to the arms of her chair. She had her zipped up purse in her lap, as though it were a cat taking a nap. She was aging years by the second, and I wasn't able to get much out of her. I couldn't even be sure that she knew I was there from the way she stared off at the dusty-green wall.

I asked my questions in a quiet monotone, stooped down into a squat so that I was peering up at her face. Eventually, she murmured about their company's merger, and something concerning the digging machines... Then she burst into hysterical sobs. Michael's father stepped closer to where I was stuck hunched over. My throat tensed as I wondered for the briefest moment if he might try to help me up. Of course not. He was too busy curling his hands into fists and vibrating, eyes bulging to offer any assistance. A vein on the side of his head looked ready to wriggle off and fall to the ground. He knew I was there to help, but his words still fired from his mouth like bullets from a gun.

"You stupid little shit!" he said. He didn't know who to direct that anger towards, so it splattered about everywhere. People in houses down the road could feel that heat. It was normal for folks to treat me with less respect after I started dying my hair blue, but this was different. It was both at me, into my eyes, and entirely regardless of me.

I blinked at him with no discernible expression before repeating my questions. My notebook was still in hand as I half-climbed the wall to get up, "Can you tell me a little bit more about your son? Was there anyone you can think of who may have had a grudge against him?"

He sighed, then ran his chubby fingers through graying hair before saying, "I don't know. Maybe. Maybe people don't like certain things he says or his lifestyle or whatever, but nobody should do this. To MY son!" I nodded. Mr. Crown quieted down for a moment, long enough to look me in the eye and say, "I just want know that he knew."

"That he knew what?" I asked.

"It doesn't matter. It's all so stupid!" Standing

before me was an angry, but not violent, broken man. A broken father.

"Whatever," he said. I noticed the tears welling up in his eyes as he turned away from me and mumbled, "I'm gonna lose everything. I lost my son, and they're gonna find out, and I'm gonna go bankrupt too."

I stepped forward, "Who will find out?"

He gestured, swatting toward me, "Oh, everybody! It'll be all over the news. No one will want to work with me again. And every time I fail, I'm gonna be reminded of my dead son!"

"Why wouldn't someone work with-" Mr. Crown stepped away from me for a moment. I didn't try to finish my question. He came around again to pass me and grab his wife's hand. He was aiming for tender, though he held her hand a little too tight, but she'd already drifted away in every other sense.

I made my way toward the center of the living room, where the snakewood table stood. It had a lacey runner across it, but it wasn't straight. The whole thing was off to the side, almost hanging off. Since the table hadn't been taken into evidence, I decided to fix the runner. In doing so, I saw it.

The letters M, O, T, and H were carved into the table, jagged and splintered.

"Hudson!" I looked around half frantic before spotting him.

He waddled over, taking his time, "You find something?"

I pointed at the table, "Is this why Michael had the multi-tool?"

"We didn't see any multi-tool. Like those Swiss Army Knifes but with screwdrivers and what-not? What makes you think he had one on him?"

I raised an eyebrow, "Well, the fiancé told me so over the phone, and these edges are pretty sharp. This seems new to me." It wasn't long before it was being tagged and bagged as well as a table could be for evidence. It was good to feel useful, I suppose.

The thought that anyone would do this to such an expensive and lovely piece of furniture shook my very core. A vicious image. Okay, that should have been a warning sign that I was becoming jaded. I was more *visibly* disturbed by the defacement of the table than by the dead man, but I was only trained in keeping my composure about death. Of course, the body was already gone anyway, so there's my excuse. Either way, the word was a clue, so I jotted "MOTH" down in my notebook.

I pictured Michael still clutching that the multi-tool, knife-out, in his cold hand. The implement used to carve the desperate message. Where was the knife? Perhaps Henry was mistaken as he had only caught a glimpse through the window. There were no signs of a struggle, according to Hudson, nor any indication of blunt force. Where was the discrepancy? When did Henry see the body, and when did Hudson? How much time had passed between? What other evidence was moved by the Crowns, and was any of it pertinent? Michael's corpse was said to be almost pristine, so perhaps he died via something ingested. Was there was a drug called "Moth" I was not yet privy to? The fact was that if Michael was the one who carved the word, Henry was right about the multi-tool.

It dawned on me that it wasn't typical for me to be in the crime scene so soon after they had moved the body. In fact, as a PI, I wasn't meant to be standing where a body had been at all. Murder isn't typically PI fare.

The family had called some favors in on this one to try and keep the grittier details out of the local papers. What was that about a company merger? Mr. Crown was afraid, though not of anything specific. It was that unbridled fear that swells in the gut and pushes hatred into our throats when we lose a loved one. It's made worse when we can't understand why we lost them. No, the feelings were reasonable, and he was under a lot of pressure beyond that. The Crowns were a well-known family with pictures always in the Society section, I understood why the whole thing was hush-hush.

They usually had a maid on the premises. She had been there in the morning, and then hadn't returned. I wasn't sure of the timeline. Was anything cleaned up before we got there? If the table was covered, the knife may have been put away too, and it might not have been part of a poorly done cover up. However, if the body was still half-under the table, the maid would have been either completely oblivious, or directly involved. That, or she wasn't there at all.

I watched Mr. Crown stomp off into his bedroom just in time for the machines to stop again and the shouting outside to begin. Out with one noise and in with another.

I hadn't been gone from the force for long, so I could still get leads from time to time, but this was my first *murder* out of uniform. I managed to keep some perks from the old job, like walking into the Crown house with little more than a nod from the two patrolmen out front. My partner, Jed, was not afforded this same luxury.

Jed could be an abrasive character, especially if you weren't used to him or had been born with thin skin. Almost as wide as he was tall, his build was reminiscent of a Viking or the strongmen you'd see on television throwing trees around for fun. He wore shorts to his knees, sometimes a little lower, but hardly ever full-on slacks. Even in winter, the best he would do was a ratty pair of baggy cargo pants. He wore a cabbie cap, regardless of weather. This was also his formal wear.

In contrast, I always wore a suit, and I generally wore an old-fashioned men's wide brimmed hat when outside - not to be confused with a trilby - over my blue hair. We were creatures of habit at best and obsessive at our worst. Next to a fit, but slim, guy of average height like myself, Jed's wide frame seemed Herculean at six foot two.

He had a limp to him, but he could be unbelievably fast if the situation required it. Jed also had a sixth sense about trouble that I lacked, and this had saved my life more than a few times so far. However, he lacked any sort of social grace, which put my life in danger almost as often. I guess it all evened out.

I'll clarify here that he had never been a cop, so much as an oddly fit accessory. Still, large, lumbering, and easy to startle as he was, Jed was an asset to the force... by proxy of being my partner, if nothing else. Everyone who ever knew him also knew that on some level.

I sauntered outside to help ease the situation.

Jed responded to my assistance with, "You'd think they'd have no problem with me here, since they already let a blue-haired, fedora wearin' jackass like you in."

"I love you too," I answered. I was lucky to talk the officer out of arresting Jed when my partner immediately threatened him. It was a miracle I had been convincing enough to get Jed into the house.

I peered into the Crown's kitchen and saw a sea of wooden cabinets, wooden counters, a wooden floor. A padded room made of mahogany. A doorless doorframe on the other side led to the bedroom hallway Mr. Crown and scuffled down earlier.

"Seriously. How do you even keep a job looking like some punk rock reject?" Jed pat me on the back as we opened the door to Michael's bedroom.

The bed had clearly been slept in since this morning when a maid had undoubtedly made it. A book on titled <u>Lepidopterology Around the World</u> sat on one of his pillows, surrounded by the frame of a grey silk pillowcase. Wait. Wasn't that butterflies and... moths?

I jotted down the possibility of some vague link. If it meant something else to Michael, I should find out. Moth could stand for something, with the letters M, O, T, and H, or a moth could be a code, metaphor, anything else. Flipping through the book granted me a definition of moths, and some fun facts, so I did my best to make do with that information. Moths are nocturnal. Was he killed in the night? Moths are pollinators, so maybe he was saying... something about spreading... things. I learned that some moths have the ability to blend in by pretending to be other creatures. It's to avoid being eaten, of course. A few even look like bird poop. Who was hiding in plain sight?

There's a fine line between finding all the little details of a case, and over thinking.

Jed motioned to the ripped and crooked posters of bands from the previous generation, "Don't think he got his feel for music from his parents, cause the kid was into *good* shit."

It was true, we would have gotten along with him, judging by the anti-establishment beat of those musicians. A person's taste in music says a lot about them.

My eyes followed where one man on a poster happened to be pointing. Michael's night stand held a small lamp, stationary, and an ornate glass and metal box. The heartbreak came upon seeing two gold rings inside that box. From the dates on the stationary, he was all set to be married in a month. The papers sported scribbles of his potential vows, love notes, and a butterfly stamp on the corner of the page. Or was it a moth?

His husband to be, Henry Shicovski, was already top of the list of potential suspects for the detectives. Husbands and wives kill each other all the time. Part of me knew it was likely the fiancé was responsible, even as my client. Common sense told me how silly it was to assume any such connection so early on. What about Michael's schooling?

Moths certainly came up in his studies. Perhaps someone from school had information. I made a note to ask his fiancé about that first.

Then there was the business of checking out the father's recent dealings. Mrs. Crown had mentioned a deal, and that turned out to be with Riverside Financial. What would killing Michael gain?

I went back out to Jed's car for a quick phone call to Riverside. That was all it took to confirm that the deal was still in negotiation. I didn't mention the murder, and no one seemed to think the Crown's had a child. Jed figured if it was intimidation, it was heavy-handed. It could've spurred the Crowns into seeking vengeance instead of folding like a cheap table. Riverside did not own the machines, as Mr. Crown had led me to believe, and they were renting. The company that made them owned the machines themselves. I crossed off the machines having much to do with anything - other than a public disturbance.

Hudson poked his head in, "You were right about the multi-tool. We found it in Mrs. Crown's purse. She said she found it on the ground and didn't think anything of it. She figured she'd dropped it at some point after using it to open the mail by the front entrance."

I asked, "When did the runner get put on the table?"

"I didn't ask. She didn't seem to know what MOTH could mean, and I believe her when she says she hadn't noticed it. If she was the one who covered the table, it may have been in shock for all we know, or Michael could have put it there himself before he went down."

Hudson didn't wait for my rebuttal before he ducked around the door frame.

As I saw it, the carving in the table was the only real lead. In this town, there were a few things to share that name. The Moth Corporation was a chemical distributor, and rumor had it they had a seedy past in street drugs. I believed it, and assumed they still supplied some to the local cooks, but no charges filed. Having a history with them wasn't going to do me any favors in this case. The department already called me paranoid any time Moth Corp came up, and they had a point. Thinking of them caused a pulling from inside of the middle of my spine to my sternum. Pulling, pressing, pounding...

In all fairness, I had a kind of connection to a lot of things that were potential leads. There was also the Moth Flame, for example, a throwback bar and club with the air of an old speakeasy. It didn't hurt that I knew the manager, Maria. Even though we had a falling out, I still kept in touch when it fit into my schedule. With those connections, I shouldn't have been on the case at all, but because of those same contacts, I didn't want to leave it alone. I knew I could be useful.

Jed found a pamphlet in one of the bedroom drawers, which had a few phone numbers jotted down in pen sideways along the full color illustrations. It was for a social club called the Moth Fanciers. A club of a half dozen intellectual types who traded pinned insects like trading cards. Michael had been a member with his fiancé.

Boy, there sure where a lot of bug-related things in this town.

Jed made a face at Officer Hudson, who was still standing outside like a mall security guard.

As we left, Hudson grabbed my arm, "Come on, Gabe. Make this easy on me. You want to be on this case, and you're a great detective."

"Thank you?"

"So, whenever you're ready to stop playing P.I. and come back to be a real cop again, you let me know, okay?"

"Yeah, sure. If that happens, you'll be the first to know. I promise." I gently peeled his hand from my arm.

We made our way back to Jed's car, a restored 1967 Chevrolet Chevelle. Red with black stripes, the mechanics were impeccable thanks to Jed's handiwork, while the outside was beat to absolute Hell.

His car smelled of the empty fast-food bags we routinely tossed to the backseat. I had cleaned his car out as a gift one year, but Jed said I was messing with its ecosystem. We started the drive over to the coroner with what little information we had.

I let a huff of air out of my nostrils and Jed noticed, "What's on your mind, Gekman?"

"Parents," I mumbled half to myself, thinking of how distraught my own were when we lost my sister, Abby.

"Ah. You should call your parents then. When'd you last talk to them?" He tapped on the steering wheel, "They like to hear from you."

"You're like my grandmother, I swear."

"Nah. She could drink me under the table." True, but that wasn't my point.

I pulled out my phone and tapped out a text warning Henry about Hudson wanting to call him again, then tucked my phone away in my pocket.

The coroner's office was located off of a main road, tucked among some other government buildings and hospitals, like the most sterile of strip malls. Three trees stood in private cage-pots within a strip of planted grass, opening to a parking lot. Cracked pavement made way for a few tiny yellow flowers, and some part of me wanted to find a metaphor in that.

The door was heavy and metal, leading to a metallic, frigid room that smelled of bleach. The coroner himself was a short, gray haired, stubby man, and old enough to have been my father. His name was Bernie, and he liked that I called him by his name. Everyone else called him Bug.

He wasn't surprised to see me so soon, and when I flashed the badge I hadn't yet handed back in, he laughed at me, "Don't worry, Gabe. I know you're a PI these days.

Even locked in this old box, I hear the goings on of the outside world! Congratulations, by the way." My cheeks flushed a bit as I put the badge back inside my coat. Bernie was someone to look up to. He was one of the few coroners who was also his own medical examiner and pathologist. He was more often than not a one-man show, yet kept a level head.

"Will you still help me?" I asked.

"I hope you realize I wouldn't stick my neck out for just anyone. But you? You're a good kid, no matter who you work for. That's rare. Plus, I'm lonely," he gave a laugh. "It's nice to see you, Gabe."

"Is it just you here? I remember you having an assistant."

"Nah. He got a new gig in another town. Honestly, I can do all this myself. It's not that busy, thankfully. You know though, I could use a scientific photographer to help me out. Somebody to use infrared, thermal imaging, that kind of thing."

"That would help you?"

"Sure. Medical data beyond notes and photos when I can physically see something with my eyeballs would always help."

"Maybe I can put a word out. Kind of background would they need?"

"For me? They'd need a degree in photography, I guess. Or mortuary science. Honestly, if someone had knowledge of both, that would be perfect."

"Okay. Does that... Is that related to this case?"

"Not at all. I'm just telling everybody in case they know somebody."

"Ah. So, what about Michael Crown?"

"Can't say much. You boys work too hard, and too fast! I haven't had the time to deal with the body yet."

"Well, you know waiting wasn't my strong suit, and Jed is even worse." Jed made his hand twitch a little to

14

emphasize my point as I continued, "I wanted to let you know that we think he was poisoned, in case that helps."

Bernie said, "I'll look into it. Now take a breather. Gonna be night soon. I'll give ya a call when I've got anything." He had a kind smile that reminded me of my dad, and we decided to take his advice.

A slight break was for the best anyway. My sinuses were dry and my eyes burned at the edges. The dustings of the Crowns, coupled with Summer allergies had punched me in the face and I wasn't thinking straight. I felt like the human personification of a fart. Or when the Sunday comic's color is a little off to the side. I felt like that as a human. I needed to shake that off and organize what our next possible steps should be in the investigation, depending on what Bernie would find.

There were other people to talk to and leads to follow, but nothing more to do at that moment. The body had made it to the morgue, but Bernie wouldn't be able to talk about the state of it until after an examination. The autopsy results would take longer, and the drug tests would take even longer than that. Henry could have been with the cops at that point, or at least with *someone* after Hudson got to him again. I figured he wouldn't be in a state fit to talk to me for a bit. He'd need a good cry and some sleep first. I wanted to talk to him before going to the Moth Fanciers though, in case he had any thoughts about any of the members.

With time to kill, I turned to Jed and asked, "Feeling thirsty?"

We got back into his car and made our way down the hill to a bar I used to frequent with the boys when I was a cop. The altitude seemed to be a general measurement of money and class. By the time we stopped rolling from the coroner, we could see the garish brick square outlined against the reflections in the harbor.

As we approached, the streetlights went dark from neglect until the neon sign of the bar was the only visible light left. It flickered red and yellow, illuminating the graffiti on nearby buildings. I could never tell if it was called The Brick House as an intended pun, or if the owner simply lacked imagination. The muffled noise of the bar was incoherent from the outside, but still loud enough to result in complaints - if the place wasn't full of cops at all hours.

We parked as close as we could, as it had a certain radius of crime reduction, but no need to take chances. I braced myself when opening the door, knowing that first wave of smells always gave me a headache.

A wet spot caught my heel and I jerked forward, catching myself with one hand on the peeling red bar top. Something about the boarded up door on the other end of the room that still had the exit sign above it was sticking to me. Like the empty condom wrapper on the floor in the back, and the giant nails sticking out of boards by the pile of tied up chairs we could see, but couldn't use, there was a lot of useful-in-theory going on. I hoped the people in the bar didn't follow suit.

Beer, cigars, and body odor saturated the air. I held my breath as long as I could without being obvious and sat at the bar. The bartender knew me well enough that a simple nod got him to work on an Old Fashioned. Jed was also able to place his order without words, but he pointed at a beer bottle and held up his fingers like a child learning to count. Different methods, same result.

I brought the drink to my face, enjoying that its proximity took the bite off of the surrounding odors. Taking a sip, I turned to take stock of who was present, and almost spit it out again when I saw Maria there.

Maria was easy to spot, no matter where she happened to be. It was like she was illuminated by a spotlight. She was wearing a long, slinky black dress and leaning on a table where a group of men in half-buttoned shirts sat enraptured.

She was laughing at some unfunny joke a man half-told, as she slid her hand on the table towards one of the heavier men. He was parchment-pale, chomping on a cigar as he placed his hand on hers. I turned back toward the bar with my lips pursed.

As far as I knew, she had been selling herself for a few years before "quitting," but she still worked for some bad people. Jed and I had met her in college. She didn't go to our school, she was a townie, but she showed me the time of my life. We hadn't even had the chance to sleep together before I unfairly, unceremoniously dumped her, disguising my fear as being for her own good. I was selfish and afraid for my own reputation.

Years later, I had made contact with her for a job, and by that time she happened to be the owner of the Moth Flame. I didn't know what business she had in the Brick House. Maybe she went back to the old ways. Maybe she just liked cops. ...Her dark eyes.

"Too late Boss, she spotted you," Jed laughed, nudging my shoulder with his elbow.

"Who?" I tried to feign ignorance.

My lie was so unconvincing, even I didn't believe myself. Jed shook his head and went back to drinking. I watched Maria's approach as subtly as I could in the smudged mirror behind the bar. By fate or chance, a big band number started playing on the jukebox and it became her soundtrack. It punctuated the movement of her hips as she made her way over to the bar.

They swayed under black silk and a silver chain-belt, which attached back up around her neck like a collar. Those dangerous hips held her leash. They held mine as well. She was magnetic in those moments, but she was also the girl I knew in college who made some poor choices.

"I didn't think I'd see you here, since leaving the proper detective scene." She carefully laid a hand on my shoulder, and I had to remind myself to breathe.

"I could say something similar. Don't you have your own joint?" I leaned on the bar, realizing the more nonchalant you try to appear, the further away from it you are. It was difficult to ignore my elbow slowly soaking up a spot of bourbon.

"Sure, but I also have friends." She shrugged with one shoulder as a short wave of black hair fell by her eye.

"From your other business ventures?"

"I don't know what you mean." She looked confused for a moment, then the smile was gone. She said, "But I suppose you are right, I should get back to the Flame," She launched herself towards the door. I followed.

I took her arm before quickly dropping it again and saying, "No, you can stay, I have to go anyways. I'm working a case."

Less than a minute and I managed to offend her. Well, truth be told, she was never the problem between us. She crossed her arms and smiled. A deserved mixed message.

I passed her again on the way out, after grabbing Jed. I opened the door into the neon-lit street and turned to Jed, but he'd stopped to say something to Maria.

I held the door open for him when he was done. As he and I walked to the car, I asked, "What did you say to her?"

He clapped me on the shoulder and beamed a smile, "I told her to be patient with you. You'll come around."

I wondered what Jed meant by that as I rubbed my bruised shoulder and asked, "How many drinks did you finish?"

Jed snorted "All of 'em!" He raised his hands in victory.

"Gimme your keys."

  If you asked Hudson why I had left for the private sector, he'd tell you I was impatient. Paperwork takes too long, we're always too late to stop anything from happening, and none of us were any good with a follow up. That's all true, but not the crux of my issue with being a cop. If you asked Jed, he'd say the politics drove me away. Bad people get away with almost anything if they have the right combination of money, connections, and skin color. This is also true, and also not the main thing that drove me away.

  I worked with a lot of rotten apples. Sure, many of them are gone now for a number of reasons, but some are still there. Everyone knows who they are. No one does a damn thing. I didn't make many friends over the years. Hudson knew that. He seemed to think I was stand offish, regardless of all the evidence I had handed our superiors. I was threatened with removal more than once. All I had done was the right thing. The thing I was supposed to do. Why was that worthy of punishment? So, I left, eager to help people where I would otherwise fail again and again.

CHAPTER 2
Old Flames

Sleep was always hard to come by during a case, and I used my stress-insomnia to carry on best I could. I needed more information before I could pester Maria at the Moth Flame, and it was still too early in the case to head back to the morgue. The body was scarcely prepped for an autopsy. Best to talk to Michael's fiancé Henry in the meantime, since Bernie needed some more time to analyze the body. Then, I would find a reason to head to the Moth Flame. The whole process would be a long one, and Jed was not useful in the morning.

He was outrageous, loud and enthusiastic in everything he ever did. The man was a powder keg, plain and simple. This is not to say that Jed looked dangerous, aside from his size, posture and the occasional mad gleam in his eye. He didn't look scary; despite what he would tell you. Though he could be intimidating in a creepy, want-to-take-a-shower-to-wipe-off-the-crazy sort of way. Of course, if someone accidentally left a lit cigarette of a slight gesture, however small, or a remaining ember of some misspoken comment behind, that would be enough. He could and no doubt would blow, if that flame was not dowsed with a heavy dose of something alcoholic.

In any other circumstance, one would assume that alcohol would make a fire larger. In his case, being the paradox of a human being he tended to be, it would squelch the problem almost immediately, like a hyper active child finding distraction in a butterfly. If he did explode, we would all go up in flames right along with him. Anyone who ever knew him understood this fact.

I decided Henry did not need such a person in his presence during this delicate time. I didn't want to push my luck. As for Maria, I would need to do that part alone. For my own reasons.

Henry was working as a chef at a high end restaurant in the city, and had surrounded himself with the nicest of everything that the area could offer. Henry didn't even bat an eye at the idea of a PI or any kind of cop at the door at this point. He had already become numb to it. He leaned into his doorframe, crossed his arms, and nodded when I mentioned the Crowns.

"They're always in some kind of crisis," he said before ushering me into his apartment, leading me to chairs, a couch, and a coffee table. Our conversation started out light.

He looked me up and down, analyzing something about me before he asked, "What are you? That was rude. I mean, what's your family history? Your ethnicity?"

I shrugged and said, "I'm Jewish. Ashki." He nodded like he understood. I wasn't sure what that meant.

Henry was dark skinned, with green eyes and very proud of his heritage, judging by the decor.

"Some of this looks like it's from India," I said.

His eyes lit up, "Yes! My mother is straight out of India, and my dad is Russian, though actually raised in Australia."

"Huh," I wasn't sure why he was telling me these things.

That's when I noticed his left hand as he offered me a mug of tea to match his own. It shook whenever Henry wasn't actively holding something.

He sniffed, "I'm just trying to think of literally anything else. I realize you're here for a specific reason. I called and you're doing your job. I'm just feeling too many things right now."

I gestured to the couch in front of me with a smile to get him to sit down. He sat with perfect posture. His composure was artful.

I took out my notebook and pen to say, "So let's talk

about who Michael might have-" Henry's wailing cry pierced through the heavy brick walls of his upscale, Ikea laden apartment. He clung with both hands to the aqua colored mug as though it was the only thing keeping him from floating into space, away from the horror I had unleashed by speaking The Name.

"Are you... I mean, obviously you aren't okay," I put a hand to my mouth, then moved a box of tissues closer to him.

"The Crowns knew about our engagement, of course, but no one called me to let me know that my fucking fiancé had been killed. How long was he like that before I saw him? I wasn't even supposed to be there. I was being nice."

"Nice?"

"I hadn't heard from him in a little while," His whole body was quaking as he grabbed a tissue to blow his nose. He continued, "I hadn't heard from him in a while, but whenever I called the house, they said he was fine and just busy. They said his cellphone was shattered when he was outside looking at one of the digging machines, but I don't know. How long had he been fucking dead? I don't even know. I went to the house to bring him lunch, because they don't feed him there. I brought him lunch, and there he was. Just... He was just-"

I attempted to bring him back to the room, outside of his head, "So, what was that earlier? It was like you detached yourself, but you were there, right?"

After a minute of hyperventilation, he huffed out, "I've been trying to detach! I keep thinking if I don't think about it, it wasn't real or something. I don't know." He took a few deep breaths, "It makes sense, I guess. They aren't good at dealing with stuff. They put stuff off, you know? They're private people anyway." He shook his head, wiping tears from his eyes with the back of his hand. "Oh God. They don't like me very much, but I didn't think they were really..." He took in a big gasp of air, "They were screening my calls. Oh God. I thought it was weird, but yeah. They were giving me the run-around for like a week." Jotting that down in my notebook felt strange. If they wanted to keep them away from each other, why get rid of their own son instead of the fiancé?

It didn't make much sense, so I bit the inside of my cheek and nodded, trying not to show how sorry I felt as I asked the next part, "I'll try to get right to it so you can be done with this conversation. Did Michael have any enemies that you knew of? Anyone who'd want him gone? If you suspect his parents, would they have a reason?"

Henry shook his head again, this time as if it were an etch-a-sketch that would reset reality, "I don't suspect his parents. I think they'd be the type to find him like that and then do nothing about it, or decide it was me and then never look into it. But Michael? My Mikey... He was bossy sometimes, but not mean enough to pick fights or get into that kind of trouble. I guess he didn't have many friends though. No enemies, but not many friends either, not even at Lotgraff."

"Did he live with anyone on campus?"

"No. He moved into an apartment by his school about a year ago. I was going to move in soon, right after the wedding. He was back with his parents for the break." He stared off into space until snapping back to his calm face to say, "He hadn't even had a dorm mate for like a year or something."

I let my head tilt to the side and kind of bounce back, "Well, what was that person's name?"

"I don't remember. I'm sorry. Danny? Danny... Something with a C sound? I'm sorry. I might have a couple old papers around somewhere. Maybe something has the name on it?" He scrambled to a desk and pulled open a drawer.

He produced a paper with the school letterhead, but there was nothing but the phone number of the head office on the housing form. This lead seemed weak, being over a year old. I folded it and put it in my pocket, just in case.

"Thank you. One last thing, and I'll leave you be."

"It's okay," said Henry as he swayed side to side and looked at nothing on the table in front of him, wiping tears away now and then. "I can keep talking. Better than being alone."

Oof. "Yeah. I get that. Well then, can you tell me anything about the Moth Fanciers?"

"Oh. Yeah, that group was fun for Michael. I didn't have much interest. Not like he did. So, I just kept track of when the meetings were so I knew when not to call him. The Fanciers don't allow cell phones because they don't allow cameras. The flash could damage the color of some of the older specimens. Anyway, they have a meeting this afternoon, actually." He told me how to get there, and the password.

"Password?" I didn't question it until after I'd written the word down.

"Yeah. You'll have to say it to the guy at the door, and then you and your partner will need to mention knowing someone in the group, so you'll say Michael." The victim was our post-mortem in, as morbid as that felt.

We walked to the door together, so I put a hand on Henry's shoulder and said, "Listen, I can't even imagine the kind of pain you're in. Do you have someone to talk to? A friend to be with right now?"

"I should see my parents. I told them that Michael was gone. I think Mom thought we'd broken up. I don't know why I didn't tell them. Denial, I guess? Like I keep thinking he's just gonna show up at the door and say it was some stupid prank or something." He started crying again. It was grossly unprofessional, but I stuck my arms out like I was going to catch him in a trust fall. He took the cue for a hug.

"Do they live far away?"

"No. I won't be that far. I'll tell them. I'll go home for a bit. I'll text you the address in case you need to stop by or something? I'll call you if I think of anything else."

Luckily for me his apartment building was right on the bus line. My timing was almost spot on too, as I was waited at the stop for less than five minutes.

Town's End, Jed's favorite bar, was not quite as easy to get to. I could ride to a stop a few blocks away before hiking the rest of the distance, crossing through some parking lots along the way. It was a nice day with birds chirping and barely a cloud in the sky, so I took it as an excuse to exercise before the possibility of excessive drinking.

A dreamy 80's pop song was playing when I walked down the little concrete steps into the bar. It wasn't a huge place, and dim enough that I couldn't tell if it was for atmosphere or if a bulb had blown and no one cared. There was zero seating left, but not because it was particularly crowded. It was a very thin hallway of a dive, with an elevated stage at the back. The show that night appeared to star a bunch of forgotten broken chairs... ah. I had found the seating. I leaned against the poster coated wall and took whatever drink Jed handed me.

"I'm surprised you're here and not chasing Maria," Jed didn't sound like he was kidding. Maria and I had a funny way of bumping into each other. We had kept in contact on and off, though I had been weird and distant about the whole thing. It always felt like ages had passed since last I saw her, but who was I kidding? She was my gravity. I hoped deep down in my gut that she had nothing to do with this case. I fiddled with my tie as I thought about The Moth Flame and the secrets held within. Christ. That club, those times... Her other job long before that... Of course, I didn't understand what was going on at the time, and something told me that I still didn't quite get it.

I remembered how much I wanted to take her away from it all. She was too smart a girl for a world like that. Too pretty for swimming in that scum. Some people don't want to change and so they never can. Perhaps myself included. I thought I had grown up since then, but I was wrong.

I grabbed a toothpick from the little green glass square container on the bar, and balled up my body as much as I could on that stool. I waited out my feelings, careful not to catch her imaginary eye inside my head. To clarify again, she was not physically in that bar with us.

The clock behind the bartender said it had been less than an hour when I got a call from our trusty coroner Bernie. I made the motions to Jed to go. He sat there oblivious to the whole thing and unmoving. He tended to assume I was an orb of panic for nothing, and he was usually correct.

"Nice to see you for five seconds, Man," he said.

"Well, I'm sorry-"

"I think you still owe me for all the times I've been right about you ditching me at a bar to talk to a lady." He was smiling as he said it, but he wasn't wrong.

I hadn't had anything to drink, but I handed him a couple of bills, "Fair enough, but this isn't one of those times."

"This in response to those multiple lost bets throughout the month, or to get me drinking some more so I don't ask questions about Maria?"

"Yes, both. Although you could come with me. The autopsy is done, and we need to talk to Bernie about it. After this, we're going to the Moth Fanciers. Things are happening that don't involve my ex-girlfriend."

"Nah. I'll go for the bugs, but not for Bug. I'm good here. You get me for part two, yeah? And don't pretend we ain't gonna see Maria eventually." He laughed and put his keys in my hand, "You take my car, then you pick me up for the other shit."

I was almost to Jed's car but was stopped short by an officer. He wiped his nose on his sleeve and eyed me suspiciously as he slowly moved toward the car. He wasn't the biggest human, but he moved himself to block the door.

"Can I help you?" I asked.

He scratched his burnt-orange head of hair, "You aren't a cop, right? You're not a detective either. I just- I'm sorry. I heard you talking in there, and you were at the Brick House before too. I don't understand why we're doing this." Oh, to have that line embroidered on a pillow for my couch.

Since I said nothing, he clarified, "This is not your case. You were hired by a suspect. That doesn't make you have any more rights to this than we do."

I sighed audibly, "I never said it did. Also, is Henry actually a suspect? I was under the impression he no longer was."

He looked at his hands, then back to me, "Okay, but why are we working together? You're still getting info and help and shit from our people. Why are we doing that? I don't get that. You quit."

Did he know me? I didn't recognize him in the slightest.

I sucked in my cheek, "Well, it's a combination of stubbornness and loyalty. I have a lot of knowledge about this case, and a few other related cases. Some of those started before I went rogue, so to speak. I suppose it's easier to deal with me at this point than to try and fail to push me out."

That came out more bitterly than intended, but he seemed to understand. He stepped aside and gestured to the door, "Fine. Just don't do anything stupid. Maybe rely on police resources less, huh?"

Going to speak privately with Bernie was not a bad idea. Bernie Lovett, or 'Bug', was not a people person, and I knew bringing Jed in again would make him nervous.

Bernie was ready for me the moment I walked in, "I did the standard tox-screen already." He shrugged, not turning around as he busied himself with various trays of tools. "Nothing came back on that. I had a couple other, less likely things to look for, and they're not here either. I don't know what to tell you."

"Then what killed him?"

Bernie waved his hands, glancing sidelong at me as I leaned against the wall. He wasn't a big fan of eye contact.

He said, "Looks like respiratory failure, but I honestly can't see what could have caused it. Logically, it was some kind of poison, and since there are no injection marks-"

"He drank it." I took out my little notebook.

He shrugged. "Or inhaled it."

None of this sat well with me. I took the toothpick out of my pocket and stuck it between rows of teeth on the left side of my mouth, nearly stabbing myself in the palate. Something seemed familiar about the way Michael died. My sister Abby had passed from an undefined, undetectable illness, but it took time. This was sudden, wasn't it?

I asked, "What could do this, but go undetected?"

"That I haven't already screened for, you mean? I'm not sure. I'll look into it. I have some friends who might have an idea. Anything else I can help with in the meantime?"

I figured it was worth a shot, so I asked, "Does the word 'Moth' mean anything to you?"

"The only 'Moth' thing around these days is the

Moth Flame club." He jutted back, as though I had shoved him with my question. "Wait. Wait. Moth."

"What's the matter, Bernie?"

"I've seen this before." A rock formed in my gut. "A long time ago."

He clutched at an imaginary necklace on his chest as the words tumbled from his lips, "A guy from the Moth Corp wanted to test this awful stuff, years ago. He called it a byproduct. Made me see if I could find it in a dead body. God. He had put this stuff in some random kid, and I didn't know any better. I wasn't in a position to question the request."

He paused and put a hand to his mouth. "Oh Jesus. Is this kid like that?"

"I don't know," I said as I put my hands in my pockets. "I wish I did."

"It's them again. It's gotta be, right?"

"Were you able to find it last time? The toxin, I mean." Pushing back flashes of little Abby in the playground, then in the hospital, then as only ash in the urn, failed to interrupt our conversation. Abby said it was some kind of conspiracy, but she said it in such a little kid kind of way that no one understood until it was far too late. My hand went into my pocket on instinct. My sister had written it all in a tiny little notebook, about the same size as my own. I kept it in fact, thinking one day I'd figure out what happened. Nothing came of it and my parents, cops, and everyone else had told me to drop it years before. I never did. I couldn't.

Bernie said, "No. I don't even know enough about it that I could screen for it now. Honestly, I thought the guy was messing with me. His credentials hadn't checked out but he was long gone by the time I figured that out. Maybe had me poke around for something that wasn't there. I hope that's the case."

Having decided not to waste any time, I thanked

Bernie and left. He was too lost in thought with his hand clutching his face over his mouth to give a proper goodbye.

Originally seeming to be a legitimate chemical company, Moth Corp was in actuality a network of uncredited labs with an unknown source of funds. More was revealed as the lawsuits began, including their ties to street drugs and illegal human trials. Breaking into any of the old labs would be dangerous without a proper plan, and I'd need Jed by my side. Through a good self-talking, I determined Jed needed only to be half sober for the Moth Fanciers, and I wanted to make the meeting that afternoon.

I parked in the same spot at Town's End, and called Jed to come outside. He didn't pick up, so I sauntered into the bar.

Jed was still in the same spot I had left him, and started to get up when I came in.

"Where we off to now? You said Moth Fanciers but like, where?" he asked.

"Henry gave us the info," I showed him the address in my notebook, but kept it in my hands as I'd be the one driving, "and they've got a meeting in less than an hour."

Jed got the door as he asked, "We gonna shake 'em down and beat up some bug nerds or what?"

"Going in with accusatory questions won't get us anywhere. We can't do this like beat cops. These guys all went to private school, you know? We need to earn the trust of these snooty bug collectors, and then ease into the uncomfortable Michael Crown topic."

"Okay, Boss. You got a plan for that?"

"No," I continued gnawing on a toothpick to help me think. "Well, I think I know enough about moths to ask intelligent questions. Then we'll find out about any drama, and then about Michael Crown."

The meetings always took place in the middle of the day on a Thursday. Jed reckoned they were either short enough get-togethers to have on breaks, or none of the Fanciers had day jobs. College students, I assumed, or retirees. We sat in the car for another minute after we got there, to get our stories straight.

"We've got to be subtle, so as not to have anyone put any guards up," I said. Jed was half listening, picking the price sticker off of an old CD case he found under the seat.

"Sure," he answered, "I can be subtle." I finally released the toothpick that had been warping from soggy weight, threatening to disintegrate between my teeth. I tucked it inside an old fast food bag by my feet.

After I gave him a nod, we got out of the car, making our way to the back entrance of an entomology wing of the Newsburg Museum. The yellow painted door of the brick building in front of us was not as disgusting as I had imagined. It opened without a squeak to a pale blue hallway lined with other wooden doors, each yellow. Toward the back was ours, the only green door. There was a moth etched in the front. Jed knocked three times, as Henry had instructed.

A young-looking red headed man opened the door and squinted at us as he asked, "Do you have the password?" He was thin, and his eyes were too big for his skull.

Jed uncrumpled the paper as best he could, "Garden tiger."

"Wonderful! Are you a guest?"

"Yes," I answered, "Of Michael Crown, but he couldn't be here. Is it all right if we join you today anyway?" He shrugged, and relaxed as he guided us inside. There were about fifteen people in total, scattered throughout the open floorplan of the room in conversations. Only a third were women, but there was a wide range in ages and ethnicities.

"Sit anywhere you'd like. Do you have a specimen today?"

Jed answered, "Just looking today. Meeting the other members to see if this is our place, you know?" The guy smiled.

The room was sealed the way curators of the Louvre keep the Mona Lisa. Had any of the folks there had the wherewithal, the rarer specimens would have been displayed behind bullet-proof glass. Some of the fancier Fanciers had climate controlled briefcases for transport. One woman suggested the use of a de-humidifier, and everyone agreed that it was a good idea. Jed and I took our seats at a long, tall, stainless steel table that was covered by white linen by the man who let us in. He seemed nice enough.

He asked, "So where is Michael, anyway? I haven't seen him in a little while."

Jed and I shared a look, but a man interrupted by saying, "Caught up in wedding planning, I'd imagine." Everyone nodded and agreed, like they had with the de-humidifier. It felt robotic, but friendly, like small talk generally does.

I turned to our makeshift guide, "You know Michael pretty well?"

"As well as anyone does in this group, I guess. He keeps to himself for the most part. Nice guy."

"I'm glad he got a break from college," said a young woman as she adjusted the beautiful, butterfly patterned hijab on her head.

I asked, "Is college getting to him, you think?"

"Oh, I don't know. I know last year was rough. Probably better that he got his own place though." Everyone nodded again. I made a note of that, thinking whatever old roommate might have come up again.

"Sooo," I trailed off, trying to think of a way to subtly bring it up. Failing, I blurted, "He did have a roommate then? A year ago. I heard it didn't end well."

There was a remarkable group-groan in awful harmony.

An older fellow in the back said, "The guy was an asshole!" and everyone agreed.

"Can you tell me in what way though?" Too forward. Screw it, I doubled down with, "I never got any details," and hoped for the best.

The butterfly hijab wearing woman said, "His roommate was trouble. He wanted to join the Fanciers, but it was to poke fun at us. He even stole some things when Michael wasn't here one day." Again, everyone nodded.

"What did he steal?"

"Chemicals. Preservatives. Random ones. I thought the worst."

"The worst?" asked Jed.

She grimaced, "I assumed he was some kind of serial killer. Making a human sized specimen collection." Jed tossed me a look.

I pressed on, "Do you remember his name?"

There was a cacophony of answers at this point. Danny, Donny, Dylan, Deddrie, Daniel, and even a Donna. Well, we already knew it started with a D anyway, and while I couldn't yet call him a suspect, I considered this roommate an official person of interest. So next would be asking the college for any records, however we could get them.

A taller man wearing a paisley tie sat down next to me, "He stole from me, actually. The roommate. I'm an arachnologist, and the only one in this club. Seemed he thought my work was particularly interesting."

"Spiders?" I asked, extending my hand to meet his outstretched palm.

"My name is Andrew. Andrew French, and yes. He took a particular kind of spider specimen." At first glance, he looked to be in his 20s, but according to his education and the life story he felt free to share, he had to be at least in his late 30s, "In any case, you want to start a bug collection?" He leaned on the table like an awkward attempt at a drug deal. "You put them in a bag or jar. Then you freeze them."

Jed piped up, "If it's a glass jar, won't condensation be a problem?"

The man tapped his finger on his chin, "Possible problem, if the specimen has scales. Of course, you'll need moisture when you want to change a pin or move a specimen around anyway. Either way, cotton balls. That's the key." He sounded like a madman.

"You need a kill jar too," said Jed. "I've heard that. What does that entail?"

"Ah! Yes. A jar with a lid that won't come off easy, and you put plaster in the bottom. Now, you soak that with ethyl acetate, acetone, or any of my personal favorites."

"You have personal favorite chemicals for your kill jar?" I asked.

"Sure! Sodium cyanide, or potassium cyanide in particular." That didn't make anything sound any better to me. Mr. Andrew French straightened his tie, "It's the vapors that kill the insect." I wrote that down and he noticed.

"Here," Andrew rummaged through his coat pocket for his wallet, then carefully picked a card from an inner fold, "feel free to give me a call if you have any questions after today. It's good to have a few contacts in this club, rather than just one. We're all friends here." It dawned on him that he was missing an important piece of information, "Oh! And what are your names?"

"Gene. This is Jim."

I felt a tickle on the back of my neck accompanied by a meek voice which said, "Your hair is like a Blue Morpho."

I turned to see a woman in a sundress who smiled before attempting to run her fingers through my hair. Jed pulled me away with one arm. He was far more aware of anyone making eyes at me than at him. In the three hours we were there, Jed completely missed the two girls who were quietly fighting over him.

We said our goodbyes, and we made it back to the car. Jed motioned for me to drive.

"Well, Crown's death had nothing to do with anyone there. They're out of the loop and in their own little world," I said.

"So what next?"

"We call the school and ask about the roommate. Then it's off to other moth-related things."

Jed rolled his eyes so hard that I thought I could hear them hit the back of his skull, "Okay, so you either mean Maria, in which case you are so on your own to fuck *that* up once again, or you mean the Moth Company."

"Well, both."

"Man, it ain't Maria, and you know it's not the company, right? It's *never* the company." I didn't answer. "But hey, you take the excuse to talk to Maria."

"Why do you sound angry about that? Do you have feelings for her? Because that's totally okay if you-"

"NO I DON'T YOU IDIOT." Sounded like all one word, the way he said it. Jed took in a breath to collect himself, and then explained, "You'd rip your heart straight out of your goddamn chest for her, but only if she never asks you to. If she needs you? You ain't there. It's been years, and you're great to her until you get all dramatic and shit. I'm all for the two of you being together, but I like her. Like... I like Maria as a person, so I don't wanna see her hurting. Now, I fuckin' LOVE you, Gekman, but you can't keep doin' this. You wanna be with her, just fuckin' do it."

"I know. Believe me, I do."

Jed's grand plan was now to have me drop him off at his apartment. He even told me to head to the Moth Flame without him, which was surprising to me. He either thought there could be a lead in the case, or he had more faith in my romantic prospects than he should have.

First was the matter of calling the school while it was still kind of daylight. We made our way up the stairs of Jed's apartment building, saying hello to noisy neighbors along the way. There was technically an elevator, but I don't remember it working.

Jed looked up the number for Lotgraff University and dialed before handing the phone to me. No one was picking up, but no answering machine either.

I was about ready to hang up the phone when someone finally answered with a meek, "Lotgraff?"

"Uh, yeah. This is Gabe Gekman, P.I." Why did I open with that? "I'm calling in regard to a case that concerns a student of Lotgraff University. Is there someone there I can speak with?" She was silent on the other end, crumpling papers now and then, before finally telling me to please hold.

Jed poured himself a drink. He offered me a swig, but I shook my head.

I was passed around from one line to another until finding the ear of someone in records. According to them, Michael lived alone, and never had a roommate, let alone one that started with the letter D.

I flopped myself onto Jed's couch, which let out a low hissing sound as if the cushion was slowly deflating.

"Yeah, Buddy," I said to the couch, "I feel the same."

"I'm gonna keep on their asses," said Jed.

"I don't know what that means. They haven't got it."

"Nah. There's gonna be copies of those records somewhere. They might have deleted them, but they aren't gonna straight up purge them."

"Why not?" I sat up as best as I could in the overstuffed seat.

"Keeps them technically compliant with the law, Man."

I squinted, "Then why pretend a student was never there? Did he do something heinous enough to warrant erasure? It's a pretty prestigious school, I suppose."

"Absofuckinlutely." Jed toasted with a bottle, "And use my car tonight. No bus bullshit. Just come back here with it eventually."

"You won't need it?"

Jed snorted, "I look like I'm driving to you? I'm drunk, not stupid."

Once the sun had been gone for enough hours, I made my way down to the street where we had parked. The air was crisp and smelled wet.

It had been so long since my last visit to Maria's bar that I got lost three times on the way. It wasn't that I had forgotten where the place stood, but I was struck by waves of insecurity as I drove on. However, I could always blame Jed's somewhat chaotic directions for how much I meandered, whether true or not.

Maria and I always met up at other bars, far away from her actual job. We'd make them dates until I ruined them with business. I expected this to be no different. Illuminated by specially made streetlights meant to harken back to black and white films, the Moth Flame was ready to put on a show. The doors were lighter than they looked, and I always expected there to be a bouncer nearby, but there was no such guard to immediately shoo me away from the premises. The closest to one was my ex-girlfriend.

Maria Lembini, lover of jazz, and ex lady of the night. She did stop, right? She wanted to change her ways, not knowing where to begin. Maybe she felt lost and determined at the same time, and that was something I could understand.

I shook my head and reminded myself that any issue I had with her was my fault, and not hers. She had wanted to explain years ago. I had failed to listen.

Imagining that we were long past old friends, I smiled at her. To my surprise, she accepted the grin and took a seat with me. A heavier, faster tempo song was booming out above our heads.

She sat with elegance and snapped for two martinis. The waitress knew what Maria was ordering based solely on the fact that she was sitting opposite a man and looked vaguely interested in me, kinda.

I fumbled with my tie, trying to avoid eye contact with Maria's magnificent cleavage. It was a problem. I felt too young. I was a couple of years older than she was, and in some ways, I thought, more mature. I was flat out wrong, and her smile alone could make me feel stupid.

Those pearls set beyond that lush red cushion of lips could send me swirling down into an ocean of confusion and an overwhelming sense of loss. I should have gone after her with more gusto. No. I did the right thing, didn't I? In a way, I mourned the death of a relationship which never happened. I took this fact out on pretty much every other woman I ever knew.

Our drinks came via a scantily clad, buxom woman. Red, black or purple corsets and bustles were uniforms. Seemed to be the girl's choice, as there was no rhyme or reason as to which girl had which color.

"So," Maria said with a sultry tongue, "what brings you to my side of town? Come to apologize?" She leaned in on one elbow.

"A case," I said. "A kid is dead and we think this club of yours may have something to do with it. It's only a hunch, but worth looking into, yeah?"

"You never are one for pleasantries, Gabe." Her smile became a sneer as she picked up her martini and swirled it around. She tossed it back and put her other arm on the back of her side of the booth. Elegant to gruff in zero seconds. She put the glass down again and gestured to the stage behind me with both a flip of her hand and a sharp tilt of her jaw. I hadn't paid the platform much notice before. The curtain bled into that which was on the walls, but they opened to reveal a quaint little theater.

"As I recall," she said, as though I hadn't spoken at all, "you have quite a fondness for jazz and burlesque."

"Only when the girls are pretty." That got a chuckle out of her.

I decided to humor her and watch for a while, throwing an arm over the back of the booth. She knew it was not only for her sake that I watch the show, as I continued to crane my neck until it felt the strain.

The dance itself had wide, swirling movements. The subtle glitter speckled the girl's dark skin, like her own private galaxy. She began to sing a rendition of an old soulful tune, and sounded like the classics you'd hear on an old 45. It was impressive. It was near the end when I noticed I had moved my position. My upper body had twisted so much to save my neck that one leg was bent onto the seat itself and I was leaning on my arms, looking over the back of the booth. From the other side, I must've looked like a little kid watching television.

"I doubt it," said Maria. She was across the table and spoke in barely above a whisper, and yet it felt like she was right on my neck.

"Doubt what?" My eyebrows went up as I turned to look at her. She smiled at my innocent, wide eyed expression. It was a rare one for me.

Maria found herself composed again after half a second and said, "That this place is what you're looking for. We don't really do stuff like that. Downstairs might be more like it. Especially if a kid's dead."

She didn't smoke anymore and hadn't in years, but when agitated, she'd still put her index and middle finger out as though holding a cigarette. That, or she was subconsciously flipping off the world. Maybe both.

"Downstairs?" I raised an eyebrow. "I didn't even know there was a downstairs."

"Most don't. Best not to know." The sadness in Maria's voice brought me back to those days where I wanted to play Prince Charming and save her from whatever life she was living. That wasn't my job. I watched her stick her left thumb between her right middle and index fingers as though she just wanted something to hold. "Everything you came here for is there instead."

I leaned in. "How do I get downstairs?"

"The right people and the right keys. So far, so good. I happen to be one of the right people. But you'll need to know more. This shady business gets dangerous and heavy right quick. If the kid was involved in something skuzzy enough to get him killed, that's what you'll need more information on."

"So, what do I need to know?"

"It's all a front, but you knew that already," she brought her voice down to a low hum, "Listen, I'm telling you this because I trust you."

She sighed, then paused and said, "And I like you. Still. For some reason." She sighed again with more of a huff and said, "I've managed to push most of what was Downstairs away to warehouses, away from the girls. I have nothing to do with those warehouses, and couldn't tell you where they are now. However, that is what you know as the MOTH company." She pursed her lips, "What's left of it."

Hah! The Flame was not such a distraction for me after all. I mentally punched myself for not putting that obvious one together years prior.

"I'll tell you though," she gestured back and forth with a lazy, titled hand, "it's not some underground gang-oriented drug ring these days. Well, it's that too, but still. Every now and then a girl gets hired for something she doesn't want to do. Sometimes boys. I've been trying to weasel them out into jobs up here when I can, but there's only so much I can do. The club is their cover. No more. No less, but it means a lot to me."

"Why tell me? If I take them down, you're out of a job again."

She shrugged, "My ex has been pissing me off, so maybe I'll throw you a bone." Shaking her head she said, "No, I don't care. I'll reopen the place. I'll make it a real business this time. Make it clean, you know? Like I'm already trying to do." There was a hint of desperation behind those brown eyes, and I had to have hope for her. I nodded. A song about romance began to play. A line about big affairs and regret tugged at me.

"God." Exasperated, I leaned back. "I don't know anything about this place. I barely know anything about you."

"There's plenty to know about me that does not concern this club, or the goings on in warehouses." She let out a quick chuckle which blatantly hid something else, "Believe me."

She put a hand to her lips and asked, "What was the kid's name again?"

"Michael Crown." I showed her the picture.

"Not a name I recognize and not a face I remember. To my knowledge, they aren't in the business of killing people, especially some random schmuck, but I can't say he couldn't have been involved one way or another."

"Well, as far as leads are concerned, this place is all I've got."

"Then that is one thing we have in common." She took another sip. I looked at my almost empty glass, swishing it around.

"I'm sorry that I'm not much help," she said.

"You helped plenty." I lowered my head down towards my glass, but looked up at her instead of taking that last sip. She smiled again and slowly, cautiously put a hand on mine. It was nice. Eventually, some people came over and she had to play hostess. I waited, listening to some more gems of the Big Band era. When Maria came back again, she looked surprised and relieved to see me still there, and we sat in quietude for a bit. It was peaceful, rather than awkward. It was a relief for me too.

Then, she had to go and spoil it by asking, "So, tell me. I know it was years ago but, whatever happened at that bar... What was it? Yeah, what happened at the Rusty Clam, anyway?"

My shoulders went up to my ears, "I don't want to talk about it."

She raised an eyebrow and held a perturbed expression for a moment, then relaxed, amused at how easy it was to rile me with such a subject. Years had passed, but the sting was still there. I felt so much older. I looked older. She looked about the same, with her dark, wavy hair never any longer than a bob. Her lips still perfect, painted in her favorite shade of lipstick, everything else about her like a photograph of the woman I met back then. ...But she wasn't the same. Maria was a woman who had survived Hell, and come out with nothing but sympathy for the devil, because she had met so much worse.

Her hair was just long enough to tuck behind an ear. She did so, which revealed the garnet earrings I had given her years before. She didn't seem to notice that she had done it but then she hadn't exactly been expecting me. I wondered how often she wore them. I felt bad, catching myself grooving to a crooning rendition of a song about a sex worker and cocaine, but Maria seemed to dig it as well. I figured, no harm done if she accepts it.

We ended the evening with her telling me to come back if I got any more specific names, and me telling her I might come back even if I didn't get them. Promises, promises.

As I got up, I took Maria's hand and touched my lips to the back of it. As I pulled away, she tightened her grip, stood up, and used her other hand to guide my face. She held her lips against my cheek for a full three seconds before letting go. When she did, it felt as though she had dropped me off of a cliff.

Leaving was no longer such an easy thing to do, but it had to be done. She sat back down with a thud after I was out of sight.

CHAPTER 3
Love Sick

Jed called.

The screaming sound of my phone at 9 AM was early enough to be late if I had a normal job. I knocked the alarm off of the table. I plummeted out of a wonderful dream of dancing with Maria, and crashed back into reality with foggy bitterness. My subconscious was hardly ever subtle. In fact, hardly anything in my life was particularly subtle. I thought about her for the whole way to the agency.

Opening the door to my office let loose a strange stench. Jed was at my desk with his feet up, chewing on one of my toothpicks.

"And the sheriff rolls back into town, eh?" He took his feet off my desk. Without thinking, I began to dust away invisible grime as I picked up a file vaguely near where he had parked his feet. He was happy to do more research, so we looked into Crown's parents.

Michael had been very close to his father, by what I gathered. I wanted to know who they knew. Look into who the kid really was. After hours turned into a day, complete with ordering and eating too much pizza, Jed and I had sifted through every piece of information we could find online. Town Hall records, public business tax filings, and social media posts helped us find nothing connecting the Crown family to MOTH, flame or otherwise. I'd have to go deeper somehow. A few too many extra hours had passed for my liking. A bored Jed threatened to leave for Town's End to "refuel" while I came up with nothing else on MOTH, but then we turned again to Crown's parents.

Jed reminded me, "There was that other company, right? What was that? The merger."

Michael's parents were no longer as rich as they had once been. His father came from next to nothing, but Mrs.

Crown was a well-to-do woman of means before everything in her life fell apart. Mr. Crown went along for the ride. This led to some seedy business of their own in an attempt to gain more assets and avoid bankruptcy. Was the new company related to MOTH? I was obsessing, but I couldn't shake what Bernie had said about the chemical. And who was the ghost roommate who had a fondness for chemicals and poisons?

I found my shattered sense of justice distracting.

I spent another day on that other company, sans Jed by my side, and found nothing beyond some funny book keeping and "accidental" money. This was of little concern to me, as Michael was not involved. Exhausted and frustrated, I admitted defeat for the time being and called Jed.

"You're overdue for a well-deserved break before we tumble any further into horse shit," said Jed. "I want you to take a break."

"This, of course, means going to get a drink, right?"

"You can't blame me."

"Jed, you're at various bars so often that I've begun to question if you even bother paying rent on your apartment anymore."

"Oh man, I wish! So where we going?"

"Literally anywhere instead of Town's End. That grimy dive bar that you go down some steps to get into is like walking down into a weird rabbit hole of shame."

"You ain't wrong. How about The Platinum Spoon? I'll come pick you up."

I liked the Platinum Spoon. I flirted with a few girls by the pool tables while grooving along to some techno dance tune. It was a lot of thumping and whistles and not a whole lot of music, but that was fun for a while. I leaned against a beam and looked over at one chick in particular. She was a pale, dainty woman with some teal streaks in her otherwise straight black hair. My smooth march over quickly became a stumble, half pouring out the drink that I forgot was I in my hand.

Before I could collect myself, she walked off with some meathead. After an hour or so, none of the other girls had piqued my interest. It was then that I began to notice how quiet Jed was at the bar. Around this point on any other day Jed would have gone on a toot and been properly zozzled. To anyone else, this change of pace would have been a welcome reprieve from the strain and tension of trying to take care of a belligerent drunk. I turned in a panic towards the bar to make sure that my unwieldy hulk of a partner was still in the building. Sure enough, there was my normally boisterous partner sitting right where I left him, calmly sipping at a glass of scotch. It was such a rare sight to see him acting almost content for once. It was *so rare* that I found myself staring in disbelief.

You see, right then a woman walked over and introduced herself to him.

She said her name was Chloe. She was a pretty little thing; I'll give him that. Brunette, with some red highlights in her hair. Her body was tan and curvy. I guessed she was about 5'7, though most of it may have been her shoes. She sat down and called for the "barkeep." Chloe pointed at the bar in front of her, and had the bartender bring out a bottle of good scotch, better than whatever Jed had. She set it down in front of Jed like an offering to an old god. At this bar, that bottle was a pretty big deal. A girl came over to me then, but I waved her off. This was too good of a show for a distraction. My partner, unsure of what to do in this situation, complained that his favorite stool was in need of repair. It was wobbly and tearing at the seat.

A somewhat dark ska song from the mid-80s came on, and Chloe wrapped an arm around Jed as she giggled.

He asked, "Oh shit. Is there a bug on me?"

Poor sap was trying to figure out why else she'd put a

hand on him, if not to dust something gross off his shoulder. He was confused. Here was this pretty girl, actively trying to buy his affection, and he was tortured by it. It kinda worked though, in a completely wrong way. She said she wanted to buy him a burger.

He responded with, "Free food is free food," downed the rest of his scotch and left with her. Casanova, Jed was not. Hell, anything that got that man laid at this point was a blessing, so I let the two go on their merry way.

I took his seat a little too swiftly, feeling the heat from his butt radiating through my pants like an uncomfortable hug to my thighs. I was thrilled he got a date. A clock on the wall ticked on. Songs changed to other songs. I hadn't asked for another drink and a couple of people started to notice. Maybe they didn't. Maybe that was in my head. Eventually, I took my own hint and caught a bus home.

That night, having no Jed and barely a case, I wrote a letter to my parents. It was hard to think, as one of those digging machines was either bafflingly loud, or closer to my house than I would prefer. They seemed to be spreading like a slow swarm of insects.

I could have called my father, or even sent an email, but this was tradition for our family. I held so few traditions sacred, I wasn't about to throw another away.

My note started with, "I'm sorry it's been a few months since our last phone call, and at least a month since I wrote to you. I'll keep this simple, just as an update. Maria's in my life again in a strange, airy sort of way. She may or may not be involved in a case I clearly can't divulge details about here. I'll say that our current case seems odd to me though." I went on to ask about Mom's mahjong tournament, and whether or not Dad had tried his new grill yet.

The door felt heavier than normal. I tripped on the steps outside but caught myself with a jolt like something small punched my throat from the inside. I didn't fall, but my knee wasn't happy. I took a deep breath and stuck the letter in the mailbox before going to sleep.

On the opposite sleep schedule, but the same as many nocturnal animals, Maria was busy signing documents hurried and hushed when the new waitress crept up by her side.

"Thank you for hiring me," said Liz.

Maria smiled as she neatly folded the paperwork to stuff into an envelope, "It's no trouble." Softness filled her eyes as she looked at Liz and mirrored the tone she used to say, "A girl like you can't live that life any longer. You should be up here with me."

Maria never had a type until there was Liz, and then she was it. Her hair was a golden blonde, long in the front to her shoulders, going at a gradual angle until it was short in the back. Her skin was pale, with rosy cheeks. Her nose was small, pierced above the left nostril, and upturned at the tip. She had a full bottom lip, with a pretty upper lip nestled on top. Heavy black eyeliner highlighted striking green eyes. She was taller and less curvy than Maria, with lean muscles. She wore pinks and purples almost every day, like Maria and her little black dresses. Liz always wore bracelets, at least three on each arm, and never the same ones twice.

"I love this club. I always have," said Liz as she leaned in to take her seat. "Saxophones and pretty costumes... It's so perfect. I'd want to have music like this play all day if I ever opened my bookstore."

"You're a reader then?" Maria took a sip of her drink and took a second one for Liz from a purple corseted waitress who knew her well.

"Sure! And a bit of a farmer. I know how that sounds! But yeah. My hope is to get enough money saved that I can take over my family's old farm. It isn't that far out of the city from here."

"And open your bookstore nearby?"

"Why not? Oh, there are a thousand things I want to do."

Maria put her arm around Liz, "You have time."

"What about you? Is this bar your dream?"

Maria shrugged, "It feels like an old habit, being here."

"You look so natural though. It's like you're meant to rule this place. If it isn't what you want though, why not leave?"

"I didn't say this wasn't what I wanted. I don't want this place to be what it currently is, sure. I want what this bar could be. Should be. That's my dream. Independent bar-owner." They clinked their glasses and made quiet vows to support each other in their endeavors, content that they'd have their perfect futures, one way or another. Of course, Maria didn't have that much time before Liz was off to start her first shift. She watched as Liz walked away.

"Helping your fellow whores, huh?" said Denny, startling Maria into spilling her drink. "Not how shit used to be." Denny was tall and slim, but his shoulders were broad, his body like an imposing upside down triangle.

Maria was unfazed by his attempt at intimidation. Her gaze shot like bullets at him, "Are you shitting me? We used to have a woman in charge, remember? Besides, Liz isn't like that. Neither was I, but hey, not like you really care."

"Of course I do, Baby. Name a boyfriend who treated you better than me." Maria didn't answer. She was too busy mopping up her drink with the towel a nearby waitress had on hand.

The next day, sharp as clockwork, I found my partner in "our favorite bar." He had only vaguely told me at which bar to find him, but I knew. Well, on the second try. There were very few places he would automatically run to, and when I popped off of the bus to find his car wasn't at Town's End, I hopped right back on my ride until it arrived somewhat near The Brick House. When I got there, I noticed that Jed was holding a bandage on his shoulder and trying to reach over his opposite arm to get the beer to his mouth.

"Jesus, Jed! What the Hell happened to you?"

"You know my date with Chloe?" He swallowed a slosh of beer, "It went bad, Man."

I failed to imagine ways this love affair could have ended in his blood being spilt. Did he get into a brawl with some hoodlum over this chick? Did he do it to himself in an effort to look more menacing and brave?

"So..." I encouraged him to continue his tale.

"So, we were getting dirty, right? All was well in the land of Jed Dean." He took another gulp. "But, see... She gets this wild look in her eye, right?" I became cognizant of what had happened like walking face-first into a wall.

He went on, "Well, half way through it all, she tells me she's into blood play. I figure, 'hey, I'll bang a dame on her period. What's it to me?' But... Ah... That wasn't what she meant."

"She stabbed you?"

"NO Man! Naw. She didn't stab me. She sliced me a little, that's all." He gestured towards his wound with his fingers and a loose wrist. "Anyway, bitch came at me with a knife, so I figured I should sever the relationship before she severs something on me that I'm more attached to."

"Ah," I gave a forced laugh as I sat down at the bar, "didn't get to finish the date then, eh?"

"No. I finished. Like I said, I was half way there when she said it, and I was pretty close when she cut me so, no. I finished, God damn it. Not goin' through that and not finishing. What do you think I am? Stupid or something?" I didn't answer, but got an old song stuck in my head.

"So, I mean..." I tried to find the words, "You were still an active participant, right?"

Jed blinked, "Well yeah. Okay, so I guess it didn't go all that bad. She's still a scary bitch though, in retrospect." He poked the bar with one finger to get his point across.

I shrugged, "I don't think I would have stayed that long. I think I would have run. Or called the cops. Or both."

Jed squinted at this, then turned toward me to explain, "No, dude. I was getting laid. Didn't you ever do anything weird with a lady?"

I mentally ran through my history Maria, trying to compare anything and everything to Jed getting stabbed by a woman. I discovered that if a beautiful woman like Maria came at me with a knife, perhaps I'd change my tune as well.

He moved on to his next line of thought, "Did you see the menu there?" Jed pointed at a corkboard behind the bar, "They have food now."

When I didn't immediately respond, he asked, "What happened? You see a ghost? Was it the Crown kid?"

"I saw Maria the other day."

He spit a little of his beer at this response, "Right! I forgot. So, did YOUR date go badly or what?" Oh, that's right. I hadn't told him how our meeting went.

He knew very well what I thought of Maria and how she felt about me. He looked at me with stern eyes and thin lips as he let his head drift farther and farther away from me. Then he forgot what I had said, or stopped caring, and went back to his drink.

Maria and Jed got along pretty well back in the day, but they didn't have a chance to become close friends before I cut her off. I had known Jed since high school, so he had to pick the side he knew better. He never outright said so, but I knew Jed had always been a little angry at me for making him choose between one friendship or the other.

After some years had passed, I became oddly possessive of them both anyway. Now though, now we were adults. Time goes by, things change, and I hadn't gotten any smarter.

"I mean, fuck." The word sounded forced, I knew. "I didn't know what to do with myself." I raised my hand to signal to the bartender, then ordered chips and salsa.

Jed told me I sound funny when I swear, "You only do it when things get dire. You say 'fuck' with some actual gusto, and I know to run."

"Aw, come on. That's not true." I shook my head as I adjusted on the stool. The too mild salsa was more like chunky tomato sauce. An old crooner song hummed behind us. Someone turned the volume up when a teen pop anthem concerning making simple things too complicated came on. I started to question if the world was trying to tell me something. Maria sprung up in my mind again. Her laugh rang in my ears. I could still remember how her lips looked when she laughed.

"Yeah it is!" Jed continued, "You say shit like, 'barking dog' instead of 'fuckin' bitch'."

"I don't!" I laughed, but I knew there was some truth to that. Someone discarded a newspaper on the bar near me. The paper screamed headlines pertaining to bombings and a lunatic couple wreaking havoc. I wondered what I'd need to do to get put on a case like that. I wondered if I'd *want* to be put on a case like that. I might swear when working a case like that.

After noting a rather remarkable sixteen missed calls and texts in total, both from Maria and Bernie, we left the bar to get better reception. Bernie didn't pick up, but he worked alone and didn't exactly have a secretary, so I chalked it up to being busy.

Jed shrugged, "So what else can we do?"

"I can talk to Henry again, now that he's had a moment. Ask him about family friends, maybe. Maria should still be working though. Maybe we try the school again."

Jed gently punched my shoulder, "I'll make the call to Maria. You get to the kid."

I left for Henry, texting him on the way to alert him of our makeshift appointment. Not gonna lie, I was proud of Jed for delegating.

Maria picked up when she saw Jed's name on the phone.

He got straight to the point, "I know you've been talking to Gekman, but who else can I talk to who ain't you?"

"Meaning?"

"Nah, I didn't mean it like an insult. He says shit to you, panics, then stops digging. I don't want you in danger any more than he does, so what low-lives can I chat it up with instead?"

Maria reached over the edge of her couch for a little black book within the thin drawer of a painted side table, "Not a bad idea, actually. People know Gabe, not you. Blindside them if you can handle this discreetly."

"I can do discreet! Gimme three hours to sober up."

"That bodes well. This is good, yeah. You know, my ex is involved. You shouldn't talk to him though. I'll give you other names."

"He dangerous? He hurt you?"

She thought about it before saying, "I don't need you to kill him, if that's what you're asking. He's just finally irritated me too much. It was almost dawn when Denny called this time. Especially strange, as his calls are usually in the middle of the night."

"Oh, so fuck him then, yeah. OH, and while I've got you on the phone here, does MOTH stand for anything? Like, it's all caps and shit, so that means it's an acronym, right?"

"You're gonna laugh. In the company hiding beneath the club, 'MOTH' stands for 'Methodological Organization of Theoretical Heresy,' and I admit that it's nonsense."

"This case is nonsense. Did it ever mean something?"

"Yeah. I think so, but I don't know exactly what. I remember finding some old books with that written out, scrawled out in red ink. Maybe it was blood."

Jed went quiet for a moment, trying to figure out if this was a joke.

Maria said, "There was a cult, way back in the day in Cornsbrook. I don't know who started it, but by the time that group became more into science than magic, it was here."

"Okay. That's fucked up. Anything else?"

"I don't know much else beyond that. Sorry." She chuckled, "So is sober-Jed going to change his mind about the whole thing? MOTH stuff gets weird and dark quick."

"Naw, Man. I'm on a mission."

CHAPTER 4
Deeper into the Flame

The next afternoon, I found myself walking into The Platinum Spoon. I hated going into that particular bar during daylight, and I could already smell my partner. At night it would be quieter and intimate, like a secret hideaway with gently glowing overhead lighting. Everything would be muted and calm. During the day, it wasn't a quaint joint so much as a filthy hole. Five men shot pool in the corner while the jukebox played some terrible pop song that was someone saying 'bootyhole' over and over. I would stop to ponder the demise of The Artist as a concept in an era where no one had anything to say later. I zoned out, staring in a direction I hadn't consciously selected.

Once I peeled my eyes from the tilted pool table, there was Jed. I'd learned not to ask "How was your day?" as the answer was never pleasant, and always far too detailed. This time, a chance to ask was not given anyway.

As soon as I sat down, he turned to me and said, "I tell you man, it's Hell. It is a Hell."

"Bad day?" I asked, half remembering that asking was a poor choice. After all, the day before, he had told me the story of Chloe attempting to cut him open during sex. If this was worse, I doubted that I'd want to know.

"Yeah. I'm like Prometheus. You know, that Greek dude whose liver got pecked out every day by the eagle."

I turned my head away from him and leaned onto the bar, looking up at no one as I asked, "Why do I keep coming here?" I held the glass as the bartender poured a rum and coke. The act granted a nice shot of cleavage, lined and cradled by a black shirt and an black lace brassiere. I was saying my hellos to her as she bat her eyes and cooed at me, when my companion piped up.

"Because I keep inviting you here."

"Yeah," I took a sip, leaning back a little, "That's not a good enough excuse anymore. I'm getting tired of bars."

Jed patted me on the back, slamming my shoulders forward and spilling half my drink as he said, "You love me. You know you do."

Gawking at my alcohol-soaked lap I said, "I must." After thanking the bartender for the towel, I mustered up the courage to ask Jed, "So, what happened today? Or last night, for that matter. You kind of vanished to Maria's, and your eyes look like you've got something."

"Yeah, Maria gave me some names and I hunted the fuckers down." Jed chuckled for a bit.

"Did I say something funny?" My partner often left me quite befuddled by simple acts.

"It's this case man," said Jed, "There's nothing. What about you? Did you get something good? All I got was threats. Stupid ones too. I'm telling ya, Man. This is crap. I ran into Zeke while I was there too. I forgot that he works for the assholes Maria works with, yeah?"

"Zeke?"

"The blonde Nazi-looking guy." When I still looked perplexed he added, "The asshole I always say I remember and don't know why."

"Ah." I didn't remember Zeke, but I remembered the fact that Jed almost had an idea of who the man was.

"Yeah. He's a menace and a shit."

Eager to get to something useful, I asked, "Did he tell you anything about the case?"

"He mentioned that he'd like to see me go to Hell, and that I'd never get near Denny. I assumed that meant Maria's ex had something to do with it, but Zeke had no idea who the freaking Crowns were. Like, knew they were some rich bitches, but that's about it." Jed ran his fingers though his hair, and then put his cabbie cap back on.

"Then why mention that guy?"

"Because he always mentions Denny. This time I

thought it worked out, because maybe Denny was Michael's roommate, based only on him having a D-name and being kinda desperate, but Zeke said Denny never mentioned a college at all, let alone Lotgraff. He's telling the truth, I can tell. Man, I even called the school again, but they don't know Denny. So anyway, turned out to be nothin'. You?"

I took a breath, "I got a little about the Crown's friends from Henry. All business partners at one point or another. The Crowns were about to go bankrupt, if not for this merger-stuff, but different people said the merger was with different companies. I don't know why their kid would get killed for that anyway. It doesn't make any sense."

We were getting more aggravated by every passing, meaningless factoid. Still, we put the makeshift pieces together to show that someone from MOTH could have known someone within Mr. Crown's company. That was it. That was all we had.

Finally, Jed's calm exploded with, "I can't believe this shit! You blueberry headed dipshit! We're in a shit storm of idiocy, Gekman! Shit!" Jed stood up and threw his hands into the air, as if trying to push off a crowd of people.

"Let's have a drink." At my suggestion, his eyes lit up. His hands went down. I had pacified him with the magical word, "drink".

I took a toothpick from a pack near a bowl of pretzels on the bar, and carefully placed it in my mouth. I let it stick to my lower lip and I laughed at Jed's immediate gravitation back to a rather decrepit stool. I took the opportunity to wander off to the blueish green covered pool table. The crowd of men had scattered like cockroaches a moment prior, and a couple of women were trickling in to take their collective place around said table.

The bar was not what I would call high class. It was nicer than Jed's usual spot, but the whole place felt like walking into a million beer ads all at once. The men weren't as suave, but the girls were plenty pretty.

They weren't enough to distract my partner, so it didn't take long before Jed was on the edge of a fight. All I wanted was to shoot pool under that green tinted light with the ladies. Was that so wrong?

"Now, you listen here, fuck face," I could hear Jed bellow from across the bar. I put the cue back on the rack behind the table and sighed. A girl giggled. I shot her a wink as I made my way to Jed. Wait, was she flirting or was she laughing at me?

"You are standing between me and the bar. That ain't a place you want to be," Jed almost seemed reasonable. It was unlike him. I began to worry much more than I was before.

The man was blond, sporting a high and tight haircut. Angular in the face, he looked like the poster boy for an old German propaganda film of WWII.

When the man stated, "I've got a right to be here, you little shit."

Jed explained, "You REALLY don't wanna be there, you fuckin-"

"Jed! Pal! Buddy!" I interrupted while putting an arm around his too-high shoulders. I used my body to wedge between the blonde man and the furious monster I called a partner, and managed to squeeze the guy away from the bar. Problem solved, or so I thought.

As it turns out, the worst thing to do when two bears are fighting over honey, is to try to shoo one of the bears away. I should have shot the man instead. Would have been much easier on him. I turned to get Jed a drink. Jed turned to DIVE onto the man.

I'll be honest. I don't truly recall what the heck happened next. I know I got hit on the jaw, but lord only knows which one of the brick-built men threw the punch. Could have been a chair for all I know, but it left my mouth open enough to catch myself drooling. My bottom lip swelled and I must have nailed my cheek against a tooth, because I tasted blood but wasn't missing any teeth.

Cue Jed by my side as we wobbled out of that bar with blood on our shirts that might have been ours, and a woman whose name I can't remember for the life of me dangling off my right arm. It was not, in fact, the woman from the pool table, nor was she the bartender. Miraculously, I still managed to walk away with a piece of napkin sporting said bartender's number. The bartender's name, apparently, was Kirsten.

"Why? Who?" I stammered out.

"THAT was Zeke!" Jed pointed at the bar behind us. "You know him! He's the asshole. GOD I can't believe that shit-fucker was here tonight! What the Hell?"

It dawned on me that Zeke did happen to fit the description of the same person Jed had been angry at multiple times before. I always failed to put two and two together on that one, "Well, I'll be sure to remember the name now, at least."

Jed shook his head like he was trying to get water out of his ears as he said, "Wait wait. Zeke. What the Hell did he do?"

"Just now? That was my question."

He put a hand up and the girl on my arm looked at me for an answer I didn't have.

Jed continued, "I think Zeke did something real bad. Why can't I remember? He looks familiar! I get this feeling in my gut-"

"Maybe you just don't like Nazi lookin' guys" I said. "I'll admit, I certainly have a knee-jerk reaction myself. Lost a lot of family to that type." Jed nodded, but I could see in his eyes that he wasn't satisfied by that answer.

He was grumbling on his way to his car when I said, "Oh! Jed, I didn't take your keys, did I? I should- Jed give me your keys!" I was too tired to argue when he got into his car. It was unlike him, and I hoped for the best.

The lady drove me home, following my mangled

directions.

"I aim to take you upstairs," I said. "This house was my childhood home, actually. I bought it from my parents when they retired."

Her eyes went from sparkling to dull as I continued to wax poetic about the wallpaper being the same as it was when I was five. We sat on the couch, and I fell asleep with my shoes on before anything interesting could happen. She left without a note. That was fair enough. In the morning, I noticed my watch was missing. That was less fair, and may have been an over-payment.

I stepped out of a quick shower to an angry vibration of Maria texting me to meet her at my place. I told her to show up whenever, almost immediately followed by a knock at my door.

Maria kissed me on the cheek in a "That's a good boy" kind of way, passed me, and made herself comfortable on the couch as I struggled to finish clothing myself.

"Did you sleep here?" she asked, gesturing to my rolled up socks and other clothing I had peeled off of myself in a trail leading from the couch to the downstairs shower.

"I passed out cold there and did not make it to my bedroom, if that's what you're asking." I walked past the island that acted as a divider between the living room and the kitchen. As I began to brew a new pot of coffee, I realized that I had no idea what time it was, or what day for that matter.

I asked, "What brings you here in such a rush?"

"A friend of mine was gossiping about overhearing a guy called Frog. He's got his hands in a lot of the behind-the-scenes drug mule stuff of MOTH. He knows people who know people, you know?" I scrunched my eyebrows together and shook my head. Maria continued without my understanding, "Well my friend Chloe said he was causally mentioning stuff still being down in the old storage units, some of it physically under my club in crates. He wants it all gone, which I'm totally for. So I looked and I found this in an old box." She took a brown bottle from her purse. "This is from the Old Days," she held it out to me.

I bent over to get a closer look at the small, maybe three-inch-tall bottle between Maria's fingers, but with no label, I had no idea what any of it could be. I asked, "Any chance you know how to find this Frog person?"

She shook her head, "I asked Chloe, but she says he's notoriously difficult to find, and manipulative enough that I shouldn't trifle with him. I believe her." There were enough Chloes in the world that I didn't assume a connection to Jed's date from Hell.

Maria continued, still holding the brown bottle out, "I know more was hidden somewhere far from my place. Probably wherever they used as a cover before my club. Anyway, it's still got a little left. Could this be what killed that boy? Maybe someone could test it and find a match."

"Maybe. I'm sorry that you found it in your club, but glad you're handing it to me. What do you think about it?" I scratched the back of my neck as I stretched out. Such couches were not meant for sleeping.

She answered with a quiver in her voice, "I don't know. It seemed like something suspicious, and I know MOTH used to do shit with poisons. Well, Denny used to, anyway. He seems to prefer guns now. And his bare hands."

"Do you think Denny could have killed this guy?"

"He could have, sure, but I don't think he did. He'd have no reason. Besides, he's theatrical. If he'd done it, I'd know. He'd gloat about it. He'd shove it in my face that he can do somebody in whenever he wants. So, no. I don't think he actually had anything to do with it. But, you think there's a connection to MOTH, and you said he was poisoned somehow, so... Here," She handed it off to me in a way that suggested she never wanted to see it, or anything related to it, ever again.

It was worth a shot, "Did Denny go to college?"

"Yeah, but I don't know where, and he never graduated. He got kicked out for, well, being Denny. Why?"

"Okay," I said, "it's kind of screwed up, but did he have a roommate like a year ago?"

"Oh, I have no idea. Sorry."

I stood up and poured some coffee for the two of us. I sat back down to immediately scald my tongue on the still steaming beverage. Maria took the cue to blow gently on her mug.

At least I was finally starting to wake up, "That's okay. And do you know anything else about this Frog guy? Even a tiny detail."

"Even Chloe didn't know much. I will say, I know a girl named Kathy. She talks about being Frog's girlfriend, but I don't think she actually is. I think she has a weird crush on him."

"So, there's a Chloe, and a Kathy, and a Frog. Okay. We'll look into it if this doesn't give us any other leads. Why is he called Frog anyway?"

She said, "From what I gather, he's called Frog because he always has his tongue out, you know? Lashing about, trying to catch whatever fly might be stupid enough to fall for his most recent scheme. He's quick with his words and can be very charming when he chooses to be. So, if nothing else, maybe you should be careful if he's really that manipulative." I nodded, looking at the bottle. I felt my brow furrow.

Didn't Abby used to talk about tiny brown medicine bottles and containers when she was in the hospital? It was upsetting how often she was coming to mind during this case.

"Okay. If you or your friend find anything else, let me know. I'm gonna run this over to Bernie in his lab. This might be a real breakthrough." I held the door for her and kissed her lips without thinking. We didn't say goodbye so to speak. She smiled.

CHAPTER 5
Frog's Breath

I got to Bernie as fast as I could, as though this practically ancient bottle of goo would suddenly expire, or the Crown boy would become *more* dead.

He was elbow deep in a body, but popped up and out when he saw me approach through the metal doors. He ran to a sink while saying his hellos, asking what I'd brought him. He'd noticed the gleam in my eye that said I had something of use.

I handed Bernie the bottle and his face contorted into a mix of joy and horror.

He said, "This is it. These were the bottles. The little bottles that man had before. Now I can analyze it. If I can find something that matches in... Oh God. This could be it!"

I felt a little bad for the now neglected corpse on the slab, as Bernie began bustling around a series of tubes and beakers. I understood that desperation of needing an old question finally answered.

"I have people I can send a bit of this to so it's being analyzed in- oh you don't care, but it's good! It's a good thing, and there's enough to do it!" Bernie took a gasp of air before he asked, "Is there anything else before you go? This'll take a while. Plus, I gotta finish up with Mr. Pager here." He gestured loosely toward the corpse.

I asked, "Well, you ever meet a guy called Frog?"

He looked startled, "No. No, I don't know any Frog. I mean, I know amphibians." He laughed at his own joke. He then sniffed before dismissing my question with, "It'll take a while to see where this goes, but thank you for this. It'll be a huge help in your case, I'm sure!"

Bernie was smiling more than I'd ever seen. It occurred to me that his answer seemed stiff, and his body shifting to shoulders-to-ears for that brief moment was telling me something. Bernie may know Frog, even be afraid of him. I needed to be more careful with the folks I brought into this case.

"Yo, Bitch," said Zeke, as he sauntered into The Moth Flame.

"Hey, Bitch," said Maria.

"Seriously?" He made a mock hurt expression.

"Well, I'm not the one taking orders from Denny like I'm his little lap dog. That would be you." She managed to maintain an emotionless visage.

"Funny." Zeke took a seat. "Denny's been complaining to everyone with ears about you talking up somebody who thinks he's like an old school gumshoe. The fuck is going on?"

"It's Gabe again. Poor schmuck means well."

"Ah. Gabe Gekman." He clasped his hands together in a mock-angel pose, "Your college sweetheart, right?"

She mumbled, "Nothing sweet about him."

"See? You are funny. Denny chose well," he reached for her chin, but Maria shook him off. "Guy come by often?"

"If you ask him, no." She gestured lazily yet with spite, "In his head, it's always been years since he last saw me. It's always some convoluted reason he's showing up too, but in reality it's about... I'd say about once every month."

Zeke leaned in, "He's here once a month?"

Maria leaned her face away from Zeke as though she smelled something rotten, "Not here, generally. Usually, he stares at me longingly in a bar somewhere for a bit. Point is, he sees me once a month. I'm like his period. I'm a little painful, but I'm a reminder that his biology still works. This was the first time in a very long while that he actually came to The Flame."

Zeke squinted, "So, not a threat."

"No. Like I said, he means well, but he couldn't find his asshole with both hands."

"Whatever. Just keep your mouth shut. The bosses like what you do here, but that wouldn't earn any favors if-"

Maria slammed her fist onto the table, causing a jolt in Zeke, "No ifs. Don't you dare question me, my loyalty, or my integrity. I don't talk. I run a clean place. You shits are the ones who track in mud now and again. This is *my* place, damn it."

Zeke fixed his ratty t-shirt as though it was a suit, "Speaking of, there'll be a truck Thursday night. We're getting some of those machines. Gonna get in on that HiEn shit."

She slouched and crossed her arms, "I don't have the space."

"Make it." Zeke pushed himself away from the table, and began to walk away.

Maria placed her words with care, "It doesn't work that way."

Zeke twisted his neck before turning his whole body back around to loom over Maria, "Sell some drinks or something, bitch. Or turn a trick. Suck Denny's dick again for all I fucking care, make it work."

Maria didn't bat an eye, questioning in silence if poison would work against someone who used his own stash so often. After all, she had thought about it with Zeke a million times before.

As if playing a game by herself, she said, "You know, you guys only come by to tell me to shut up and make room. Won't you stay and have a drink?"

"Maybe next time."

She called out to him as he turned to leave, "Only good advice my father ever gave me was, 'Never trust a man who doesn't drink'."

"You should be a fucking stripper comedian or something. Denny would fuckin' love that." As he walked out, Maria slumped forward.

"Never trust a man who doesn't drink." She lowered her voice as she gazed into her martini, "Or a woman who does." She took a swig and slammed the empty glass down. Liz had overheard the conversation, keeping herself scarce and quiet in a dark corner.

She sat down by Maria, scooting the chair over inch by inch, until Maria finally smiled.

"There we go," said Liz. "You busted your ass for me. I can't have you frowning and shit. None of that. Here..." She took Maria's hand in hers, "Let's go to my place. I've been making some new jewelry, like you suggested, and you know what?"

Maria smirked, then let out a chuckle, "What?"

"You were right. I do feel better. Old hobbies really do help."

Maria swished the last drop of her drink around in one hand, while refusing to let go of Liz's hand with the other.

Maria said, "You're good at it, from what I've seen. I bet you could even sell some pieces. When I've got this club to myself, we'll set you up a little store front." Liz gently kissed Maria's cheek, and helped her up.

"Everything is going to be okay," said Liz. "Just wait. You'll see."

A couple days passed without much sounds from underground, until a text came from Maria. It wasn't my phone buzzing though, it was Jed's. His fingers were a flurry as he texted back, a determined look on his face. I stretched my neck out to see what was going on from my office chair.

"What are you two chatting about?" I asked.

"Heh. Maria's asking for love advice, believe it or not."

"From you? Why?" I sucked my cheek between my teeth, "Is it about me?"

"Nah, sorry Gekman." He wasn't sorry, Jed was laughing, "Looks like you lost your shot! It's this girl she's working with, Liz Ramond. Sounds cute." Another buzz lead to, "Ooh! She IS cute. OH man, Gekman, this chick is WAY cuter than you are!"

He was grinning, so thrilled. I couldn't tell if he was messing with me. I figured it was about time to have some fun sans Maria anyway, at least until we got a better lead for the case.

"Did you wind up calling that bartender yet?" asked Jed. I shook my head and told him more than I expected to. He soon learned that I would think of Maria while with other women. He elected to give me advice, assuming I needed to win Maria over.

"Talk about her eyes and shit." Jed tilted his head back and made an awful noise like somewhere between a belch and vomiting, then said, "You gotta be a poet to woo her, man.

"Her eyes are brown. Nothing good is brown." I knew well enough how to woo a woman, and even how to get Maria. Something else was always blocking me.

Jed put his head in his hands, "Whisky is brown. Chocolate is brown. Maria's fucking eyes are brown. Those are good things. Fuck! YOUR eyes are brown, and you pretend you love yourself, right?"

I wanted to think that deep down, lovers were playthings for Maria, and not much else. This wasn't true, but I told myself it was. To have a real connection with her was frightening. Society had told her a lot of things, and very few of them were true or had anything to do with her own feelings. This rang true concerning her feelings for Liz or myself as well.

Bernie called me at around eight PM. I walked outside of Town's End to get better reception, and was surprised that Jed followed. He appreciated the time to cool down outside in the crisp night air.

"I got it!" Bernie screeched into the phone, "I finally found the toxin! HO I feel like my life's work has come together, you know? That old case- ANYWAY, yes, there is something in Michael Crown's system! Not normal drugs you see on the street though, or even hospital grade. Honestly, chemically speaking, this stuff looks more like Rohypnol in combination with some kind of serious toxin. This was specially made, I think."

"Well, now what? Does this mean there's a definite link to the MOTH Company?"

"Yeah. Find Frog. You mentioned him last time, right? I... Frog knows where all the stuff in this town goes, including everything through MOTH. I'll keep looking into this toxin."

"How'd you find out about Frog? I mentioned his name, but not much else. Do you think he's got a connection to the company?" I tried my best to be delicate.

Bernie seemed unsure if he should answer but said, "I got a call soon after I ran the tests from some... old friends of mine. I asked, and they told me who Frog is. Said he's in chemical distribution." He could have been lying to me, but it didn't matter. Bernie sounded unsure. I didn't doubt his info, just his description of its source.

"That's it then. We keep going into MOTH." I gave Jed a chummy pat on the back, and he looked at me quizzically, as he hadn't heard any speck of Bernie's side of the conversation.

I hung up the phone, looked to Jed to tell him what I had learned, and saw one eye get larger than the other.

I asked, "What's wrong Jed?"

He was looking past me, at a little store across the street, "It's her! It's the chick from the bar again! Christ. Was she always everywhere?"

I shrugged, "The bar? Which bar? You spend most of your time in various bars."

"The chick with the knife!"

"Oh. From THAT bar. Wait. ...Isn't that this bar?"

"Her name's Chloe! Remember her Goddamn name! Bitch is out for blood," His voice became high pitched as though he had inhaled three balloons worth of helium, "but I think in a sexy way?"

"Then... What's the problem?"

His tone dropped back down again, "I... I don't know." He was wrecked by her very presence. Chloe wasn't a big woman, but she could hold her own in a fight, and often did, by the look of it. She walked with a determined gait, head held high. She'd smile at passing folks on the street, then scowl if anyone made a comment she didn't approve of.

"She hangs out with Maria, by the way," Jed whispered.

"Really? Did that come up, or-" Jed hushed me silent, then swiveled his head on his neck as he searched for a place to hide. Chloe wanted romance, even if it ended badly for Jed. He was still half-debating if he was willing to take it, but chose to gracefully hoist himself into a nearby dumpster instead. She wandered off, having seen me, looked for Jed and been unable to find him.

Jed clawed his way up, scrambling out, then flopped onto the ground in front of the thankfully freshly emptied dumpster into which he had thrown himself.

He grabbed my pant leg to pull himself to his feet and said, "She's like a PhD or something. Really smart. It makes her worse, Man! She can find anything and anyone. She's like if a comic book hero decided to be an evil, crazed woman!"

"So, a comic book villain."

Jed ignored me and continued, "Her mother designs tanks and shit, and the digging machines with the little grabby hands." He gestured with t-rex arms, "Which is cool, but Chloe is freaking crazy, Man."

"She can find anything or anyone, huh? Maybe we could use her on the team." When I said this, my partner's face went pale and drooped.

"You crazy, candy headed shitter. The blue dye has infected your brain!"

We had to find Frog, and if her mother could find us something big to use, the more the merrier.

"I'm gonna ask," I picked up my pace to cross the street.

"I'll stay here!" I heard Jed say before the dumpster slammed shut again. She hadn't gotten far.

"Hey, Chloe right?" I said.

"Yeah, who's askin- OH you're Gekman, right?" She put her hand out for a shake.

"I am. Gabe Gekman, Jed's friend. I assume that's how you know who I am?"

"Well, and Maria talks about you. There aren't many guys in suits that have blue hair around here," said Chloe.

"That's fair. Listen, I know we don't know each other, but Jed was saying you can find people. He and I may need your help for a case."

"Sure! Anything for my Jeddy teddy. What do you need?"

"We're looking for someone who calls himself Frog. Could you help us?"

Chloe shook her head, "Frog's not easy to find. I may be able to get some information on him to get you there. Anything specific you wanna know about him?"

"Does he have any connection with the MOTH company that you know of?"

She thought about it for a second, then answered, "Not directly, but then, everyone kind of does, right? I mean, Mom's selling some machines to people I know are gonna be sending them off to MOTH, but as a company or whatever, MOTH doesn't really exist anymore. It's technically disbanded, yeah? Like, from a legal perspective. People still know and use the name though, and right now, digging for HiEn is big business, and it's good to have a name."

"Now I'm wondering how to get a giant drill tank of my own."

Chloe smiled at this, "As Jed's friend, all you gotta do is call me." She handed me her mother's card and started to walk off.

I caught up, "Hey, I know this is a long shot but have you heard of a Michael Crown?"

To my surprise, she nodded, "If you mean the kid obsessed with butterflies, yeah. He came to our factory to protest twice, but like I said, we don't know what gets done with our machines. We couldn't help him. I felt real bad."

"Who was he protesting?"

"Uh… Shit, I don't remember. A farm site. I think the second one was closer to home, cause he was real mad about it. The places they were gonna dig was upsetting this rare butterfly habitat in the area. I remember that much. OH and the farm was in Newsburg!"

She took a moment to nod before clarifying, "I remember that because the family that owned the farm came to us to stop the protesting. What the fuck did they think we could do about it? But yeah, I don't know what happened to either side of that, let alone the butterflies. Sorry." She shrugged, "If you need anything else though, like a machine, you call us, okay?"

She gave a little wave, and walked away. I guess that was the end of the conversation.

Jed invited me into his apartment for a breather, and to play therapist about his whatever-the-Hell with Chloe. He paced and drank while I mostly sat on his couch flipping through old magazines for a couple of hours.

We heard a faint scrapping sound. Shoved under his door was a large envelope.

"Is it a death threat?" asked Jed as though that was common for him. I opened it.

I said, "It's a file. HAH. Must be from Chloe." Taped to the inside-front of the manila envelope was a polaroid of Jed sleeping, with hearts drawn in permeant marker and "call me" but I decided not mention that part to him. I flipped through the papers, "It's a list of clients Chloe's mom has had for their machines, Crowns included. Ramond sounds like a familiar last name too. That's somebody..."

Jed pointed at the paper in my hand, "It's Liz's last name. Her family farm used the machines." I put the papers down to pick up my notebook.

"Chloe mentioned a farm that Michael Crown had been at, trying to protest against the machines destroying a butterfly habitat. We gotta talk to Liz," I said.

"What's that?" Jed walked over to the folder and flipped it over, revealing a USB drive taped to the back. He also noticed the polaroid. "Shit," he said, handing the whole package over to me. "Is this gonna turn out to be weird porn? Maybe you should look at it first."

I had no fear of Chloe, so I ripped the USB off of the folder and marched up to my computer. It took a minute for the machine to recognize that I was asking it to do anything.

The window opened to ninety-eight files, and nothing was labeled. I hesitated, so Jed took the mouse from me and clicked.

"Holy shit," said Jed. "This is a bunch of stuff on Frog! Why does she even have this? Does she have a file like this on me?" The answer was probably "Yes," but I didn't respond to the question. Instead, Jed and I spent a few hours perusing the files, printing some to spread out on his coffee table to pore over in detail. They were mostly typed documents, probably from gossip she had collected over the years. Every now and then there was a blurry photo that didn't tell us much, as though he was some kind of cryptid.

I'll give Frog one thing: His plans and his puzzles and his often convoluted tricks and conspiracies? They were elegant. Maria and Chloe were right though, as he was also very difficult to hunt down. Even his looks made for an easy time blending in. His suits were ridiculous, but he was a good looking guy of Italian descent, not much shorter than I was. In those padded shoulder suits, he came across as about the same build as I was, but he lacked any semblance of muscle definition otherwise. As eccentric as he attempted to be, he was average. While I may have both pitied him and seen myself in him a little bit in a different life, at that moment, he was the enemy.

Nothing gave me any clues to where he might be. However, the name "Kathy" came up a few times. I sent Maria a text assuming this was the same Kathy she knew. There were a lot of Kathys in the world, sure, but everything in my life came back to Maria.

She answered near immediately with, "Yes. Come

over. Do you remember where I live?"

Jed left for yet another drink. He figured I'd like time alone with Maria. I did not. I was nervous. I took a bus and wound up at Maria's place faster than planned.

She was wearing a fuzzy bathrobe, and clearly nothing else. It drooped off of her shoulder and revealed pale skin as she stood in the doorway, looking more entertained than annoyed at my far-too-early knock. My being there wasn't my fault. We had to find Frog, and Maria knew his maybe-girlfriend, Kathy. This led to me standing awkwardly in the hallway of her apartment complex. Of course. That was reason enough, right? I bit my lip when I caught myself staring at her bit of exposed flesh. She took note of that and gestured for me to come inside. Soon, she was pouring drinks and leading me to a couch.

After she mentioned that she had known Kathy for a long time, I laughed, "Ah. She's one of you despicable types, huh?"

Maria frowned at my half serious question, sitting close to me. "She isn't exactly a MENSA candidate," she said, "but I think she's your best bet for someone who would know where to find Frog. You be nice to her, okay?"

"Should dump Frog in a pond." I took a swig of whatever was in that glass, thinking about all the people who had been hurt by what he had peddled for so long.

She crossed her arms and said, "With cinderblocks."

"'Kathy' blocks will have to do." Maria rolled her eyes at my joke and accidentally let a half smile escape her lips. She always smiled at my terrible jokes. With that, Maria stood up to give Kathy a call.

I got up soon after to look around. I spied a pair of chrome handcuffs having decided to make another joke. You see, occasionally I get a bad case of Stupid, and mistakenly find myself humorous.

I smirked and said, "I had a pair like these once. Did

you secretly become a cop when I wasn't looking?" as I dangled the handcuffs from one finger. She laughed to the point of a snort when she attempted to stop, but not at my joke.

"Everything in this room," she gestured at a few ropes and whips, "and THOSE are what you pick out to make fun of? Still, better than some other things you could have said, I guess."

I raised an eyebrow, "About your previous employment?"

"You're wrong about that, you know." As I asked how, she shushed me, dialing the phone for Kathy again, but to no avail. This wasn't an issue, she said. Maria had an idea of where to find her. We'd have to go out into the city and collect her. I agreed that this would be preferable, given the amount of time that had already passed since Michael Crown's murder.

Maria meandered behind a modesty curtain. Good thing too. I was about to make an even bigger fool of myself.

It was at this point that I got a good look around the massive apartment. She had lived in a studio loft for so many years that having the entire first floor of a townhouse seemed excessive by comparison. The layout was like a classic penthouse, and could have been a single family home. I didn't feel the need to ask what went on in the "maid's quarters" but it still struck me as a huge living area for one woman. She filled the place with Halloween decorations, paintings, sculpture, interesting furniture, and some objects that I wasn't quite sure about.

Three different whips hung on the walls, there were medieval looking things on black shelves, rope of varying length and color and... God only knows what that thing was. I felt very young. When I had gotten caught up by what I *thought* she did, it never occurred to me what that would entail, nor did she herself ever actually say. There may have been a good reason for that.

I took in a deep breath and desperately tried to let it out again. I stuck my hands in my pockets and couldn't help but let my mind wander. I started wondering how to use half of that junk, and whether or not I could possibly like it. This was an awful thing to start thinking. The way the light poured in from the wide window behind her, I could see her nude silhouette, almost beckoning beyond the screen. I whipped around and turned my back towards her, as though she could see me, and started to whistle poorly. Even just the outline of that chassis... Jesus. Every now and then, my eyes would gravitate to her form and turn my head along with them. She wasn't someone I could really be in a relationship with, right? Or... Well, was she? I tried reasoning with myself in both directions as I eyed more toys on shelves. God, what was wrong with me? It was like I couldn't turn off a speaker spewing garbage inside my skull. She probably didn't even view me as a real- What was THAT thing for?

She took her dress from where it had been draped, but her panties fell. I picked them up for her. I was being a gentleman, in fact. They were lace, and would barely cover anything. I swallowed air and tried to calm myself down as I tossed them over to her. She thanked me. When she came out, I appreciated the dress. It was a sexy, slinky black number. Most of her dresses were black, but this one was particularly alluring, with a slit up the side to the top of her thigh. It gathered across the waist and up on either side like a layered "V," and her breasts sat perked inside the halter neck bodice. Dumbfounded, I questioned internally how she could breathe in such a dress.

I swallowed, trying to ignore the dress as best as I could and ask about her earrings instead.

"Do you like them? Liz made them for me. She's even teaching me to make things too! See?" I had never seen Maria so excited as she ran to her coffee table and held up her blue and purple creation.

"That's really cool, Maria." I was happy for her. I was so blissful that she was laughing and looking full of joy in a way that I had never seen. Perhaps she hadn't had very many real friends before then. Perhaps it was something else entirely, like Jed had said.

I had a knot in my stomach as I asked, "About Liz... Her family farm. Chloe said there was a protester once, and said protester was Michael Crown."

Maria asked, "Is Liz a suspect?"

"I don't know," I was being honest, "but if nothing else, maybe she'll have some details we're missing. We're still following the poison lead though. If there's nothing connecting her to that, then she's fine anyway."

Maria's eyes darted around for a moment, looking for something inside her own head, "Liz hangs out with me and works for MOTH. She was a mule for a while. ...And her farm had this Crown kid on it, yeah? The one that died, but she wouldn't-"

"I'm not saying she did anything. She might know who did. That's all." Maria jotted down Liz's number for me and asked, "Don't suppose I'd be allowed to hang out during this interrogation."

"I don't think it'll be an interrogation, so I don't see why not. I'm not considering her a suspect. Crown was there a long time before he was found dead. Plus, her farm isn't the only place he protested. I'm thinking maybe one of the machine operators could have been at both sites. I don't know." I shrugged.

Maria decided to give Kathy one last call, just in case. I wandered around a bit as I overheard her say "Corner of Brensten and Canary?" Clearly, she got through. I didn't hear her hang up or say goodbye, so I was a bit startled when she caught me staring at something phallic next to what looked like a pre-made noose on the wall.

She calmly stated, as though she had read my mind

the whole time, "I've never fucked for money, by the way. Never even touched my clients. That's not the kind of thing they asked for."

"Wait. Really?" I was an idiot for many years, apparently. Stuck inside my own head, I hated myself too much to ask.

"You know," she said seductively in my ear, "now that we know where she is, we have some time if you'd like to..." She gestured towards a large rod on the wall.

Without thinking, or perhaps while thinking too much, I started, "Well, maybe. I mean, I never really thought about-" I caught myself. "NO! No. That's uh... That's okay. I mean, aren't I on the clock?" I tried to laugh it off, but my chuckle was openhandedly a ruse, "So let's get going, right?"

She held out a sticky note with the address for Kathy, raised an eyebrow and said, "I'm not going with you. I got dressed for work, and to tease you."

She smiled slyly as I grabbed the note and fled the room. I wanted to stop and turn around to find out what her clients got instead, but I had already gotten into a sprint. The sticky note said I had at least half an hour to get there before Kathy would wander off again, but nothing mattered so much as leaving that apartment in that moment.

CHAPTER 6
Upside Down and Backwards

Kathy was awful. Jed had practically melted into the brick wall on the same corner where we found her. She still hadn't told us anything of use after talking to her for over an hour. She had a laugh so irritating that every time her lips parted, I wanted to grow an extra flap of skin inside of my ears that I could close on command, to prevent that awful sound from reaching my eardrums. She kept talking, yet said nothing.

"I love your hair! Hahaha like is it natural? Hahaha! Like, is your mom's like that?" She in total asked me about twenty times if my hair was naturally blue.

I tried to answer differently with, "Maybe," but that didn't stop her.

Kathy only got worse as she became more comfortable, noticing that her audience wasn't going anywhere. She called Jed ugly to his face and I was amazed she still lived. She also peppered a few choice anti-Semitic statements into the conversation that may have actually been her attempt at being politically correct and supportive of me. I worried about my teeth as my jaw attempted to clamp even tighter into a grind.

I took in a breath, "I just want you to tell us where we can find Frog, okay?" I wanted to be done with her forever.

"Um yeah so I go with Frog pretty much everywhere and we saw each other like yesterday, well it wasn't yesterday, it was like a month ago hahaha but yeah we text all the time so it's like we're always in contact, you know and Hahaha yeah, like, hahaha so um Frog likes those uh Whachamacall them, you know the Latino restaurants so we should go to there."

Jed looked at me sideways. His shoulders rolled

towards his ears as he said to her, "The only vaguely Mexican restaurant around here is Burrito Baron. Not even Mexican. It's Tex-Mex. Is that what you mean? Tex-Mex at the Burrito Baron?"

"YES! That's the place! Hahaha! Let's go there! Please please please? Let's go to the Burrito Baron! It's Frog's favorite, I promise!" Kathy jumped up and down. If she was adorable, or at least cute in personality, her leaping in the air with joy would have been a lot of fun to participate in. Unfortunately, she didn't even have that going for her. It was a right shame. Someone that irritating should at least be attractive on some level. Or funny. Or something nice. Anything nice, really. I'm not usually so mean, even in my thoughts, but something about Kathy brought that out of me. Okay, that's not true. I was always judgmental, but not out loud, of course. It didn't help that Kathy was like nails on chalkboard as a person.

I said, "All right then. We'll ask people around there." I looked at Kathy. I looked right into her vacant, blank stare. I looked so hard that I could have seen her very soul, had she had one. "Don't you know a more specific spot than just hoping he's at this particular restaurant, today of all days? I mean, he's your boyfriend, right?"

She jutted and titled her head to the side. I think she was trying to look cute, but it came out all twisted and strained. Layers, wrinkles, and extra chins appeared on the one side of her throat as she said, "Of course he's my boyfriend! Hahaha! He and I have been sleeping together a really long time, yeah."

"Okay. Oh. Kay. Well." I had to know, "What does 'boyfriend' mean here?"

"Um, duh? Someone who doesn't have to pay! Hahaha!" She hung herself on my arm, putting all her weight into it as she said, "You can be my boyfriend too, you know. I know Maria doesn't treat you right. You should be with a real woman, like me!" We continued walking. She coughed before adding, "Like, Maria is fine, but she's a moron."

Normally I'm much more passive. Normally, I can take a beating like the best of them, and still have a witty comeback. But this... This was not normal.

As a result, I said in perfect, robotic monotone, "I hate you. I hate you with every fiber of my being." To this, the dumb quaff chuckled even more. I turned to Jed and said, "If the dame starts screwing a burrito, I'm having her committed on the spot." He nodded, glaring in her direction. Jed and I were both remarkably kind for how we were feeling on the inside. She was mean, and thought she was funny. She assumed every man wanted her. She was... Oh. She reminded me of how I viewed myself in the worst possible ways.

Dragging Kathy with us into the restaurant, we sat down at the first table we saw. It was nice and close to the door in case we needed to leave in a hurry. This was especially good because, after we had already ordered our food, it became evident that Kathy was not exactly a brilliant conversationalist. Well, more obvious than we had already witnessed. I stared at that door for a while. It was lodged between a giant, singing cactus, and a happy, personified sombrero. Green, yellow, and red burned my eyes under flickering fluorescent lights.

Boring at best, Kathy spoke of drugs she'd "like, never do," yet knew exactly how they all worked and how long they'd last in someone her size. Then she started about past sexual exploits. That second one could have been entertaining, but I disliked her as a person. She wasn't physically ugly, but every now and then she'd wink at me and emit a sound that could have been an attempt at a sexy moan in my direction. She made me feel dirty, and not in a good way. Where was Frog? Would we recognize him if we saw him come in?

She kept talking in my general direction about many

things until she landed on, "So how much money does a P.I. make? Like, are you loaded, or are you like a squatter somewhere? It's totally punk rock if you're homeless, but like, you dress nice, so you probably make bank, right?" She blinked at me a few times, trying to flirt for God only knows why.

"Depends on the case," was all I said in response. It wasn't what she was hoping for, and yet, she persisted.

I called her names, but I must have said it too fast. I kept only closed-off body posture, but I must have looked aloof and thus alluring. It all appeared to contain a double meaning of something very positive, by how she replied. The bright yellow and guacamole green of the walls caused a migraine to teeter on the edge of my brain as she spoke. Eventually, I had stopped responding altogether. I assumed my silence would lead to her talking less. I was wrong.

Somewhere in that nightmarish, one sided conversation, the waiter came to take our orders. I don't remember saying anything, but I know something was said. I was too busy being unhappy.

Frog was nowhere to be found. Kathy was laughing at the phone in her lap. I wondered who she was texting, yet didn't care enough to ask. Then, in walked Chloe. Huh. I guess that's who she was texting. How did they know each other? Did *everybody* know each other? Jed dove under the table in a fluid motion, but when I kicked him, he peeked his head up.

"Whatcha doin' down there, Honey?" Chloe inquired.

"Uh... dropped my fork." Jed clutched it for dear life. Then he paused and thought for a moment.

Jed looked at Chloe as if he didn't find her utterly terrifying and said, "You know how to find people right? You hear things..."

"That I do. Your buddy here already tried this." She smiled as I chuckled to myself, thinking she sounded like she was admitting to suffering from auditory hallucinations. She hears things.

Jed straightened up. "We're here, looking for Frog. Kathy said he'd be here." He gestured desperately towards Kathy with the fork.

Chloe scrunched her eyebrows together and thought for a moment. She put a hand on her hip and shook her head, "By what I've heard, Frog hasn't been around here in months." Chloe turned to look at Kathy, "I told you that earlier, didn't I?"

"Oh," giggled Kathy, "I know!"

I was furious. I was so mad that I couldn't even move. I was paralyzed with an intense loathing for this muddlehead of a girl. I broke out of it, unblinking, to shove a fistful of cold, soggy nachos into my mouth once the waiter presented the family-sized plate in front of me.

Kathy, sweet as candy continued, "I took them here because I wanted time alone with Gabey-Baby Gekman here. I figured he's a detective, so if my Froggy won't tell me where he is, these guys'll find him for sure! And if not? I'll fuck Gabe!" She laughed again and stated, "Yeah like honestly, I'm kinda surprised Jed hasn't gotten bored and wandered off."

Jed asked with one eye closed, "Was that part of your master plan, you lunatic?"

Chloe took this as an invitation to sit down. She pulled up an empty seat from a nearby table with very little regard to the people still sitting there. They glared at her, but didn't argue. She then swung the chair right next to Jed's. Chloe and Jed made a cute couple, when he didn't look like he was about to scream and set himself on fire.

After a while of this double date from Hell, we'd consumed too much spicy and cheesy food, and Chloe was sound asleep on Jed's shoulder. It looked like a hurricane wouldn't wake her. She even snored, but it was hard to hear over the generic mariachi music. Kathy was still talking a lot about nothing. At one point, her voice consisted only of a buzzing to me, mingling with the buzz of the lights, as though a bee had tucked itself into my ear to drown out her incessant nonsense.

"There's no reason to still be here, right?" I started to get up, but Chloe opened her eyes and looked remarkably sad at the prospect of our double date ending. She had a death grip on Jed's arm anyway, so I sat back down and picked up a churro to devour.

My partner had his hands clasped in front of him, very businesslike as he asked, "So, when we're chatting with Frog... How long before I can cut off his little toe?"

I waited patiently for the day to be over with my head leaning on my fist. When the waiter came with somehow even more food, I smiled and thanked him. I took another churro. Jed was still deep in murderous thought. He was an all or nothing kind of man, so torture wasn't really his thing. Still, I suppose an idle mind wanders where it will.

The decision to humor him was a poor one. I said, "He doesn't *need* his toes I suppose."

He continued his hypothetical mutilation, "I can use my butane torch to cauterize the wound."

I paused, my churro hanging out from my mouth like a cartoon mobster's limp cigar as I said, "You scare the crap out of me sometimes. You know that?"

"He wouldn't even need to go to a hospital!"

"Seriously. What the Hell is wrong with you?" Quietly, I leaned over my quesadilla and emulated my mother, "We are in a *restaurant*. There are *children* here."

"He doesn't need the toe, Gekman. It's a superfluous body part."

When Kathy chimed in, I assumed she was going to complain about how infantile, brutish and crude my partner and I were being. No such luck. She put her hand on my arm. I wanted to catch fire so she'd take it off.

"Sweetie! Sweetie." She sounded like a nagging old woman as she pointed a finger at Jed, "Nobody's gonna understand that. What's super-flatulence? It's a made up word, Honey. Don't be childish."

I looked at Chloe. She grimaced, realizing that Kathy was being weird in a mean way. Jed and I were silent, with clenched jaws. From anyone else, in any other fashion, this would have been reasonable, even funny. I would have calmed down and told the person the definition. I would have used it in another sentence. I wouldn't have judged the person at all. But it wasn't a regular person saying that they did not know this vocabulary word. It was Kathy.

Jed and I slowly turned our angry faces to glare at her. She giggled and stood up. She said something about getting that "tasty" waiter's number. She was standing, said she would leave... But she didn't leave. She stood there in soundlessness for a moment, and in that instant, she reminded me of my little sister. Silent, confused, lost. It was off-putting. I tried to shake the image from my head. Why then? What was wrong with me?

As she started that awful laugh about nothing yet again, Jed reached for the fork once more. I let him. If he wanted to use the thing like a mini trident, I didn't care anymore. I looked to my food.

Kathy heard a sound from outside. She turned her head to look, smiled, and then bolted out of the restaurant and into the street. I got up as fast as I could, chair tumbling to the ground, but it didn't matter. Jed was still half-under a semi-conscious Chloe, and I didn't see it coming. Neither did Kathy.

After the blur of it all, I reached out my hand as if to warn her of what had already occurred, or stop it with a touch of air, or hit some imaginary rewind button. Kathy didn't deserve that. I was useless in that moment. I was too late. That tractor trailer full of digging machines wasn't stopping for anyone. In that moment, I became intimately aware of my breathing, praying it was painless. Maria had asked me to be nice. If I had been nice, she wouldn't have... What was I saying? I didn't want to go back in time and force myself to do something I didn't want. I could have gotten her to sit back down. What was the sound? It was all at once too much and far too little air. I touched my chest, as though searching for the leak.

Chloe was awake now, confused and not quite processing what had happened, a hand on Jed's back. I managed to force my head away from the door, and back to where we had been sitting. Jed in his chair, cradling his head in his hands, his own vomit in a puddle by his feet.

Chloe and a waiter helped clean him up. Jed looked out at the mess. He pushed his plate of mini tacos away, his expression blank, as if stuck in a dream. His choice of cuisine had made him look even more behemothic, but now, he was small. I stood, looking at him for a response. A girl we were just speaking to was now splattered all over the road, and neither of us wanted to talk about it. The waiter brought to-go boxes. No need to ask.

Someone from another table said, "Guess her mother never told her to look both ways, huh?" and Jed nearly got up to clobber him, rattling our bolted-down plastic table, but Chloe pushed his shoulder down.

Jed noticed my expression and said only, "Splat." He then went to the counter by the soda machine to get the napkin dispenser and bring it back to the table. After grabbing handful of napkins to blow his nose into, he sat on the ground and sobbed with little sound. I packed up our leftovers because I felt like I should do *something*. The other patrons were leaving. We didn't have the time but I felt it was only right that I stay there and give what I knew of the story to the person answering the call.

Jed forced himself to his feet. He looked empty between bouts of running to the bathroom, or finding a garbage can to vomit into. It was rare to see his trauma affecting him this way, rather than as drinking. He made his way over to me while I jotted down what had happened for the cop working the scene.

Jed said, "Bitch had it coming," then looked at what I had written and gestured with a hand at the pad of paper, "No no. Write that down. Bitch. Had. It. Coming." Chloe hit him in the shoulder. I hoped that it hurt.

Jed was never one to deal with what he was feeling, unless it was rage. A situation like this was completely out of his element, but that was no excuse to be an ass. He needed to go home and rest. He needed to take his head out of his own history, which was obviously something I had no right to tell him. The least he could do would be to shut up about this one, for his own sake.

I called Maria, unsure of what to tell her. "How'd it go? Well, we killed her. We didn't. I'm a little screwed up right now. God. I'm sorry. Your friend, Kathy? She's gone." I told the officer what direction she came from as I started to hyperventilate.

Everyone could hear Maria screaming on the other line, "You- Wait, WHAT?"

I caught my breath and tried to be gentle about it, as I hadn't yet processed it all myself. "Well, technically the tracker trailer killed her. ...Truck? I'm not sure what it's called. Is that right? It carries other vehicles."

Jed piped up with "Fate-Mobile. The Karma-Cab, if you will." Chloe hit him again, even harder than before.

Jed started to cry into her shoulder, rather than going off alone like a cat about to die. It was a step in the right direction. Chloe thought she had caused him physical pain, but that wasn't the problem.

Maria didn't hear him, "A truck? Wha- Why was there a truck?"

This conversation continued for a while, interrupted by bouts of hysterical yelling, tears, cursing, and denial from all the parties involved. Finally, Maria hung up, and I turned to Chloe.

"Do you know where Frog is? Honestly, I'm hoping that's why you came by." My left hand was shaking. I stuck it in my pocket.

Chloe swallowed, looking at the spot where Kathy last stood. "Frog has been spotted in front of an old ranch house. Could be a safe house, could be a contact's place. But... I mean, that doesn't mean he's still there. I'll give you the address though." She started to cry, and then shake a little, vibrating from some innermost part of herself.

Jed put his arm around the freaked-out driver, referring to him as "Ass-Face," and telling him about nefarious "employment opportunities" for a "cold killer" like himself. The driver was tearing up, wide eyed at nothing in particular. Chloe had walked away, come back, and walked away yet again.

Jed wiped away his own tears as he continued, "Listen, there are a lot of assholes in this world. I mean, shit, look at you, right? Ran over a goddamn pedestrian. All I'm saying is, if this is the path you're goin' down, Kid..." Both having tears in their eyes made them look like they were bonding, but Jed was more or less torturing the driver as he swung from sad to angry and back. Jed had his own accident-related trauma, but that was no reason to drag a stranger into it.

The officer on scene began to notice what was going on. As he stepped towards them with a suspicious look, I ushered Jed away before he could get himself arrested.

Chloe then grabbed Jed, seeing that he needed a shoulder, even if she didn't fully understand why at the time. I set out to find Frog, presumably on my own, until I thought better of it. No use taking this out on anyone else.

Instead, I went straight to Maria's in an effort to iron out our emotions.

She wasn't happy, but she didn't seem to be falling apart either. She took some deep breaths. I did my best to play psychologist and see how much she was bottling up, but I was never any good at reading her.

Finally, she said, "I'm glad you came. I'm not going to ask for any more details about what happened. I don't want to know and I've already decided that it probably wasn't your fault. Probably."

I took off my hat, "You seem to be taking this all oddly well."

"Oh, with my upbringing, I've learned to rationalize pretty much anything. That doesn't mean I'm okay with it. I've done my crying, and I'm sure there will be more later."

I went to her kitchen to brew some tea. Chamomile with honey, I remembered. That's what she liked for her nerves. Maria took the time to snatch my coat from the chair I had draped it upon, to move it to the coat rack where it belonged. In doing so, she found something.

When I entered the room again with two mugs, she was holding the small notebook she had found in my overcoat pocket.

"I'm sorry," she said. "I didn't mean to pull a Chloe and pry, but... Can you tell me about this? I thought it was your work notebook, but it's not. It's a little girl's diary, but there's hardly anything in it." The book was no more than four inches by three inches, and a light, pale purple. Sort of a dingy lilac. The spine of the hard cover was worn.

My sister had opened it many times, though Maria was right. Abby had only written in it twice, with a few scribbly doodles after that. There was a distinct Before and After of her normal life within those two pages. That first had a little something about a little girl's typical day jotted down, and a few lines under it said, "black candy" followed by nothing. The second page was about the hospital. It was about other children dying, bottles, and needles. It wasn't terribly comprehensible, but it was the page I had formed my cult-like obsession around. My parents figured it was a sick little girl's overactive imagination, trying to make sense of everything.

"Yep!" I slammed myself onto the maroon chair in Maria's living room, swiping the book from her hand as I went, "I usually keep it in a box in my room, but I sometimes put it in my coat for luck. Some odd thing. It was my sister's. Abby. She's come up a lot for me lately... I don't know why I kept it."

She raised an eyebrow and said, "For sentimental reasons. She was your sister."

"Well, yeah, but..." I looked at Maria for a moment in silence, trying to figure out what the Hell I was trying to say. Maria didn't need me to defend my case. She understood. What on Earth was I arguing?

Feeling the need to say something anyway, I said, "I have no delusions of her coming back to add more pages of writing, but I kept it. If my sister had it with her in the hospital, maybe she no longer had the strength to add anything."

"That's a thought," said Maria.

"More likely," I continued, "she knew that her dopey older brother would cling to it like a religious text, and she didn't want me to ever know what pain she had been going through." Maria pouted a bit when I said that, which was understandable.

"What was 'black candy'?" she pointed at the book in my hands.

I sucked in air through my nose and let it out again. "I found a woman by the name of Candice Black years ago that may have had something to do with a much larger conspiracy. Vaguely concerned the MOTH company that I think got a lot of kids killed." Maria straightened up at that, and I continued, "but I never had the evidence to pin her to my sister, and then she disappeared. It turned out to be unrelated, I think. That woman to Abby, I mean. I was told that those kids were dying anyway, and it was some experimental treatment that unfortunately didn't work. I never believed that."

"I remember that name, Candice Black. She was in charge of almost everything back before my time in MOTH. Did you ask about her a long time ago? And, you're right. She vanished. I'm so sorry. We all assumed she died. No one brought it up after that."

As she put her hand on my shoulder I said, "My sister... She tried to warn us, and to let us know what they did to her, and my parents and I chalked it up to childish fairy tales. She was sick and she didn't understand." I turned my head to face Maria, then swung back to the book, "I still think someone took her from the hospital, and then gave her back when they didn't need her anymore. That's what she said. I don't know why no one believed her." I stroked the text of "black candy" with my thumb, wishing it would rub away the pain and reveal something useful. Maria put her fingers through my hair, gently petting me as she said, "I hate to make you talk about this more, but how did your sister wind up in the hospital to begin with? She must have been sick before the company got to her, right?" "Yeah. Abby had Lupus. Weird and rare thing for a kid, but she had it. She developed what's called a Malar rash," I gestured to my nose and cheeks, not looking Maria in the eyes, "like a butterfly shape on her face. She couldn't be in the sun too long, and she kept saying everything hurt." "Poor kid."

I could only offer a somber nod as I continued staring into a wall's cracked paint, "Then her kidneys started to go, and we got desperate. Mom and Dad found this study going on for kids like her, to find a cure, or treatment, or something for kids with any kind of autoimmune disease." "Was the study the real deal then? From what little I remember about your parents, they seem like the type to look pretty closely into that sort of thing." "Yeah. She got transferred a few more times than it seemed anyone else in that study did though, and at some point during that, they got to her. I know they did." Maria squeezed my shoulders with her arm.

I spent a few more minutes in Maria's cozy living room while I absentmindedly flipped through the tiny, thin, pre-lined pages. Each had a pale drawing of a flower printed in the bottom right-hand corner. I wasn't looking for anything, but I stopped short when my eyes glanced over a quick scribble.

Turning back the pages, something clicked deep inside my brain. I questioned how I had ever missed it before. It was a tiny map, drawn in some kind of chalk on a random page deep within the book, but of what or where?

Maria asked if I needed more light, and flicked a switch before I could answer. Having the book pressed so close to my face, she must have thought I was going blind. It said "hospital" in tiny lettering above the floor plan.

"It's the hospital." I said.

"You need a hospital?" She put her hand on my forehead.

"No. This picture." I shoved the scribble of an image at her, as though it was about to slip right off the page if she didn't look at it quick enough. "She's telling me where to look to save her."

Maria turned to go into the kitchen.

"Save her," she repeated as I heard an appliance door close. She came back in the room with a package of peas from the freezer. She wrapped it carefully in a thin dish towel, then plopped the whole thing onto my head.

"Well, okay, not save her. But..." I put the book down and stared off at the wall, trying to picture a bird's eye view of a memory, and compare that to what I had just seen. "It's not the floor plan of the hospital where she died. It's someplace else."

I sighed then said, "Maybe she made it up."

Half out of some mustered up and wrongly placed anger, I tore out the page and closed the book. I had every right to be frustrated, but I felt stupid. Maria was my friend and she was being completely understanding, yet I still felt like everything was upside down, or like she should be mocking me. She was worried with good reason. None of that was her fault. Too much happened that day, and I felt like my mind was melting.

"How about you rest for a while?" Maria pressed a button to my left that I hadn't noticed. The comfy maroon chair was evidently a recliner. She got a blanket for me and gently tucked me in until I complied and closed my eyes.

CHAPTER 7
Amazing Mazes

Chloe managed to confirm Frog's last known whereabouts via connections I'd never want to meet. She sent Jed my way as errand boy along with the directions. Getting to Frog was still a challenge though, as a bomb going off had caused traffic to slow to a halt. Where did the bomb come from? It was the third seemingly random explosion in the area in two months, and I hadn't heard a word about the first two until the third. Everything was hush-hush given the amount of property damage done. We didn't even know if people had been hurt.

Jed and I were both on edge, imagining how the reign of the mysterious bomber would do us in. The police were handling the man Hudson referred to as "The Blue Bomber." Still, it felt like we were running from the darkness of it all as we left the noise of the city and watched the countryside open up before us. Would the Blue Bomber follow to attack such a quiet area? Not our problem.

Frog, however, *was* our problem. We had time to prepare for whatever he had gotten mixed up in.

"Shall we speculate on what we're going to find at this place?" I asked.

Jed shrugged with one shoulder, "Why bother? Chloe said he's a weirdo in a zoot suit. How much damage can he do?"

"Technically, Chloe said a plaid zoot suit was his formal wear, so thankfully, that implies he only wears it on very rare and special occasions."

Jed nodded, "Yeah well if a special occasion includes getting his way through some ridiculous trap or whatever, according to what little Kathy told us, it happens kind of a lot."

He wasn't wrong. In fact, Chloe said it was

especially empowering for Frog if his trickery almost didn't fly. Even better if the con could have easily gone in someone else's favor instead of his. He wasn't the type to handle disappointment well, but he loved the thrill of nearly failing and winning at the last minute. The land looked deserted aside from this lone home.

Jed let the car crawl up the gravel drive to Frog's place, dimming the headlights. We crept up to the trailer-office and peered through the picture window. We saw photos of mushroom clouds framed as though they were beloved family members, a neon yellow legal pad beneath florescent lights, and the thin man in a suit a size too small for his arms, hunched over his folding desk with his fingers entwined in his hair.

He was seedy, slithery, and he never quite stood up straight, shoulders and thin neck strained under the weight of his thick skull and heavy ego. Frog resembled the bastard child of an old-fashioned gangster and a used car salesman, so Chloe and Kathy where both spot on in their descriptions.

I let Jed go into the ranch house to talk to Frog without me. It was unorthodox, but it was the smart thing to do. Send a guy who takes no crap from anyone to deal with a guy who only dishes crap out. Crap attracts more flies, I suppose. Frog should've liked that.

I chuckled to myself at the thought as I let my eyes close. I listened to the crickets chirp as the sun began to set. Being so used to the metropolitan area made moments of tranquil stillness an extra kind of peaceful. I felt the gentle wind pass me by. The air smelled crisp, but it wasn't cold enough yet to be uncomfortable. Voices were raising behind me through the wall, but I was trying very hard to enjoy the peace while it lasted.

It didn't take long before Frog was hopping right out of his establishment, via a vehicle of shattering glass, right through the picture widow. He smashed head first onto the overgrown lawn, and I expected Frog to be missing half his face when he got up. Surprisingly, he had only a bloody nose, and some decorative scrapes across his left cheek. Luckily for him, a ranch house meant only one floor.

"All right, all right!" Frog flipped onto his back and raised up his hands in front of his face. He cracked his neck and then stood up slowly, his hair slick and flat with sweat against his forehead, "Can only smile so long before it's a grimace, you know? Fine." He spit on the ground. I glanced to see that it was clear, no blood. Jed hadn't damaged him too much.

Frog said, "Right. I know... I know where someone might, MIGHT score the stuff. I know, like, the kind of people who work in those... areas. Bad shit goes down man. Bad shit."

"Bad shit, eh?" I asked.

"Yeah, dude. They used to take kids in. They used to experiment on little kids and shit. They did real bad shit to them. I won't tell you what specifically, of course. I don't wanna die. I can't talk about it, they can't know I told you, or I'm gonna die."

Something snapped inside of me. I can't explain it. Before I knew it, Frog's neck was under my hand, and I was pressing him into the faux outer brick wall of his safe house.

In almost a whisper, as though some part of me was calm, I said, "What kind of bad shit?"

Jed put a hand on my shoulder, a shocked expression in his eyes. Still, our impromptu "bad cop, worse cop" seemed to do the trick.

Frog whimpered, "Testing drugs, mainly. Told people they were developing cures. Got to do it in a hospital, all legal-looking, but figuring out where to go was rough. It was some riddle to get to where the kids were kept." I let go of him. "Some higher ups had codes left all over town. They used to change when they needed to, but if you go to the first place, that one's always the same."

"Nothing you just said made any sense." I chewed

on a toothpick from the pack from my inside jacket pocket.

Frog took a deep breath, "If you follow them, if they're even still around, that'll bring you to wherever the old stash was. I assume that would be evidence for whatever the fuck you guys are trying to prove, if it's- I don't even know if the shit is still there!" Frog turned as though he was going to vomit a little, then looked at us again instead. His tongue ran across chapped lips before his mouth drooped into a slack jaw. He stared at me, panting, then refocused. No words, no judgment in his eyes. He didn't like me, but studying me for a hint of a crack.

"So, it's like some horrible, bad guy scavenger hunt?" I asked. Jed laughed while Frog looked around confused like he had missed some bigger joke.

I handed Frog my notebook and a pen for the place to start. It was less of a sketch and more of a scribble with no discernible features.

"Close enough" Jed said. I walked away with the notebook in hand as Jed threw one last punch into Frog's stomach. It wasn't a strong hit, just something shocking. Frog was starting to stand back up as we backed out down the dirt and gravel road.

The address led to a small hole in the wall. Literally. A brick wall stood before us at the wrong part of a dead-end street. On either side were doors to restaurants and a side door to a sleazy motel. None of them were what we were looking for, and everything was closing down for the night. However, in front of us was a small sign, beneath that tiny hole, in this gargantuan brick mass of a wall.

The sign read, "Lower East Level, 22 Boulevard" on rusted metal.

"Well, that doesn't make any fuckin' sense!" Jed bellowed. "I'm gonna kill that fuckin' Frog-swamp-bullshit-"

"Hold on, Jed. Mix it around here. There's an East street just that way, right? 22 East street is that big ol' dilapidated building."

"That hospital? Well, used to be a hospital. It's all run down now." Jed shook his head, "Some gangs tore the place apart. It was like, 'The St. Jude Massacre' or something. Rough."

"That was years ago. I remember it being on the news. No one knew how it started."

"Yeah, but a lot of kids died there." I cringed when he said it. Then Jed continued, "You think this cryptic shit leads there?"

I shrugged. "Why not? Worth a try, right?"

Jed stuck a finger in the hole in the wall, then peered through with his flashlight. "There's a piece of paper stuck in there, Gekman."

"THAT could be our clue, huh?" Agreeing, Jed whipped out his old lock pick kit, and took from it a little hook on a stick. After some maneuvering, he managed to fish out the piece of paper.

He straightened up, as if like a herald announcing a queen's royal ball, "Room 302... Actually, the rest is all melty."

"Melty?" He showed me how little was left of the paper after years of deterioration in porous brick. "Room 302 is still something, maybe."

It was getting windy as night took hold. I shivered thinking of how turtlenecks, long coats, and scarves were never enough once the leaves were done turning color, done falling. Our Winters were bitter.

"Okay. Okay then. 22 East street, we go to the old hospital. On the lower level, so... The basement, right? Why would room 302 be in a basement?" I asked.

"Because you're stupid and reading into drug dealer's mumbo jumbo bullshit. This is a joke, man! This is nothing!" Jed was often baby elephant-like in his movements.

"Worth a shot cause it's all we got."

"I hate when that logic works." Begrudgingly, he trudged forward and followed me back to his Chevelle.

I gestured to him as I got in the car, "We'll go to the hospital. I'll go inside and look around, and you scout the perimeter."

For once, Jed was cautious, "No way, Gekman. We're partners. If you're right, I don't want you alone in any of that shit. Besides, we still don't know what else would have been on that little paper, and it doesn't feel good."

"Jed, you aren't exactly a ninja. In fact, you are the opposite of a ninja. Loud, blaring..."

"So?"

"So, if MOTH, or whatever bad people are still in there-"

"I'll fuck their shit up."

I couldn't argue with that. "Okay. Fine. We both go into the hospital."

The transition between somewhat-nice-area to liquor stores, gun stores, and the kind of roads that may as well be made of dirty syringes was not a pleasant one. The hospital fit in well.

Saint Jude Hospital. The Saint of lost causes, according to Jed. Fitting name. Erosion of the urban jungle had consumed the "O" of "hospital" long ago. Cracked concrete lined the ambulance drop off entrance. Shards of glass littered the dying grass next to a plastic bag window. The area had been struggling for a while. Once the hospital went, no one even bothered to bulldoze it for the land, so it sat decaying.

An emaciated girl leaned against a dirty pillar, smoking what I wanted to assume was a cigarette, or maybe pot. Her scavenger eyes never left me once on my approach. Jed coughed as he sidestepped fresh blood on the ground and walked up to the doorway to be by my side. The girl took the "cigarette" out of her mouth and spat brown-grey liquid. Broken people outside a broken house of healing.

With our guards up, we opened the double door. It had been forced open before, perhaps by the woman outside, or others before her. Jed went ahead as I fumbled with my back pocket, lifting out the map Abby had drawn in her little notebook. I unfolded the page with care, wondering if this was the place. I felt an old force pull me upstairs, rather than towards the basement. I thought I saw a shadow on the stairs. A sign scribbled in mock crayon on the wall pointed towards where the children's ward had been. I went that way, following in a daze.

I remembered when I was a teenager, and I had visited my little sister in a children's ward, miles away. It was a very different experience, yet some remnants remained nestled in the folds of my brain. Here, it was all dust and cobwebs. Everything was grey. The place I remembered was brighter, and cleaner. Time had ravished this ward before me, yet I remembered it all like looking at a photograph. It was so much like this place. The ceiling seemed to go on forever as color tumbled into the room, filling the vast emptiness. A few adults trickled in while their well-watched children ran across the polished, glimmering floor. I tried to picture that old scene over the new one. I tried to erase the gloom and have the light wash over everything. It did not work. That was years ago, and a different hospital. An odor of mildew and caked-on dust permeated my senses. I could smell a hint of cleaning product too, muted but present even after all these years. I wondered how toxic it was to still be lingering like that.

Like a spider, I snuck on silent feet to another dim,

obscured room. If anyone else was around, they were being just as quiet. I couldn't even hear Jed, but I felt like I could hear the old echoes of the hospital of the past. Sounds of laughter and songs of praise singing how brave everyone was grew to a rumble throughout the halls behind me, but when I turned, the voices were gone. My memories were playing tricks on me with old ghosts.

Jed finally caught up, closing the heavy metal door. Peaceful solitude took the petite room into a whisper, no longer bludgeoning me with sight and sound from my past. Jed was acting as a shield, protecting me and pulling me away from my own mind.

"Why does a children's ward need a fucking blast door?" asked Jed.

Though beautiful and haunting in its age and wisdom, this engulfing place seemed so fragile. I could feel someone else's memories under my skin as I gazed upon the dust covered books and tiny chairs. Children used to sit here. Children used to wait to die here.

"Look, Gekman!" Jed held up a hollowed out book, "It was on the shelf with all the other kid's books. It didn't have a title, so I looked inside. There's a bottle in here! Looks empty, but it's like the one with the shit that poisoned the kid. Is this room 302?"

Not turning to look, I said, "Good job."

"Let's bring it back with us. Oh. Hey what's this writing?" Red permanent marker bled through a few pages. I watched as Jed flipped through to get to where it read "Mrs. Rosenbury and Craven, Central Air" in clear letters.

"This a second clue for MOTH shits? Otherwise, why hide a drug in a hospital like this? In a book even."

"You've got a point. I wonder who was supposed to find it."

"Don't know what the fuck it means though. Central Air, Craven, Mrs. Rosenbury."

My eyes lit up, "Central Air... Craven. No.

Rosenbury Boulevard! There's a heating place. They do air conditioners! I bet someone in the air conditioner place has information."

Jed, expressionless, said, "I wanna say you're pushing here, but you keep being right."

He turned to leave with our prize. I couldn't. Not yet. Small toys sat trapped inside boxes, screaming for their long lost children. It was as if they could hear the small ones on the other side of that door like I could, laughing. The cold floor was not as welcoming as the small soft rug, which had been so carelessly thrown onto the other side of the room. While my eyes wandered around the sculpted ceiling and forgotten walls, I noted that this place was meant for play at one point. Abandoned. Why was it tossed aside in this manner? What happened at this hospital that made it all worthless?

"GEKMAN! You coming, you sky-toned shit head? Still gotta check the basement." I jerked back into reality and rushed up to my partner.

The basement was hardly that anymore. It housed tents and people. Too many quiet people with angry, sunken eyes reflecting the campfire in the middle of the room. When they all turned to face us, Jed opened his mouth to ask a question, but when every person started to slowly rise toward us, we backed away and closed the basement door.

We needed to head over to our next possible hint at the central air place. Jed was right that it was a long shot, but it was all we had, and if it led to another clue, so be it. It was also getting very late, and would most likely be closed.

The wrecked central air place was much closer to the hospital than I had anticipated, so we made it in no time. I was no longer worried about working hours, as the building seemed to be about as run down as the hospital. I tried the door.

"Locked, and it's not the type we can pick." In

retrospect, it was a poor choice on my part to then add, "No way in, unless we break in some other way."

Without a word, Jed picked up the nearest metal trash can off of the street, and sent it flying through the window. I waited for a response from passersby after the crash, but no one cared. I suppose we were in that sort of neighborhood.

"There," said Jed, "like magic, the window now doubles as a door." With a shrug, I followed my partner.

"Right," I was suspicious. "Though I guess an alarm won't sound in an abandoned shop."

We walked, or rather, crawled and stumbled like hybrid dogs and crabs into the building. Dodging shards of broken glass was never fun. We got about five feet before the alarm finally sounded.

"Huh. Still works," I said as I put a new toothpick in my mouth and my hands in my pockets. I took a breath out of the side of my mouth. Jed began running around in circles, with his hands above his head, flailing about in an effort to poke fun at me.

He said, "OH no, Gekman! I can't go to jail right now! Not again, this month! This is what you look like every day."

"Jed?" He ignored me and kept on running. The circle was getting tighter.

I tried again, "Jed, I've never gone to jail, and you know that." No use. He still didn't answer. He tripped over himself and fell down instead.

The alarm shut off. Standing before us was a woman, early fifties at least. She was irritated with good reason, shotgun in hand. Possibly the owner of the store, I should have shown her some respect... rather than trashing the place. She had a noticeable scar over her left cheek and a small eye patch on that eye. Green clips held her red hair back. I showed my old badge. Hudson figured I'd be coming back, and I'd use that fact to keep the badge as long as possible.

She said nothing and her face remained expressionless but for angry eyebrows. I imagined she'd have her arms crossed if she wasn't holding the gun.

I asked her, "and your name is?"

"Tabby Craven. Why are you here? I've got a license for the gun."

Jed piped up, "We're... Uh, looking for more of this." He fumbled with his pocket, then held up the bottle he had found in the hospital. "Not for our jobs, mind you!" He was quite entertained by the shotgun, not making eye contact with Tabby, "Gabey here just likes flashing the old badge, that's all."

She seemed unimpressed, so of course I had to make it worse by adding, "I think I'm nervous. It might be the gun."

She groaned, "So you're looking for me? I am not in business anymore, boys. I've got nothing to give you when this store is closed."

"How about information, rather than product?" I tried so hard to be charming.

"You are so full of shit that I can't even- What?" She took the tiny bottle to have a closer look, putting the gun by her side in the process. After a moment, she glanced up and said, "If you're here for Denny, he ain't here anymore. He used to talk to cops, right?"

"Did he?" I was taken aback by that. "For what?"

"Hon, are you made of wet paper towels? Wait. You aren't with him, are you? Well. That's different then. Anyway, you'd never need more than what comes in one of these little bottles, unless you're looking to off your whole department. Is that what you wanted to know?"

Jed retorted, right in her face, "And anything else you got. Is this Denny guy still involved in this crap or what?"

She huffed, handed the bottle back to him, and then glared at me. "If you want to find him, you'll have to find his family. They're all close. Well... The ones that are left. The stuff you hold there? They got rid of most of them years ago. I remember taking pictures of the bodies. I still have those photographs."

"Photographs?" asked Jed.

"Sure. Got a degree in mortuary science with a minor in photography, and I wound up owning an air conditioning place. What else was I gonna do? Gotta find your joy somewhere."

Ignoring the creepy photography thing, I nodded and said, "What else can you tell us about... Uh, this stuff? Anything?" I pointed at the bottle, as though she had forgotten to what I was referring.

She shrugged and put the gun down on a counter. "You guys seem funny about all this. Who are you really?"

I collected myself now that the weapon wasn't near my face and said, "My name is Gabe Gekman, and I'm a PI. This is my partner, Jed. A boy died. We don't know why he died, but it seems this stuff was involved. We already know some of the common characters in MOTH, so we've come to you to find out anything else you know."

"You're lucky that I like cops."

I smiled, "You do?"

"Sure. Never had any trouble. Regarding the bottle, it was commissioned. The idea didn't even come from anyone within MOTH, as far as I know. It was a byproduct of some medicinal chemicals. A mistake. Someone I once knew got involved... Anyway, the guy who originally got it made was Eli Addams. He's dead now, but he's got family too. The only one left in charge of any of it, as far as I know anyway, is Denny. Sometimes his thugs come here to harass me. I thought you were with him."

"Not to be brash but, how do you know so much about it? Why the AC shop?" Tabby was interesting, and I wanted to help her find that joy she mentioned.

"Someone I knew was one of the first people

involved. I was never deep in it myself, but I was there, you know? I was around and I knew everybody. I went to all the parties, back in the day. Now, I'm for them exactly what I am for you. I'm here because I know things. The shop is my job. Literally. That's it."

I didn't feel the need to stay there bothering her any longer, "Fair enough. Oh, how do you spell ol' Denny boy's last name again?"

"C. H. I. T. T. L. E."

"Chittle. Right." I don't know why I felt the need to check. I knew it was Maria's ex-boyfriend. Well, crap.

"Listen..." I wrote out my information in my notebook. I handed her the torn-out page with, "Bill me for the window. Thank you."

We left through the door. Jed wanted to stay and look at the photographs, but I urged him to plod on.

I didn't wait for her to bill me. Instead, I came back the next evening with an envelope filled with what the cost of the window would be, plus a bit extra, and Bernie's information. He was looking for someone with her skill set, right? She counted the money, nodded with a smile, and I left again in silence.

CHAPTER 8
Understated Seducers

I was starting to worry, having not yet heard back from Bernie about the toxin. If this was truly the same stuff he couldn't find before, I shouldn't have expected this to be an easy task. I went to his office early that morning to check things out. He was there all right, but slumped over at his desk. At first glance, I thought he was asleep.

I approached with light steps when I noticed an uncapped pen, a few staples, and binder clip on the floor to the left of the desk. He must have pushed these off of something, but the other staples were on the shelf. Had he grabbed the shelf to steady himself, before taking a seat? I took his pulse. Nothing. He was cold. Then I felt cold. I hadn't taken a breath in too long, so I gasped before calling for an ambulance, mostly sure that wouldn't help him now.

I said to the person on the other line, "It looked as though he had suffered a heart attack, but then I noticed the blood beneath his fingernails."

"Is it his? Someone else's?"

I sighed as I wiped the tears from my eyes with my sleeve, "I can't tell yet. I'm going to keep looking around for clues, and I'll call the police. I'm staying here until someone shows up, but I'm hanging up now, okay?"

Bernie was a good guy. I wanted to introduce him to my father and have them play poker together. I noticed, upon further inspection that there were tiny holes under his nails, not quite where the blood was. It looked as though someone had injected something there, and the skin tore when he struggled against it. There were bruises under his sleeves, which means someone may have held him down long enough before his death for such a bruise to form. In his front pocket was a bottle just like the one we had found in the hospital. Bernie was a message, but what was it trying to say?

Officers and EMT arrived. I put my shaking hand into my coat pocket, then led an EMT to everything I had noticed about the scene. An officer I didn't recognize took notes.

I said, "Oh, that teeny little bottle is the same kind MOTH used to use for their toxins. I think it's all related to this case I've been working-"

"You'll send over what you've got on this stuff?" asked the officer.

I blinked, "Well, yeah. I mean, I have other information."

"This is considered a new, open case until we know otherwise. We'll appreciate any information you were working on as a PI, but please don't expect to be on the team with this one." That hurt, though I'm not sure why.

Bernie felt like a friend to me, I had clues I could have offered up if I had the chance to do so without paperwork, and this guy had mustard in his goatee. Who the Hell was he to tell me who was on the team? I agreed with a nod anyway.

The bus was late, but I managed to make my way to Jed's place. He was in the bathroom, yelling for me to come inside the apartment. The door made a sad creaking as I opened and shut it again. The couch made a similar kind of sigh as I sat down.

My companion had no trouble communicating while on the toilet, as he began muttering something about Chloe.

"I'm an understated seducer," he said, "I don't mean to do this. It just happens!"

I heard a flush, and out walked Jed from the bathroom, "I shat out something that looked about the same shape and size as your head, only a healthier color."

When he saw me, I must have been making a face, because he stopped short. "What happened, man?"

I clasped my hands together, squeezing a little too tightly as I said, "Bernie's gone. I went to see if he'd found anything else and he's dead. I thought it was a heart attack or something, the way he was slumped over, but someone killed him. He had these marks…" I started absentmindedly picking at my fingernails.

Jed sat down by me, "You call anybody?"

"Sure. The whole shebang. It's still on us, but I'm letting them have a go at it first. Like, I was specifically told Bernie isn't my case, but that's rough for me. Somebody will tell me if it's related to MOTH or the Crowns." I looked at my hands, "I feel guilty."

Jed scrunched his brow, "Guilty? For what? You and Bernie were both doing your jobs, and you gotta talk to people for yours." He took a moment before adding, "You feel this bad when you talk to Maria?"

I nodded.

He continued, "Don't. She knows. Everybody knows. Listen, we're getting closer to whatever this is that got the Crown kid. We need proof of Denny doing shit beyond people talking about it, right?"

"Is that it? Is that what we've decided?"

Jed nodded, "I called Lotgraff University while you were with… When you found Bernie. You'd left that school stuff Crown's fiancé gave you here, so I called. His dormmate was Denny Chittle. That's what they said."

"I knew it! How did you finally get confirmation?"

"Easy. I just lied a lot. Got the desk woman into a conversation, and then the dude in files into a conversation. I told ya they didn't throw anything out, just in case. Got copies of something with his name on it too, if we need that."

I blinked a few times, "Okay. We need motive. We need to find out the why and how of it, and then find the solid proof that he was the one responsible. This could still be a weird coincidence with what little we've got."

110

"The red head lady said to go to his family."

"Tabby. Yeah. Okay, so would Maria know where to find whoever?"

"I assume you don't wanna try to look them up then?" Jed laughed, "Gotta do things the hard way, right?"

"Yeah," I said, "and you aren't coming."

I gave him a smile, then took a deep breath through my nose. I wanted comfort.

"You okay?" asked Jed.

"Yeah. Just thinking. Everything is kind of a lot, you know? Anyway, I'll see Maria alone about Denny."

"Any excuse to see Maria."

I sighed and then chuckled as I put on my hat and began gnawing on a new toothpick. "That ship has sailed, like you've said. No dice. I figure she's more likely to know if someone shouldn't be spoken to. A phonebook won't tell us that."

Jed stood from the couch, slipped on nothing, and fell down cursing the entire time as he regained his footing. He was bent. I hadn't noticed before. Christ. Was he always so drunk these days? He hadn't been like this years ago, but trauma does things to a person. Dark things.

He rolled onto his back and looked up at me as he said, "Ugh! Why is the sky so fucking blue?" I was about to leave him there with no qualms, when he grabbed my pant leg.

"Something you need, Jed?"

"You know I only do, like, anything cause of you, right?"

I sat on the floor, "What do you mean?"

Jed stared at the ceiling, "I mean, I didn't kill myself, I didn't flip out in a really bad way. I feel it getting worse now, and I'm scared. But I'm not scared enough, I think." He didn't move his head, but his eyes drifted to mine, "I'm gonna stick around cause I think you need me. I'm not gonna fall into nothing, because I might help somebody.

You're my boss, kinda, but you're my best friend before anything. You're my family."

I didn't say anything, and instead kissed his forehead without thinking.

He laughed, "Talk to Liz too. She's been hanging out with Maria, so she's probably there. Don't take my car though, cause I won't remember you've got it in the morning. I'll think somebody stole it."

I took the bus to Maria's. According to her, for 18 days, Liz had been switching through her usual assortment of bracelets, except for one. The blue and purple bracelet Maria had made for her rested on her left wrist every day, even when all others changed.

I was unsure how to approach the case with Liz. Maria had already told me about Denny before, so all I had to ask was about the farm. Otherwise, my questions were more prodding at Maria. I didn't want to do any of it. I said hello, and made small talk as though I was on my way to somewhere else. She guided me to the couch and then immediately got up to make tea.

When I mentioned the bus, Liz said, "Oh! Are you a non-driver too?"

Maria answered for me, "No. You choose not to drive. Gabe here has a license. He even had a car, once upon a time. Didn't you, Gabe?"

I heaved a sigh and started, "Yeah. I at one point had a car of my very own, not six months ago. Almost needless to say, Jed Dean is the reason I no longer have a car."

Liz asked, "Do I know Jed?"

Maria laughed as I said, "If not, that's probably fine."

"Sooo... How did he wreck, steal, or whatever your

car?" Liz asked.

I took a seat on the couch next to Liz. "You see, it was April 1st. I had cleared out Jed's entire apartment, so when he came in, I told him that there had been an awful robbery, right? Well, I got a good chuckle out of his reaction, all throwing up his arms and blabbering about 'those horrible beasts! I'll skin the bastards alive!' and so on. Finally, I let it be known that it was April Fool's Day."

"And how did this Jed person react to that?" Liz was highly entertained.

"Oh, without skipping a beat, he punched me in the face." Liz burst out laughing, which made Maria smile too.

I continued, "I didn't lose any teeth. However, I did wind up in front of a doctor, and my nose had to be surgically relocated to its original position on my face."

Liz gasped, "Really?"

"Yeah. Jed footed the bill. When a nurse asked him what had happened because I could barely speak, he said, 'Hey, I only hit him once.'"

"That was true," said Maria.

I said, "In any case, I assumed we were square. That it that was the end of it. It wasn't."

"Right. So, what happened to your car?" asked Liz.

"I was all healed up by the time I was making my way over to said car on this particular sunny day. Birds were chirping and everything. I had just gone shopping, so my arms were full of brown bagged groceries. I used the little remote to unlock my restored blue 1969 Shelby Cobra. It had silver stripes. I was very proud of this car."

"And then?"

I paused for dramatic effect, leaning in close to Liz before saying, "...and then it blew up."

"HO-WHAT!"

"Yep. The moment I hit that tiny unlock button, the whole car went up into the air and exploded into chunks of metal and various other pieces. And there was Jed, seemingly from nowhere, laughing hysterically. He was downright maniacal as he said, 'APRIL FOOLS, FUCKER!'"

Maria put her arm around Liz as Liz said, "What did you do??"

"I stayed silent and still. Maybe I was in shock. Finally, I slowly turned my head to say, 'Jed... It's July.'" That got another laugh out of the girls.

Maria said, "Gabe had a motorcycle for a while too." She turned to me, "Whatever happened to that?"

"I had two." I shifted in my seat, "One got stolen in college and was never found. The other I crashed in such a way that the bike was totaled, but I barely had a scratch. I figured I was invincible." I looked at Liz, "For the record, I have since discovered that I am not."

"Do you still have your license?" asked Maria.

"Yep. I keep my licenses renewed and updated at all times, just in case I'm ever not dependent on Jed and the bus."

Maria poured three mugs of tea. It was nice to sit for a moment thinking of nothing but the warm mug in my hands and the smell of the herbal brew. I listened as Liz showed me the jewelry she had made that week, and explained the different stones involved. They each had meaning, like flowers in a bouquet.

She said, "So if I wanted to make you something with a blue stone, like lapis lazuli, angelate, or sapphire or something, I'd try to find one that might have meaning to you. Or one that could be useful to you, if you believe in that kind of stuff."

"Useful?" I took another sip of tea.

"Well, some blue stones are said to have a calming effect. Tranquility and all that."

"Tranquility? That sounds like something I could use." I put my mug on a coaster and began to stand up.

"Where you going?" asked Maria, a hand jokingly on her hip.

I lied and said, "I really have to get going, but this was nice." I began to leave. Liz nudged Maria with an elbow, and so Maria begrudgingly got up to follow me outside the door.

"Hey. Did you need something? You don't normally show up unless you want something. You okay? Is the case going okay?" Her hand was light on my arm.

"Well, I wanted to ask you about some Denny details, and talk to Liz here about her farm. I didn't ask because..." I looked at Liz. She didn't look nervous. I turned back to Maria, "I want to be friends with you guys. You shouldn't just be informants. I can find another way to get the information."

Liz said, "Maria mentioned you might want to talk about the farm. I remember the protest. It wasn't violent or anything, and honestly? I agreed with him."

"You wanted to save the butterflies?" I asked as Liz gently pulled me by my sleeve back inside, leading me back to the couch.

"Yeah. The butterflies were pretty. Plus, those machines weren't for us. There was another family that owned a chunk of land nearby, and they started digging. Then my dad saw the little grabber-arms and thought he could get one for harvesting stuff. That was the start of the farm going more automatic, which is good, in theory, but Dad couldn't keep up with payments. It's not really my family's farm anymore, is my point." She paused and sniffed, tears welling in her eyes, "I want to buy the last bit of land, but there really isn't anything left."

Maria put her arm around Liz and pulled her close, "You didn't tell me that."

"It was a silly idea, I don't know. But the place is a quarry now. It's for the Hi-En, and we get a piece of that, so it's not like my parents are hurting financially, but I don't know. It's like I watched Chloe's machines kill my childhood-WOW that was dramatic. I'm sorry. I don't blame Chloe for it, or her mom. I swear I don't. Anyway, I can't imagine who would hurt Michael. He was really nice. I didn't know him, but he still seemed super nice."

I asked, "Are you okay?" as I handed her a box of tissues from a nearby coffee table.

"Yeah. I'm fine. Sad about the farm, you know? It happened a year ago, so that's still fresh. Like I said though, my parents are fine. I'm selfish. I wanted that farm for myself." She kind of chuckled at that. She sniffed, "I wish I had more to tell you. I know he said his family was gonna have the same problem. Did anything come of that?"

"Same problem?"

"The butterflies. Michael said they were set to drill by his house within the year." It occurred to me that Michael may have been protesting at the home of his own parents.

Maria smiled at Liz, then turned to me with, "Did you have any other questions?" Maria seemed expectant, but for a moment I wasn't sure what she meant.

"Yeah. Yeah, I'm fine. You're busy. You girls have a good time. I'm-"

Maria blurted out, "What did you need to know about Denny?"

I sucked in a breath, "Okay, yeah, I was gonna ask some more stuff about Denny's family and... I mean, I can tell you about the case if you want. That's up to you."

Maria scrunched her eyebrows together, looked back at Liz, who grinned knowingly, and then back at me. "Meet me in three hours at Grubs. I can grab a late lunch, early dinner, and you can talk to me then, okay?" She smiled as she walked me out. Liz waved happily to me as Maria closed the door.

It was only after walking to a nearby dive bar called "Boots" that it occurred to me I may have developed a similar addiction to Jed's. Constantly wanting the attention of women around me may not have been as obviously dangerous as alcohol, but it was certainly self-destructive.

I spotted a brunette with a low-cut top and immediately started chatting her up. She giggled and touched my arm, then kissed me on the cheek and called me cute. Everything was going swimmingly.

Then, another woman walked over. She looked familiar. Oh. I'd slept with her. Was she coming over to slap me for never calling again?

The second woman said, "I see you've met my daughter."

I may have audibly gasped, "Wow. Yeah? I thought maybe sister. ...That wouldn't have been much better." Everything was so heavy with awkwardness. "Sooo... How long have you been her mom?" I left with my cheek stinging.

What a crappy afternoon, made worse by a phone call.

It was Chloe, "Kathy was texting me, you know? That's how I knew where you were."

"Right. You'd said that then."

"Well, I've been thinking about it-GOD I can't stop thinking about it... But I get the impression that Kathy was also texting other people, based on what she said to me. I'm wondering how much the guys you're after know about you." Chloe bit her lip, "This is so fucking morbid, but did the phone make it? Like, can you look at what was on the phone?"

"Do me a favor? Please call Jed, and tell him all of that. Have him figure out if that phone is with her family, trashed, at the coroner, at the funeral home, or wherever else it could be. Can you do that for me, please?" A couple hours left to wait before Grubs with Maria, but still not enough time to deal with any of that. I also didn't have the wherewithal emotionally.

"Of course! I'll forward what she was texting me too, in the meantime." I thanked her, then went to sit at the bus stop in silence for a while.

Grubs was not a fancy place. There were baseball jerseys and soccer pendants haphazardly hung to cover any of the wood-panel walls. I wouldn't have been comfortable in a more upscale place anyway, but I was overdressed wearing a tie. In this sports bar version of a restaurant, we would be able to hear each other without shouting. Also, no one would come up and try to steal one of us away, provided it looked like a date. Then, in she came, wearing yet another little black dress. It felt nice for a moment. Normal.

The air was murky. Heavy even. Every time she looked at me with those big brown eyes, I felt like I was suffocating. I'd fiddle with my tie or stick a finger between my collar and my neck, but nothing helped. Those eyes took away my air. Maria was not a tall woman by any means. In fact, she was rather short. Still, I felt as though she towered over me.

She sat down, and the waiter came right over to take our orders. I had already gotten our drinks set out for us. She ordered filet mignon, having the money to pay for it. I ordered a Reuben. This was pretty typical for the two of us.

Maria cut to the chase with a stabbing, "Why are we here right now? I like the idea of hanging out, and I honestly can't think of anything I haven't already told you."

"You can get in places I can't. You know things that I don't. I figured, being old friends, you would be willing to help me, which is how I dragged you into this whole thing to begin with. I'm now entirely willing to not have that particular conversation and be buddies. You seemed to want to tell me things though, so I'm leaving it up to you. We did find out that Denny was our victim's college roommate."

118

There was silence for two minutes as she drank, gave me pained looks and contemplated what she could get away with telling me.

Then she said, "I want to help you. That's the problem. After the case is solved, I do want you to hang out, and until then, I want to help you, regardless of any obligation I may feel. That having been said, the people you want me to talk about are dangerous. I assume that's why you're trying and failing to back me off of the case?" She took another drink, eyes wandering across the other patrons. "I'm sure you're aware that everyone already knows that you've been hanging around."

"Actually, no. I knew I was being rude to you, but I didn't realize it was that bad."

The movement she made was more of a twitch than a shrug, "And maybe it isn't. I'd like to think no one wants me to get hurt, but I'm fairly certain those who know me don't care about me that much, aside from Liz, and I'm not even sure HOW she feels about me, if you catch my drift. For the club though, I might be a figurehead in some respects, but I do run a damn good club." She raised her eyebrow while sucking in her bottom lip. "I'm not sure, really."

I clasped my hands together on the table in front of me, "That's fair enough. Keep to your instincts. Don't tell me what you think could get you into trouble. Send me off to someone else if you need to. Trust yourself, if not me."

"I wish that were more reassuring."

More silence.

I couldn't take it, and so I said, "Look, I need your help, okay? That's true and I realize you know that. There's no one else to turn to. Anything else I do for information is gonna be a long, winding road of crap. I'm sorry for dragging you into this but-"

"I dragged my ass into it myself, you know Gabe?" Words stopped coming out, and yet my mouth hung open. She smiled, but not with her eyes as she said, "Honestly, I guess I was hoping this would be a date and that you were using the case to get close to me. You're obviously rooting for Liz though, which I appreciate. It's just that I know you wanted friendship here, but I can tell you're struggling. I'm going to help, and there isn't much either of us can do about that."

Quietly and pained she said, "So, why not use me to your advantage?"

I stuttered on a sentence for a long while until it came out as, "I didn't mean to imply anything like that." I leaned into the table, half begging. I was using her. I was, and that was terrible. Of course, she was right too. I really did want to be around her. Both were true. I should have told her that. I kind of tried. "It's just, you're here now so, yeah. Okay. This can be a date too though! I didn't even, I mean..."

She let out a horrible grunting noise and folded her arms, "I mean, I don't want to make this all I am to you now. Some kind of informant? But I want to feel like you need me too."

"No." I was telling the truth. "You've always been more than that." She didn't seem convinced.

Even more silence followed. This time, the stillness burned. My stomach turned and flipped. My throat tensed. I wanted to whisper something clever or comforting, but thought better of it.

The food came at this inopportune and awkward time. We looked mid-fight. The poor waiter quickly placed the food in front of us and didn't dare ask if we needed anything else. Maria thought about her next move.

I said, "Breathe. I'm not going to leave you again even if you don't help me out with the case. After all this is over with, I'll prove it to you." What? What the Hell was I saying? What did that even mean? My mind started spinning with ways in which I could, in fact, prove it.

Whatever I meant, she smiled and said, "I'll hold you

to that, you know. Like I said, I do want to help. So. What do you want to know? What else can I tell you specifically?"

"Can you tell me anything about Denny? Or his goons. Or tell me about the old hospital. Please. The abandoned one. We found drugs there, hidden in books. It's gotta be by MOTH, right?" Christ. I was obsessed.

"That was true, a long time ago. It had been taken over by drug dealers rather suddenly. They rampaged the place. Killed a lot of people. It was all over the news, years ago. Not even MOTH uses that place now."

"I'd ask where they do their business these days, but you've already said you don't know. Warehouses somewhere, right?"

She tilted her head, as if looking up the information from slightly beyond me as she said, "Well, the rumors were that there was this warehouse people called 'The Factory'. Years prior to now, I mean. I was a kid then myself and I don't really believe all the stuff people used to say about it. It all went by pretty fast. I don't know where anything is now, true. I think most of that... project, if you will, is done with these days, no matter what it really was. Maybe it was all for show. You know, intimidation and whatever."

The Factory. My sister had mentioned that a few times. No one had listened. We figured she was playing games, making the worst kinds of imaginary friends. Or delusional. Was it all real?

She pointed at me and stated, "You'll have to talk to the guy who used to make the stuff if you want any more up to date info. He'd have it."

"Denny Chittle?"

"No. I meant a man named Eli Addams."

I shook my head, "Eli Addams is dead, from what I hear. You mean his family?"

"He had sons, yeah. It's worth looking up, right? Though, I guess Denny might know something. Going right to him for some kind of interrogation will get you killed, and no one within the company will out him for that same reason. You mentioned at the house something about Denny's family though."

"Yeah. I've been told to talk to them, rather than him. Could you help me get in touch with whoever that may be?"

Maria nodded slowly, "Yeah. You'll want to talk to his grandma. Nothing like him, of course. You know, I don't even know where Denny lives these days, but I remember Grandma." She gave a cute little laugh. "Oh, but try not to say anything obviously bad about Denny to her. The woman is completely in denial. She'll just shut you out."

"I assume even if you knew where he's been staying, you wouldn't want me going there. Do you happen to have Grandma's address?" I said.

"Nope. I was never the one driving, and it's been so long that I honestly couldn't tell you where she is. Somewhere around Bellevue, not far from you. Looking her up may not be useful either. She had a different last name than Denny. As for him, if you do wind up confronting Denny, like for an arrest or whatever, do it away from the club. Away from anything related to him business wise, okay? I don't like the idea of you going head-to-head with him while he's got so much back up."

"Better to catch him off guard." I took in a breath and said, "Thank you. Believe me, I appreciate everything you're doing for me." I stood up and brought my chair over, closer to her. I kissed her on the cheek and said, "I always have."

"Oh, and you asked about his goons, right? I only know one of them. Zeke."

"I feel like everyone knows him except me."

"That's true," she gave a subtle smile as she said, "He's mostly harmless. He talks big, but he'd never hit someone unless Denny told him too."

That made me feel better. We finished our meal in peace.

Maria pointed at me and said, "Hey, you know how Chloe likes to eavesdrop?" She let out a chuckle, "She's good at it too, and she's been giving me a ton of useless information from all over town. There's never any malice behind it, or any real intent at all, to be fair."

"Has she always done that?"

"Oh sure. It's like a compulsion. She occasionally pipes up to engage the strangers in conversation, and she's never felt like it was spying. I've tried to convince her of how rude and creepy eavesdropping is, but that doesn't help." She laughed again.

"Try saying it's something only drunk men and bored housewives do."

"Oh, it would be to no avail. Chloe simply likes doing it, and I'm thinking, it's been useful sometimes, hasn't it?"

I chewed before saying, "Oh?"

"Yeah. Sometimes, she goes so far as to jot down notes to force feed me the more amusing or juicy bits. I hear all these conversations had by folks Liz and I would never meet. I guess it's a meaningless hobby, but yeah, it has been useful. That's how she got you info on Frog."

A man came by, completely ignoring me, and handed Maria a small box. At first, I thought it was the waiter. I mean, we came here for some privacy, right? She didn't even glance at the box. She nodded at him with a smile, and then proceeded to ignore him like a tired aunt might a small child. When she noticed my tight faced expression, she looked surprised.

"I guess they find me everywhere. Hey, you aren't bothered by what just happened, right? I mean, it's not like we were on a date." She winked. "Oh. You were bothered. See, I'm always receiving gifts from strangers. Some are tacky, some are pretty, and some are clearly meant to be heirlooms, but they're all pretty meaningless to me."

I looked at the box, "But why? Is it something about your club?"

"Sometimes. Sometimes it's old clients who remember me fondly. Sometimes people confuse me with a famous heir to a fortune that I'm not."

"Huh. I wonder who you look like?"

"She's in France, I think. In any case, I keep very few of the gifts. Remember that big charity auction we had at the club a while back? All the stuff came from strange men. Sometimes I'll sell them to consignment shops. That gets funny."

"Funny?"

"Yeah!" she beamed. "Every now and then, an item will find itself re-gifted to me from a different suitor, and I take pride in relating exactly which thrift shop the man must frequent. Then I sit back to watch the man's eyes widen in horror and embarrassment."

I got quiet, looking her in the eyes, "You still wear the earrings I gave you."

"Of course. I like you."

We spent a couple more hours talking beyond when our food was gone. When it was time to go, I paid. I didn't know if I had the money to but the card didn't decline, and I figured that it was the least I could do. She rushed after me, and stood still, then I kissed her square on the lips, staying there for a moment. We said nothing about it, but smiled before she escorted me to her car.

"You took a bus, right? Let me drive you home." I liked Maria's car. It smelled like memories and the seats were comfortable.

My phone vibrated angrily when Jed called. I put it on speaker so Maria could hear.

"Did Chloe talk to you?" I asked.

Jed responded, "The new coroner is a prick. She's got Kathy's phone though."

"They couldn't get Bernie help, but found a new coroner quick."

"Yeah. Family hasn't claimed the phone, and whatever shitty funeral home doesn't want it either. This chick has it locked up in her office, and she ain't letting anyone get it unless we prove we're somebody to Kathy."

Maria said, "Will this be an undercover case? I can't imagine that going well for either of you."

"Hardy har har," Jed said. "Look Gekman, Chloe said Kathy had her phone on all the time. Always had the most advanced tech, but never used a password."

I rolled the window down to feel the cool air, and I asked Jed, "What good does that do us if we don't have the phone?"

"I'll figure it out. We just need a clear signal is all."

"Well boys," said Maria, "sounds like you two need to get going then. Gabe, I'll drop you off wherever Jed needs you to be." It was drifting into late evening, and we all hoped that meant the new coroner would have gone home for the day.

Jed parked the car farther down the road, away from the coroner as best as he could, while still assuming a close enough distance to where the phone may have been. He took his phone out and looked as though he was a thirteen-year-old texting his crush.

"It's like short-range wifi," Jed explained, as though I understood what that meant.

I pointed at his phone, "Wait. Why would her phone still have juice so many days later?"

"Coroner said she plugged it in for the family to get stuff off of it." He shrugged, then got out of the car and put his phone up against the wall of the coroner's office.

"Act casual," he said.

"Jed, we're behind a closed strip mall close to midnight. We look suspicious."

Kathy's phone was 70% pictures of her own feet, and games to play. Then, we found the most useful thing I could have ever hoped in a series of unanswered texts to Frog, or at least, to what she thought his number was. They read in excited tones, "Did you hear? I got called in to do a favor for Denny! He's the next Eli! This is so thrilling. Jealous?? You should be. It's a real easy gig too. I'm supposed to hang out with his grandma, his ONLY family that's left, and take a bullet or whatever for her if need be. Easy peasy! Oh, if you wanna find me," followed by Denny's grandmother's address. Perfect.

CHAPTER 9
A Mouse in The Cathouse

The only man still living who might be in charge of getting the toxin made was Denny Chittle, that we knew for sure. The name Eli Addams came up now and then, and he had sons, but that seemed vague to me as there was no mention of said children taking up their father's mantle after his death. We kept Addams on our list, but Denny was priority. I knew I had a blinding vendetta for his being Maria's ex, but I had a feeling he would know who killed Bernie. Kathy seemed pretty sure he knew all the other goings on of MOTH beyond that. Hopefully, Michael Crown would follow. According to Kathy's texts, Denny had no family left, besides his grandmother, and now we had her address. With our crappy luck, she was most likely senile.

We plopped ourselves back into Jed's car after a quick regroup to process what we had found. The ride didn't take long before the overgrown yard and colonial style home came into view. An off-white door, beige roof, and strange yellow siding made the whole house look like it wanted to puke. We got out and began to walk along the haphazardly lain stone path.

Looking at the lone apple tree in the yard, I asked Jed, "Hey, wanna come with me to my parent's place for Tu Bishvat?"

"Sure, I'm down. Isn't it not for a while though?"

"Yeah, it's in January. Dad's always been into that one. Wants to go all out for it."

"Fuck does that even mean? It's one of your, like, eighty fuckin' arbor days. What's he gonna do? Build a tree house?" I shrugged and rang the doorbell.

The door creaked open. There we were, standing on the doorstep of a woman older than most fossils. She looked like she was about to fall apart.

"Hello Ma'am," I said with a tip of my hat, "I'm Glenn Gaiman, P.I., and this is my partner, Jeff Davis. We'd like to ask you some questions, if you don't mind."

She looked like a light breeze would carry her off at any moment as she said, "Oh! Detectives! That's nice. Like on the television."

"Yes Ma'am!" said Jed with a smile beaming as he politely removed his cap, "Just like on the T.V. shows." He puffed out his chest as though there were cameras nearby.

The woman was a moldy antique. Glassy eyes, thin white hair, and the smell of mothballs and cat pee overpowered every other stench within a five-mile radius. Yuck. Old people. Jed liked her immediately. I could tell that she reminded him of his grandmother, and I had to admit there were similarities, though perhaps not in personality.

Jed's grandmother was a woman who would beat the crap out of me with a broom for being "snippy" when Jed and I were in high school. Not much changed about her up until the day she died. While Denny's grandma didn't seem quite as aggressive, they looked and sounded similar. Though I suppose they both looked and sounded like general, pale, old women.

If you're wondering how I felt about my own grandmother, she was different. She could be found gambling with men about my age late into the night, and as much as she got older, she never seemed *old* in the traditional sense.

Also, my grandmother was the only one of the three to not smell like cat pee.

Denny's grandmother invited us in. The distinct cat crap odor intensified and came forth from the couch when Jed and I sat down. This was particularly disturbing, as there was no cat to be found. Furniture from the forties sat stained and dingy. She started talking, but I was a bit...

distracted by the house itself. It was somehow both out of date and hoity toity, like a fine cake coated with a layer of dust. Jed, however, was utterly enthralled. He was like a nerdy boy who had won a date with the head cheerleader. He was hanging, downright dangling off of every word that came out from between her gums. In front of my face shook her bumpy, spotty, boney hand holding a silver, ornamented tray.

I stared at the thin, stretched flesh she called a wrist, and the gnarled branches she took to be fingers as she asked, "Would you like a cookie, Deary? I made them yesterday right after I visited Cornsbrook. Lovely place, that is."

I took a cookie and smiled as I said, "Nobody should stay in that town too long. Rots the brain."

I took a bite. The cookie exploded into my mouth, and not with flavor. This was not a pleasant explosion, like an orgasm or an overwhelming light show. No. This was a bad explosion. Not a devastating bomb in an undeveloped country mind you, but awful nonetheless. This explosion consisted of a dry crunch, a poof of dust, and shards of cookie shrapnel assaulting my unarmed tongue. Pretty sure the confectionery was meant to involve chocolate. From the taste alone, I would never have known. Oh God. Oh God. Was this covered in dust like everything else in her house? She said they were only a day old.

Squeamish and sheepishly, I smiled again and said with my mouth still full of powdery cookie mush, "Delicious!"

"Oh, I'm glad you like them, Deary."

I mocked wiping the corners of my mouth with a napkin, attempting to stealthily drop the clump, and bundle it up in a nice little package of terrible in my hand. In an effort to distract myself from the cookie, I began asking her questions about Denny.

As she poured some tea for us, she chuckled and said, "Oh, my son is long gone. Dead like his father.

I wanted this over with, "Your grandson, actually. Was he a Denny junior?"

"Oh yes. My dear little Denny. Oh, makes more sense someone your age is asking about him, yes. Well, he went to college at Lotgraff University, and then he fell in with a bad crowd, I guess. Not much more to say about that."

"Lotgraff University..." I trailed off as Jed and I shared a look. We knew he had lived with Michael Crown. That connection made Denny a likely suspect, but what if Michael was simply caught up in that group himself? "Uh, what kind of 'bad crowd' was Denny involved in?"

"He used to hang around a boy they called 'Toad' or something..."

"You mean, Frog?" said Jed.

"Yes. Frog. Silly thing to call such a sweet boy."

I was going to need a new notebook soon, "How did they meet?"

"Some club. They called it... Oh... Some kind of bug fire."

"The Moth Flame?" Jed asked. I was glad to have him as a willing translator.

"Yes. Yes that's what it was. He hangs out there sometimes, he tells me. Talks about it all the time. He has a girlfriend who runs it, you see." I gave a shudder. "Later on tomorrow though, he'll be at the Bunny Inn, just outside Newsburg. He likes the ladies there." I wanted to question why his grandmother would know all this, but I guessed some families are just that kind of close.

The Bunny Inn was a sleezy motel known for sex trafficking that the vast majority of cops conveniently ignored. It was also where some legitimate sex workers used to get their jobs as well, though some weren't so lucky as to stay alive longer than a month. Everything blended together, and it all depended on who considered them "high class."

Maria had worked there for a long time, if apparently not doing what I had thought at the time. She had told me years ago that she had done her best to suss out which women were there by choice, and which were too afraid to leave. She saved a lot of would-be victims back then, though Maria would never think it was enough.

Letting my mind wander, I looked into my tea cup in that cat fur coated little room and noticed a small bug with too many tiny legs, occasionally twitching, floating. I grimaced, then shrugged it off and decided to hold the cup and not say anything.

"What do you do with your time, with your boys gone?" asked Jed.

"Oh, I work for an orphanage. We do wonderful things for these children."

"Oh yeah? That's really nice." Jed had no issue with the deserts.

"Mhmm. Oh! They always take toy donations, so if you boys have anything from when you were little, we'll take it for the children."

I piped up, thinking of the hospital, "Toy donations?" I was not thinking clearly when I reached for another cookie and popped the damn thing into my mouth. I have never regretted anything so very much. To quickly get the dry, brittle, whatever-the-Hell-it-was taste out of my mouth, I chugged the rest of my tea. Looking solemnly into the empty cup, I realized that the possibly dead thing was no longer to be found. I placed the cup and the rest of the cookie onto the plate in front of me, resting precariously on the edge of the table. I put a hand through my hair and the other on my hip as I said, "Well, it's getting late. We should be going. Thank you for your help."

"Oh! Going so soon?" Denny's grandmother scrunched her thin lips together in a pout, "I know you two must be very busy. I understand."

"No, we can stay a little longer," said Jed. We

wound up staying long enough to play three games of Parcheesi. I had to conk out once we got back to our respective homes.

That night, I didn't sleep terribly well. My nightmares weren't the usual fare of abstract hospitals and dead but walking children. Instead, there was no gore or screaming. There were no hands made of wallpaper, reaching at me from my old room, making me question the sanity of wanting to purchase my childhood home. There were no worms coating the ground, or protruding from beneath my knee caps. No. In this particular nightmare, there was only an intense sadness and caustic frustration in my chest.

In the dream, I was trying to talk to Maria. She said she was with some other girl from my past, my first girlfriend in fact, and they were talking. They looked over old files of me from this giant bin that required a ladder. They found they were similar people, so Maria decided she didn't mean as much to me. The logic was that they both found me attractive, and I found them both attractive, so they must have been a dime a dozen in my eyes. I couldn't tell Maria otherwise, because I was suddenly in the rain then, and the droplets were eating away at my phone like acid. I could see her sometimes as though through heavy fog, but I was too far away to reach out and talk to her.

I ran inside, desperately trying to tell her that I loved her more than anyone, but I still couldn't. All my old friends I had lost contact with after high school came to swarm me. I couldn't get past the wall of people to call her back. When I finally did, the door she had gone through was locked, and she had blocked my number. I had taken too long and I had missed her.

The dream shifted and I was with my parents in their new house post-retirement, instead of in my own place. We'll move past the fact that "my place" is my parent's old house. Either way, I called her on the house phone. This meant that I was in another state yet again when I called her up to try to tell her. I wanted to tell her that I was so happy to hear from her, and so afraid, and I never wanted to bother her or ruin her perfection with my awful everything. She picked up the dream-phone and told me that she was staying where she was, away from me. She had moved on from the stupid something we had never even had, whether she wanted to or not.

When I awoke, I felt sick and guilty. I felt like someone had kicked me in the stomach and then immediately wished that had happened so I'd feel something other than whatever crippling sadness was eating away at my gut.

I picked up my real phone in actual awake-life to text Maria. I typed in, "Ever wake up from a dream feeling awful about what was in your head?" but it wanted to autocomplete to "in your heart?" I thought about leaving it, since it would have still been accurate. I never hit send.

Four hours later, Jed and I were in his apartment, getting ready to go to the Bunny Inn. It was still daylight, far from when active hours would have been. We were counting on that. We knew it was possible the whole place was deserted too. Neither of us had kept track of the Bunny Inn enough to know how bad it had gotten, but we knew it wasn't great to begin with.

I didn't see the point of showering before going

someplace that would require a good scrub after the fact, but Jed said he could smell himself. He mocked vomiting as he removed his shirt, threw it into the corner, and made his way to the bathroom. His shoulder tattoo caught my eye. It was old, faded. Must have been there for a long time.

"What's the letter-number combo for?" I asked.

"You've seen it before, haven't you?"

"No. I haven't seen you without a shirt on for many years, even at the beach." Of course, the only beach was by Cornsbrook, so avoiding it entirely was undoubtedly more sanitary anyway.

"It's the license plate of the fucker who ruined my life."

I could feel my head attempt to retreat into my neck, "What purpose... You knew it by heart enough to get the tattoo? Or you wrote it down at the time and just... What?"

"Darcy wouldn't let us go to the cops. She didn't want to know who it was. Took so long, not like I could prove any malice anyway. Then she was gone. I've got this to remind myself that nothin' is forever." I dropped the conversation like it was made of lead.

While Darcy's spine was never the same, Jed often made it sound as though Darcy had died in the accident. If I were her, I would have been even more insulted than she was. He hardly ever saw her, and she hated to see him drunk. It isn't hard to see why she left him.

Jed drove.

The Bunny Inn itself was much worse than I remembered, which was saying something. It was what you could call an old school motel, with an inner courtyard surrounded by a squared U shape building. The courtyard had what used to be a pool in it. The "pool" was now a mostly drained hole with a little black, stagnant water in the bottom. Mindless graffiti splattered all over the place, and not the artsy kind either.

As for the inner workings of the area, a few permanent residents lived in the East wing. On the West was where all the business happened. Most of the rooms we checked out were outright dirty.

As filthy inside as they were outside, they stunk of sex, vomit, alcohol, and various smoke-related drugs. The windows were caked with dirt and smudges from God knows what. Some had definite signs of meth along the edge of the floor and walls. Some of the people in those rooms had the same signs. There were bubbles in the wallpaper and most of the beds didn't have sheets. Just bare mattresses. There was no working plumbing and hardly any functioning lights.

Jed always refused to call the place a brothel. He much preferred "cat house" or even, "Casa Del Pussy" and I hated hearing it. The last time we showed our faces around there to follow a lead that the department would then ignore, Jed had found himself being propositioned by a pretty lady. Then, he realized how young she looked and changed his mind. He managed to finagle her into the car and get her to safety instead. Last I heard, she had gone back to school for library science.

I remembered he had said, "Even if I wanted to, and she was of age, it goes against my rule" with a lifted finger.

I had replied with a raised eyebrow, "You have rules?"

"One. I have *A* rule."

In any case, the room up front was where all the girls with a specific job tended to gather. Maria had said she'd see the girls line up like cattle, to then be picked and sold to the highest bidder. It was the nicest of the rooms. The wallpaper was all intact, the glass was clean and unbroken, and the bed was always made. That was of course where their pimp used to hang out. When we arrived this time, it was Denny's room for whenever he decided to visit.

We were headed straight for his castle when I got a phone call from an unlisted number. My heart dropped inside my chest, Maria said only, "He's got me. We're in one of the warehouses and-"

A man's voice came on the phone, "Hang up with your friend, Maria" followed by a click. Denny Chittle. It had to be. I swallowed, wide eyed. What warehouse?

I turned to Jed, "Did you catch that? Denny has Maria in a warehouse! She's in danger and I don't which place he took her or why she needs to call for help and-"

Jed grabbed me by both shoulders, "So we gotta keep going. Someone here might know where Denny is today, right?" I nodded, verge of tears.

Frantic, we continued on, praying Denny's room would have some clues as to where he took Maria. We both doubted Denny's grandmother would have a better idea.

Blocking the path, the man standing in front of us was huge. A white, tanned and burnt in all the wrong places, behemoth of a man. His shoulder length, light brown, scraggly hair was pulled back in a rather neat pony tail. He had a goatee, with a heavy emphasis on mustache. His upper lip spoke more of tequila binges in Mexico than it did shoot outs in down town Newsburg. He dwarfed Jed with his barrel chested, bear-like presence. Staring at his long, mostly blond goatee, I hoped to God he wasn't a good friend to Denny. Evidently, I wondered that out loud, but the beast misheard me.

He tilted his head back a little and wobbled slightly as he said, "Oh. I'm not Denny."

He wore a black, long sleeved v-neck under a short sleeved, colorful Hawaiian shirt. Bermuda shorts, combat boots and what I believe could have been argyle socks completed the ensemble. It occurred to me that he was drug-addled and therefore probably harmless, if we knew how to handle him. He teetered as he spoke, as though he balanced on an invisible wire.

"I'm Puffin. Harlo Puffin." He was at once both terrifying and humbling, while a bit hilarious. Must've been at least six foot seven, and something about his demeanor made him downright monumental. Still, I wondered what he might be like at a party.

"Well, Harlo... Any idea where Denny is?"

"I can't tell you that." Harlo's voice dropped and he barreled towards us at top speed.

"Why is he charging?" I called out.

My companion, without missing a beat, grabbed a small gun from his left hip and shot Harlo with two tranquilizers. I didn't question why it hadn't been a normal gun. I was glad that Jed had them on hand. Unfortunately, I am not a terribly fast man. Harlo the Nordic Sasquatch fell, and when he did, he landed on me. We heard some ladies scream in the distance, and figured they must have been tucked away in whatever area Harlo had been. Since we weren't out to hurt any of them, and I was at that moment incapacitated, this was fine. Let them yell. I wasn't sure there was anyone else around to answer them anyway. When I got out from underneath Harlo, everything was terrible.

Sharp, shooting, stabbing pain shot up through the arch in my right foot, up under my knee cap. Searing, awful pain. The throbbing was jarring and disorienting. I could only see black in my peripheral vision. Realizing I'd have to rely on Jed until it went away, I decided it was best not to mention it at all.

"Let's get him somewhere to ask some questions. Here we'll just be freaking everyone out." I wasn't entirely making sense, but Jed didn't question it.

I spent the time Jed took to drag Harlo to his car's passenger seat to search and hobble around Denny's room. It was mostly empty, aside from used tissues and other such objects I did not feel the need to touch.

Once we got the monster into the car, I crawled as

best as I could into Jed's back seat. There, I spotted an electric guitar, a bag of sex toys, various fruit, both wax and real, and three balloon animals. I believe they were a rabbit, a turtle, and a monkey.

"Jed," I asked, not necessarily wanting to know the answer, "what the Hell is all this for?"

He shrugged as he turned the key. "I had a good time the other night."

I thought about getting my leg x-rayed. Thought about pumping Harlo full of more sedatives just-in-case too. I did neither.

Jed looked at me through the rear-view mirror to say, "We manage to get him onto the shitty wooden chair in your office, we don't know if he'll talk or kill us if we ask him questions."

"Questions?" asked Harlo. "You my lawyer?"

"Yeah," Jed replied. "Now talk to the nice blue haired man in the back." Well then.

Still doped up from whatever the Hell was in those tranquilizers, Harlo was pleasant. Downright serene. I thought about capturing and domesticating him, like a pet that was once a fierce wild animal. Exotic and intimidating. Good for picking up women. I wondered for a brief moment, how Maria would feel about that. Then, I debated if the pain in my leg was making me delusional.

I gave it a shot, "We have to find Denny. Do you know where he is?" Harlo shrugged.

I tried again, "Do you know about any warehouse he may have gone to?"

"Where's the house?" We weren't going to get anywhere like this, and I was getting frustrated.

"I could hurt the information out of him," said Jed.

I glanced at Harlo who looked truly confused. "Screw this!" I threw my hat off and ran my fingers through my hair, grabbing a chunk and holding onto it. "He's not gonna give us anything! She's gonna die!"

Harlo perked up and asked, "Who's gonna die? A girl?" It was like he had no idea who he was or how he had gotten to this point. In fact, that may have been totally accurate.

Jed realized he could use Harlo's confusion to our advantage and said, "You *would* fall in love with an ex lady of the night, wouldn't you?"

Not realizing at all what Jed was trying to do, I said, "What? No. I'm not... I am not in love with her."

"Oh yeah? Then why are you so upset?" He clasped his hands on the steering wheel like an angry mother who was ready to pull over.

Harlo looked back and forth between the two of us with great concern.

"Listen to me, you blueberry idiot," Jed pointed back to my face, "I see the way you look at her, Man." His tone turned sarcastic with, "I also see the way you become a brilliant conversationalist if she is so much as within thirty feet of you."

I'll admit, that jest stung a bit, but I couldn't argue. He continued with, "It's painfully obvious that your blue balls take over when she's in the room!"

Actually defensive, I said, "Well, what do you want me to do? If we don't get information on Denny, she's going to die!"

Jed gestured to Harlo, "So, if you want, I'll beat it out of Harlo here so we can get the twinkle back in your eyes. Take his fingernails off and shit."

I huffed out a, "After that, he'd say anything. No telling what's true. Oh God. She's gonna die before I ever get to tell her-"

Jed got louder, "Tell her what, Gekman?"

"Tell her that I love her, okay?"

Harlo blurted, "I'll help!"

Jed pointed at me again and said, "You owe me twenty bucks."

Harlo sat up straight. "I'll help you find her! I'll shoot Denny myself if I have to!" I questioned this, but hoped he'd guide us. We were already driving in circles.

Harlo looked right at me and said, "I don't care if she DID get involved with Denny!"

I responded, "Exactly! Maria's still a human being!"

Jed added, "And a hole's a hole!"

CHAPTER 10

A Chortle For Chittle

I'd never taken a ride with a drug-addled man as a
navigator before. Drunk, but not this. There's a first time
for everything. As far as first times go, it was an interesting
experience to say the least. Harlo switched seats with me
and directed Jed from the back to several of the hot spots he
knew Denny used for illegal dealings. Holding a woman
against her will would certainly count as such. Harlo was
horrified by the idea that Denny, or anyone, would do such a
thing. I wondered how he knew Denny without knowing his
nature. Was Harlo at the Bunny Inn during the trafficking?
He huffed into my ear about how horrible the whole thing
was as often as he'd change his mind about which direction
to take, which meant he never stopped mumbling to himself
and to us.

Harlo didn't know the address but claimed he knew
the way regardless. We checked two warehouses out, and I
wasn't sure Harlo knew which planet he was on. Yet, we
plodded on.

The next place he brought us was a couple of storage
containers by an abandoned amusement park. What
followed immediately thereafter was a very out of the way
storehouse that had a weird hookah bar inside of it. I
couldn't tell if he was trying to help us or looking to satisfy
his chemically fueled state of mind. Jed wanted to stay and
interrogate some people in the green, smoky hookah bar, but
changed his mind when he started to get dizzy.

On the way to each area, we managed to get some
more information out of Harlo. By the end of it, we knew
that Harlo had absolutely no idea who Michael Crown was.
He thought he knew everyone Denny knew, but he didn't
know who Maria was either. Denny may have been
dormmates with Michael before his death, but Harlo didn't

even know that Denny had gone to college. A lot of people within MOTH didn't seem to know, which made me question if certain kinds of intelligence were looked down upon in their community.

I took over driving about half way through the journey. This allowed Jed ample opportunity to continue giving Chloe reports on our whereabouts via text to try to make her stop asking. I let the car crawl up to the most dilapidated warehouse we'd seen yet.

We removed ourselves from the vehicle in a slow and reserved way, in case this was the place, as we had done for all the others. It may have proved as fruitless as the other however-many locations, but I was sure to have my gun on me just in case this time. Something felt different in my gut.

The inside of the building was a maze of hallways and metal rooms, each filled with a copious number of wooden crates, varying in size. A large surplus of those crates trickled outside of the building into a concrete backyard, too bumpy and full of rocks to be useful as a parking lot. There was no fence around this back area, so at least we wouldn't need to go back inside to find our ways back to the car. Instead, on the sides of us were walls of the warehouse itself, in a square U shape. Here and there was also your random green storage container, and no sign of Denny or Maria.

I would have been quick to continue on, but I stopped short when I noticed a small hole dug into the ground. There was another little hole nearby, followed by another. Some of the holes were more like scooped scuffs, like something was digging in before being dragged back out in one direction or another. I followed the holes until I got to a lone shoe. A black high heel. I alerted Jed with a tug on his arm and a point. His face became stern as he whipped his head around, looking for any other signs. We had checked all the rooms inside the building. The two of them must have been tucked away inside one of the compartments, if there at all.

I turned back toward the car, and not to anyone in particular said, "At least this wasn't another immediate bust. We've got a clue, haven't we? So not another useless trip. Let's call some back up in case this is it, get inside and clear the place as fast as we-"

Before I could finish my sentence, Jed was pulling his gun from its holster and aiming it directly at my head. This was not the tranquilizer gun. As any good detective worth his salt knows, when a man is waving a gun in your face, it's best to keep your cool. This holds true, even if the man with the gun is your partner.

I realized then that he wasn't pointing his weapon at me, but beyond me, past the left side of my head. A delighted laugh echoed behind me. A sick, malicious cackle that left a bad taste in my mouth. He had been waiting for us. He had made Maria call, even if he'd given us no real clues as to where they'd be.

"Took you long enough!" said Denny from behind me. "My fault, really. I assumed you were better detectives than you clearly are."

He sounded vile and made my blood boil.

I started to do what you see in the movies, a slow turn to give the bad guys a cool look, followed by a fear-inducing one liner. Very Clint Eastwood. Okay, I probably looked more B-movie like Bruce Campbell. Before I could think it out, we heard a pop like a loud engine backfiring. It felt as if my leg had burst into flame from the inside. I went down. Apparently, in real life, the bad guys just shoot you when they get the chance. No monologue required.

My leg wouldn't obey my brain, just limp and bleeding. Lots of bleeding. I could feel my heart beating fast inside my head as I dragged myself behind one of the mobile storage units so I didn't become a sitting duck. As I did, Jed took cover behind a nearby crate and started to return fire. The gun that would take two hands for most people to fire looked like a child's toy in his hands. Following his lead, I pulled my much smaller gun from its home in my side holster, happy that I had pushed aside my typical hesitation about firearms.

I pushed the pain to the back of my mind and tried to return the favor between the sounds of Denny's bullets hitting wood crates and concrete around me. Denny ducked behind the crates easily, despite his being almost six feet tall. All photos I had seen before made him look pasty and half dead. Here, he looked like he could hail from California with his unkept light brown hair, tan skin, and hazel eyes. His jawline rivaled my own, and I'll admit for a second, I saw that he was the type of handsome that made him look dangerous. I steadied my aim the best I could with my leg throbbing and my head whirling, and pulled the trigger. One. Two. Three times. Each shot missed the mark, due in no small part to my injury. My lungs couldn't quite get a full breath. I wanted to vomit.

Denny started out with three goons. One was missing. Was he dead? No. My vision caught up with where my eyes had gone, and I spotted Denny handing Zeke a piece of paper.

Zeke looked down at it in his hand, then looked back up at his boss to say, "I don't like that you hurt Maria so bad. You didn't say it was gonna be like this."

"You turning on me now, Zeke?"

"What? No! Of course not!"

"Then take what I'm giving you and GO." He didn't announce to where the paper would be taken. Zeke ran off. I fired at him, but missed entirely. Denny started firing again, forcing me into cover.

Denny was the only one wielding a hand gun with a much smaller clip than that of his lackeys. They were both tearing up the crates we were using as cover. He barked out the names Nick and Rex, but it took a while for the sound to catch up to my ears. It was as though everything around me was moving too slow, like in a dream where you can't quite push yourself to run. I pulled my head back in, as a barrage of bullets sprayed the spot it had just occupied. I hoped that whatever was in these crates and storage units would hold up.

Looking over to Jed, he seemed to be taking a different approach. He fired in the general direction of Denny and his two goons, rather than taking care of where to point. I soon figured out which goon was which. Nick was a dark man with thin dreads all pulled neatly back. He had the body of an Olympic runner. Rex on the other hand was as tall as Harlo, but pasty, with thinning brown hair. If I could've caught one of them, it would have been Rex. My plan was to do so before the chaos of my partner ensued.

Still no aiming whatsoever that I could see, Jed would unload the magazine as quickly as he could, eject it and load up a new one. There was a significant amount of damage happening around the three gangsters, with dents and holes in the storage containers as well as bits of wood exploding into the air every time one of the rounds bore into a crate. I caught a panicked look on Rex's face. Jed ejected the third magazine in the span of a minute and loaded in a fourth.

Just as I was about to question the point of his technique, I heard one of the goons let out a howl. I looked out in time to see blood spray into the air from his gut. Rex was knocked clear off of his feet and laid on the ground groaning. Seeing Rex go down, Denny ran to his left, directly into what looked to be a stack of crates. Except instead of face planting, he disappeared inside of them. He had disguised a damn storage unit, that sneaky son of a gun. He came back out dragging a very bloody and battered Maria by the hair. He threw her to the ground and looked in my direction. She was half awake and barely aware of the situation at hand.

Denny yelled, "Is this what you came for? This dirty

little whore who doesn't know how to do her job, and keep her mouth shut?"

Before I could stop myself, I shouted back, "You scumbag piece of shit!" Clutching my leg with one hand wasn't doing much to help me. I could feel the warm liquid pour through my fingers and down my leg, getting colder as it went.

Maria dragged herself behind a crate. With two fewer shooters to worry about, and Maria tucked away, I stuck my head out again and popped off five more shots at Denny. The last two bullets must have taken some of the crazy luck that allowed Jed to take Rex down, because one knocked the gun clear out of his hand. The other hit him square in the right shoulder. I wanted to run to Maria and get her out of there, but between my leg, and an unseen Nick still laying down cover fire, it didn't seem like I had much of a chance.

Harlo decided this was the perfect time to step in. I had somehow forgotten the giant was with us. He grabbed a crate which would have taken three of me to lift, and started sprinting toward Maria. He braced himself and lunged the crate directly at Nick who was clearly not expecting such a ridiculous thing. He swung his gun toward the flying object but the panicked spray of bullets didn't stop the momentum. The wooden death box hit him right in the chest, sending him back a couple of feet and laying him out. Continuing his charge, Harlo shoulder checked a surprised Denny aside, and grabbed Maria in one fluid motion that I would never have thought possible.

Out of the corner of my eye, I saw Jed toss his gun aside. Out of bullets. He pointed at Nick, who was getting back up and said, "Stay here." Strangely enough, the man complied. He had a look on his face that suggested that he simply knew no other way to react.

Jed ran to the trunk of his car. He flung it open and started rooting around in it for something.

"Harlo, get Maria into the car, and get her the hell out of here! A hospital. Get her to a hospital," I shouted. Immediately after, I realized how much trust and responsibility I was having in someone who in any other situation would not be granted such. I started grabbing my stomach from feeling sick, rather than my still bleeding leg.

As Harlo daintily pranced Maria over to the car, Denny tried to goad him from the ground. "A lost confused lap dog, that's all you are Harlo. I took you in, gave you whatev-"

He would have kept going had I not shot the ground near his arm as he pushed himself back up. I was aiming for his head, but I guess you can't win every time. I glanced back at the car to see it pulling away, a slight bit of relief washing over me. I noticed then, that Jed was now barreling toward us whilst wielding a medieval battle ax straight out of a Renaissance fair, as if it were the most normal thing in the world.

I was only able to spit out, "What... The... What?" Then, "How long have you had that in the trunk of your car?" dropped from my mouth.

Instead of a verbal response, Jed glanced my way, grunted, then charged at Denny, who had almost gotten back to his feet. Denny rolled to his right, grabbing his gun off the ground to stand up with his gun trained on Jed. Bringing a battle ax to a gun fight couldn't end well.

"All right, all right. So, you got the girl. Whatever, I can deal with that for the time being, especially since once I take you two out, I just have to deal with that brain-dead gorilla," said Denny. "You two aren't even shit."

I retorted, "I do still have a gun you know, and a pretty clear shot on you."

It was at that moment that I felt the barrel of a gun press to my temple. Nick had used the events of the last couple of minutes to make his way around some crates to sneak up on me. We were looking pretty screwed, and once again, time slowed down as my mortality took hold of me.

The feeling was interrupted by an Amazonian-like battle cry blasting over a speaker system. This was enough to distract everyone, giving Jed the chance to slam his ax into Nick's right shoulder. Seemed to bludgeon more than slice, probably an unsharpened prop, but Nick dropped gasping for air. I was able to grab the gun from Nick's hands, as the man crumpled to a moaning pile on the ground. Whatever adrenaline Denny was riding on must have subsided at that point. He vomited, then so did I.

The source of the sound was made clear when Chloe came riding in, half way out of the sun roof of what looked to be a futuristic tank with elements of a pickup truck. I recognized it as one of the digging machines converted into a cargo haul, the legs replaced with metal treads. A flame thrower was strapped to the top. The machines really were random parts smacked together.

"You can thank my mother for the rental!" She gave the vehicle a pat. "I suggest you get in the machine before you become part of this barbecue." Chloe stated this with a nonchalance that sent shivers up my spine. How did she even know where we were? Jed.

"Wait!" I said.

Jed grabbed me and helped me hobble into the vehicle, where I could watch the show. I was more concerned with any information we were missing out on by ending their lives. Besides that, we now had the upper hand. Would they surrender? We could get an arrest for what happened to Maria, and then question Denny about Michael Crown.

Denny had run into his disguised storage crate, and Nick was trying to make his way there as well, and Rex was nowhere to be found. Nick was taking his dented shoulder worse than Denny took the bullet, and I had to assume Rex wasn't doing so well with the hole in his gut.

Chloe wanted to fire at the storage crate, sending

wood, metal, and Nick flying through the air, but she tossed the thought aside. Instead, she took up the flame-thrower, dousing everything in sight in flame and a napalm like substance. The stench was overwhelming. She pounded the roof of the machine twice, signaling the driver, her own mother, to leave while she continued to spray as much wood as she could.

I wheezed out, "But, wait! Shouldn't we see what happened to Denny, and Nick? What about the other guy? Rex might be dead! And Zeke is just OUT THERE somewhere, and-"

Sitting in the back, there was a sudden, awful, all-consuming pain. I did not notice it at first. Only the nausea. I wanted to throw up a second time, and then I once again realized what had happened, and it made me even sicker. The rushing slow-motion had kept me busy, and had refused to allow me to ease into the knowledge of the situation.

Right. Oh yeah. Shot. Shot in the goddamn leg. Well, at least it wasn't my stomach, or my chest for that matter. It's hard to stay positive when the world is spinning and everything is going dark from blood loss.

CHAPTER 11
Wine Comes Later

I needed to go to the hospital for my leg anyway, but I wasn't the most important person. I had to find Maria first to know if she was okay. I imaged how I looked to the lady at the front desk; I was a bloody, battered man with shredded clothes asking about a different person entirely. I was pale, leaning on every available surface to hold myself up, and distinctly unwell, so no one would answer my question until at least handing me a pair of crutches. I'd be billed for them later.

There was a door, a hallway, and then Maria's room. At that first threshold, I took a step on the borrowed crutches, and then rocked back. In an effort to prepare myself, I thought of what she may look like. Tubes everywhere, half dead like I last saw her. That's what I immediately pictured. Her makeup would be smudged, or off completely. She was still beautiful without it, though I knew she hated to be seen that way. She'd be unconscious, struggling in a quiet place inside her own head to survive.

Jed took the paperwork to fill out while I made my way down the hallway. I heard someone call out about waiting for my name to be called, but I was a man on a mission.

She was here because I failed. I didn't get to her in time. If she was dead, it was my fault. I may as well have beaten her within an inch of her life by my own hands. I dragged her in. She was on her way to the top of the food chain, and I yanked her back down to the ground.

I took another step, and took a breath along with it as I limped down the hallway, clutching the wall for support. I was no good on crutches.

I opened her door.

Drenched with sarcasm, Maria said, "What do you

mean, there's no wine?"

My entire body sighed in relief. She had refused to wear a hospital gown, so there she sat on the starchy white bed, in a little black dress, jokingly complaining about the service. She had a slight cut on her bottom lip, and a black eye, but it wasn't swelled shut anymore. Liz was standing with her, attempting to be the mediator between the nurses and Maria, and mostly failing. I wanted to muster up the ability to run to Maria, but keeping my cool seemed to be the better option.

In the hallway outside of the room, Jed was anything other than "cool."

"Fuck you! I may as well be family! She dead? Is she fucking dead? Cause I gotta find Gekman again before he blows this fucking building up if she's fucking dead!" The nurse looked horrified.

Soon Jed was tossing folders around and over turning gurneys, thankfully without people on them, in order to get his answers. I decided to step in before he could be restrained and taken away somewhere.

"She's fine! Upset that there's no wine." I smiled as I reached for a toothpick from a pack that was no longer in my pocket, and then I collapsed unconscious.

The nurse was very sweet. I wouldn't have minded her giving me sponge baths, if you know what I mean. She was gentle as she tended to my wounds. She was also endlessly entertained by me, so I could tell her ridiculous stories, wilder than what actually happened, and she'd be happy to listen. I liked her.

Jed came into the room as I was watching the nurse leave with a smile on my face.

"You okay, man?" He was concerned enough that he pet me on the head.

"Yeah, I'm okay. I mean, it hurts, but it was a clean shot. Nothing is left in my calf, they're replacing the blood I lost," I gestured to the tube in my arm, "and it didn't even break a bone. Through the muscle and right back out again."

Jed nodded and said, "Okay then. We got the bad guys, right? No harm, no foul."

I didn't have nearly enough morphine, and so I shook my head, "It's all foul!" I started laughing in a weird, creepy way. "We got *some* bad guys. Not THE bad guys. We still don't know why Michael Crown is dead!"

Jed stared off into the distance as he said, "We still have that sidekick of Denny's..."

"Harlo? Or do you mean Nick?"

"The rat, Zeke. The one who ran off so fast, right when the good stuff started. Harlo may know where to find him."

"You really do have something against that guy, don't you?" I reached over to review my new prescription. After my leg was drained to avoid infection, I was still going to be taking those antibiotics for a while. So long as I had pain killers, I'd take whatever else they gave me. The pretty nurse came back in and un-hooked me from any machines.

Jed said, "Zeke reminds me of something bad. I can't place it. I feel like he did something bad to me. Or really bad to somebody else."

"Any clues at all as to what it may have been?"

Jed scratched his short beard more than his cheek, "I don't know. I keep having weird dreams about Darcy though. I think I keep smashing all the bad shit together in my head."

"Well, let's talk to Harlo." I began to stand up, out of habit more than a want to be upright.

"Oop! Sorry, no no no," said the nurse as she chuckled. She placed a wheelchair under my butt, and then left the room once again.

Maria, thankfully, took the reins of wheeling me around from Jed. It was one vehicle I did not appreciate, but I was only to be stuck in it for a couple of weeks.

Sitting in my new metal throne with my leg up, Maria was taking care of me as best she could while Jed was sleeping off whatever he had drunk the night before. Once Liz showed up, both Maria and Jed gave Liz notes on how best to deal with me, like a dog owner would give a pet sitter.

Liz handed me my phone when it buzzed.

It was Hudson, "Well, it's interesting. You aren't wrong."

"Obviously," I answered, "What am I right about?"

"Crown was killed by whatever was in that bottle. You suspected that when you found the coroner's body. You said it was from the MOTH company, right?"

"YES. You believe me now? You believe MOTH is killing people!" Maria didn't like the sound of that, so she wandered away from me to get a refill of coffee.

Hudson responded with a cold, "No." I felt punched through the phone. He clarified, "I believe that this concoction came from MOTH years ago, and that it was used as a poison to murder Michael Crown. There is still nothing directly connecting the company itself to Crown, especially since the company was bankrupted and sold off years ago. Nothing."

I held my breath.

Hudson said, "Check your email though, okay? Your coroner friend had some interesting notes pertaining to your case. We've gotten what little we could out of them, so I thought you'd like to have a look."

Rocks filled my lower intestine and frothing acid swarmed my throat. My ligaments were taught rubber bands. I was a half-pulled zipper, unsure of which direction would be most useful. I had Liz wheel me over to my computer.

It was jargon explained by more jargon.

"This guy talks about spiders a lot," said Liz. When she noticed my eyes light up, she said, "Oh! Did I say something useful? What were the spiders for?"

I made grabby-hands toward the pile of paperwork on the ground and said, "I have to rummage through that nonsense until I find the business card of one Andrew French."

Maria popped in to yell, "You're not doing anything. We'll do it."

Liz cheered, "Yeah! What are we looking for? Just his business card?"

"Yeah," I slumped back into the chair, out of breath. "He was the arachnologist from the Moth Fanciers. I'm thinking that he'd be able to decipher these notes."

Liz and Maria were diligently organizing the chaos that was my paperwork on the floor when Liz said, "His card doesn't have a giant spider on it or anything, does it? Because if it does, you'll know I found it by my blood curdling scream." My laugh was more of a snort.

Maria found it, and no, there was no spider on the card.

"How you feeling, Gabe?" asked Liz.

I smiled, but my words weren't on the same page, "I'm in a box of agony, made from my own skin. Just flesh, and bone, and pain."

"Well, you're obviously in better spirits, at least!" Oh, Liz tried.

I dialed the phone for French. I heard Maria whisper to Liz, "Why does he need to call the spider expert?" Liz shrugged and then gestured wildly to the mess we'd all made.

I caught them cleaning up the place when I hung up

with French.

"He'll be coming over for me to ask some questions," I said. "You guys are free to leave whenever. Thank you for everything."

"We're not leaving," said Maria. "Jed's gone home, but Liz and I will stay in the other room. You need anything, you either tell us, or just make sad little sounds and we'll figure it out. You do not get up."

"I'm not going to whimper like a-"

"Understood?"

"...Yes."

French was thrilled to come over and chat. He pieced together why Liz was the one inviting him in once he glanced at my leg. He didn't ask, and I didn't offer the information. We got to work.

"My research. The stuff Michael's roommate took from me was all on this spider! This is my work! My notes. You have any idea how much of this I had to reorganize before I could get published?" He got loud as he said it, but not in an angry way. His eyes were wide and so was his grin. He was pleased, like a ghost learning of his great legacy.

I pointed at the screen, "Can you explain it to me? Never know what might help the case."

French squinted and tilted his head to the side, "Case?"

"Oh! Yeah. I'm not a Fancier, I'm a PI. Michael Crown is dead. Surprised no one in the group noticed. Fiancé wanted a third party to investigate, so I was there to find out if anyone there knew anything, and the answer was no." Pain killers plus the fact that I was tired of literally everything made my professionalism non-existent.

"Did... Was this used in... for that?" French didn't look so happy anymore.

"Maybe, but understand that if this was taken from

you by Denny, it's on him. This isn't your fault. Ever. Okay?"

He turned to look at the screen again, "It mentions the chemical compounds. It's not anything you'd find interesting, I don't think. It's a shame too, because this spider is something really special."

"You're here. Tell me about the spider." All I wanted in that moment was for this lanky man to look less desperately depressed so I could go back to being doted on by my beautiful lady friends and looking miserable myself while wondering if my leg would ever feel normal again. I enjoyed people passionately speaking on subjects I knew little about.

"One big female and thousands of small males. It's extinct." He started crying as he was explaining, the reality of Michael's death setting in. It sounded as though he was mourning each and every last dead spider. "So there's a coconut sized lady spider crawling with tiny males like a walking army ant-hive. The female lays eggs, the males secure the eggs, fight over fertilization, gather food, and cover her area in webs. They do everything, and she's like the city where they all work and live."

He sniffed and I wobbled to get up, but Liz appeared. She got us the box of tissues from the bathroom, and I winced as I adjusted myself in my seat again.

French kept talking, half in a daze, "The female is tan and brown, what sets her apart is her size. Big! The males have red rings around each leg joint and their face fur is much more bright than the abdomen. God, I sound dumbed down when I'm upset. I probably sound like an idiot, I'm so sorry."

I handed him the box and nudged the trash can out from under my desk with my good foot, "No. I wouldn't understand a word if you weren't dumbing it down."

He laughed a little before continuing to explain, "It's all theory anyway. We don't actually know any of this.

156

Educated guesses."

"Still neat."

It was good to see French smile, "The males are what you'd think of as typical spider size. Maybe slightly smaller than an average Black Widow. Fast moving and extremely venomous. They also coordinate basic tasks like defense, hunting. Well, they did. They're extinct. That's why it's all theory. You can't ask them! We think scouts sent messages back to the hive via a relay squad, like a game of telephone."

"When did they go extinct?"

"Yeah, they really only existed pre-dinosaur, but couldn't adapt to a low oxygen earth. That's the Achilles heel. The size of the female means she needs to be in an extremely oxygen rich environment."

I pointed at the screen, "Any idea how anyone would have gotten venom from the spider then?"

"You've probably seen it in movies, right? Rehydrate tissue from amber. I don't know if that would actually work. I don't know. It would take so much time and so many steps. Wait. Oh my god it wasn't D- You said Denny was his name and that's right but it wasn't him."

"You just started talking very fast." I reached for a glass that wasn't there, "Would you like a glass of water?"

"Who is Eli? There was an Eli who sent Denny. I remember that name because that's who I wound up talking to. Denny's boss, I think. Older guy. Eli said that they had to buy almost every sample found over the last 50 years to get a feasible double helix! I was going to get paid a lot of money, but then Denny stole it and-" Andrew started hyperventilating. Maria found him a paper bag from the kitchen, which he made quick use of. Liz brought him a glass of water.

He thanked them, then took in a large gasp of air, "WHAT ABOUT the Japanese hornet that melts flesh?"

"Pardon?" …The what?

"Totally illegal to import so that's why it was really

hard for them to get. That was part of the talks too. Eli Addams. That was his name. He wanted to know if I could procure one and the answer was obviously a big fat NO. They're the size of a thumb too. Like MY thumb." He held up his thumb to show me. He indeed had a rather large thumb. "Oh, and they decimate bee hives. Not good."

"Listen, I'm gonna send you to a friend of mine. Officer Hudson is a good man. I want you to tell him everything you told me, okay?" Andrew nodded, and the three of us were quick to set up a meeting for them. If the company did find a Japanese hornet, that would be yet another illegal act to add to the list.

I wanted to be in my own bed that night, and that's what I got. A bed with a pillow top mattress and flannel sheets sounds like a brilliant plan for colder weather building up outside, until you have to get out of it. Then the bed becomes the softest of prisons, and sometimes creepily damp from my own sweat.

A cold breeze found every aching joint once I could mostly walk again. Any icy walkways became utter terrors, and I'd imagine snapping my leg in half if I fell. I missed autumn. Every now and then, the snow outside turned to showers of sprinkling ice and I could hear the skitter echo against the window like Hell spawn mice. The weather would change again soon after, which made it difficult to complain about. We had ways to entertain ourselves inside.

For example, we made Harlo an "honorary deputy." We weren't sheriffs, but Harlo didn't know that. He did notice that his badge was made out of cardboard, but so many temporary licenses are paper that he figured he'd get a real one in the mail. I couldn't say why we adopted him into our little group, other than a combination of curiosity and pity.

When I asked about Zeke, Denny's left-hand man, Harlo shook his massive head, "Nope. I told you. None of this crew knew your dead kid. I wish he did. Really. I'd love to fuck up his stuff. Zeke's a nasty guy. You can't do anything legal though. Besides, he's a chicken. We were in a gun fight, and he just runs away. Bok bok bok!"

I was expecting him to yell nonsense at any point. He didn't.

Instead, he continued, "I could beat the shit out of him, but even I need to be provoked."

"Or on the right shit," poked Jed.

"Or on the right shit. Yes." Harlo looked as though he expected us to give him a pill. He thought for a moment, "Nick might know something, if you can find him. I heard he was trying to get out of all this crap though."

"So where would he be?"

"Wherever the machines are." Harlo shrugged, "That's what he wanted to be doing. Making stuff." Jed picked up his phone to call Chloe and put her on speaker.

She answered, "Jed! What's up?"

"Hey, Nick wouldn't happen to be with you, would he?" Jed was measured in his question, "I know it's a long shot since he's obviously not one of the good guys, but we figured we'd ask."

"Nick will help. Whatever you need. He'll answer whatever, just don't go after him, okay? He's a good guy. Nick's a good guy who just got in over his head, okay?"

"How do you know that?" I asked.

"I know him from college, and yeah, he's here with me right now." Chloe took in a deep breath, "That day after we saved Maria, I went to help Mom sort some pieces of old machines and tanks and other horrible things to make into better things."

"And Nick was there?" I asked.

"Sporting a bandaged shoulder, no less. He walked into our facility with a paper in his hand, saying it was for my friends."

Nick spoke up at this point to clarify, "I got myself to a good hiding spot before she showed up with fire on one of the machines, but I saw that it was Chloe. I told her that I hoped the guys who took Denny down were her friends."

Chloe said, "If I had realized you were involved with that maniac-"

"Didn't have much choice, but thanks to your friends I have another chance. So, yeah. I don't know if it's gonna be helpful for anything. I took it from Zeke. He and Denny both thought it was important enough to drag around."

I asked, "So what is the paper?"

Chloe said, "It's the Addams' family tree. Different members have notes jotted around their heads about MOTH and roles they'd play. Little stories and connections are circled, while the dead folks are scribbled out."

"Okay," I let out a sigh, "Nick, how did you get this from Zeke then? Also, how long have you been there with Chloe?"

"Well, Zeke panicked. He got this from Denny, but didn't want to hold anything. He was afraid of being a target. He handed me everything, but most of it was garbage. This looked Different. I thought it could be useful." Nick went quiet for a moment before, "I don't want to be in it anymore. I never did. I want to build the machines with you and your mom, if you'll have me."

Chloe took the phone back and told him what part of which machine to get to work on.

"I planned to text you that I had the paper. I got distracted, checking on Nick's shoulder. It was an intense bruise, but little else. He'd already been stitched up, and nothing was broken. Jed called like right after, I swear."

"I believe you," I said.

Jed got the paper, and Nick told him where to find Zeke's house. I was glad Jed came back to me first, rather than slamming himself into more chaos first.

"We should go check it out, right?" Jed asked.

"You know, I've been mulling it over for a few hours, and I might actually agree with you."

"What? No, you shouldn't agree with me." He waved his hands in front of my face like someone asking a group of people to stop, "I mean, yeah, agree with me, but like, don't come with me. I gotta go. I gotta check this out."

"If you're going, I'm going. I can walk now."

"Barely. Every time you get better, you fling yourself into more shit. Stop it."

I knew I was saying the wrong thing, but I couldn't place how. I tried a different approach, "I made the decision to check out Zeke's place. I may have made this choice out of sheer determination, or perhaps the high of pain killers. Either way, Harlo is passed out in your apartment, right? So, if you needed back up, who else would you call?" It would be a near impossible task to wake such a man once he had oozed his body over too small a couch.

"Fine. Here's hoping Zeke isn't too difficult to handle on our own."

"Let's not tell Maria."

"Of course not. She'd kill me if she knew I was taking you on a fuckin' raid, man."

I made it to Jed's car before he effectively placed me into the passage side of the vehicle, followed by my crutches in the back.

Once outside of Zeke's shabby little shed of a house, Jed looked at me with the closest thing to puppy dog eyes the man could ever have, "See? Nick remembered where the Nazi fucker lives. I'm glad the ax was shitty, so he's not too hurt. Nick was helpful. He's not on my shit list anymore. This is it."

He was white knuckling the steering wheel, then let go to say, "What do we ask?" Then he took in a sharp breath, "We still have another two hours before last call."

I chewed on a toothpick as I said, "The way we work, we don't get a 'last call,' Jed."

He stretched his neck, "You're on antibiotics anyway."

"I don't understand. You wanted this, right? Pull up closer."

Jed did as I asked and pulled up, blocking in the only car in Zeke's driveway. Jed got quiet and we jerked to a stop. His face went pale.

"You okay, Jed?"

"It's him. It's him, unless he stole that fuckin' license plate." Jed pointed at the used-to-be-white Buick. Calmly and with complete serenity in his voice, he said, "You know what? This fucker ain't worth the time. There's no connection between him and the kid. He was a go-to guy for Denny. You're right. You were right about everything. I've been obsessed with this piece of wet, hot garbage because it's HIM. He's the guy who took Darcy away from me."

Jed took in a breath, and slowly let it out again. I can't say that I was afraid of Jed, but I was scared in that moment of something. I wasn't sure what exactly had me by the heart.

I asked, "If you knew his license plate, did you report it back then?"

He shook his head, "No. I got the tattoo, and I remember the ass of that car. I KNOW that stupid fucking plate cover. This is it. This is the car. I swear to God, this is the fucking car, and he was the driver."

"But I don't see how you-"

Jed continued like a mother would speak to her child

162

who was waiting in the car, "Hold on. I'm gonna finish this, and then we can go to the bar."

I was stupid enough to respond with, "What are you gonna do? Gonna tell him off? If you know the license plate, couldn't you tell somebody, and get him to do time for whatever? I don't understand what's happening. Is this because of those dreams you've been having about Darcy?"

Ah, but then, I noticed what was in his hand.

I was exhausted, but tried to scramble my way over to the driver's seat. I stretched out one arm to steady myself, and the other straining toward Jed, trying to grab his belt, his arm, anything to stop him. My leg felt like it was screaming. Once he was already away from the car, I knew I wouldn't be able to hobble over to him fast enough to stop what was about to go down.

The grenade was small, but it would do plenty of damage. Did I take an extra pill and slip into a bad dream?

Jed called out half to Zeke and half to God, "April Fool's, Bitch!" He pitched the explosive like a major league baseball player with a fastball, and at first, I thought it was a dud. There was nothing but a smashed window.

Then blazing heat swatted at my eyes. My ears were boiling and ringing. I lifted my arm up as if to block what would soon be raining down, but no debris hit me. If it had, my arm wouldn't have been much of an umbrella inside the car. Somehow, I didn't have the heart to tell Jed that Zeke had run out of his house the moment he stood up with the explosive. I kind of hoped Jed actually knew that.

Jed had done enough property damage that I figured it would keep Zeke from going forward in any direction. Frankly, I assumed Jed and Zeke both would be less of a problem after that. I thought about how I'd have written it all up in a report if Hudson still required such a thing from me. I was glad he didn't. I couldn't have figured out a good way to say, "and then I let him blow off the stinking roof."

Jed got back into the car in total silence. The drive to

Town's End was a slow one. We chose our bar stools carefully upon our arrival. He ordered the scotch. In celebration of my last night of antibiotics, I ordered an iced tea. We sat for a while, in solitude, yet together.

"So," Jed said, "what do we do now?"

"Well, we wait." I answered him, but looked at my glass.

"We wait?"

"What else can we do?"

"I don't know. I guess I figure-"

I turned my head and belted, "Where the HELL did you even GET a god damn grenade?"

Needless to say, I didn't get a straight answer. After a while, I changed my question to, "Do you think whatever that did to Zeke is like what he did to Darcy?"

"He smashed my life up with his fucking car, then drove off to keep on living."

"Right. I know. The hit and run," I rubbed my forehead. "Why didn't you talk to me? Why keep all of that inside of your gut forever? And does he even know who you are? What you just did was crazy."

"Man, Darcy is GONE because of him. I know it's him, even if he had no idea who I fucking was. He didn't CARE who I was. He didn't care who SHE was. Meanwhile, I just blew up his fucking house, and you let it go. You wanted to know how long I had the grenade or where I got it or whatever. Asking why I did it was a fucking afterthought. I know you ain't afraid of me. That means YOU are the psychopath."

I didn't have a fair argument for that. I knew he wasn't angry with me, and he knew I was trying to do the right thing. We finished our drinks in silence, until Chloe sent me a text which read, "We found him" and I responded with a phone call.

"You found Denny?"

"He's alive. His grandma said he had a burn, he's in

the hospital. I don't know if it's that he's been there a long time, went back, or that he just finally checked in. She couldn't get him to tell her anything else. I don't even know which hospital."

I nodded, as though she could see me do so, "We'll have to look around then. Hopefully he stayed local."

CHAPTER 12
Mixed Messages

Maria and Chloe were hanging out at Maria's when Chloe, curious critter she was, happened upon a black and red notebook. It was placed on the dining room table which also served as the kitchen table, simply due to lack of space. Chloe put a hand on the book and looked to Maria sheepishy for approval. Maria nodded and smiled, then wandered deeper into the kitchen, thinking there would be no harm in a look. Chloe flipped to a page, then became giddy within a minute of reading.

"You write poetry? Will you read one to me?"

"I write a lot of things about a lot of things," said Maria, "so you'll need to be specific."

Chloe shrugged, "Read one about Gekman. I bet you've got one."

Maria said nothing, but walked over to her from the refrigerator.

"Please?" asked Chloe.

Maria rolled her eyes and sighed audibly, snatching the book from Chloe.

"Yay!"

"It's really old though." Maria cleared her throat, adjusted in her seat at the kitchen table and began,

"What I would give to have one day... To see him again in more than a photograph, to hear the sound of his voice directly from his lips to my ear without the assistance of a telephone. To feel his hands on my body, and his breath on my skin and have it be so much more than childish fantasy... His hands, his lips, and even his flaws are beautiful.

"...But his eyes." She paused, and in her stillness, Chloe's smile faded away as she began to realize that Maria wasn't joking around.

"Oh?" said Chloe, trying to coax her. Chloe put her chin on her fist.

"They are terrible," Maria explained. "Sometimes they are gold, a deep, rich gold sparkling like the deepest, most hidden treasure beneath the waves of the sea. You see, he also keeps secrets and is a mystery, and like the ocean, he can drown a person when too blunt, all at once. A giant wave I never see coming. His eyes are terrible because they are beautiful, and that masks their danger. A siren song."

Maria took in a deep breath, then continued, "And sometimes... Sometimes his eyes turn to black holes and he is cold, aloof yet mystifying as the moon. He is the moon. Beautiful and inexplicable and impossible to reach.

"And sometimes his eyes are rigid and wooden and he is like a ghost. An incorporeal image of himself drifting along. I reach to try to touch him, but it's as futile as trying to touch the moon, or as trying to hold onto the sea."

Chloe hummed, and then said, "Something about this makes me muse about what Jed and Gabe are doing right now."

"Oh? Do you think they write poetry about us?" They laughed, but in truth, I did write poetry about Maria, though mostly in my own head. I wasn't ever brave enough to write it down. I was never as brave as she was.

Maria said, "I've written better things since, you know. Stuff about other people." She smiled coyly, as if she wanted to give vivid details, but said nothing about it. Instead, Maria said, "Gabe Gekman. I feel bad for him. This case has him all riled up about his little sister, and that Crown boy is a mystery death."

"I think it was someone in his family," said Chloe plainly. "He was protesting; they were trying to expand the business. Besides, Denny may not have had a real motive, and Michael still knew other people within the company, didn't he? Seems oddly specific that he'd know two people related to MOTH, but no one remembers him. I bet his parents knew people too, is what I'm saying."

Maria brought over two glasses from the counter, followed by a white wine to fill them.

"Gabe already talked to the family though. I assume he would have found something," said Maria.

"Maybe he's just bad at his job." Chloe had no malice in her voice. She was simply stating what may have been fact, and Maria offered no disagreement.

Meanwhile, Jed and I had spent a few hours at the office doing the paperwork and being very particular about what I wrote in. I knew if I could still wander over to the police evidence room, there'd be something I didn't see before.

I told Jed, "I wish I could see those files, like the forensic team's photos of the scene. I don't have access to my old account though, since I'm out of the game."

Jed stopped chewing on the jerky he had stashed away, "Yeah you do. I've logged in as you before. Where do you think I've printed shit from?"

"What?"

"Yeah. You tell me you need something, I figure you're asking me to go into your account, if I can't call somebody. Ain't that my job for you?"

I blinked a couple of times, "But how are you doing that?"

"Technically, they never turned off your account, you have to backdoor into the server to access the application, but you're there. I've even told it you forgot your password once and just reset the damn thing to get in."

Clearly more than only Hudson assumed I was eventually coming back. This would be one Hell of a sabbatical if that were the case, but I knew I'd never be on the force again.

Jed got me set up on the computer, then wandered off to get a coffee. The website made me feel like I was in the evidence room first hand. I could almost feel the dampness of the air, the cold on my arms, creeping its way up my sleeves. The room always reminded me of a morgue, all grey and lifeless, with things shoved into boxes and files, never to see daylight again. A morgue for pieces of a person's history. A morgue for things.

I found the scans associated with the Crown case. I got to the digital photos of the snakewood table, still locked up in that sad little closet of a room. It said "MOTH" all right, followed by another ding in the wood. Being a long sliver, I called it out as suspicious, and zoomed in as much as I could. If only I could reach into the screen, my finger could push back the two tiny, thin folds of splintered wood. Upon closer inspection, there was a tiny bit of something reflecting the light. It was sharp. It was a part of the blade broken off inside the groove. Crown had been mid-carve on another letter. Thoughts raced through my mind. Eyes darting around the room, searching for an answer in the back of my skull, I yelled for Jed loud enough that birds scattered from the tree outside.

He looked at what I saw. At first, I got no reaction beyond a sidelong glance at me, then back to the table. I put my finger on the offending mark on the screen, dragging it across to what I envisioned.

"Hey, Jed?" I swallowed, trying to stay level headed as I asked, "Could you please hand me my phone?"

Jed got up from his chair and leaned in to see what I was looking at as he placed my phone on the desk in front of me.

Then Jed shot up into the air and screamed, "Jesus' tits! Why didn't he just say 'Mom'?"

I called Hudson, and told him what I'd seen. He

didn't mention the fact that I was still able to get into the system, and instead walked into the evidence room to have a look in person. He kept me on the phone while he did so, leaving me privy to his self-mutterings.

He finally said, "Yep. This is something. You two meet me at the Crowns'"

"I'm surprised you'd want us to come along at all," I said.

"Well, I figure you should see this through. Your client is gonna be off the hook for good now, after all. I'm just glad you're letting me do things proper."

The car ride was less than pleasant, with Jed mumbling and blathering in my ear, "Seriously! If I was dyin' and I had a knife and I had to cut a message out to somebody- Well, first of all I'd cut the prick that fucking killed me. But if I had to write a message to the cops, I'd be like 'Mama' or just 'Ma', you know? My mom wouldn't do that though. My mother, she was a SAINT."

Inside Mrs. Crown's purse was the multi-tool, complete with a mother of pearl M in the handle, with the tip of the flathead screwdriver scratched to Hell. I couldn't wrap my mind around why she hadn't thrown the damn thing out. She'd given it up so easily right at the start.

Mr. Crown was screaming as we took his wife away. No words, merely loud noise. Mrs. Crown didn't put up a fight, and seemed calmer than ever. She said nothing, but looked brightly aware as she ducked down to get into Hudon's car. The ride was silent, and in the rearview mirror, I could see her almost smiling, like she was finally getting something she had been waiting patiently to receive. I could see Jed in his car behind us, singing along to something that required a lot of screaming and tapping on his dashboard with imaginary drumsticks.

"You know," Hudson said to Mrs. Crown, "we're taking you to the station, but you're not going into a cell or anything. You're not gonna give us too much trouble if we question you in my office, are you? It's much more casual, but still important that you be honest with us."

"Not a problem," said Mrs. Crown. "I'll want you to cuff me to a chair or something though. Is that okay?"

I turned to look at her, "Why do you want that?"

"Because if I panic, I can't run then." Hudson nodded to me, but I had to wonder how she was keeping so calm while talking about potentially running away in a panic. Her pupils showed no sign of distress. No sweat. No shoulders shaking. I wondered if she was in shock.

I didn't like seeing Hudson handcuff Crown's mother to the wooden chair in his office, but she had asked for it to happen, so there we were. She wanted to be sure we knew she was being truthful, and that she wouldn't run. Fine.

Jed and I watched Hudson set up the audio and video equipment as a pretty officer I didn't recognize walked in to join us. She winked at me, but no introductions were made.

Neither officer had a chance to use any interrogation tactics. About five minutes of expressionless yes and no answers from Mrs. Crown broke into, "I know it was awful to do. I killed Mikey."

Jed and I gave each other a look that was mostly made of raised eyebrows.

The unnamed officer said to her, "If you want me to un-cuff you, you can make a real statement with a lawyer in a more comfortable-"

She was interrupted by Mrs. Crown saying, "I killed him. It was planned. I didn't think... I didn't think it would be like that. I don't know." She was stuck in a monotone voice, but she was crying now. Maybe they were real tears. I wondered if being locked up induced this sort of thing. Hudson handed Jed the key who then took the cuffs off of her.

Mrs. Crown rubbed her wrist and continued, "I think... God. I want to believe that I didn't think it would kill him. I wanted him sick so that he'd stop trying to ruin the business! That's all. Then he could go on with his questionable lifestyle in peace."

I cringed at how she regarded her son's life, a life she ended. I did my best to swallow my opinions. Instead, we asked her about other strange things involved in the case and believed her when she said that she had no idea who Bernie was. It seemed we still had an unsolved murder on our hands. In the back of my head I thought of Abby, and Denny, and everyone else.

She downright sobbed as she said, "I got the poison from that man at the nightclub."

"How did you get in contact with this man? Do you remember his name?" asked Hudson.

"I asked Denny, the boy who used to live with Mikey. I was snooping through some of his things when they shared a dorm, because he mentioned drugs. I was just looking out for Mikey! Anyway, that's how I knew Denny had something that could help me. I asked him, and he gave me the number for that man at the nightclub. He gave me a special note to hand the man, like a password. I didn't understand it. I don't remember it. He said it was impossible to trace. I poisoned him. Oh God... I poisoned my SON."

"The man at the nightclub. Do you remember his name?" Hudson's tone was measured and stern.

"Denny called him Frog, but I don't know if that's his actually name."

"Okay. I think that's all for now. We're going to

take you into another room, all right?" Hudson began helping her stand up.

"So, you didn't mean to totally get rid of your son?" I asked.

"I figured if it made him sick, we'd be able to continue drilling. I won't lie anymore. I thought if he died, that would be okay too. It was a last-ditch effort to gain his assets either way. Oh God, it sounds so stupid now. I- I did it so that I would have more when I left his father after the merge."

"How was that going to work, exactly?" I was having trouble following, and neither officer stopped me from asking.

"Mikey was in line to take over the company. The way the business was laid out, it would be his, but he was going to screw everything up. He wanted the merger to fail and to put Ben's Hardware, another company we use, out of business. He kept saying they were racist and homophobic. He had examples at the ready of how the owners treated their workers, wooden signs they were selling, all kinds of stuff. Who cares? It was money! Besides, if I left his father when Mikey was going after all these good people and their businesses, I'd be penniless. I have to leave the man though. He's awful. Dirt under his nails, and he didn't care what our boy was doing, who he was going with. None of it."

"Marital problems aside," said Hudson, "I don't know that any of that warranted the murder of your son. Can you explain that connection a bit more to me?"

She took a breath and continued, "We don't have marital problems! He's not abusive. Not in a screaming at me, hitting me sense. He's not even manipulative. He's not smart enough to be. I just... I don't love him anymore. I don't know if I ever did. He's a man who should be digging ditches, not heading big companies. Oh God. It's only a matter of time before he has another heart attack, so he took out an insurance policy and wrote up a will. He was giving everything to Mikey. As soon as Mikey got out of school, I'd get nothing if I wasn't legally with his father anymore. If he was dead, and I left, I could get something in a settlement and none of this is making sense anymore, is it? But... But oh... I can't. I can't go to prison. I will die if I go to prison. Oh God. Why did I think that would work? My poor son!"

Jed, expert at tact as he was, said, "If you don't go, it sounds like you'll rot from the inside out anyway. They got you on tape, and you murdered your own son, and you know it."

That's when she went completely batshit. She started whipping around until she got out of Hudson's arms, picked up the chair and smashed it against Hudson's desk. Jed got a hold of her before she managed to hurt herself, and the officer I still didn't know the name of put the handcuffs back on Mrs. Crown.

Hudson pointed at the camera and said to me, "We caught all that. Might be enough to recommend her a stay at Cornsbrook Mental Institution, rather than prison."

He turned to Mrs. Crown, "We wouldn't know the real outcome of that for a while. Justice is slow. Still, if you'd rather be in a mental hospital rather than prison, we can try to make that happen for you best we can."

She was sated by this. I wasn't. A mass deinstitutionalization had happened in every other city, county, and state, but not in the town of Cornsbrook. Everyone in Cornsbrook Asylum was crazy, and half of them weren't before they went in. If anything, death would be a nicer sentence.

Mrs. Crown was taken away and I said to Jed, "You wanna call Henry Shicovski to let him know, and I'll send him the final invoice?"

"On it."

Hudson turned to me to say, "Frog, huh? Well then. I'll look into Frog and Denny from here."

"Why?" I asked, "The case is closed, isn't it?"

"This one, sure. What's got me thinking is that Denny and Frog had access to that poison, like you've been saying. It's what killed Bug, right? Maybe you're right about MOTH not being totally disbanded."

"Just like that, huh?" Some concoction of resentment and joy bubbled up in my gut.

Hudson looked at Jed, then glanced through his office window farther into the station, "I'm gonna come clean here, Gabe. I've been looking into some stuff on the down low. I found which hospital Denny's at. He's still there, if you're curious. We have more on him now, and I'd like to know what he knows about Bug."

I said, "I'm glad to be of help, and it's great that you're helping me, though I'm not sure that's how this whole PI thing is supposed to work. Look, if you let me have a conversation with him, you can do the arrest with no trouble from me."

Surprisingly, Hudson agreed, "I figure you have to get all this out of your system."

"What do you mean?" I wasn't sure if I should be offended.

"This whole... This sabbatical you're on. It's not a hiatus, cause you're still working. I can't do much for you. Rules are rules, but figure once you're done, your desk will be here at the station."

"I can't picture coming back. Honestly, I don't know what I'm going to wind up doing to get this case solved."

"And which case might that be, Gabe? The one about the Crown boy, the one about an underground drug ring, or the one about your sister?"

"Well, it's all one case. It's all intertwined. Related. You get that now, right?" I knew how I sounded.

Hudson huffed, "Did you become a PI just to follow your conspiracy theories?"

"It's not a conspiracy! I'm RIGHT, goddamn it!"

"Sure." He jot an address down on a pad of paper at

his desk, then ripped it dramatically to hand it to me, "Get to the hospital. I'll be there to meet you soon."

Jed and I drove to the hospital, and Jed mused about how it would go down, "So, they send guards there to hang out until Denny gets released? It could be days. I mean, how bad are his burns?"

I shrugged.

Once Denny was officially a "forensic patient," I effectively demoted myself to Hudson's sidekick. Jed waited in the car outside.

A nurse stopped us before we entered the room, "I know you're here to talk to him, but I need you to understand what this man has been through." He clearly didn't realize that I was there when it all went down, and so handed me a copy of Denny's chart.

The bullet stuck inside of his deltoid, then the flame must have licked quickly up his shoulder, to the left side of his neck, under his jaw, melting his left ear to his head. His polyester shirt had melted into his shoulder's flesh as well, and needed to be surgically removed, replaced with a skin graft, after the bullet was taken out. Well, that explained why he'd been in the hospital so long. I wondered if he would be able to communicate with us.

The nurse opened the door and led us inside the private clinical room. Denny was not happy to see me, yet smiling with the uncovered side of his face, "You take my girl, you take my good looks, you take my freedom, and I don't even get a chance to take your fucking life? How rude." The nurse had him propped up, still attached to tubes giving him fluid.

I rolled my eyes, "In all fairness, you had plenty of

chances to kill me. It isn't my fault that you're a terrible shot." Hudson nudged me in an attempt to keep me on track.

I sucked in my cheek, "I'll get straight to it. We know what happened with Michael Crown. Now I want to know what happened to the coroner."

"Ah." He wobbled a bit on the bed, "The Highest Up ordered Bug's death to make shit harder for you. It was a message I knew the real cops wouldn't take, so instead it was like a gift for Mr. Gabe Gekman. You love being the hero in a good murder mystery, right? I didn't kill Mike, by the way. He wasn't quite that bad of a roommate." Denny laughed wickedly.

"You mentioned a higher up. Any chance you'd tell me who that is? I'm a little tired of mysteries, to be honest."

"Nah uh, Pretty Boy. She's The Highest Up. Even wandering off with her new toy, nothing happens without her say. And no, I'm not going to tell you who she is." Denny learned forward as much as he could toward my face as he whispered, "I don't have to anyway. I know you've been obsessed with her for years, like we all have."

Hudson went in for the arrest, and I had to assume someone else would get more information from him before he could be released from the hospital that evening.

That night, I checked the mail and found a letter from my father. It said only, "Don't be stupid. You never know. Love, Dad." Well, if that was about Maria, it wasn't exactly subtle. It was also unhelpful. Thanks, Dad.

CHAPTER 13
Moving On

Jed and I went to Town's End. We sat in our usual places, and Jed was quick to grab us the little basket of pretzels and a stack of napkins.

"You know what I've realized, Gekman?"

"That we need to do things more exciting than going to bars?"

He made a finger guns gesture, winked, and clicked his tongue before saying, "Yeah that, but also I think Chloe is the only one who's ever consistently on the case. I don't know if it's just like, finally having a useful application for gossip or what, but it's true."

He wasn't wrong.

I poked him in the arm, "What about Maria? She's done a lot for us, even while hanging around Liz a lot. They're probably off complaining about men right now."

Jed mumbled as he got the bartender's attention, "I doubt it."

"Why? We spend half our time talking about them..."

He put his finger up to shush me, ordered and then downed his beer, immediately asking for another before he finally lowered his finger and said, "First off, cause Maria has more important shit to do, and second, Liz is gay."

I had one of my many ignorant moments as I took my own drink and asked, "What do you mean? You weren't kidding about all that?"

"I mean she bones other chicks."

"I know what that means! I just... Why is Maria hanging out with her so much? I mean, obviously they can just be friends, but I'd feel pretty bad for Liz if she-"

Jed cut me off with, "Neither woman has many friends beyond us, but honestly, it's pretty obvious there's a

mutual attraction. Dude, you know this! AND you know
Maria swings both ways, but from what I've seen-"

I interrupted him in return with, "Wait, they have a
what? Mutual- I mean, I did know that. It's just that I
thought she and I were-"

Jed's phone rang on the bar, getting a call from
Denny's grandmother. I answered it.

She didn't mention her grandson, let alone the arrest.
Instead, she started talking about the orphanage being
thankful. I hadn't told her that I was the one who donated a
few ancient toys of mine from my childhood home. I wasn't
done yet, which was another thing I didn't tell her. I had
also decided to go through the old hospital and send any
unsoiled toys to those kids, and Jed was going to help me
whether he knew it or not.

I handed the phone to Jed who made conversation
with her for a bit. I only half paid attention, but I could see
his smile widening now and then. I tried to lean in when I
thought I caught "Denny" through the phone, but couldn't
tell if I was imagining things.

After he hung up, Jed turned to me to say, "Denny's
grandma said the orphanage needs a couple of new workers
too, which is perfect."

"It's perfect?"

"Yeah. Maria's gonna be fast on her feet getting the
club back up on better pretenses, especially with a certain
newly placed bouncer named Harlo," he nudged me with his
elbow.

I tapped the table with one finger as I thought about
it, "Yeah, but The Moth Flame is gonna be out of
commission while every last piece of MOTH paraphernalia
is removed. Hudson's on that. I'm just glad Maria gets to
keep the place."

"Right! So, Maria and Liz should take the orphanage
jobs for the time between. Maria likes the old lady almost as
much as I do."

"That's fair." My shoulders went up as I hunched over my drink.

"What's up? This is happy shit! Why aren't you thrilled?" He took a fist full of pretzels.

"I am! I am, it's just that I have a bad feeling we're missing something important. Denny's grandmother didn't mention anything about him to me. What about you?"

"Ah. Yeah, I was gonna tell you later."

I shook my head, "I knew it. What's happened?"

"He ain't gonna stay in jail very long. Everybody at the Brick House was talking about it last night. Dude got a deal. No loyalty among the MOTH company."

"Who said he's getting a deal?" Jed rattled off a list of cops and most of them were names I hadn't heard of.

"It's a weird deal though," Jed waited for the last few drops of liquid to lazily drip from his glass onto his tongue before he continued, "There's a stipulation that Denny is gonna have no contact with anyone else from the company."

"I can't imagine how that would be enforced, but we also have no say in the matter." I suspected Denny was going to be a bit of an issue in the future. He had made clear his wish to murder me, after all.

Maria, Jed, Liz, and I took a small crowd of Moth Flame waitresses to the hospital to collect and clean the toys for donation.

When Denny's grandmother came up in conversation, I warned Liz, "Don't eat the cookies. Don't do it."

"Wha-" started Liz.

A stern look crossed my face as I said, "Never mind. No time to explain. Promise me you won't do it. Tell me you won't eat the damn cookies."

180

"I won't eat the cookies!" She put her hands up. My shoulders finally relaxed. "All right then. Good."

Maria came over and laughed, "Is this boy bothering you, Liz?"

I asked Maria, "If you're hanging around his grandma now, she's not going to try to see Denny, is she?"

"I don't think so. By what I was told, Denny wasn't spotted until he went to the hospital, and in all that chaos, his grandma found out more about him than she bargained for."

"She's had no contact at all from him?" We moved down the hallway, leading Liz and the others to sort through other rooms as we went.

"One phone call, as far as I know," said Maria. "It was about medical care. He's paying his own way, at least."

I opened the last door of the children's ward. Jed stayed outside for a moment to help guide stragglers to the right locations. Maria and I got to work, sorting through some bins.

I don't know why I felt the need to say it, but I did. "Abby died here. Well, not this hospital specifically but... My little sister spent a lot of time in a children's ward just like this before the end."

Maria put a teddy bear down and came over to me, "Before these last few months, you rarely ever mentioned your sister. Are you okay?"

I felt a pit in my stomach. My eyes welled up. I didn't want to cry. Not right now. Jed approached, then backed away. I paced my breathing and managed to keep myself in check. The incessant giggling of children of the past slowly died away from my memories, as did their fast-paced footsteps. I started to get up from where I was squatting.

Jed grabbed my arm when he noticed my wincing, "Not used to having a bad leg yet, eh? I can give you some tips later! For now, let me help you up."

My hand placed itself upon a fallen volume from the shelf. Jed let me go as I took the book out, sat back down on the floor, and flipped through the pages.

The drawn-out attempt to decipher much of anything within that cover was quite a failure. I was surprised by my own disappointment. It was written in an ancient language that I vaguely remembered how to pronounce, but I couldn't remember what any of it meant. With no transliteration, I simply admired the complex lettering. It was Hebrew. I hadn't seen a copy of the Tanakh since I was a kid.

After my sister passed, I suppose we all lost faith. I sometimes told myself that I could have a Bar-Mitzvah one day, but decided that I'd never have time to study. Those curls and straight lines, thick and thin were of a kind that I could never hope to produce with such flare and awe-inspiring beauty. This was typed out, of course, but I remembered the scrolls. I remembered chanting, knowing full well I didn't want to go through with the ritual back then. Still, good memories. What a peaceful distraction.

"I think I'd like to take up calligraphy," I said. Jed pulled me to my feet.

More people came in and helped to clear the place out by taking anything useful to the orphanage. Maria put her head on my shoulder and I put an arm around her waist. She kissed my cheek. I turned to kiss her properly, and missed as she took me in for a hug instead. It was nice. I started to pull away, but she pulled me back in to initiate her own kiss, a peck on the lips. Then she let out a giggle, and we left.

She took Liz's hand for the walk to the car, whispered something to her, and then Liz joined Jed, and Maria was to take me home instead.

182

On the way back to my place, I asked Maria to pull into a parking lot where an old antique shop stood. Actually, it was a little too old, and so it leaned more than stood. I had reserved something and decided now was the time to pick it up.

"Sort of a congratulations to myself for a job well done," I said.

"A table?" She was confused.

"A *snakewood* table." I don't know why, but I thought suddenly she would understand the significance if I emphasized what the damn thing was made out of. She didn't.

I paused, then blurted in an effort to clarify, "I'm redecorating the house. I feel like it's finally mine as of this week. Have you seen the place, since I left the apartment? It had been my parent's house, before they moved. Now that I've taken it over, all the style just went right out of it."

Another moment passed, then I kept talking, "When I ordered this, Jed made a joke about it, but it's a good table. Solid. Pretty."

She laughed and took my hand. Her skin was soft, smooth, and warm.

"Of course," I continued for some unknown reason, "if I had any taste, I wouldn't start with a table, right?"

She laughed again. It was then, that I finally kissed her. I mean, *really* kissed her. We held each other and touched our lips together warmly.

"You know," I continued on, "I think it's about time for you to move into a real house, and you could bring all your toys and stuff with you. We could set you up your own room! I wouldn't mind." I think, looking back, that I was as surprised as she was.

Nevertheless, it was a good decision to suggest us moving in together, even if she said no.

She said, "Believe me, some part of me wants

nothing more than to wake up in your arms every morning, and know in my heart that we love each other, but..." She looked at me with the saddest look a mother might give her child who has just dropped an ice cream cone. "But I don't believe that you can right now. I think you might love me. I think you want to." She paused again to find the perfect words, and I didn't interrupt. "But I don't think you are ready to be in love."

"You're probably right. You have every right not to trust me. Especially after everything I've put you through."

"I trust you. I don't think you know what you want, and I don't want to be tangled up in that. Also, quite frankly, I don't know what I want either. I seem to be head over heels for two people, and that's never happened to me before. Either way, we both have some growing to do, and some learning to do when it comes to each other." Then she took my hands and said, "Don't worry. I've waited this long. I'm willing to wait some more. We'll figure things out, one way or another."

"Yeah," I said. "I understand."

"You aren't going to hold that against me?"

"Not this time." I shook my head, "It's about time I acted like your friend anyway. I am your friend. I want you to know that."

She put her hands on her hips and asked with a coy expression, "What if I were still selling myself? Would you think so little of me again, and run off?"

"I don't know. I think I'd get jealous and weird about it, if nothing else."

She kissed me gently on the cheek. "At least you're honest about it now."

She smiled, and went on to say, "Would you like to know what a dominatrix for hire actually does?"

"Yes. Yes, I would." Surprisingly, it had very little to do with sex. She never even took off her clothes. It was good to hear, but I felt silly for what I had thought. I felt worse that I ever made her feel like she had to explain herself.

Jed had gone home to The Platinum Spoon. He found the place where his stool normally sat. It was the same, yet nicer and fixed up. Fancier, even. He placed himself on top of the stool and noticed that it was significantly sturdier and much more comfortable. Before he had a chance to ask from whence this magical stool came, out walked Chloe from the back. She had a smug look on her face. He chuckled as she kissed him on the cheek and poured him a drink.

CHAPTER 14
When it Rains

April had been an odd month. The Winter snow was melting into the first pangs of Spring, which had caused a bit of flooding on its own. Then rain became the dominant weather, and it had been anywhere from drizzling to pouring on and off for weeks. Everywhere was damp to drowning.

Even though riding it in the rain would prove a bit more difficult, and I needed to wear a leg brace to ride it at all, I loved my motorcycle. Jed bought me the "crotch rocket" as he called it, as a gift for April Fool's Day. Yeah, I know how that sounds. I'm sure having me describe it as such was part of the appeal for Jed.

Worse than that, he had it delivered in such a way that I couldn't tell who it was from. This was not done on purpose, mind you. Very little of what Jed ever did was on purpose. As I inched closer to the giant box, I realized that it could easily be from an enemy... Or worse. It could be from a friend. Memories of my perfect Shelby Cobra exploding apart in a fiery burst came to mind. As a result, bright and early in the day, there I was, freaking out and assuming that the box was going to shoot bear mace into my eyes or blow up. After finally opening it, I found that it contained the motorcycle. Me, being totally rational, asked Jed to come over so that he could start it up for me. Just in case.

When he lumbered in, he said, "OH FUCK YEAH! THEY GOT IT HERE!"

"This..." I pointed at the bike. "This is from you?"

"Yeah man, did that shit you put in your hair finally cause permanent brain damage? It's my April Fool's gift to you." He started it up and asked, "Why were you so scared?"

I looked at him with my eyebrows scrunched together, "I don't think you understand how this holiday works, Jed."

But that was two weeks prior. Now, I loved my motorcycle, and missed it dearly as we sat in Jed's car. Out of his sound-system came *The 20 Long and Sharps*, a new band Jed had befriended. Their music was a combination of a number of things and pooled into "Jazz Metal Fusion." I asked how this was even possible.

Jed said, "Well, what do you expect from a band named after sewing supplies?"

I didn't have an answer, so I moved on to asking him what his phone was vibrating about.

"OH yeah! We got something big earlier!" Jed tossed his phone at me. I managed to half catch it, juggling the phone until I could see his texts. "It's Chloe!" He drummed on the steering wheel along to the song, "She said Liz has been making little metal pieces like for jewelry and stuff. Commission shit. Nothin' full time, but folks know her now."

I squinted and asked, "Why are you so excited about jewelry? You thinking of getting something made? Looking for my opinion?"

"Why do you always have to be so full of yourself? No. Look at what Chloe said! Liz made a little gear thing, and Chloe said it's exactly a piece her mom and their people use in the Hi-En excavators. It's like a little three quarters of a clockwork gear. It's really specific to what Chloe needs, but she gets them mass produced. That means-"

"Liz is making pieces of the digging machines for someone, but it's not Chloe or her mom. Is there a bootlegger? How does someone bootleg a tank?" I shook my head.

"Piece by piece, apparently."

I called Chloe and put her on speaker phone.

Maria was saying hello in the background as Chloe handed the phone to Liz who explained, "But the tiny gear pieces are being sent to a PO Box. I got scared after Chloe told me what it was for, so I asked. They wouldn't tell me who owned it though."

Chloe took the phone back, "We got the less-private investigators involved. Mom's got repo-men types that can get information. Here's the kicker," Jed pointed at his phone, as though telling me to concentrate on what she was saying, "You gotta read the newspaper. Next day and reporters got this stuff published! I guess Mom's people went a little far and scared some people. Anyway, it worked because they figured out who was asking for the piece when the Post Office gave up who had the box."

"So more private would have been better?" Chloe didn't think I was funny. She handed the phone to Maria.

I took in a hard gasp of air when Maria said, "The Blue Bomber. His name is Rayne, by the way. I don't know if you heard that name during all your MOTH hunting over the years. Anything else you'll be able to read for yourself."

She hung up, so I handed Jed his phone, and he stuffed it into his pocket.

"I'll have the paper at my place," I said. I needed a change of topic to cleanse the palate of my brain, which led to my asking Jed, "So, you're talking to Chloe a lot, huh? That's good. How are you two doing? I haven't gotten any updates from you recently."

He looked a bit forlorn by the question, "She likes me. A lot."

"And that's a problem?"

He shrugged, "I don't WANT to be alone. I don't know any other way."

Jed hadn't been doing too well in most ways, and romantically was no exception. Flashbacks of that crash had infused his life with angry panic. He wasn't always the lovable drunk I called a partner. He used to just be Jed the genius weirdo. He was always a bit off his rocker, even when we met in high school, but at least he was less smashed at the time.

The car rolled up to my house, and we stepped out. The sky poking through the clouds resembled blue painted paw prints on textured gray paper. I picked up the newspaper from the porch and took it inside.

Jed pointed to a photo in the living room before the turn to the kitchen, "Did you have this hanging before?" It was a framed picture of Abby and me on her birthday. We had the same green and purple party hats on that my goofball mother always made us wear on birthdays. In front of Abby was a cake that probably said her name before we got our fingers in the frosting.

"No," I answered. "I found it in a drawer. I've always liked this one."

None of the lamps seemed bright enough as we walked through the doorway to the kitchen. My family's once polished walnut table was now dingy and pale with age and use. The enamel was worn away from where my father's elbows dug in while worrying over Abby's hospital bills. Memories like that were why my parents didn't take the table with them, and I assumed it was why they hid old photos away.

I unfolded the paper and handed it to Jed. Chloe was right. The front page was a story about the man Hudson had been tracking for a month or so, Rayne. His last name was unknown, and we only assumed that Rayne was his real first name, yet someone at the post office had found his previous apartment just the same.

"I know how they did that," said Jed. "When you get a PO Box, you gotta have two forms of identification, usually with a picture. One of those could have been a lease as ID. I don't know how the last name got away though. Maybe he's only got one name?"

I pointed at the words "The Blue Bastard Bomber" stretched across the top of the page and said, "The name was either simple alliteration or a poorly thought-out homage to comic books. In any case, you think it's an honest moniker?

A mad bomber, hell bent on taking over the cities in the area from Newsburg to here in Bellevue, and even Cornsbrook, right?"

"Yeah. Eyewitnesses say he's got blue hair like yours. I gotta assume you are also a bastard then." He grinned.

It was true, though Rayne's was darker than mine, more like a navy color, and shaggier, dusting by the edge of his jaw. Most witnesses didn't live to tell the tale, so I had to question the validity of any descriptions.

A police rendering revealed Rayne to be a bulky, shabby looking man overall, though still remarkably clean shaven. Even his chest was hairless, and we only knew that by the impressive, if somewhat grotesque, amount of detail in said composite sketch. He was said to be tall and broad shouldered, though he slouched and hunched over. He was usually in suspenders, black pants, and a dirty sleeveless undershirt with little else.

"I don't know how much stake I have in this part," I said pointing to the paragraph about Miss Blue. She was someone portrayed by the newspaper as Rayne's assumed companion, a mindless sidekick, and maybe-girlfriend. It seemed Miss Blue did everything Rayne told her to do, like a puppy dog, yipping at his every whim. I wasn't sure why the description didn't sit right with me.

Hudson called, so I answered, "Is this about the Bomber?"

"Yeah. I got the clear to bring you back in. We're gonna say your friend Chloe hired you, since her mom has the patent to the Hi-En machines Rayne's trying to replicate. Sound good?"

"Bring me in where, exactly?" Hudson gave me the address to Rayne's suspiciously empty apartment.

They had found his domicile, but he was nowhere to be found. I blamed the aggressive repo men causing loose lips for Rayne's disappearance as Jed and I scoped the place out with Hudson and the forensic team. What was I even looking for?

I felt my eyes drift without me and wander aimlessly around the dingy palace of shame. The meant-to-be-white walls had been painted and re-painted so many times that it was thicker is some areas than others, and half covered all of the outlets. A cockroach ran from the tiny orange kitchenette to under the wooden chair parked in front of the thirty-year-old television, which sat atop a partially collapsed milk crate.

My bladder, or perhaps my lower half over all, decided that there must be some all-important clue in the bathroom. I urinated, then flushed, then put the lid down in order to sit upon it to think. I attempted to wash my hands first, but only black and brown slime came from the rusty faucet.

Sitting, there was a lone lime green towel dangling in front of me lifelessly, helplessly from a half-busted rod, arbitrarily jammed into a wall it did not match. An interior decorator's nightmare, I understood that towel as it sat there resembling a wild hunk of snot, gooing from a wailing infant's nostril. A knock at the door jolted me back into reality.

"You taking a shit in there, Gekman?" Startled still, I opened the door for Jed. Now facing the door, I saw it. Inexplicably nailed, instead of tacked to the wall to the left of the mirror.

"What's this?" I asked Jed, as though he'd miraculously know immediately.

"A crumbled piece of paper nailed by a maniac to an ugly, defenseless wall."

Heavily laden with sarcasm, I squeezed out, "Thanks. Give it here."

He tore the page down as he said, "Looks like scribbles. Maybe a map of wiring to something."

I held it up to the light, too close to my face. I could smell feces, but what I saw was too important. I couldn't bother with silly little things like my sense of smell or dignity.

"It's a map all right," I grunted more gutturally than I meant to. Made me feel like an old cowboy, though the voice occurred in my struggle to not breathe in the stink, let alone vomit from it. I did not wish to do either, and surely one would inevitably lead to the other.

Jed became my scrappy sidekick as he said, "Held up, with the light behind it... Holy shit. You brilliant, blue headed weirdo. See both sides like that..."

It was true. One image on top of the other side reversed, became a map of our not-so-fair city. Circled were some key points. Schools, hospitals, even prisons. High population areas.

"Gather the troops, Jed." He gave a salute instead of a comeback. I was pleasantly surprised.

Jed grabbed Hudson and dragged him in to have a look.

I said to Hudson, "It would be impossible to evacuate all those areas, and we have no idea when the strike might occur anyway."

"Sure," he said, "but we could barricade if we have enough police assisting us. We have to be everywhere, absolutely everywhere all at once."

"Do you have that kind of man power?"

"Probably not."

I frowned, "Could we find Rayne before he blows anything up?"

Hudson titled his head back to think, then said, "That's even less likely, if I'm being honest. We have to search each area to see if charges of any kind were set up. Guy like that, crazy as he is, could be brilliant enough to have everything go at once. He wouldn't even need to be at the site. That's what's horrifying."

Hudson sent me home with all the details in a neat little folder.

That night while I sat mulling over it all in my kitchen, Jed was off finding whatever file he could pull on anyone who had ever come in contact with Rayne, our blue bomber.

CHAPTER 15
Gratuitous Everything

Days passed with nothing. No new leads, no new possible places he could be. There was nothing we could do but plan, search, and recoup. Higher up state authorities had the map, and I explained to the kind-of-intimidating police ladies how we figured out the way to read it. They would mark the possible bomb sites and take whatever steps they could from there.

Jed closed himself off as the days wore on, no matter what Chloe tried to do. Maria and I had been spending more time together, not as a response, but as an inevitability. Liz had been hanging out with other people she knew from farmer's markets and craft shows, and Maria took that as a cue to see if I could mess up less. She'd also check my leg once in a while to be sure that I was as healed as I said.

I found Jed hunched over some files in my office. He looked broken and beat. I knew what had been in his head. More nightmares, more worry, and blowing Zeke's house up didn't make any of it better. I put a hand on his shoulder.

Jed put his face into his hands, "The image is stuck there. It fuckin' haunts me, Gekman. I'm trying to put it out of here. Trying to concentrate. I swear, I'm gonna do my job. I'm gonna do it well. I won't let this fuck shit up."

He wasn't really saying it to me, so much as to himself. It was his mantra, attempting to remind himself that he would be okay. He'd get through this patch of emptiness and suffering once again. Jed spoke these words aloud in much the same way as I wrote letters no one would ever read.

Some letters I kept as reminders of whatever it was I had wanted to say. Some of them I burned as effigies to another year wasted, another thought that should never have passed through my mind. Embarrassing or depressing, each served a purpose, even if that potential was never fully realized in a productive manner. Every time I didn't send those letters, it was another moment in my life as a coward. Every time Jed repeated that he wouldn't mess up again, we knew it was too late.

"Jed," I near whispered it, "I don't pay you. You don't have to call any of this your job if you aren't up for it. I appreciate everything you do, always, but please don't lose sleep on my account, okay? We can just hang out or something."

"I know you don't pay me. I've got more money than God. Doesn't matter. I don't need any of that. I need something to do. Something to think about. I need to be by you, Gekman. I gotta make sure you aren't alone." He poked me in the chest.

I pulled up a chair, "Okay. So, what next?"

"Next, you get the fuck back up and let me do this."

I squinted, "You just said you want to make sure I'm not alone."

"Yeah. You go to Maria. Bring me back either a snack, a drug, or some clue we missed about the Blue Bomber. Dealer's choice." He waved me away.

"Okay then, well, you call me if you need anything."

I had made the mistake of trying to baby him a thousand times before, and it always ended in my tears, rather than his. I took a hold of his shoulder for a friendly, loving squeeze, and then turned to wander over to Maria's place.

She had mentioned drinks, so I left my bike in the garage. The air was balmy, warmer than usual for that time of year, but that made the walk to the bus stop less of a hassle. I popped my headphones on and listened to a specific pop song I would never tell anyone I liked, waiting for my diligent ride. It always got me into a Hunter S. Thompson sort of mood. I didn't know what that meant exactly, but I could feel in my gut that it was a thing.

Hopping up the grimy steps, I passed some chewed gum, as though the walls of the bus had been painted with the floor of a dirty theater. A wave of body heat and stink hit the side of my face as I slid my bus pass through the machine.

After three more songs, I switched out of the mix and hit random when Maria's corner came up. The final song blasting past my eardrums was a quick paced ditty from the mid-sixties. It was the kind of song that sounded happy until you sat and paid any attention to the lyrics. I hopped off the bus.

When Maria opened the door, I let the headphones sit around my neck so she could hear it as I sang some lines to her. I was never the greatest crooner, but she beamed and took my hand as though I had said the sweetest words in the world. She led me up the stairs to her floor like we were back in our college years.

It wasn't long before Maria and I were necking on her couch. We would have preferred a night of holding each other and talking, but somehow that always failed. We both had things to say, but nothing we wanted to talk about.

"You feel so good," I said as I ran gentle fingertips over her red corset-covered stomach and half-stocking-covered thighs. In another mood, she would have bit or kicked me.

"You make me feel beautiful," she said.

"Good," I replied. "You are."

She giggled and snuggled up into my armpit.

"Honestly," I said, "I don't know why such a pretty

woman like you would find me attractive."

She lifted her head out of my armpit enough for me to see the incredulous look on her face.

"The great Gabe Gekman, the cockiest man on the planet, doesn't understand that I find him attractive? Are you making fun of me?"

When I didn't answer her, she realized something very important. Something secret that only Jed knew. "Holy shit," she said, "You project everything, don't you? It's all crap! You force this shitty image of badassery because you have some weird self-loathing? Gabe! Look at you!" She was smiling as she said it, but the words lacked a joyous tone.

My eyebrows raised up, "I look at me all the time. Doesn't change anything. I obsess over my hair, how well I've shaved, all of it. In the end, I'm spending all that time on my appearance because I feel like I need to, not that I want to."

She pouted with giant eyes, "But look at you!"

"You're a goth, and I'm a guy with blue hair."

Her mouth got small, "I don't dive onto every asshole who looks like a freak."

She straightened herself up only to fall back into my armpit. "You're special to me. ...and hot. That's why I put up with so much of your shit." She laughed, so I laughed.

Then she finished off the point with, "You're just eyes, jawline and arms. Of course I find you attractive."

After a moment of cuddling quietly and peacefully with my hands calmly meandering around to the sound of soft whispered wishes and promises of what we would do to each other, Maria moved and placed herself straddling my lap, facing me with her dress hiked up enough to see the top of her thigh high stockings. She began to grind against me very slowly as she kissed my neck.

"Is this what you wanted?" she asked with a coy smile. "I am going to do so much more to you." She grabbed a fist full of blue hair and held on tight as she whispered breathlessly in my ear, "When I'm done with you, you won't be able to feel your legs." It was always better than feeling my injuries. I didn't say that to her.

I grabbed her backside with both hands and gave it a good squeeze while answering, "I think that's my favorite thing about you. You are unapologetically yourself in all the best possible ways. You don't care what anyone thinks."

She moved her head back in front of me and gave me a look, so I said, "Okay, you care, but you don't show it." She smiled and I said, dead serious, "You are so classy," I interrupted myself to gently place my lips against hers. "...yet so filthy."

I planted a deeper, longer kiss on her mouth. I grabbed her thigh and lifted one side of her as I scooped the other up until I was holding her in my arms. One arm beneath her knees and one around her waist and upper back. As I walked, she wrapped her arms around my neck and I left little kisses along her face and neck and shoulder. She giggled as though it tickled, even when it didn't. Happy little giggles.

Without her shoes on, Maria was petite. Her frame was almost Barbie like, mostly leg and breast. I certainly didn't mind that. Being made up of the best parts was certainly not something to complain about. She made silly, playful whines as she reached for her black octangular bed stand. I complied not by putting her down, but by allowing her to get close enough to reach what she wanted. Her skull lamp and the old phone that was covered in eyeballs stared at us as she grabbed her tiny remote. I was surprised it had not also been adorned with something gruesome.

Her music player was already set to shuffle when she hit play. Heavy metal, pop, industrial and a menagerie of other songs started playing bits and pieces in a row until she found the one she wanted. Maria made little peeps of delight as I not-so-gently plopped her onto the bed. I moved us so that my legs were between hers, though we were now near to laying down, both still clothed. Clothed was never something I wanted when it came to Maria. Her dress was a wraparound pretty thing, black of course, and had been held in place by the under-bust corset. Wanting only one of these items to stay on, I set about carefully pulling the dress out from underneath both itself and the binding garment wrapped around her torso. I bit into my bottom lip as I did so.

I had her down to only her panties, a choker which sported a silver bat, and that red under-bust corset by the time the next song came on. The cold breeze from the slightly opened window wafted past the lacy, dark purple curtains. I was thankful for the newly cooled air. I kissed her lips, propped myself up with my left arm so as not to crush her, and slowly utilized the calloused fingers of my right hand. I wanted to savor this. By the time a modern prog rock tune had come on, I decided against keeping her corset on. I wanted to feel as much of her skin as I could. She tossed it to the ground. Without words, I looked up to the handcuffs dangling on one post of the four post bed. Everything about her bedroom was grand and rich and decadent. Like the music, it was all deliciously appropriate and somewhat silly to me in any other mood. I was still dressed, and noticing what I was looking towards, she tugged on my tie as though she needed to further grab my attention.

She handed me a silk rope from an ornate box by the side of her bed and said, "You use handcuffs in a very different way. Perhaps this will be more comfortable for you?" She was sly, yet reasonable. I nodded. Taking her hands in one of mine, I guided her up to the bar which went across the middle of the headboard, seemingly for this purpose, and tied her up. I wanted to make it loose enough for her to easily remove if she wanted to, but she argued, saying a slip knot she can get out of would be good enough.

She understood what I was trying to do and called me out on it.

"Come on. Do it right. If you're worried about the rope, we can get something else."

I furrowed my brow and sat up with my hands on my thighs for a second as I said, "Honestly, I'd sort of like to use my tie, but no. I don't want to hurt you."

She slipped herself out of the rope and handed it to me again saying, "See? No problem. Besides, I *want* to hurt. I trust you to hurt me the right way. That's what this is all about. Trust. I know you don't want to hurt me. That is exactly why you get to do it. For once, I'm letting go and letting someone else have control."

She whispered, "I trust you" in the most exquisite tone.

"I will. Not yet though." I winked. I was surprised at myself for winking, but I did it and there was no taking it back. I placed the rope over the bar to wait until the right moment.

I looked down, past my arms at her face. She smiled with those full lips and big, dark eyes. I leaned back on my feet and sat by her for a moment. My fingers trailed down her bare stomach until they graced the silk of her black and white striped panties. The last of her clothing aside from the collar, which was little more than decoration.

I huffed out a harshly whispered, "I want you."

She said, "Conveniently, here I am. Take me." She sat up to kiss my ear and left little kisses down my jaw and my neck until taking a big hunk of my shoulder in her mouth. She bit down hard through my black dress shirt. Somewhere along the line, Maria taught me to like the pain when I knew it was done in the act of pleasure. Of course, she preferred teeth in flesh, rather than fabric, but I had no intention of taking my clothing off at that moment. This was about her. For once, something I was doing was all about her. Her hand wandered down to take a grab of my crotch.

"No." I pulled her hands back above her head and held them with one hand again, my left hand, remarking in my head on how small she seemed underneath me. "I want to make you finish first."

"Oh?" Still sassy, with eyebrow raised and sly smile mocking me, even while completely under my control. I suppose she knew that I was never in control. "Then you really will have to tie me up."

"I will tie you up." I put a finger to her nose playfully. "And yes, I will make you finish before anything else." I put up three fingers to illustrate, "At least three times."

"And how will you accomplish such a feat?"

I moved myself over, rolled my sleeves up to above my elbows, and placed one hand between her legs, resting on top of where she wanted me to be. I kissed her and began lazy one fingered circles. I entertained myself with her little gasps between serious toned words, while I still held her tiny wrists in place. When a heavy gothic mix of a song we used to dance to came on, I took it as my cue, and so I bent down enough to drag the tip of my tongue along her neck, hands unwavering from their positions.

I smiled a vicious grin and said, "Oh, in any way. Every way I can. I'll start with my hands…" She moaned and raised her hips a bit as I moved her underwear to the side. Everything about her was so small in that moment. I felt her whole body hug my fingers. "And then I suppose I'll use my mouth…" I kissed her lips, kissed her neck, and then returned the favor of the bite. She got louder as I sped up the pace of my thumb and fingers, my teeth still digging into her clean and supple skin.

I waited for a snarky response. I got nothing for a while until she asked between somewhat pained gasps, "And then what? And then what will you do, huh? Will you fuck me?" She sounded both desperate and demanding.

I grinned. I couldn't help it. I moved my thumb

against her faster, and gripped her hands above her head even tighter.

I pressed my body against hers and said very calmly, matter-of-factly, "I'll touch you everywhere you've ever wanted to be touched."

"Hah! You say that like it's… You say it so nonchalantly. Like it's a normal thing on the menu." She tried to laugh but her sleepy eyes closed again as her head titled back.

"It should be a normal thing. Why on Earth should making a beautiful woman reach orgasm be a special occasion thing?" A bruise was forming where she had almost rend flesh from bone in my shoulder. Holding myself up with my left arm the way I was slowly became an agony, but I didn't care. It didn't matter. I did not want to move that arm as it held her in place. I told myself I'd use the tie later.

In response to an utterance from her that may have been words, or possibly a tiny demon possession, I calmly reassured her with another touch.

She let out a singsong groan as I reached my goal. I smiled again. I kissed her stomach, her breasts, her neck... her lips. I let my hands peel her poor panties off as though I was unwrapping a gift.

I let out a hot and steamy breath onto her as a tease, then moved up again to grab the rope. Thinking better of it, I took off my lilac tie. I used it to secure her to the headboard as tightly as I could while letting circulation flow through. "Now don't you dare move." My voice had found a stern, gruff sound, but the smirk on my lips left her smiling.

She asked in a playful way, "What happened to you being my bitch?"

I shrugged, "The people rebelled."

"Revolution is good. Gets things done." She started to say something else, but was interrupted by her own gasps and whimpers as my tongue began to explore its ample surroundings... Licking and sucking depending on what her moans were telling me to continue doing.

I did my best to hold on to her thighs, sometimes her rear, until she reeled and arched her back, making sounds that made the music in the background do nothing more than gently hum in comparison. I let her cool down for a moment as I loosened her bonds. I began to undress. She shot up, pulled me in for a deep kiss, and removed my shirt for me with passionate aggression, trailing little kisses and nips of her teeth down my chest.

When I asked her if I should continue stripping down, she nodded, then made a lazy gesture to my pants like a queen might give to a lowly peasant. Off with my pants or off with my head.

She, as if in slow motion, cascaded down again onto her back. Beautiful. I liked the false power she gave me. As in most of my life, I liked pretending I was in charge. I wanted to take my time. I wanted to tease her, for once in a good way. I unwrapped the condom, though she diligently put it on me. I placed my body over hers. It was more "vanilla" than she'd like it, but I had a plan. As much as I appreciated being shown the other side of the coin, I wanted romantic. Something told me Maria had never so much as had a taste of such a thing, especially from me. There was no argument from Maria. I wondered if this was sort of a kink to her.

My lips grazed hers. My tongue followed. She tasted like strawberries. I lightly nuzzled her neck with my nose and lips. Took a deep breath and let it out as I smiled against her vulnerable skin which smelled of lavender. Her hair, of jasmine. My hands caressed her.

Gently, lightly, slightly pushing. Little by little I'd push deeper, then remove myself entirely. Slowly, steadily, painstakingly, I let myself rub and prod until she moaned a command which sounded more like a pained begging.

Letting her have what she craved was a joy to us both. My lip quivered and my shoulders shivered as my eyes rolled back inside my head.

"Hah." Maria could barely speak in her flustered, blushing state, "You are certainly enjoying teasing me, aren't you Gabe?"

I huffed into her ear, "Oh," then bit and sucked her earlobe, "you have no idea."

I moved us onto our sides. My teeth chattered for a moment. Twisted, she let her mouth hang open, breathing and huffing out sounds of heat. She looked at me, smiled, and then reached up. She held me towards her by my neck and kissed me, then released me to look at my chest and drag her nails across my flesh, making me grunt. Maria's tongue stuck out at that between her teeth with childish abandon.

I flipped her over and took her from behind. I changed my tone to match the pace and heavy strum of the music. Fairly slow and powerful pulses. This was not a normal position for her, and she relished the opportunity, asking me to pull her hair. I did as I was told, taking almost all of her hair into my fist and pulling her head back far enough to take her neck between my teeth. She rocked back into me.

Another song came on. It was the most achingly appropriate of any song before that. By then, we had switched to another position, simple and elegant enough. I put her on her back and had her legs up high towards my head. I kissed her calves and held her body as though dipping at the end of a dance. She did a kind of split, taking me by surprise, and pushed herself up while pushing me down. Straddling me, she had a mischievous grin, clearly she was done playing around. She put her nails into places no one should ever dig, and yet, I did not mind. I bucked right along with her and let my jaw clench until my temples throbbed.

About an hour or so later, when both of us had found ourselves finally spent, we held each other, drenched in sweat and the heat of our collective breath. The smell of the room had changed and the world felt soft and blurred. She had turned off the music, but neither of us could remember that happening. Her head stayed tucked beneath my jaw, her whole self curled against my chest and stomach, with her legs swooped over mine. I held her right hand in my left, allowing my thumb to move her thumb ring around lazily. I hadn't noticed that she was wearing it before that moment.

"This is a nice ring," I said. "Where'd it come from?"

"Ah! Liz gave it to me a few days ago." It had little curls throughout the otherwise Greek inspired design. My index finger brushed against her middle finger, which wore another ring. It was small and delicate with three amethyst stones set in silver. The ring I'd given her years ago.

"You seem to be collecting jewelry from your lovers," I smiled.

She laughed and nodded.

CHAPTER 16
Heavy Rain

By the time I woke up, Maria had already begun pouring over her desk to do the monthly Moth Flame accounting. She wanted to be left alone for that task and I was okay with that. Still, it seemed oddly cold. I wondered aloud if I'd done something wrong, but Maria shook her head.

"It's not you, trust me," she said. "Do you want a ride home?"

"No, I've got it."

"Try calling Jed before you take the bus though. I should have let you take your motorcycle!" She looked guilty.

"We drank a little last night. Wouldn't have been great if that was my only way home and you had to kick me out before the morning."

"I'm not kicking you out. I'm just boring right now."

I felt kicked out. I got dressed and stepped outside.

Calling Jed didn't do much. He didn't answer with his usual crack about me being his boyfriend. He didn't answer at all, but that wasn't immediately worrying.

I crawled my butt onto the bus. Sliding into a seat by a window, I watched the next passenger feed the machine bills like it was the finest of strippers and he was a lonely man. My music was the mix Maria had handed me a couple of years prior. I could tell when a chick-band grunge song from the 90's came on. I listened to the lyrics carefully while leaning on the too small edge of the window. Words of needing someone and wanting so much more than she can have echoed in my head. Maria's mixes had always been like secret poems she couldn't bring herself to write. She had never said so, but it was easy to tell. So, I listened, and I remembered.

I tried to call Jed again, but it went straight to voicemail. Every time the bus made a stop, there was a slight move and change to the stench. The strange heat remained, making me feel like I was swimming in someone else's sweat. Outside of that weird little terrarium of the bus, flowers were starting to bloom on the trees. There had been a light dusting of snow for a moment the day before, but that was how the weather was for us. Ever changing and hard to keep track of, like everything else in this town. I got off the bus, got onto my bike, and made my way to where Jed might be.

Normally, I don't worry if I haven't heard from Jed in a while, because he's easy enough to find at one of the bars. That day, he wasn't in any of them. Not the Platinum Spoon, not Town's End, not the Beer Bandit, not the Brick House, not the Crooked Canteen, not even Mama's Old Time Barrel. After looking in every single bar, dive bar, club, and almost-bar-like-place to no avail, I called Chloe. She hadn't heard from him either, and was also worried. He wasn't home. She suggested that we take to the streets, and so I rode my motorcycle around town for a couple of hours, unsure of what to do.

I stopped on a corner when I felt a vibration in my pocket. It was Chloe, "I've been asking around and Jed might literally be in a ditch somewhere. Are you still down town?"

"Yeah. I've got a few more streets to try. He's here?"

"Fit the description anyway. Closer to Cherry, I think. You call me if you find him!"

I made my way as slowly as I could around Cherry Ave, and there he was. Face down in the street. My partner, Jed Dean. I got off the bike. He reeked of vomit and alcohol. That wasn't unlike him, but being found unconscious on a random street was. I checked for a pulse, just in case. He was alive, but not exactly kicking. I debated calling 911, but I couldn't afford an ambulance. He could pay, but I knew he'd be angry about the ride. If I could avoid it, I should.

Jed was passed out, and I couldn't move him. I knew I should've hit the gym more often, but I didn't think it would come to this. I knelt down to try to get some leverage in order to get him standing. It was no use, and I was only hurting my leg.

"Gonna need a crane," I said aloud. "Maybe a wrecking ball." I removed my helmet, then felt a cold splash against my forehead.

"Crap." It was raining. The way Jed was placed, literally in the gutter, there was a real possibility that he'd drown if I didn't get him flipped over quick. My leg stung on the inside, reminding me how little the brace really did. A stabbing, piercing pain shot through my back as I tried to heave him over. Luckily a couple came over, noticing my sad, fruitless struggle.

I didn't catch their names, nor did they throw them. They were good people, and strong too. We got Jed to their truck with much heaving and hawing. If Jed were conscious, I'm sure he would have laughed at us all. The man propped up a 2X4 in order for me to walk my bike into the truck bed. They were more than happy to follow my directions to Jed's place, and even offered to then me get him up the stairs after I mentioned his rather gross apartment complex.

The road was getting wet and hazardous. I wondered what horrors would occur if a hung over Jed woke up in a stranger's truck. "I've been kidnapped!" he'd yell. He'd grab the wheel and drive it off the road... Oh God. I hoped he'd spot me first.

Fortunately, he didn't wake up during the trip. Unfortunately, this meant that he was still dead weight, dragging along as we attempted to push him up his rickety, now slippery from our drenched shoes, half ready to collapse beneath our weight, steps. I felt like I was molesting him as I groped around for his keys. When I found them, the half of him I was supporting thunked to the ground.

"Woah there!" said the man. I felt the need to defend my friendship with Jed.

I said, "No, it's okay. He can take it. We do this all the time." This was thankfully a lie, at least to this level. He always found cabs or I drove unless he sobered up. I never had to find him a way home. I hadn't seen his place in a few days, but I knew very well what to expect.

When walking into Jed's apartment, to the right was the green couch, a coffee table and a boxy television. To the left, a book shelf filled with everything from porn to Tolstoy. Through the doorway was the kitchen. Beyond that, to the left was the bathroom and to the right was the bedroom. I knew that I was not going to make it to the bedroom. The couch would have to do.

I opened the door to chaos.

Everything was thrown about. Food of every color dripped along the yellowish walls. They were white once, years ago. It was hard to tell anymore what color anything was. Jed was never big on light. One could confuse the man for a vampire what with the use of blackout curtains. Still, this was abnormal. The dirty glasses, old Chinese food containers, and the coffee table full of empty beer bottles was typical, but the portraits that were shattered or off of the walls all together were something else.

His couch was entirely inside out. It had been a real couch the other day. It had been the most pristine thing in the room, as a matter of fact. What happened? Either a great party or an awful one. I got Jed onto his sort-of-still-a-couch. It was couch-shaped, anyway. When I turned around, my new friends were gone. Their adventurous evening of being Good Samaritans had perhaps gotten a little grosser than they'd anticipated.

Using my detective skills and my vast knowledge of

the inner workings of Jed, I began to piece together what may have happened. This was all fairly recent. The food wasn't terribly rotten. The only fowl smelling thing in the room was Jed himself. No, this was probably all done the night before. It looked as though he had been urgently searching for something, but hadn't found whatever it was.

Then I heard a soft voice behind me say, "Hello?" Darcy. She was in her wheelchair peering out from the hallway into the apartment. We rarely had a chance to get to know each other well over the years, as our phone conversations were almost exclusively about Jed. It had been a long time since I saw her in person, but I remembered her black hair cascading down her shoulders, strikingly thick eyelashes, and her nose that came to a little point. She was more tan than last I'd seen her. Good. That meant she had started going out more, like she wanted.

Preparing myself for a slew of excuses as to what was going on, she interrupted me to say, "The elevator was broken last year. I'm surprised they fixed it."

"They fixed- Oh. I should have checked that."

"You walked all the way up here, didn't you?" Her left wheel squeaked as she moved closer to look at Jed's half dead body. She said to me, "Thanks for dragging him home. I was beginning to worry."

"How did you know to come here? Have you got a sixth sense about Jed these days?"

"You know I check in on him now and then. When he doesn't respond, I usually text you. Sometimes I just show up if I'm nearby, like today." She managed a fairly tight turn in order to maneuver out into the hallway again. I followed.

I said, "You got married recently, right? Does he know you're here?"

She laughed, "Believe me, he knows. Jed's part of the reason we eloped. Art was worried that Jed would come in, guns blazing, even though he knows Jed means well."

"I'm sorry that you're still stuck looking after him. I should be doing a better job of this."

"Jed should be doing a better job by now. Not you, and not me. It's funny. I left him for obsessing over me. But now I seem to do the same, in a different way. You know that though. You're Gabe Gekman, Ace Detective, right?" Her sarcasm was heavy, but not cruel.

"Yeah but-"

"Then you know all there is to know. And now I know he's gonna be okay again. Like I said, I was in the area anyway, I swear."

"Convenient."

"Yes and no. Art and I are looking for a new place. Around here would be closer to Art's job, and I wouldn't mind being closer to Jed. Maybe we could finally rekindle a friendship." She put a hand to her chest when Jed's shoulder moved, "Okay. I'm panicking. This was a bad idea."

She lowered her voice to a whisper, "I don't want him to be conscious while I'm still here, so I'm gonna go. Please, let him think I was some kinda fever dream, okay? Don't mention me. It'll make him even sadder."

I closed the door behind me and followed her to the elevator long enough to ask, "Why not have a real conversation that doesn't revolve around what he should be doing? You obviously love each other. I don't see why you couldn't be friends. He could get to know Art. I could meet Art. You could text me funny jokes, rather than just asking if Jed is alive. We could all be friends. I don't even know how you met Art!"

She held pity and amusement in equal parts within those deep green eyes as she answered, "We met and instantly fell in love at a book club. You know, a place Jed would never go. Listen, just because two people love each other, and are great separately, that doesn't mean they're any good together, even as friends. It's like ketchup and chocolate syrup. You don't want them on the same sandwich." With that, she was gone.

I went back in and closed the door behind me.

"I need a shower, don't I?" moaned Jed from his heap of used-to-be-a-couch.

"NOW you wake up! Some help you were before!" I navigated the shambles of his kitchen in order to brew up some coffee.

"Black" he said.

"I figured."

"No," he sounded half sober now, "her name was Black. Candice Black."

I knew the name, but I figured he was still drunk. Candice Black was the name of a woman who might have been involved with MOTH in some capacity, but she was long gone, probably dead, and her only real connection with anything was a lousy excuse for detective work on my part. Abby had written "black candy" in her little notebook and I had wanted it to mean something.

I poured coffee into the cleanest mug I could find and asked, "What are you on about, Jed?"

"She's Rayne's girl. It ain't him. She's the big bad. She's Miss Blue."

I gestured towards an imaginary bomber standing beside me in my mind, "He's got the bombs. He's the one killing people."

"She's the one who sent your sister and all those other kids to be experimented on. It's her. I saw it. I had the goddamn proof. She's alive under a new name."

I didn't even feel the mug leave my hand. I couldn't hear the crash. The news hit me with a hard slap, followed by a ten-ton pressure on my chest as I shot back to grab the countertop. I felt like I was falling. They had found at least fifteen kids with symptoms just like Abby's. They'd been used as lab rats by what my sister tried to tell us. Sick, she went to the hospital, got sicker, and never came out. Even people within MOTH didn't believe it had been real, that it had happened.

"I'm sorry Man," he continued, "It was here. Chloe's mom had old files about Rayne because he designed the machines, and there was a name in there that I saw in that Addams file before, and so I just followed this shit. I just kept going, trying to piece stuff from all that to stuff you already had. I talked to whoever higher up in MOTH, and I put it all together. Like, it made sense! Bits and pieces from all over, from people even Maria barely knows. I got it! She's had a bunch of names, and she's got a pattern with them. I had it! But somebody took them. The proof is gone. I even asked for the stuff from your old co-cops, because I knew that part was only copies, but whoever took them from my damn HOUSE took the originals from the department. Hudson's trying to figure out who did it. Nothing on camera somehow. I don't even understand. I don't- We had the proof but not her, and now we've got the bitch back in town, but we can't get her for that old stuff! We can't get her for your sister, Gabe. Oh fuck. I'm sorry."

"Not your fault." I very slowly shook my head while I thought things through as best as I could. Squinting at the wall, I said, "She's pinning this all on Rayne then?"

"Not exactly." Jed kind of pushed himself up from where he was sitting on the floor, but failed. "Not what it looks like anyway." He half burped, half vomited in his throat. "I don't know what she's got in this one. I know that Tabby knows her though."

"Tabby Craven?" I turned around to face the oak cabinets and the sink, putting my hands back on the counter. Hunched over, I debated placing my head down on the cold, stained countertop. I was dizzy. Everything was rushing forward all at once.

I found myself sitting on the dingy tiled kitchen floor, trying to process what my partner was saying from the other room, "Yeah. Remember, years back, we heard there was a girl who knew her way back when? It was Tabby.

They served together. I went back to everybody we talked to for the Crown case, because I had a theory. She knew her."

It all made sense in some strange, dream like way. I wanted it to make sense.

I looked around with my hands on my hips, "What say we get some help with this place?"

"It's pretty bad, huh?" Jed rubbed his neck. "I only did half of it."

"Whoever took the proof tore your place apart?"

"Yeah. Then I did worse looking for it, and then I got angry, and then I left to get drunk and die. Now we're all caught up."

One phone call and Chloe came running over to help clean up. She even stood in the rain with an umbrella that wasn't much help as she waited for her hired help to arrive. They brought up a brand new, oddly maroon couch.

"Only the best for my Jeddy!" said Chloe.

"I wanna be drunk again." Jed slouched.

"Can't do it, ol' boy" I said with a forced carnival-barker-like smile as I grabbed my helmet from the floor where I'd thrown it. "We've got a case to solve." Then I looked at my helmet, looked at the door, looked to Jed and said, "Think they took my bike off of their truck?"

"Who?"

Chloe took my helmet from me as she said, "Yeah, I was wondering why your bike was parked all awkward. It's out there, unscathed. You're not riding in this weather though, right?"

"I guess not. I'm honestly surprised my bike is safe. That's a win," I put a hand out to help Jed up. "Knowing that Miss Blue is really Candice Black will help, believe me."

Jed, flabbergasted and guilty, put his hands out like he was waiting to catch something falling from the sky, or that he was hoping something would. "We don't have the evidence." He grabbed my hand and I failed to hoist him to his feet. He sat back down again with a thud.

"So long as we bring her in somehow, I don't care." I added a toothpick to my mouth from my pocket.

"Why don't ya just kill her?" asked Chloe. "Find her when she's with Rayne and snipe her down or something."

I'll admit, I considered it before I said, "We'd never find out what happened to the other kids if I found her and shot her immediately."

"Fair," said Chloe, "I'm just sayin' that folks like that are ingrown hairs of society. Sure, they could have been useful, but instead they hide out, undermining what everyone else is trying to do, until they finally become painful enough to deal with in the most violent of ways. Bang."

Jed mumbled as he tried to stand again, "None of us are the smartest cookie in the knife-shed, but we can pick our battles. Usually."

That's when Jed's door was busted down, landing on Chloe's head. I worried she was knocked unconscious, and next thing any of us knew, there was Harlo, wearing a pork pie hat that was ten times too small for his gigantic head, saying, "The sharks wanted to get me off the cheese and into the candy canes but I said FUCK THAT cause I'm following the gecko man to the Jed."

I had learned to ignore most of what came out of his mouth. He bumbled over to Jed, and I stooped to see if Chloe was okay. She was rubbing her head, and only opened her eyes after I fetched her an ice pack. I felt a large finger tap on my shoulder.

Harlo handed me his phone and said, "Play the recording. You'll hear it all."

"Hear what all?"

Jed, Harlo, Chloe, and I, crammed in this modestly sized, trashed apartment, were all still soaked to the bone when Maria came to the door. She looked like she wanted to knock, but there was no door. It took her a moment and she was adorable, standing with her little purple and grey striped umbrella, the only dry one among us, with her little fist up, and eyes darting around for a door to knock upon. None of us explained the missing door, and she didn't ask.

Harlo pointed at me and said to Maria, "Get him to play the tape!"

"What am I about to hear?" I asked.

"Oh," Maria stepped inside, "Harlo went on a mission of his own today."

He beamed with pride as she continued, "He was trying to work his new phone, and he got excited that he could record his insane narration of the whole thing."

I pressed play. The recording was as follows:

Harlo: There I was, with the beautiful but also hideously taken Maria.

Maria: Huh. Gabe says Jed didn't pick up his phone...

Harlo: See, it had been gettin' around town that Jed was falling apart and people were getting worried. Even me. Even "Harlo Puffin: Deputy P.I."

Maria: What?

Harlo: I had to find and save Jed Dean.

Maria: Uh... What? Are you talking to me? ...Are you talking to yourself? Where are you going? What the Hell is happening?

At this point, we hear a door slam and then a child's bike bell. This is because Harlo had a very small bicycle, and he was riding it as fast as its tiny wheels could go under his massive weight.

Harlo: Jed and Gekman are my best friends. We have known each other forever and I MUST help him.

About two minutes of nothing but road noise.

Harlo: There's Gekman! ...No. No it's not! It's a giant gecko man-animal, riding a motorcycle! What's that? My cufflinks told me to follow the gecko. The gecko will tell me where I must go.

A woman screams, but continues yelling at him, so we know he didn't kill her.

Harlo: The road is made of cheese! How am I supposed to drive in this? Sharks with wheels... They call themselves cars owned by pretty people. I know. I know what they are. ...Oh shit. Chasing me. Don't be cops! Pot holes! Pot holes made of swiss cheese! The cheese road is made by the Swiss! Candy cane lamp posts! I'm hungry. Everything is too wavy and delicious! I'll never make it. Gecko Man, go on! Go on without me!

The recording ended about there, which was fine.

I handed the phone back to Harlo and said, "Good job." Then I walked over to the window and gazed through to see the water rolling by on the street. No one was going into the shops across the way and all the apartment windows were darkened by shades. Some poor sap was getting into his car. His window had been left open, probably all night. I wondered what would have happened, had I not been able to get help for Jed. Well, I would have called Chloe, Maria, and an ambulance. What if I hadn't found him at all? Would Jed have survived? I didn't like thinking about it, but the images were there, stuck inside my skull.

Chloe was fully up and moving around. We listened to the rain clacking against the roof. After we filled Maria in the best we could on the rest of the day, she asked why we were all drenched. Something about the amount of rain made it impossible to dry off. I debated stripping down to ease the process, but I thought Harlo might get the wrong idea. Chloe's normally wavy hair was beginning to dry and form ringlets. I felt like a wet cat, sitting on the floor with one leg out and one bent, my left arm resting on my bent knee. My other hand held my helmet and twirled it around from time to time. I was about as miserable as the weather itself was. Apparently, it showed.

"What got your knickers twisted? You were all

bubbles and sunshine like a second ago. You aren't turning into me, are you?" Jed was back to normal now, for the most part. Next to him, Chloe was sitting on the new couch, rubbing her head, noticeably in pain. Maria had gotten a fresh ice pack from the freezer to help fight any lingering swelling. If I had been a cartoon character, that's when a light bulb would have popped up over my head.

"Chloe, Harlo, can you two connect with Frog and the rest of Denny's old crew? The ones that are still alive, I mean."

"Sure," said Chloe, "but why would you want to?"

"I've got a theory. You find them, and find anything you can on what was commissioned. The stuff that killed Michael Crown."

Maria squinted, "His mom had nothing to do with MOTH, I thought."

"She doesn't. Kind of. Denny knew Michael Crown. Besides, that toxin still has plenty to do with the case and MOTH. Heck, given the timing of it all, Black might have had something to do with Crown's death after all. I'll talk to Tabby Craven myself. I'll see what she can tell me about Black." I had said her name so many times that it was starting to lose its meaning as a paint color.

Maria stood up and walked over to me, "I can help. Send me with Harlo and Chloe. I know the old haunts inside and out."

"Absolutely not." I stood up and put my hands on her waist. "I keep putting you in danger. I've got you out of that garbage and I'm not throwing you back in now." I looked at Jed, who was still a bit wobbly, then back to Maria. "Actually, I've got a better job for you. You're on babysitting duty." Maria turned to look at Jed who waved with a weird grin.

I borrowed Jed's car and found Tabby at her old store. This time, I came in through the door, rather than the window. She half smiled at me when I arrived, knowing I had flat out lied to her last time we met.

"Well, if it isn't the detective." She smirked, arms crossed. Her red hair was gently tussled, half in front of her face as though she'd just taken a nap. The black eye patch was barely noticeable beneath it.

Pleasantries were shared, as well as halfhearted flirting. The half-heartedness was on her end, meaning I could have dropped dead at any moment and she would not have taken the time to call to have my body removed.

"I'll tell you why I'm here. You spoke with Jed, right? You told him you knew Black."

She shrugged with one shoulder, almost turning from me, "Yeah. I don't see what good it does to know that now though."

I leaned in towards her awkwardly and unbalanced, as though telling her a secret, "Did you know Rayne too?"

Tabby scrunched her neck up, trying to get her head away from me without moving her body, "I'm offended by the assumption that I'd waste attention on every Tom, Dick and Harry who had the gall to call themselves interesting. You know what? You may think otherwise, but you're just another boring guy too."

"You could have just said no. I didn't mean to offend you. I'm sorry," I said, taking another toothpick to my lips. "So, how did you know Black then?"

"We're veterans of the same battle. I don't mean that as a metaphor, I mean a war back years ago. I think you would've still been a kid. It was a war no one should have been fighting, least of all dipshits like us from a country that didn't have any skin in the game. We had become fast friends, out there in the muck. Somewhere along the line though, after we got home..." She folded her arms again and looked down, "See, it was a desperate attempt to reintegrate into every day society."

I raised an eyebrow and titled my head, almost nodding, "I'd imagine."

"Right. So, we both cracked, just in different ways."

"Cracked?" I removed the toothpick as though somehow that would help me hear her better.

"I shut down. Thought about dying, but that felt cowardly. I wanted to care about something again, so I opened this place, and then I fully stopped caring about everything else. After I lost my eye, I stopped dating too."

"But it's been-"

"Years." I felt sorry for Tabby.

I wanted to tell her that she was beautiful, even with the scars and the eye patch. It wasn't my place though, so I didn't say a word.

She continued, "You know, I still tell people that I lost it in the war."

"You didn't?"

"A cat fight would be more accurate. In a bar of all places. I still can't drink Guiness out of a bottle without cringing. That shit is no good in a can for me. Candice can have my eye, but ruining a favorite beer is a shitty thing to do to a person."

She sighed as though slowly deflating, "I guess I'm ashamed of it. I feel like a broken heap of a woman whenever I look in the damn mirror."

I opened my mouth to argue, but she stopped me with, "Black, on the other hand, cracked outwardly. She got bored with not fighting, hence what happened in the bar. Somewhere along the line, she got it into her head that no life was good life."

"I know you don't know him, but any idea how could

she be connected to Rayne, the bomber? Could she be?"

"Sure. She liked poisons though. She liked to watch someone be taken over by death slowly. An explosion wouldn't be enough for her."

"That doesn't seem like something that would come up in a battlefield," I said.

"You'd think that. Truth is, she was a hero. It's not something that made the papers back home, I think we were supposed to keep it hush-hush. Technically a war crime maybe."

"Technically?"

"Well, she snuck into a camp with some big wig officers of the opposing side, but she didn't do the deed right away. She told me she had started sleeping with one of them to get in. I guess taking the lives and reputation from the men she's with gives a good reason for her to be involved with the bomber. It's always been her thing."

"Any chance you'd give me a thought on how to find her?"

She looked me up and down, then said, "If you're really looking for her, look for clubs. Small, expensive, exclusive clubs. She hates pretty much everyone, but even nasty sociopaths crave attention from time to time, and only the best of the best are allowed to give it to her." I nodded, thanked her, and called her pretty. Before she could respond, I was out the door and back in the car.

CHAPTER 17
A Day in September

Still in Jed's apartment, Maria had a hand on Jed's shoulder as he hung up the phone, "They found something."

Black had last been seen at a secret club called "September." After the Moth Flame went legit, less legitimate characters needed a new place to lounge about on their off days.

"Kelvin," said Maria. "September is located beneath his mansion. He won't be a problem for you. Kelvin is a well-to-do criminal who fancies himself important among the other criminals. Of course, that makes September technically considered a private residence."

Loop hole that it was, that wasn't going to stop Jed or myself from showing up and crashing the party. We would wear our best suits and pretend as though we were heavy hitting, posh rich men during the Prohibition. Like we knew where to get the best and only gin in town. The concept didn't hold much weight in present times, but the attitude sure did.

Jed asked Maria, "Should you come with us?"

"Oh, absolutely not. I effectively kicked out the few people who couldn't afford Kelvin's time. They can't go to my joint anymore, remember? That means you're just as likely to see high class snobs in September as you are to find coke dealers. I can't imagine they'd go anywhere else now. Also, Bernice hates me."

I asked, "Bernice?"

"His wife. She thought she'd gotten the best deal, you know? She married into one system to get out of another. I managed to avoid both sides of the coin. Anyway, wait a few hours and go tonight. No one knows you know yet. You know?"

I took a pain killer, then set out to get my costume,

including a quick temporary dye job. It would be strange to have black hair again, but perhaps it would help me stay in character.

As we stepped onto the giant white porch with the stars above us, I studied Jed. He looked decent. Too decent. I hadn't noticed in the car. As such I said, "You own a suit. When the Hell did you buy that anyway? And how the heck has it lived to this point?" I was particularly surprised that his tie was not a clip on. I yanked on it to make sure.

Jed chuckled more politely than he ever does and responded by asking about my suit, "What about yours? Is that Armani?"

"A gift from Maria, years ago. Who are you and what have you done with Jed?"

He didn't answer, beyond a weird, possibly possessed smile. That was strange enough to convince me that he was fine, so I knocked on the door.

A maid opened the door and looked us up and down, "I've never seen either of you before. I assume you're here for the little get together?" She tapped with long, acrylic nails on the door frame as she waited for our response. She didn't ask for our names, but she didn't seem to have an exclusive list either.

"We figured it was about time," I made a show of slowly looking her up and down like she had done, but more methodical, "and I see coming here wasn't a waste."

She rolled her eyes, smiled, then led us up the rich mahogany staircase to a hallway lined with peeling flowered wallpaper. The doorknob was cold and echoed the disdain coming from the poorly lit living room on the other side. A brown leather couch tried desperately to speak of an owner with class, taste, and old money, but fell short once the stubby man and his beautiful, purchased wife entered the room. Her eyes told of an intelligence of which her mouth dare not speak.

"Ah!" Bellowed the short, round man. He had black hair, slicked down against his head, and a strange, thin mustache. He continued, "I see you made it! I am your host, Bartholomew Kelvin. This is my lovely wife, Bernice. And you are?"

The bead-draped woman stood with significance tattooed on her lips. She was tall and shapely with long, strawberry blonde hair trailing over her left shoulder and down her side. According to Maria, like a strike anywhere match, she once dabbled in relationships with strangers, but Kelvin settled her down long ago.

As I said, "Name's Mortimer Steadman. Real Estate. This is my associate, Hunter Jones," another man entered.

His name was Donald Washington. I remembered his face from a file I had seen when I was still a cop. His trade was uncut jewels with a side of overseas child labor. He was known for roughing up his underlings as well as his own wife. Apparently a good friend or business partner of Kelvin, Don was also a party of interest for Bernice. They eyed each other like old lovers do. Jed and I found what was going on obvious, but Kelvin didn't seem to know. Maybe the poor schmuck just ignored it?

The ballroom was large enough for a pool table and ten square tables, each sporting a different color table cloth. There was a fully stocked bar to the left with a snooty looking, well dressed bar tender behind it, religiously cleaning the same glass again and again like a mechanical animatronic display. Hired dancers swung around, landing provocatively on the tables, and occasionally on guests.

We sat at one of the three long sky-blue couches against the far wall. Chit chat and idle banter swirled around. I began to get bored. Noticing this, Kelvin took out a small bag.

A bit of ash spat, burning my forearm as two men passed a long cigarette above me. They were lighting a small contraption on a short table I hadn't paid much mind to before. Out of the bag, Kelvin pulled a small, greenish-brown sphere. A hand flicked on a tiny aluminum fan above the flame, which fit into this hour glass looking device. In the middle of that was where the greenish brown sphere lay in a tiny concave dish. As the sphere began to heat up and start smoking, the fan condensed the smoke into ribbons. My new companions casually waft some into their noses with a wave of the hand as I tried to subtly dodge being hot-boxed with this bizarre opium circle. I watched the smoke form a ring of petals, like a flower around the middle of the hour glass frame.

The conversation about nothing continued. I wondered what the point was, talking to these people. Savages. Back in my younger days, perhaps I would have partaken in the mystery drug. Adult Me was less than thrilled about the notion. I brushed the fleck of gray off of my arm, noting that the pain had subsided quickly. The throbbing in my head due to the blasé company I was keeping, had not. The worst part about these people was that they honestly, truly believed that they were part of the intelligent elite. Money does not make one smart, though it did seem to keep them out of jail, even when caught red-handed. Jed did not need to suffer this way, as he had quickly fallen asleep.

Don and Bernice got up, holding each other's hand. Then Don let her go, as if letting a boat slip off onto the vast ocean, so that he could mingle and sell his personality and jewels. In that mouth of a bar, he was the teeth. With harsh words, he bit and snapped through whole discussions, yet was pearly, straight, and white enough that no one dared to question. Forced, fake smiles filled the throat of it all, dancing from palate to tongue. Kelvin was the uvula.

Bouncing around when needed, he'd sink back into the darkness of that secretly rank pub, unseen, forgotten, and perceived as creepy when briefly revealed. Without him though, the whole place would choke.

Avant-Garde music blared. The lead singer was mumbling noise that could have been words. This went on for a few minutes until a new band took the slightly raised plank of a platform called a stage. They played a song about hallucinations and drugs, and I watched an old man in a beret as he nodded along. I'll admit, I liked the song. It was catchy, clearly inspired by songs of Woodstock, but I couldn't help but wince anyway. It was the kind of touch too loud where I'd be lame if I complained and in pain if I didn't.

Kelvin said, "Oh no. That guy." He pointed to a drunk man sitting at one of the square tables. This one was covered in purple. Purple napkins, flowers and everything else, all on top of a purple tablecloth. The man was waving around a bottle in one hand and an empty glass in the other as he moved about like an electrified noodle.

"Who is he?" I asked.

"Stanley Addams. He was a good regular here. Eventually, another paying costumer started coming by and he flipped out. We removed him a few times, but I couldn't ban him. He was such a good customer for so long. He claims the nice lady is his step mother. She says she doesn't even know him, but rumor is that she killed his father. Since he freaked out, she stopped coming. Honestly, I'd much prefer her company to his."

Stanley Addams spoke very loudly and drunkenly to the maid about that woman who had frequented the club. She called herself Carla Blue. I pieced together who that probably was, given the naming convention. In retrospect, she wasn't terribly clever about her aliases. I elbowed Jed to ensure he was awake.

"And that's Carl, Stanley's brother," Kelvin gestured to a man who looked like a larger version of the dark haired, pale Stanley. "Their father was Eli Addams, I'm sure you've heard that name."

Eli was the man who had ordered the toxin that had killed my sister and so many others. That meant that the man who originally asked for Denny to create the toxin was married to, and later killed by, Black.

I was about to ask a question when Carl sucker punched Stanley to the gut. Carl continued walking out as his brother doubled over onto the ground.

Poor Stanley, the only non-schmuck of the family was about to be thrown out when I jumped up and said, "Hey, Hunter! Isn't that the guy who owes us money?"

"Uh... Yeah!" Jed ran to him and flung him over his shoulder.

The maid nodded and held the door open for us, pointing up, "Head to the main hall, and then go up the spiral staircase. You should find an empty room upstairs to rough him up. No one will bother you."

She smacked my butt as I followed Jed.

The staircase was a tight fit for Jed alone, and he didn't put Stanley down until we got to the second floor. The floorboards creaked as we walked. Stanley looked at me with worry and confusion.

"It's okay," I said. "Let's talk."

We found an empty room, just like the maid had said.

"Okay. So, what are we talking about?" Stanley removed his coat and took a seat. His arms were covered in small, halo shaped burns.

Jed asked, "Are those from cigarettes?"

"Yeah," said Stanley. "From a long time ago. My brother used to do it when I wasn't doing what he wanted." He shrugged, then looked at me, "So what do you want to talk about?"

I swallowed, "Candace Black, or whatever name your stepmother went by. We know she's a monster, and we're looking for her. What can you tell us about her?"

"Wow. You're just coming out and saying all that, huh? I've never met cops like you guys before!" He seemed a little more excited than one would expect.

"We didn't say we were cops," I sighed, "I'm tired. Please just tell us what you know."

"My father kept files on everybody. Even my brother and me! Dad's got shit on her still. Well, I got shit on her. My brother always liked her. He didn't see what she did to us. Our family. I'll give you all the stuff! It's more than I remember." Still very drunk, he sloppily attempted, and failed to give us an address and time to meet him before wandering off. Content by our stroke of luck, and having no desire to return to the party, we joined him instead, hurrying behind him to get the information before leaving.

"Why'd you keep coming back to this place?" asked Jed.

Stanley squinted, "I wanted to kill her? I don't know. I wanted something. I'd keep my nose hidden, but then I'd need to get some liquid courage, and then I'd screw it all up."

He led us to his car, and handed us a box from his trunk.

I called him a cab, and Jed paid for a tow.

An hour or so later, Maria and Chloe joined us at my house while we were looking through the haphazardly thrown together piles of paperwork and newspaper clippings from the Addams household. Jed, and I joked about old times and wondered when we might find something useful.

"Any day now, I'm sure. Did you find anything at all so far?" asked Maria.

Chloe took a seat as though she'd been there the

whole time, and pointed to an ad for "The Rusty Clam," a bar Jed and I used to frequent back in the day, on part of an old newspaper clipping. Jed grabbed it and hastily shoved it into his pocket, hoping no one would notice. We all did. Chloe chuckled having heard very little of the story.

Looking at the files on Black, Maria mused, "She's pretty."

"She's evil." I paused, then added, "You're pretty. ...and you're not evil."

"Oh!" My memory conveniently interrupted, "Tabby said Black was into poisons, right? And Rayne made the machines. I saw something about Hi-En in here," I flipped through some pages until I found it again, "This one. Hi-En in a bomb. I thought it was just an article that happened to be on the back of something about Addams, but I think it was kept for another reason. Check it out."

I handed the clipping to Jed.

"Yeah," said Jed, "Hi-En is nasty shit if it's used like this. You think Addams wanted to make a bomb?"

"Or Black. No idea! Let's keep it though, right?"

Jed nodded.

We collected the bits and pieces of maybes and who-knows from the files, and came up with a decently sized list of places Black would go and people she may still know.

"Shame we can't load all this onto your bike," said Chloe. "Then you could go one way and Jed could go another and you'd both have the info, and you wouldn't need me or Maria to drive too. You need a basket!"

"A basket for my motorcycle? I can still only ride it when my knee and ankle brace are doing their jobs. Otherwise I'm stuck asking for rides anyway."

Chloe straightened up, "You know what? You should get a crappy car, and then paint it up 'til it looked like a Porsche. You'd never total a piece of crap but you'd refuse to drive something that *looked* like a piece of crap, right?" I ignored this proposition, knowing that with my luck, she probably had a good idea.

I called Hudson, "Any chance you could send me a report on the last places Rayne was spotted? I've got another lead scheduled, but for now, we've got all we can with what we have."

"I'll send it in an email. Hold on." He hung up, and a few minutes later came the email from Hudson. Time to find the Blue Bomber.

Jed said to Chloe, "If you girls have a problem with driving Gekman, we can stop asking for your help."

"Woah!" said Chloe, "I didn't mean anything like that. I like helping! I just know Gabe would like a little more autonomy, you know?"

"That being said," Maria added, "We do have our own lives. I've got errands to run for Liz, and Chloe could help me with them." Chloe nodded with a grin. We used the somewhat fractured case as an excuse to let them go.

Errands did not take long with Maria guiding the event. Chloe had been texting Jed throughout, and after achieving their goal, a rest stop at Chloe's apartment was in order.

Maria made tea. A lot of tea. She tended to drink tea when agitated. Chloe remained blissfully unaware as she ranted about Jed's strange behavior towards her and their "relationship." Now it was Maria's turn to do the texting, also to Jed. He was feeding me information as it came to him while I stuffed my face with the whatever-fusion food we'd ordered, and studied the file Hudson had sent.

Liz raised an eyebrow, "There has to be more to it. I mean, he looks sweet around you."

Chloe shrugged, "He is sweet, most of the time. And

then he says those awful things. He assumes I'd screw anything and that I must be some kind of idiot."

Maria waved her hand in a circular, lazy gesture, "So, according to Jed, if you like him at all, you must be a moronic, rampant slut who can't hold her legs together any better than she can read a dictionary?"

Chloe gestured wildly, "Evidently. I mean, Jeez! You'd think I was Kathy or something."

At that, Maria passed her a stern look. Apparently, it was still too soon since we had let her get smashed by a truck... Or a trailer. Whatever it was. Liz didn't understand, but decided to quietly sip her tea.

Maria shook it off and said, "Well, I'll give the boy credit for one thing. He's fully aware that he's being irrational. Knowing that is as good a place to start as any, right?"

"Sure, but it's about the follow through, you know?" Chloe slumped down onto her chair.

"Believe me, Hun, I know."

Maria's phone gave a buzz. Her ho-hum expression upon looking at her phone gave way to wide eyed panic and dread.

"Who is it?" Liz leaned in as Maria answered.

Maria took in a sharp breath through her nose, "Hi, Mom. ...No, I didn't call on my birthday." She lifted the phone away from her ear while her mother screamed about her being an ungrateful little monster.

"Well," Maria continued in a paced, calm voice, "It was MY birthday, so I thought I didn't need to make any calls out. People typically call the birthday person, right?"

Her mother began to screech about what a spoiled child Maria was, and how she'd never amount to anything. Eventually, the random and angry rant turned to talk of breaking her bones. Then Maria would need her mother, was the woman's reasoning. Chloe sat befuddled by this. An unnecessary and unplanned birthday call seemed like such a strange thing to threaten your daughter over. Maria was on the verge of tears, and so Liz took the phone from her hand and hung up.

"Wait-" Maria sniffed.

"We aren't picking that up again if she calls back," Liz held Maria's hand. "You understand? No more talking to your mother until she calms the Hell down off of whatever the heck she's on."

"Oh, you don't understand." Maria huffed out a laugh, "She isn't on anything. She's just like that. That's how my mom is."

"That's where it all started, isn't it?"

Maria didn't answer.

Liz said, "Sometimes it's hard to know what we're worth if no one ever told us while we were little. It's okay to say no sometimes."

Maria had a look on her face like she was having a flood of epiphanies. The idea that she was in charge of her own life and her own happiness was daunting. Chloe handed Maria a cookie.

Jed sent a text to Maria which read, "Gekman misses you, we aren't getting anywhere in this shit unless I follow one way and he goes another, so and he needs a ride. His leg is being all screwed up. Oh, bring a cassette player if you have one. You up for it?"

Maria read the text aloud, and then asked the others, "You coming or staying?"

"I'm home for the night," said Chloe.

"She's gonna teach me how to bake those cookies," said Liz.

It was late afternoon when Maria left Chloe's

apartment to come pick me up. She hurried as a woman with a mission, and within fifteen minutes, she was at my door.

Something about the light, Maria's hair resembled the finest silk.

She said, "I don't have a cassette player. I assume you have a tape?"

I handed Maria the audio tape I'd found inside my mail box about half an hour prior. The tape had a note attached from which read only, "Listen. It's proof."

"Who is this from?" she asked.

"Not Stanley. This isn't his handwriting. Jed thinks it might be Tabby. He's already back at his place." I went blank for a second, "I just realized he has a tape player. He's got one in his apartment. He could have just- Whatever. Want to go to Jed's with me?"

We got into the car, held hands on the gear shift, and tried to sing along to a couple of pop songs on the radio, even though we didn't know the words. It made for a nice comedic break until we got to Jed's apartment.

Maria sent a text before we entered through the door to let Jed know to set up the tape machine. Who still had tapes? Jed and Tabby did.

I got there and almost immediately booked it for his bathroom. The whatever-fusion food had found its mark, and my body was the victim. Turns out, Hell is the bathroom of a dingy little apartment on the fifth floor of a brick oven building which sported no air conditioning and had broken pluming. I did my best to hurry myself along.

As soon as Jed heard the flush, he put the tape onto the player and we sat around it like it was a campfire and we were roasting marshmallows. Presumably, the recording was of Black, telling her plans to a man who sounded like an older Stanley. Eli Addams.

I felt like we were all in a scene in a horror movie, listening to an already dead man read lines from an ancient, forbidden text. It didn't tell us very much, except for one crucial piece. Now we knew where Black planned to go and how Rayne would be used. She'd done this to others before him, and swore up and down that Rayne meant nothing to her. This plan was years in the making, all the way back to when Rayne first developed the Hi-En digging machines. She knew he'd be able to finagle her perfect bomb.

Rayne was a scapegoat, like Jed thought. Black used him for the knowledge he possessed, as though she was the owner of his mental library. She sat beneath his infamous handle as though it were an umbrella, shielding her from her own sins. I almost felt bad for the guy.

Maria looked at the file Hudson had sent and said, "Rayne keeps hitting bigger and bigger targets, and the bombs are always clustered in threes."

"What?" I walked over to her.

"See?" She pointed and scrolled as she did, trying to show me what she had glanced at, yet gleaned. "And look at the dates. If it's a pattern, wouldn't there be another one today?"

I picked up the map from another file, "And if he's going in a line, with bigger and more important targets, he'd be hitting City Hall today!"

I had Jed call Husdon to let him know, since neither of us had a direct line to a bomb squad, and wanted to check it out just in case Rayne was nearby.

I turned back to Maria, "Listen, the smart thing here is to take two cars, in case someone is there that shouldn't be. We could separate out, you know?"

"Good idea!"

"So, I'm gonna take your car, okay?"

"Wait, what?" Jed hung up with Hudson, and we ran to get to the cars, leaving Maria to decide if she wanted to go home or hang out at the apartment. I'm unsure how we thought she'd get home, in retrospect.

She called Chloe, "You baking right now?"

"Nothing in the oven, why?"

"Come get me from Jed's place. Gabe stole my fucking car."

Chloe laughed, then realized Maria was serious.

I slammed the car door a little too hard as we exited the vehicles and stomped towards City Hall. The building was still standing, but for how long? Hudson and his crew were in charge of being sure everyone was evacuated.

"Is it safe for us to go in and find the charges?" I asked Hudson.

An armor-laded woman behind me said, "Not at all. That's why we're here. Step aside, Sir."

The bomb squad was on it, setting up a perimeter. I turned when out of the corner of my eye, I caught a glimpse of a woman running. Gone. She'd left in a direction the road wouldn't immediately lead to. I had to go on foot. I ran to the fence, climbed it, landed on the other side, and felt my knee cap move sideways. The pop sound led the way for the shooting pain up into my hip, and back down into my burning ankle. I collapsed, and had no idea where she had run to from there.

Jed asked the bomb squad, "You seem to be having some trouble. Need a hand?"

"Not sure what you're still doing here."

"The bombs are rigged with HiEn."

The person he was speaking to stopped, then put a hand up and told the others to halt as well.

They said, "Hi-En?"

"Yeah. Explosive enough to need special machines to collect it. I know how they put these things together. Let me show you, or we all blow up and die. Okay?" Jed was right, and Rayne must have needed the special gears hand crafted by Liz in order to build the machine to collect the Hi-En to begin with.

Jed went on to explain to the expert, "These charges were set up like tubes within tubes, so to disarm it, you'd need to get into the inner part, which could also make it go off. You ever play Operation? You're gonna need a magnet." I wasn't entirely sure how that all ended, as my head felt heavy and blackness rushed my vision, but no one died and nothing went boom, so I had to assume they figured it out.

I woke up to Jed propping me up against the fence to try and get me back on my feet.

"You're coming with me," said Jed. "Chloe dropped Maria off, so she could reclaim her car. Figured I should make sure you weren't dead."

"I want," what was I trying to say? "I want to spend the rest of the day gathering any evidence I can find that might relate back to the tape."

"Yeah, that sounds great, but I don't think that's happening."

"I just have to readjust my leg braces."

Jed rolled up my pant leg as I spoke, and saw that my knee looked too many different colors.

"I'm gonna carry you around this fence, and we're gonna get into my car."

"Okay. Where to then?"

"Gekman, we're going to the hospital for your fucking leg." The walk back was a short one, but humiliating for me. He didn't have me over his shoulder, but instead held me like one might a bride. I was cold, and worried that it wasn't that chilly out.

I looked out the window of the passenger seat, not thinking of anything in particular. It was just past midnight when the last unbroken streetlight finally gave up with a sad little flicker and spark. My eyes were having trouble adjusting and I could swear I saw a little girl out of the corner of my

eye. She had pigtails and a flower print dress like the one
my sister used to wear to temple. The streetlight sparked
again, turning on for a second to temporarily blind me when
I looked straight at it.
I didn't wait for Jed to open my door after he parked. My
walk forward became a wobble in the parking lot and I
stopped rubbing my eyes long enough to dart out of the way
when Jed tried to pick me up again. The bench was wet, so I
thought better of sitting. Instead, I plodded on. I saw her
again, when the light went out, but she was gone just as
quickly as she had come. I glanced behind me to find that I
hadn't made it more than a foot away from the car.

 Chloe brought me my laptop, which means she
absolutely broke into my house. Whatever. I sent all emails
I could from the hospital bed with the promise that I had
more in store in person, but that would have to wait until
anyone else was awake. I wanted to pour myself a drink,
take a hot bath to soothe what hurt, which was everything,
and then attempt sleep. I failed to do the only part of that I
had access to. Instead, I listened to Jed and Chloe talking in
the hallway.

 Jed took out his flask for a swig when a nurse
approached him, "Sir, you can't drink here."

 He looked her dead in the eyes and said, "You think
you got the cojones to take this from me?"
She briskly walked away, less from fear than from not
having the time to deal with Jed.

 "Why do you drink so much, Jed?" Chloe said to
him, curled up on the plastic-coated bench as she read an old
magazine she had found on a nearby rack.

 He poured another gulp into his mouth, "I'm an
alcoholic, and it's delicious, bottled happy."

 "Well, stop that." She rolled up the magazine and bat
him on the nose.

 "Oh. Gee. Will you look at that. I'm fuckin' cured."

 As soon as morning hit, the detectives were there for

visiting hours. I showed them the only thing I had found. It was a connection between three files and a specific date. That date happened to be the next day. There were some options as to what area the bombing may be going down, and I had already sent all that information off to the department. In return, I got a note from some of the higher ups telling me to find Zeke, the guy who got away.

He may not have known Crown, but he certainly knew Denny, and Denny was deep into Moth. That was the logic of my far-distanced-from-this-case-colleagues. Still, they wanted me to follow up, and I was glad they accepted me on this case. I figured I'd appease them, provided I could bring Jed along.

My pseudo-bosses knew fully well that Jed was not a detective, but he helped me out on so many occasions that no one ever said anything anymore. Besides, as a P.I. I was effectively doing them a favor by still keeping in touch with my "bosses" at all.

My doctor came in and shooed the detectives away.

"We're gonna send you home now," she said.

"Oh? My prognosis is that good, huh?" I was thrilled.

"No, you're causing a scene with all your friends coming in and out, and you won't die resting at home. So go home. Now." She handed Jed my new prescription, and that was that.

Maria was waiting outside when we got back to my place.

"Here to help tuck me in?" I asked.

"You stole my fucking car, left me stranded in Jed's apartment, and then nearly broke yourself on the other side of a fence where no one could see you. Is that everything?"

"Well, yes."

"Did you even need my car?"

"...No."

Maria unfolded her arms, then asked Jed, "So what's the plan?"

Jed took my key and began to open the door, "He's got to relax until his knee stops being purple, and I don't even know what's happening to the bone that got shot near it. I don't know. They gave him some fancy new pills, and he's got the cops on the case, so here's hoping he'll actually stay the fuck in bed for a bit."

"I'm right here," I said as we walked inside.

Maria said to me in a motherly tone, "Gabe, it's so good that you're learning to delegate." Abruptly ending the trend of giving others work to do so I wouldn't constantly feel about to keel over, I told Maria and Chloe to go keep safe for a couple of days, and that I'd take Jed to scout out Zeke's place.

"You will NOT!" said Maria.

Jed and Chloe were busy gathering blankets for my bed without my input.

I said, "You're right. First, on a gut feeling, I gotta rethink a place I didn't mention to the department before."

"What does that mean, Gabe?" Maria looked ready to scream.

I wobbled, then slammed down on the couch, "I'll send Rayne's old library card to some other folks on the case. It might be meaningless. Something picked up with everything else and stuck in, but there's something about it which spoke to me."

"Sending it to someone else though?"

"Yeah. Either way, for now it's not my problem."

Maria put a hand to her chest, "Oh, thank goodness."

CHAPTER 18
The Lost Boys

Zeke's new home was less than classy, and there were at least twelve other people living in this ridiculous hippie commune. Jed noted that the reek of patchouli, sweat, and marijuana soaked into every surface. It was so very wrong for Zeke. Unless, of course, a certain near-death experience had changed him.

"Do you know this man?" I held up the picture of Zeke to the grungy thing of a person that answered the door. Just a pile of rags and mats the white man called dreadlocks. I hoped Zeke hadn't given any of his new companions descriptions of the men he had attempted to kill before they threw a live grenade at his house. ...As that would have been us.

"Uhhh... Yeah. Zeke lives here now. One of us. Come on in and hang out and you can wait for him. He'll be right back."

"Oh joy." I handed the picture to Jed, who put it in his coat pocket.

Candles lined every surface. Some were electric and struggled to stay flickering, like most of the house's inhabitants looking half awake. The others were nearly burned out. As pretty as the ambiance was, I couldn't help but think of the fire hazard.

A light pressure against my good leg introduced me to the house pet. Vince, an adorable gray cat, purred whorishly at whoever would grant him a pat or a scratch behind the ears. He moved onto my lap, which happened to be seated next to him on the daybed, and it was only then that I noticed that he had three legs. The left hind stub did not go beyond the top of the thigh, and sucked in and out of his body as he attempted to stretch the missing limb. His nose, chest, and remaining three paws were dipped white.

When a clattering sound came from the kitchen, he leapt away. Vince was remarkably fast for a three-legged cat. I wanted to steal him back to my house.

Beyond the day bed, some built-in wall shelves, one desk and a horde of random, mismatched chairs, there was no furniture in the house that I could see. No kitchen table, no real bed... Only space. It was remarkably clean, and according to the man who was giving Jed a tour he had not asked for, the walls held art done by one of its inhabitants. I'd met plenty of artistic types through Maria over the years, and they were generally eccentric and not great with people. Off the bat, this felt different.

Conversation from the group of hemp wearing people sitting in a "love circle" on the floor made my teeth hurt. They spoke of the need for more animal rights, which I agreed with on a certain level, but then went on to remark against rights for various human beings. Love, my ass.

A bald man wearing a brown tunic startled me. His movements were silent.

"Would you like some organic vegan hummus on organic wheat crackers? You don't have to worry. It's organic and vegan." I shook my head and wondered what the Hell was wrong with this place. He said not to worry as though there weren't a thousand other things to be concerned over with that platter. Besides, telling me something is organic has very little meaning. Arsenic is organic. I walked into the living room.

Huh. Another piece of furniture. Well, a television from the 60s on a small, beat up wooden side table. There was no couch to sit on to watch it. The conversations in that room were even worse.

Over a metal pan filled with gummy bears, one man said to another, "They can do all kinds of positions, which is interesting as they can't actually spread their legs."

"Oh! Gummy bears!" Exclaimed the second man.

A girl chimed in at this point to say, "Gummy bears

make me pee."

"Why?" asked the first man, "Are you allergic to something? Maybe it's too much gluten? You should do a detox diet and try acupuncture. It'll cure it."

She answered, "I don't know, but if I were a guy, I'd hang to the left. I pee that way."

At this point, someone else came in from behind me, and pushed me to the side like I was another beaded curtain.

The second man said to this new one, "You might not like this movie."

"Why?"

"Cause it's old, man."

"Oh. Like, how old though?"

"Like, really old," said the man as he took another handful of gummy bears into his maw, "Like dinosaur old."

"Is it black and white?" asked the new guy.

"No, but it's from like, 1985."

I felt so very ancient. This was particularly odd, as a couple of them were older than I was by twenty or so years.

I turned to face Zeke, who had been standing behind me. I looked right at the guy, but he looked through me. His eyes were empty and glossed over. He was thin. Too thin. His once blonde hair was lifeless and dull and had grown long enough to graze his now protruding cheekbones. Jed took me by the shoulder to pull me away.

He didn't say a word, but he knew as well as I did that we had already ruined Zeke's life and he wasn't hurting anyone but himself now. We'd tell Hudson the truth. Zeke wasn't aware enough to give any answers, so we walked away, out of his new home. The detectives thought they were covering all the bases. They couldn't have known they were wasting our time.

I called Hudson to tell him such.

"I'm not sure what my boys were expecting you to find. They haven't been as privy to everything you've done as I have. Sorry if it was a wild goose chase."

"I don't suppose you have any news?"

"I do, actually. You were right. I just had to call the bomb squad again."

"Where is it?" He said the bomb was exposed and looming on the side of the library. However, the bomb wasn't set for the next day. It was set to go off in half an hour.

"Jed and I should go and make sure they know how to handle it."

"What makes you think they won't know?"

"If they aren't the same exact people, we don't know if they were given the information we gave the bomb squad last time." I hung up as Hudson was asking what I meant.

Jed and I walked briskly to the building once we pushed ourselves out of the car.

He started, "If you're Dick Tracy, does that make me The Kid?"

I didn't even turn to look at him as I answered, "I never said I was Dick Tracy."

Jed shrugged, "Didn't say you said it."

We stopped short, noticing the giant mound of wires and flashing lights so haplessly stuck to the wall of the building with a wad of now dried clay. This one was definitely Rayne's work. I picked up my phone to ask if the bomb squad was on their way. Shouldn't they have been there by now?

Jed took a breath, and then continued towards it.

"What are you doing?" I asked, terrified that he was going to blow himself up right along with everything else.

He waved me off and said, "If it's got electronics, I can figure this out. Look. It's like a puzzle box. I got this.

I need a magnet."

I put my hand on his chest as though that would ever stop him. "Wait, what? Why? How?"

"I have a PhD in this, remember?" Jed smiled smugly, with a cool confidence I hadn't seen since we were kids. "Besides, I watched them do it. I helped them through it last time."

"You what? I thought you were kidding. I was half conscious with a busted leg while you were in actual danger!"

"Nope. You silly true blue numbskull. Heh heh. I was never at risk. This one is my thesis." He handed me a small book from seemingly out of nowhere. "Complex Distributed Neural Network Controlled Detection Systems." It had his name etched in the front. Holy Hell. Jed Dean was a published scientist, and I was a bad best friend.

Jed reached into a hidden pocket on the inside of his coat, and pulled out a small yellow rectangle that had wires coming off of it in every direction. It looked like a device you'd see in an old Sci-Fi movie. He clipped it onto bits of the wall-bomb and started stroking his chin like an impression of Freud. Digging through another one of the many unknown pockets he had in his coat and pants, he fished out a length of wire, a pair of wire cutters, a tiny but strong magnet, and a small propane powered soldering iron.

Dumbfounded, I asked, "What? What the Hell? You just carry this crap on you all the time? Where have you been all this time?" Louder, and with much less of a joke in my voice, I asked, "Where have you been?"

Jed replied with a smile I have only seen in the most mischievous of situations and stated, "You never know when you might need to re-wire something." The chuckle that followed sealed the deal. Something was going to go down and soon, and I wasn't entirely sure that it would work out in my favor.

I called the department when Hudson didn't pick up

at his desk. The person on the other end of the phone let me know that the bomb squad decided it wasn't a threat they could do anything about.

I said, "But we helped disarm the last one! The bombs on City Hall? They didn't go off! Didn't anyone say-" The person on the other end cut me off. They weren't coming, and they knew the building was going to blow.

The last thing they said over the phone was, "If they aren't all evacuated by now, I'm sorry. We sent people to handle that already." Was there anyone left inside? I hoped not.

I stood there by Jed's side and let him continue. God knows I had no clue how that device worked, and I assumed that this would be the appropriate end of me.

After another few minutes of careful consideration, squatting down and staring deeply into the eyes of possible death, Jed started feverishly clipping wires and splicing them together in a mad rage.

He took in a deep breath and gestured toward the device as he said to me, "It's a metal cylinder full of chemicals suspended in another cylinder full of chemicals. That's what the magnet is for. This is the tricky part. If I can use this magnet to bring the cylinders into contact so that I can pierce them without the chemicals mixing, it won't blow up. I can, like, drain it."

I asked, "Are we going to die?"

"Yeah, probably. But you don't have to be next to me while this happens. You can take the car and go to Maria."

I shook my head, "Absolutely not. I'm here with you."

He worked the magnet like the worst magic trick before stabbing a pin through the side of it. Fluid dripped out.

And then, just like that, he was brushing off his hands and saying, "All done!" Finally, Jed pulled out his knife and pried the now disarmed monstrosity from the wall as he cheerfully exclaimed, "This is going to come in handy later, I think. I'll hold on to this." Then a chunk of it disappeared into the cartoon hammer-space he called a pair of pants.

I sent a text to Hudson alerting him to what happened. He was furious and apologized profusely. I asked him to have Jed added to the bomb squad as some kind of consultant. After all, no one else bothered to show up.

Hudson asked around, but no response came about why the real bomb squad had given up and was nowhere to be found. Of course, even if we didn't all blow sky high, I was thankful that Maria was at Chloe's apartment, blissfully unaware of how close Jed and I had come to The End. We decided they never needed to know.

On the other side of town, Chloe asked, "So you've got two love interests at once? I can't tell if you're lucky or not."

Maria sat down on a stool with her cup of hot cocoa in Chloe's almost organized and yet still disheveled kitchen and said, "I already had abandonment and trust issues. Dating Gekman on and off hasn't helped. I have Liz, but she and I can't be exclusive, because she said she isn't ready for that. I still remember the first sunrise I saw with Gabe. The first time he ever really made me laugh. I have all these great feelings for him, you know?"

"But then, he has to ask you when you'll trust him, because you cringe when you're not expecting him to touch you. I'm not blaming you for that."

"No, you're right. I do the same thing with Liz,

which is why she started backing off from me. I always feel bad about it. How do I fix that?"

Chloe leaned in and put her hand on Maria's knee, "It's a lot for you to work though. Honey, it's going to be okay. I know they both love you. As far as the Gabe problem goes, you've only dated two guys, right? And like eighty bazillion women. Are you even sure you like men?"

Maria took a second to stare off into space before responding, "Well, I'm not exactly straight as a rail, no, but I mean... It takes so much for me to like a man, so I guess I get kind of attached when I do."

Chloe pushed off as she said, "Dude, you should revel in the fact that you don't have to only be with men. They are super dumb."

"And we are crazy, right? Look, blanket statements like that don't help anyone." She shook her head, "I know he cares about me. I know Liz cares too, but she isn't up for a relationship with me, and I don't want to take it personally. I mean, it's because I'm the way I am, but yeah. I want to know what I should do to get over my own history. It isn't Gabe's fault that I don't trust him."

"It kinda is," Chloe sipped her drink.

"No, it's my fault."

"He stole your car."

"I mean, he's done some weird things, especially while he thought we weren't together, but when I've been clear about it, he doesn't screw up. He's busy. How do I make it so I'm not upset that he's busy? I'm not a jealous person."

Chloe gestured as she walked towards her stove, "Honestly, Sweetie, I understand that it isn't your fault, but I think if you really wanted to be with him, you'd already trust him more. If you don't want to believe that, that's fine... It sounds to me like you just want to be with *someone*. Denny's gone, Liz isn't on the list right now, and Gekman is half-here."

"Actually, that's a thought." Maria let out a laugh, "I've been avoiding being alone, yeah. Might be good. We'll see how I do."

Chloe's phone gave out a squeak. It was me, texting about a proposed date with all four of us at a coffee place.

Maria was happy enough about the idea, but said, "Hey. Why did he text you, and not me? See?"

"Shh. We have time to make cookies before we go. That will make everything better!"

Seated on that small stool, Maria tipped her whole body in an effort to dodge the cabinets frantically opening and closing, as Chloe tossed herself around the kitchen and began to bake.

Maria said, "I feel like you're always making cookies."

"Think of it as a chase with Gabe! He's a catch, right? I know I'm running circles trying to get Jed, but it's fun in a way."

"No." Maria folded her arms even tighter against her chest, "No it is not fun. You ever try chasing in heels? You fall a lot."

"Why do I think you mean that literally?"

"You know what else? What the Hell is he running from? Am I so awful? He drops off the Earth, and when he does, it's only MY Earth. Wait. What do I do if Liz changes her mind?" Maria turned her head to glance at a sullen looking Chloe. "Okay, I'm done ranting about him. Thank you for listening. I probably need therapy, but I shouldn't forget that he's sometimes also an ass. Both are true."

Chloe went back to her tossing of ingredients around the room as she said, "Relationships. Terrible until they aren't."

"So, what are these cookies for, anyway?" asked Maria.

Chloe tore through another cabinet as she said, "Gekman let it slip that Jed likes these nose print cookies.

Salt! Ew! Where the fuck are you?" Flour poofed out of one container as sugar spilled onto the counter elsewhere, "Plus, I've had a craving for the fudge and what the Hell are you doing there? You belong over here by the nutmeg! So, I figure, why not?"

"Nose print?"

"Yeah, cause they wind up looking like little puppy noses and AH! There you are! And with Gekman always getting hurt- I'm gonna put a shit ton of you in here! It'll be nice, now that we're buddies."

Maria very causally watched the chaos ensue, with spices dropped and bowls thrown and various utensils used, then subsequently forgotten until outright lost, then found again too late. She looked to the side and mumbled under her breath that I hadn't "been so bad lately" but Chloe didn't hear it.

Chloe sliced into her finger, "MOTHERFA!"

"Huh," mused Maria as she got up and grabbed a paper towel for Chloe, "I didn't see blood on your ingredients list."

"It'll be our little secret." Chloe held her finger and went to the bathroom for a bandage.

Maria sat back down and said, "Just a happy little accident like you're like the Bob Ross of baking."

"New topic," said Chloe as she continued her mixing, "My mother is driving me insane and I don't know how to make it stop."

Maria asked, "She's talking about marriage again? Kids? A job? Which is it now?"

Chloe nodded as she stuffed a hunk of batter in her mouth with the unharmed hand.

Maria chuckled, "All of the above?"

"I'm dying. She is the nicest momma ever but oh my god the pressure." Chloe fiddled with a drawer until she found yet another spoon.

"Have you talked to her about it? I mean, does she

even really understand what Jed... is?"

Chloe finished scooping the last cookie blob onto the baking sheet and said, "I don't know. I mean, I try, but it goes in circles. And no. No, she doesn't fully grasp the Jed Dean."

Maria leaned forward until her elbow was on her thigh and her head rested on her fist. "No real way to explain him either. Maybe once you two get serious, she should meet him?"

Chloe flinched, "Ack. No. I mean... They've seen each other at the garage, but- Oh god I hadn't even thought about that possibility."

"Well, what kind of a lady is 'ol Momma? All I've heard is frazzled insanity."

"Yes. Exactly." Chloe placed the trays in the now preheated oven and took in a long breath, "She likes to delegate, and that's not a bad thing, but she put shit on me that has nothing to do with anything. Things that aren't important are the things that blow up in her head and become huge." Chloe put her hands on her hips and nodded at her oven for a job well done, "But, delegating is good. You should learn to do that with your club."

"Ha! No. That is a complicated situation. I do technically own the club, but other people are still pulling the reins. I need to cut the strings. I'd leave and start my own club, if I had the money, but that's the trick. They've managed to put me in this weird position of pseudo power. The only way out is to control the whole damn thing. As far as delegation goes though, I've certainly managed to hire some competent workers."

"Ah. I see. Like Liz, right? Hey... You aren't in some kind of trouble, are you? I mean, we're kinda dating detectives, right? Would they be helpful or...? I mean, I don't want you to get in trouble again. You almost got-"

Maria shrugged as she interrupted with a flippant, "I've been in trouble for years. I don't care anymore."

"Well, that's not true. I think you care a lot, you just have a good sense of it."

Maria picked at a bit of old dough that had hardened like cement on the counter, "I like the affection and the real friendships I've gotten lately, like with you. I don't want to go back to being alone all the time. Or worse, being around my ex all the time."

"He's missing a chunk of his shoulder now, isn't he? That's who you mean, right? How did that, I mean, I got a weird text from Jed that day and flew over in a pyro-prototype. Proto-Pyro. I never got the full story, and then I set your ex on fire."

Maria let out a sigh, "Denny used me as a trap. You know, you've got a point about women. The only super dramatic exes in my life are the guys. I wish it hadn't been a dick measuring contest, and was just about the digging machines, or new energy sources, or something business."

Chloe twirled around, "Fun fact! HiEn was going to be called Die Lithium as a joke." She put her finger to her lips, "I actually don't know what HiEn means, but I know it's short for something. Something Energy." The cookies were done just in time for the ladies to leave and meet us at the coffee house.

This coffee joint was more my style than our favorite bars, and Maria was certainly content grooving along with acoustic guitars and high-end coffee and teas. Jed and Chloe were both pretty pleased by the amount and quality of the booze.

The walls were a deep orange. Red, overstuffed couches and mahogany tables oozed warmth. The lighting was soft, and certain areas were highlighted by yellow and orange candles, but it was not so dim that one couldn't see the details in the abstract paintings of dancing women and beverages on the walls. Occasional mirrors of various sizes and shapes, surrounded and hugged by antiqued frames, opened up the fairly small room.

Curtains, cloth and bead, separated each area. Every other room was fairly similar, but the people and the songs played changed. The whole establishment was round on the inside, like a horseshoe. The kitchen sat in back, and the coffee area right in front of that, so that any orders could be placed there, but only drinks were readily viewable. There was a large statue of a topless mermaid, which happened to have a tail starting right below her butt, right in the middle of it all, and then the other lounge rooms made up the horseshoe around that.

Maria was especially enthralled by the arched middle eastern feel of the front and back doors, musing about an imaginary future home.

"Tell you what," I said, "We could have a statue of a nude, merman Jed in the living room that doubles as a fountain."

"Oh, of course, but he'll pee in it every time he comes over."

We could faintly hear the guy in the area next to ours, and so I said, "Boy, they must be listening to some classy music. I mean, he just rhymed 'Yo' with 'ho' and everything."

"Well, aren't you the ray of sunshine?" Jed met my smirk with a smile and his middle finger. I laughed.

A waitress came over to us with samples. She asked, "Would you like some fish paste on a rice cracker?"

Jed responded, "Woah there. That sounds disgusting. Sure." He grabbed three and shoved them into his maw.

"Careful," I said. "I think that one's still mooing."

She pivoted rather gracefully to turn around and walked away.

I realized how far away I was from Maria, so I scooched closer to her. I leaned in and put my arm around her, but her shoulders went to her ears and she shrugged me away.

"What's wrong?" I asked.

"You're going to ask that now?"

Truly, I was baffled, "I know I was kind of distant lately, but that's why I'm taking you out now." I thought I was going to cry, "This is me making up for it?"

"Oh god, I'm sorry." She rolled her eyes and then corrected, "I know that. I'm sorry." She cuddled up to me, but I moved my head to keep talking.

"Wait a minute. There's a problem and we should figure it out."

"Here, now? No. I made a mistake, got snippy, took it out on you."

I looked at Jed when she said this, and he nodded, as though telling me to push it further.

I asked, "Is it about the club, or about me?"

She folded her arms, "It's kind of sad that I only have those two things in my life."

"I'm sorry you perceive things that way." Oof. What did I just say that for? She clenched her jaw and closed her eyes as the words came out my mouth, as though they were going to fly forward and hit her.

She fiddled with the fabric of my sleeve between two of her fingers. "Family stuff. It isn't you, but I'm lonely and frustrated and I don't know if I'm safe or not. I'm tired of it, you know? Also, you stole my car."

She was talking at a rather low volume, so Chloe and Jed had begun to lean in like we were all child detectives talking about a suspicious case concerning the neighbor's cat. Hell, that wasn't too far off.

"Family stuff?" I put my hand on hers, forcing her to hold mine back as I said, "To help, you gotta talk to me, whether family or club stuff. I want to help you. I want to keep you safe."

"I know you want to keep me safe, but I also want you to be safe. I should get to make the choice like you do." She looked at the man playing guitar and said to me, "My job got in the way before, when you didn't even know what I did. Now I'm sitting on a ledge, wondering who might push me. How am I supposed to assume this will work now, even as friends?"

I shifted in my seat, "Those were different circumstances."

Chloe stifled a snort.

Maria poked me in the chest, but smiled, "You think so much has changed, huh?" Then she put her hand gently on my face. "I'd of course choose you over anything from my past, but you have to admit, my past was consistent."

She smiled again, but not with her eyes. "From day one, I knew where I stood and how things were going to be overall. When things changed, it meant something horrible was coming." She laughed as though it was a joke, but I knew it wasn't.

"Aren't we comfortable?" I thought I was, at least.

Chloe interjected with a sharp, "You almost got blown up at least TWICE, Fool! Your leg is messed up from a bullet and fuck knows what else!"

Strangers looked over at that, so Jed glared until they went about their own business again.

Maria said, "Yeah, there's that. Also, we skipped over an important step for me. Both then and now, actually. Especially then. Years ago, I realize, but it still grates on me. Besides, something is missing."

Stale memories left crumbled bits all over the work she and I had done for our relationship.

I asked, "And what was that? What did we miss?"

"The honeymoon phase. Usually lasts a month or two. We had about a week, and even that ended with me in tears and you going right from 'What's your dream wedding?' and 'We're going to be together forever' to 'You're too clingy. Back off.' See, it's the inconsistency that kills me. And then I was gone for a couple months. Since you hardly ever called or wrote, regardless of how often I did, which you said you liked to receive, I figured our relationship and the honeymoon phase were on hold. But when I came back, it was already over. I had missed it. Now it's something else entirely and-"

I took over the conversation, "That was a long time ago, but if it still hurts, we should do something for it." I adjusted to get a better look at her, and to try to ignore Jed's intense ogling of the situation.

Maria sniffed, "I don't even know if we're in a relationship. I mean, we're dating. Right? We go on dates?"

"Yeah," I was so confused, "I'd like to be exclusive, if you do."

Maria nodded, but then shook her head, "When we met, I was a kid. I was barely the right age for college. Then later on, you could only be romantic when on a case and seeing me on the side. I wasn't enough. I tried to blame Jed for it all, but it was you. It's like you were so miserable without a case, and I could do nothing. That is why I freaked out a little… When was it? I think it was two years ago when you said you would leave it all and take a desk job. It's not that I didn't believe you. In fact, I think you'd do it. But you wouldn't be happy. I'd hate myself for being selfish. Even now, the job is your wife, and I'm your mistress because I don't know what else to do."

Chloe looked at me and gestured to Maria, as though I wasn't about to answer.

I said, "Even when I sometimes forgot about dates and stuff, I knew I'd see you, because you matter more. You were like my default."

We both cringed.

I shook it off, "That sounded terrible. No. I mean, I

knew I was always going to come back to you. You were a given. When we broke up that first time, it's because I wasn't ready. I was young and afraid and I didn't understand what was happening. After that, I was an asshole because I already had been an asshole and I didn't know I could do anything else with you."

At this point, the guitarist was still playing, but also listening intently to our conversation over his acoustic Martin. Chloe and Jed had turned to watch a long time before then, and they had somehow managed to get a bucket of popcorn when I wasn't looking.

Maria said, "Didn't tell me that. It's nice to hear it now. So, thank you for that."

"Anything else?" I leaned in for a kiss. She dodged.

"Yes. Why did you fail to ask me what I did for a living? You assumed I was a sex- well I was a sex worker, but a different kind! Also, even if I *was* some other kind, so what?"

"I know. I know and I'm sorry. I swear to God I'm sorry. I think about you all the time and I know I should start telling you that. I don't want to sound creepy. I do over-think things and I know you are busy too. This shouldn't just be on my schedule. You run a club and-"

She nodded and kissed me on the cheek.

"You're right." She ran her fingers through my hair. "It is different. I'm afraid. I don't want to lose you now that I finally have you close to me. I want to feel like I won. It's not a game though. I know I can't do much without getting my head in too deep, but even Chloe is on this case with you. I'm one of the guys enough to play poker and sit in silence while you talk about things I'm not a part of. I try to participate in conversation and I feel so small and silly."

"It's dangerous. You were already so deep in it and I already almost got you killed before. I can't do that again."

She pointed at nothing on the ceiling, "Technically, I almost got you killed by Denny. Not the other way around."

"What?"

She shrugged, "Never mind."

"But, you've tamed me. You're my girlfriend, and I'd like it to stay that way."

She looked up at the ceiling as if searching for my logic stuck somewhere between the faulty lamps, then down at her hands, then out past the guitar and its player. She cast her eyes at me and asked in the most pain-stricken whisper, "I'm your girlfriend?" It was the kind of tight, barely audible but beautiful sound one might make right before a stream of tears.

"I'd like you to be, if you aren't. I mean, I think you are. Are you?"

She grinned, then grimaced as she looked around, then back at me to grin again, "...Yes?" I kissed her deeply and heard Jed and Chloe clap.

I said to her, "Things are chaotic, but now I've got you."

She let out a kind of wistful sigh and said, "I never thought I was asking for much."

She was right. She didn't ask for much, I did know she deserved more. How unfair of me. Maria was practically losing her mind because I had managed to push the most patient woman alive to the point of breaking.

I answered, "You deserve everything. That's the problem. You don't want everything, but I get frustrated when I can't give you the whole damn world all at once."

Suddenly placated, she cuddled up to me like the discussion had never even taken place.

We continued listening to the music once the befuddled guitarist shook off our conversation.

"Oh," Maria whispered in my ear, "and thinking of me as a given is the same thing as thinking of me as granted. Like, you were happy to literally take me for granted. People don't think about that phrase enough."

She poked me in the nose and said, "On second

thought, maybe I shouldn't be anyone's girlfriend right now. I don't want anything to change between us, but I need to figure out who I am on my own, sans romance."

"Okay," I said.

I went through the events of the couple of hours we were there. We fought, made our relationship official, and then kind of broke up. What did that mean? We walked out together.

Jed and Chloe left soon after, and she didn't spend the night at his place either.

CHAPTER 19
Dropping The Bomb

It had been a couple of days since the coffee house, and I hadn't heard much from Jed, so I invited him out.

"I'll pick you up," I said.

"You ain't drinking with me?"

"It's a little early, right? Painkillers and alcohol don't mix well anyway, so I'm just gonna be there to hang out with you."

"And be my DD?"

I got to his apartment and knocked on the door. He answered, wobbling and drunk already.

"Jesus," I said, "Did you miss the part where I said it was too early for this?"

I gently moved him aside to enter the apartment.

"We goin'?" he asked.

"No. Why bother going anywhere? Look at the state of you. Let's just hang out here. Let's talk, okay?" He nodded. We didn't talk. We watched a couple of science fiction movies while he attempted to sneak more drinks. He had to try, as I was routinely moving glasses and bottles away from him throughout the viewings.

We heard a click from the door. It was six PM, and there was Chloe.

I stood up and gestured to the couch, "Ah! I didn't know you were coming! Here, take a seat." I took the bags of Chinese takeout from her hands.

"Wasn't the door locked? I have it auto-lock when you close it." Jed scratched his head.

"Oh," Chloe looked towards the door sheepishly, "I got a copy of your key."

"Got?" I didn't understand, "He didn't give you that?"

"No. I got it myself, but with good reason! What if

Jed's in danger or something?"

I nodded slowly, "But today was Chinese food."

"Yeah, my idea was to surprise him with Chinese takeout from his favorite place and a six pack of beer."

"And you let yourself in," I looked back for a reaction from Jed, but he was unconscious on the floor, with several empty whisky bottles next to his head. He was clutching a photograph of Darcy. I wondered aloud when he'd gotten that out.

Chloe rolled Jed over with a heave, a huff, and then a sigh. I took my awkward leave as she got water from the kitchen in a large plastic cup to splash on his face. It woke him up part of the way. Her crying out woke him the rest of the way.

"You shouldn't do this to yourself anymore, Jed! There are people who CARE about you! You ever think about that? Huh? Just STOP!"

I closed the door behind me. The loud click to indicate the auto-lock rang in my ears as I reached for my keys, slowly realizing that in my haste I had left them, and my wallet in the room. I didn't even remember my hat. It wasn't a good time to retrieve them, so I just sat down and listened through the door.

"Don't fucking tell me what to fucking do." Jed wobbled, but sat up. "The only reason I'm not dead right now is because I refuse to take my own life. It's a selfish, pansy ass way outta this bullshit the world puts you through."

"And this is better?"

"I'm a grown-ass man! I'll do what I want." He rolled over in an effort to climb onto the couch. It didn't work.

"I don't get it! You're always so distant! I've done everything for you. I'm willing to do anything! Tell me what you need!"

"You don't owe me anything. You're not my girl."

Chloe stomped and said, "We go on dates! I brought you food! You've said you want to be with me! You've told me I deserve better, which I do! What does it take to be your girl then? When's the last time you even had a real girlfriend?"

"Five years and three days."

"What?" She quieted down and stepped towards him.

"I never asked for you. You're the one who keeps hanging around me."

"I want to."

"Well, I got news for you. You should run the fuck away while you still got time."

She placed a hand on her chest to emphasize her point as she said, "I can take care of myself. I want to be with you."

"Stop."

"No. No, I won't stop. Tell me what you want from me. Anything other than stopping."

"All right. Sit."

She plopped herself down on the couch like a dog obeying a master. Jed pulled air in through his nose and quickly huffed it out again as he failed to wrangle himself a piece of the couch to sit upon. Giving up, he adjusted on the floor.

"All right. Okay. You deserve to know this." He winced and then continued, pacing himself, "See, once upon a time, I was engaged."

Chloe's eyes got wide.

"It was five years ago." Sitting on the floor by him was an open bottle, and so he picked it up and held it, as though for comfort. "I had a real job then. I was an engineer. I had a good, steady job and was the best in my field. I designed detector arrays for particle accelerators. Gekman never understood that junk, but back in the day, I was damn proud."

261

"So, who was she?"

"Darcy. Her name was Darcy. Her name *is* Darcy. Gekman's right. I talk like she died, but she ain't dead." He looked to the side at nothing but wall and sat in silence for a moment until he continued, "We met in college. We were perfect. I don't say that lightly. But, like Gekman says, Fate wasn't too keen on Darcy and me staying together."

"What happened, Jed?"

"We were coming home from a day trip to the museum. She loved the museum. She liked the dinosaurs. Anyway, we had to cross a huge mountain on back roads to get home, and it was night time. So, I was driving, and next thing I know, some asshole in oncoming traffic has his brights on, and I failed to see the FUCKING turn, and he just rams into us. Just fucking whips his car into us!" Jed threw the bottle across the room. It smacked against a piece of rug and managed not to shatter. It would have been more satisfying if it had shattered.

"We plowed into the side of the fucking mountain. Darcy was... ejected from the car." Jed finally got up to sit on the couch. "I... I scrambled out of the car. God. I clawed my way out the window cause the door was fucked. I was bloody from broken glass. I've still got the scars all down this side." He gestured to himself and began to stare off into the distance again.

"And I see Darcy laying there... And there's that car. It's like he waited to make sure we were fucked. And I see Zeke's goddamn license plate before he zooms off and there's no one else around. The cockbag with the brights is Zeke. I know where he is now and I just- ...But yeah. And there she is just bleeding, cell phones have no fucking reception, all I can do is hold her in my arms and watch her die, only she doesn't. A car came by."

Chloe put her arm behind Jed, but didn't dare to touch him, "Someone came and helped?"

"Yeah, but after that night, I wasn't the same. I got

really shitty to her. I was trying to… I don't know. I wanted to save her. I wanted to protect her from everything."

"So, she left?"

"I SWORE to protect her. I fucking promised that I'd be there for her." Jed took a breath and found another beer from the kitchen.

He sighed and said, "All my hope for the future died when she left my life. Hope gone with Darcy. Gekman wanted me to find a new reason to keep going, but I never did. I spent the next three months locked away in this apartment, drinking. Pretty sure Gekman still texts her about me, like keeping tabs. But yeah. That's when I blacked out all the light. ...And when I lost my job." Jed plopped back down on the couch.

Chloe inched closer, "What happened after three months?"

"What?"

"What got you back out there?"

"Gekman." Jed popped the cap off the bottle and took a swig.

I knocked on the door, "Hi! Speaking of me, can I get my keys?"

I was busy buzzing about in my old childhood bedroom, which was all set to be an adult guest room, but for my overloaded closet. Time for organization. I took a mildewed two-foot-wide cardboard box out. It had water damage along the bottom from a mild flood in the basement when I was a kid. My parents didn't know that I had stolen it away to my room. I placed it on the floor, beside the new box of papers from the MOTH case.

It was all there, laid out before me like three different

puzzles all jumbled together. Abby had been telling the truth. There were drawings of "the Factory" which looked exactly like one of the old MOTH buildings, and a list of things that happened to the kids next to a list of what was done to "subjects." My sister was a guinea pig for the MOTH corporation, and we all ignored her, thinking she was just trying to make sense of being sick. Kids make up stories to survive.

Feeling tears well up in my eyes, I called Maria.

She could hear the hitch in my voice as I said, "Hey. I'm trying to kill two birds with one stone. I'm trying to organize some stuff, get it out of the guest room, and maybe piece some things together for the case? I just saw the same things I always see, but there's a box of stuff from when I was a kid, and I seem to have started crying and-"

"I'm on my way." She came over in a flash. Without me explaining a word, she opened the door, closed it, marched right up to me as she stripped off her coat and kicked off her shoes, and held me in her arms as we sat on the floor. Thank God for Maria.

After a long while of silence, she piped up, "I was thinking, even bad guys keep things to remember people. Usually more like trophies, but it's something. Have you looked in any of the places Black used to live?"

Fact was, we hadn't. We were so concerned about her old hang-out spots and new places of residence, we had managed to not even glance and the old places she had actually lived for extended periods of time.

I called Tabby to ask if she had any thoughts on the matter.

Tabby took in a deep breath to let out a slow sigh on the other end of the line, "I can think of a couple of places that meant something to me once, but I don't know what they meant to her, and I can guarantee she ain't there now. I can't imagine she'd have left anything behind, or that she even had anything to leave to begin with."

"What do you mean by that?"

"I mean she wasn't sentimental. She didn't collect things, or decorate. She never expected to live places for very long, even when she got these big houses. They were just to live with somebody until she left the somebody's body behind. I don't know any place after we stopped talking. You know though, I got one in mind she was at for a while. We weren't really together then either, not officially anyway, but she was there a long time."

I wrote down the address, and then sent a text to Jed, but Chloe responded, "He's out for the night. I don't mean he's gone somewhere, just that he's asleep."

"Fair enough. I'll wait until tomorrow so I can have Jed with me." I put my phone on the counter, and Maria and I moved to my bedroom.

We didn't do the gymnastics of our normal bedroom routine. Instead, we remained clothed. The skin of her slightly exposed hip was soft as we lay there, breathing in sync, her head on my chest. We were quiet in a peaceful way.

Maria was never the one who needed to change. I was always the problem, and now it was time to start being grateful. I drifted off into a restful sleep.

Black's old house was now a condemned shell. The painted brick had all but entirely peeled back to reveal the dusty, cracked red meat of the foundation. The inside wasn't much better, but a void. Either she had cleaned everything remarkably well, or she had lived there only briefly. A two floor, one family home would have been an odd place for Black to have kept for herself, especially as such a temporary fix, but Jed was right. He mused that the whole place was one big spider web for her to catch mates and devour them.

Jed wandered upstairs. I headed through the front foyer to the kitchen, where I could hear his steps, followed by a crack and a smack.

"You okay up there, Jed?" I called out.

"Yeah, this place is falling apart, so be careful!" This was emphasized by the small crumbles of ceiling that sprinkled to the floor in front of me. I made my way into the dining room. It was a large area that also encompassed the living room. There was a china cabinet to the left, stocked with old ornate plates and cups. To the right of a large bay window, a Bombay dresser held a too big terracotta pot with a too small, dead plant.

A letter sat on a blue tablecloth covered oval table, surrounded by stationary and crumpled up papers. The other papers were a different handwriting from the middle paper and all had the beginnings of letters with no end. I picked up the yellowed paper in the center. It was old and worn and looked like it had been folded and unfolded and refolded hundreds of times. Stained and carried around. This was clearly precious to her, so why leave it here? She had left only this, as if burying it in a tomb. It had one of her old names on it, of course, but what was remarkable was who it was from. Tabby. They had been more than bunk mates in a war, and according to that paper, they had been lovers. Tabby had implied as much in conversations with us, but the things she wrote to Black weren't anything I would repeat in mixed company.

Jed called down about not finding anything in the bedroom, so he was off to rummage through the bathroom. I starting thinking about love notes I should send to Maria, and making up stupid reasons why I'd never get around to doing so.

My all or nothing mentally left me smothering her with affection one day and then completely ignoring her the next. She must have thought I was crazy. Meanwhile, Tabby and Black seemed to understand how to write love notes. Maybe crazy people wrote good love notes. I could dream.

Over thinking to the boiling point of a potential meltdown, I announced my find to Jed. He came down to find me looking at the half-written letters Black had started, and comparing the writing to a tiny note written in the corner of Tabby's letter.

"Whatchu got there, Gekman?"

I showed him, "I thought she kept this because she actually cared, but look at the corner. Is that an address? What is that?"

He shrugged, then called Tabby, "Hey, we found a letter from you to Black."

"What? I'm surprised. Which letter did she keep?"

"I almost covered by ears as Jed said, "The one where you talk about putting her legs above her head."

"Oh!" She gave a hearty laugh, "That's a good one! Wow. That letter was from ages ago. What did she need from it? I assume she used the back of it to write something important."

"That's not too far off. Holy shit. Yeah, it's a note in the corner."

"What's it say?" On speaker phone, I could almost hear Tabby cross her arms.

Jed said, "We think it's an address. It's all smudged, but it says something about Bellevue."

I piped up, "The ink looks recent. Any chance she would have come back here with Rayne, or that he'd be at this new address?"

Tabby hummed as she thought, then said, "We had a couple safe houses in that area. I'll text you some thoughts. I don't know that you'll find Rayne there either way. Not alive, anyway."

Jed thanked her, and Tabby said, "Once I get that to

you, I'll get back to writing my book. Maybe I'll send you a copy one day."

I said, "I knew you were a photographer. You're an author too?"

"I will be if you leave me alone long enough." She chuckled, to lighten the harshness of it all, then continued, "Non-fiction writing is a lot like photography. Yes, a person shows what is there in reality, but one also has to be careful about the lighting in order to truly capture what we are trying to say, regardless of that reality. This book is really gonna piss a lot of people off, is what I'm saying."

"Well, thank you for your help."

She sent two addresses, both in Bellevue, but in opposite sides of the town.

I listened to classical music to help me think and process information in Jed's car. That or the bops from the fifties, or eighties rock and roll. So, music in general. On the ride back over to the station, I blasted a few tracks off of a "masters of music" collection that included Bach.

I clicked it off to say, "I should tell Hudson, right? I should give him one of the addresses to check."

"Why?" asked Jed.

"Because otherwise I'm overloaded." Jed nodded, I sent a text to Hudson, and Hudson was thrilled. Jed tapped me on the shoulder to look up through the windshield. We had come to the old gutted apartment complex. It looked as though it had tried and failed to be a home for a couple rich families instead of a hundred shoddy living arrangements.

Up on top of the building was a shadowy figure. Someone was looking down at us. Who would be on the roof?

"Could be someone fixing something up there, right?" said Jed.

"Looks big, bulky, and blue to me."

"You think it's Rayne?"

"I'm thinking we should investigate."

I had thankfully remembered to pop a pill that morning, as there was no elevator, and so we took the many rounds of staircases up to the roof.

He didn't notice our arrival, but right past the entrance to the concrete roof was Rayne the Blue Bomber, with no sign of Black. We hid behind the large, metal air conditioning unit.

Rayne was bigger in real life than the eye witness reports had implied. Bulkier and a much taller than Jed, Rayne was a fit man, broad shouldered with an oddly white, toothy grin.

As grungy as most of him looked, apparently his dental hygiene was immaculate, though his giant canines had to have been fake. His tousled, dark blue hair was poorly kept and shaggy. A few mats, rather than dreads. He looked like a punk rock vampire. Rayne slouched, but it did nothing to hide his size. His jaw was less angular, with his chin more protruding. He was a fantastical man, with a fleshy, aquiline nose. A bumpy scar across the top of his right hand, and a matching one on the left side of his face from his cheekbone down made me question what he had lived through. What makes a man grow up to blow up buildings?

We stayed back, noting how he whipped his body around a machine on the ground, looking downright manically giddy, then dead serious, then back again as he tossed himself and hopped around the device. After the dance, he hunched over the explosive thing, trying to get it operational.

In stepped Black.

"Oh fuck" Jed whispered. I put my hand up to let him know we were not about to pounce. We stayed hidden behind our large, shed-shaped, metal shield.

Black sauntered over to Rayne, like a jungle cat approaching prey as she said, "I'm bored, Rayne. Entertain me."

"Not my job to entertain you." He kind of smiled with one side of his face as he said it.

She gnawed on the inside of her cheek, "Then I'll entertain myself. How about a game?" When he didn't answer, she stepped closer and asked in a seductive voice, "Do you still love me now, Rayne?"

"Yes." He did not look up from his work.

She laughed wickedly, "Am I the love of your life??"

"No."

She stopped, looking strangely hurt, "No?"

"No." He stated plainly as he fiddled with something on the ground, to pick up and place inside the device, "The love of my life cast me aside years ago, and with good reason."

With heavy sarcasm, she said, "Oh yeah? Do tell."

"Yes," he answered, ignoring her tone, "I ruined myself. Now I am only good enough to be punished by women like you. Not loved."

"Hey, I can love." She gingerly stepped forward, ever closer. I was starting to pity Rayne.

"Can you?" He turned to look at her with puppy dog eyes.

"Sure. Just, you know, not you." She continued her cackle as he shook his head and went back to work, clenching his jaw as he went.

Black put a hand on her hip as she said, "You know, something just occurred to me. See, you don't feel like entertaining me anymore, and you've done such a good job of teaching me how all this works, so you aren't too much use to me anymore, are you Rayne?"

Rayne titled his head down and to the side to get a better earful of what she was saying, as he asked in his deep, gruff, and whispery voice, "What?"

Black threw her arms over his head, holding an end of piano wire in each hand.

He dropped his tools, jumped up and began to panic,

waddling backwards into her as she attempted to strangle him from too far down below. The size difference was working in his favor, and he was smart to have stood up as quickly as he had.

She said, "It was easy to lay the charges without you, especially with everyone looking for you instead of me, but I'm bored now!"

It was happenstance for us that they were both here together for the assumedly last time.

Black pulled tighter, drawing a bit of blood as she said, "You know, it's kind of a shame. You're a pretty handsome guy, when you remember to bathe!"

With Rayne struggling and her clinging to his back in an effort to choke him out, Jed burst forward when I gave the cue.

Jed startled Black by saying, "Holy fuckin' Moses on a rocket pogo stick, Gekman! This bitch is stealing shit outta my playbook!"

I stepped up, gun drawn with sights set on Black, "I've got her."

She dropped Rayne, or rather, dropped down from Rayne and put her hands up. He was going to survive, but he'd have a Hell of a scar across the front of his throat.

"Huh." She eyed me with the kind of look a drunk frat boy might give a pretty girl, "Where you from? I bet you came from a long ways away."

Jed had pulled a gun on Rayne at first, then re-holstered it to tend to Rayne's neck wound. Jed called Hudson, hoping he had a car nearby. We needed every kind of help.

I told Black, "We've been after you for a long time. You've killed a lot of people. Some of them, I was pretty fond of. I'm wondering if you killed Bernie too."

"What's a Bernie?" She giggled. It was disgusting.

"Bernie was the pathologist looking at the MOTH toxin."

"Oh! Bug! I remember him, actually. Yes. I absolutely killed him. Well, I got someone else to do it, but for me." She seemed proud. Probably just to rile me up, and it was working.

"Why Bernie? Because he'd found the toxin? Wouldn't he have been useful in making it even less detectable?"

She put her hand on her hip again, leaving the other one in the air and said, "You know, I hadn't even thought about that. Too bad."

The hand on her hip reached for something in her pocket I hadn't noticed, and she tossed it at me. Thinking it was a small bomb, I dodged. It was a compact for makeup. She was running away, down the stairs, and out the door.

With no time to tell anyone, I burst into a run in pursuit of her. Jed saw right away what I was doing, and boy, that big bugger could run.

Jumping the fence wasn't a problem for me, hopped up on determination and long-lasting pain killers. We came onto a boardwalk attached to a dock, just in time to watch Black shove a man from his tiny fishing boat. He fell, slamming his head onto a rock. He bounced right off and made a splash with his unconscious body.

Jed dove in after him without a second thought, leaving his heavy jacket in the water as I stood there helpless. On the bright side, unconscious meant that the man couldn't panic and struggle. Jed hoisted him up to me by standing on rocks by the dock. I scooted along, dragging him onto dry land. An officer who came with Hudson began to give the man CPR, so I ran back and gave Jed a hand.

Paramedics came soon after and said the man was going to be fine.

Jed looked at me, as I stood there in a state of half-shock, and he said, "Right, I forgot. The blue haired man is afraid of the fucking water."

"I'm not afraid! I never needed to learn to swim."

Jed waved back at the man as they loaded him up into the ambulance. He was awake and content that he had survived.

Then Jed said, "If you had gone in, I would've had two scrawny shits to save."

I shrugged, "When all this is over, I'll let you teach me to swim."

He half joked about getting me a pair of inflatable wings, then stated, "Well, it wouldn't have helped now anyway. An Olympic swimmer ain't gonna catch that bitch."

He waddled over to the edge of the dock. I found a stick, and with great skill, we managed to snatch up his jacket from the water.

CHAPTER 20
Taking Steps

We went to the first floor of the building, dejected and disheartened, and watched Hudson and the other officers gather around Rayne. He was effectively detained by the EMTs as they struggled to stuff him onto a stretcher. He needed to be strapped in to avoid escape, though he looked to me like a man who just wanted a break.

We made our way back to the roof with an officer Hudson pointed in our direction. The officer in question looked like she could play an Amazonian warrior in a movie. We searched for any clues to where Black might have gone next. Nothing, but the bomb they'd started. Jed analyzed that chunk-of-explosive until he found that it must be triggered by a detonator that either wasn't made yet, or was nowhere to be found.

"It would be a main hub," said Jed.

"A main hub?" I kicked a piece of broken concrete as though something might be underneath it.

"Yeah. It would be a detonator for a bunch at once. We just have to find it, if it exists. Possible he hadn't put one together yet."

The statuesque officer said, "I'm not sure how we'd get Rayne to talk, if he even could talk at all after his throat was opened."

"That's a fair point," I said. "Maybe it's not as bad as it looked? He's not dead, so that's a start. You're right though. Best case would be if he also told us where to find Black again, as well as all about our ghost detonator."

She nodded solemnly, "Save hundreds, if not thousands of people." Then she looked down at me with piercing blue eyes, "You know, Hudson's got every detective in this county and the next on Black. He told me what this case means to you, and as someone who spent too many years of my life too close to a case myself, I'm asking you to go home. Hudson has this covered, and clearly has what's best for you in mind."

    With that, I went back to my house to pack up all my work, and then went with Jed to his apartment, hauling the boxes along for the ride. I didn't feel like being home. No one lived there with me. I dove back into my copies of every file I could and began to organize them into categories which made sense only to me.

    Jed and I made each other drinks, and he was careful to make mine non-alcoholic. We sat on the floor in front of his couch with all of it. Maria sent me a text saying she sent Chloe on a mission. I asked her what that meant, but she only responded with a smiling emoticon. After we'd been at it forever for little to no result, Jed went to bed, offering me his couch.

    My mood was silly, in retrospect. Everything seemed tragic and dramatic and blown right out of any reasonable proportion. I took a pill. I couldn't feel my feet or where I was going. I had very little sense of self as I got up and vanished into the deep blackness of the unlit hallway right outside of Jed's apartment that smelled of stale incense and booze. The floor was misshapen and oddly bumpy, or maybe it was my feet. I went back into Jed's apartment, but I knew I couldn't sleep. We still had one last place Tabby had mentioned, just in case it led us to anything new. I sent a text to Jed so I wouldn't forget, then put my phone on the couch. I took a pill. I made my way to the fire escape through a window.

    I awoke the next morning to Jed hovering above my

head, and the sun piercing every part of my brain.

"What the actual fuck?" asked Jed. He pulled me to my feet, and half carried me down the fire escape back to his window.

"Get your shoes on," Jed threw a bundle to me made of my coat and shoes, "We're gonna look at the other area Tabby mentioned, like you said to me in the middle of the fucking night, you lunatic."

"Just us?"

"Yeah. Get your shoes on, and then get in my fucking car."

It was once a brewery in an area of Bellevue that most people had moved out of years prior. The parking lot was gravel and small, not built for many guests at once. Dead trees and weeds grew against the brick and yellowed siding. The door was stuck shut, but not locked. Jed hip-checked it open.

Light streamed in from the East into high up windows to reveal large, rusted tanks, some barrels, and pipes dotted with valves and pressure gages draped around the building like discarded snake skin. The concrete floor was difficult for my leg to contend with. I swallowed a pill while I inhaled the lingering smell of stale beer. Jed tilted his head to visualize how one might have used the moving carts, the scaffolding, and the ladders to get to the top of the tanks.

"You hear that?" he asked. There was a faint pinging sound coming from deeper inside.

Guns drawn, our steps light and as silent as we could muster, it got hotter and hotter the closer we got to the giant, metal container.

"What is this?" I asked Jed, looking around to see if there was anyone nearby.

"It's a pressure cooker."

"It's huge."

"Probably about 100 gallons, yeah. Should we open it up?" Jed climbed one of the ladders to reach a button on a control panel. A hissing sound followed and I hoped it wasn't about to explode. Jed pointed to a valve and a large faucet.

"You want me to see what's in here with this?" I asked him.

"Yeah. Just to see if this thing is even brewing something."

I turned the valve as Jed instructed. A churning sound precluded a clunk as red and brown goo fell from the tap.

"That doesn't look right." I closed the valve, trying not to breathe in through my nose.

"That looks like blood." Jed climbed down and picked up a piece of rebar from the floor to prod and gently poke through the viscera. One small, thin chunk held a gaudy ring.

"Wait," Jed continued to try and clean off the object with the steel rod. "This looks familiar. This... Gekman?"

I had already turned to call Hudson when Jed finished revealing Frog's cooked and severed finger. It smelled like rotten pork.

"Fried would have been better," said Jed.

"Fried?"

"Frog legs are better fried." Jed was a very light hearted soul for a raging lunatic.

Hudson was on his way, I was ready to vomit, Jed was... Jed, and I realized something important, "This place is one of Black's secret hideouts. Here's Frog, dead. She just tried to kill Rayne, which is just a thing she does in general."

"Right," said Jed. "She's a murderous little-"

"She's seen our faces. She knows who I am."

"Oh." Jed took out his phone to call Chloe.

A minute later, he hung up and told me, "Liz. We're going to her family's place. Her folks ain't there. They use it like a vacation spot now, so we're effectively gonna rent it for as long as we need, only free, 'cause Liz is with us."

"It's arguably the only house we have that doesn't have a direct tie to Black. Yeah. Okay. Plan made. I want my stuff from your place and mine, and then we bolt there."

The farmhouse was bright and flowery in all its décor, from the pathway up to the house, to the wallpaper in the living room. I could see how easy it would be to rent it out to vacationing families, if not for the mining operation next door. Jed, Maria, Liz, and I got set up and unpacked in our respective areas of the house. I wanted a nap.

Jed laughed from the kitchen and announced that Maria was going to help him shop while I slept the prior few months off.

"You're going shopping?" I asked, bemused.

"What if I need a disguise during all this?"

"And you need Maria for that?"

"I need to know that I don't look stupid, and I don't want Chloe to see me if I look stupid. Since your blue ass would stick me in a three-piece suit, I'm kidnapping your woman."

"I'm so pleased that I am given so much choice in this wonderful modern age." Maria said, grabbing her purse.

I was amazed that they continued to let Jed into any mall at all. There had been so many incidents at least facilitated by him, if not his fault to begin with. He was quite the gentleman with Maria though. He respected her on a level that most people could never achieve with him.

In fact, once there, Jed opened the door for her and everything. It was by hitting the handicap button so the door opened automatically, but it was the thought that counted.

They had managed to find a few things and ignored the strange looks and glares from people in the men's dressing room while Maria sat on the floor outside of Jed's stall.

She shrugged with her legs straight out, crossed at the ankles. "Hey, if boyfriends can do this, why can't I? It's not my fault this store doesn't have a bench or anything nearby."

Jed's frantic voice came from beyond the door, "Hipster shirts don't fit me! They're all too fucking small. 'Extra large' my ass."

Maria picked at something underneath her fingernail. "Well, yeah. You ever see a wide hipster? They're harder to find than records of bands no one has ever listened to."

"...No, you're right. I have never seen a fat hipster. Don't hipsters eat?"

"Nah. Too mainstream." Maria waved to a stranger who was staring in her direction. The man turned red. When she winked at him, he ran away.

"It's true. I mean, it's like EVERYBODY fucking eats. That's about as mainstream as you get." Jed stepped out and modeled a pair of pants. "Do these make my calves look chunky?"

Maria asked, "Are you screwing with me?"

"I just wanna be better for Chloe, okay?"

"You know clothing isn't the problem, right?"

Jed let out a sigh, "Yeah, but I figure if I look better, and I smell better, I can trick myself. I can be like I'm a new person."

"Fake it 'til you make it, I suppose."

The light may as well have been pepper spray, by how my early morning eyes, struggling in afternoon waking, responded. Humming, fake electric nonsense called the overhead lighting mocked me and laughed openly at my predicament. If I had been hung over, at least I would have had the pleasure of knowing that a groovy time had occurred the night prior. This was an attack of the senses, as if to say, "How dare you have anything to do this morning!" A stinging tingle at my shoulder proved irritating, but not enough to warrant madly swatting at whatever bug might have been sucking at my very life source. I gulped a glass full of water, then looked at my phone notifications.

It was a text from Darcy which read, "Your friend Chloe is the one who builds weird vehicles, right? Any chance you could give me her number? I might have a job proposal for her."

I complied. I could have asked Chloe first, but I figured she'd either roll with it, or yell at me in person once she got back to the farmhouse. I took a pill, then stumbled, vaguely remembering what I was looking for. I was missing a box.

Chloe had come and gone sometime in the middle of the night, and done something Jed assured me I had asked her to do.

Beyond the mess and various junk Jed had piled into the closet he'd be using during our stay there sat the boxes of my papers. I did not remember a conversation occurring, but Jed said we had spoken about the closet situation, and I believed him, and so there I was. I was losing time. It was not so much that I was running out of time, as blacking out and losing hours of my life that supposedly had happened.

Hangers adorned a metal rod, but any clothing had fallen off into stomped and wrinkled piles on the floor. On a top shelf sat board games and a large jar of some unnameable substance that would on occasion jiggle and move as if laughing at the closet's over all condition. Maybe that last part was imaginary. Either way, the shoebox of various knives was certainly real, if coated with half an inch of grey, sickly dust and grime. I wasn't sure if that was something Jed had brought, or left by Liz's parents. Spiders and their extended families with no sense of human cleanliness or property had made roost quite comfortably throughout the area.

Turning to the left, vomiting into the trash can from the overwhelming stench of god-knows-what was the only viable option. Of course, the box of papers was next to said trash can, a few feet from the broken, dangling what-was-left-of-a-closet-door. The whole venture into said closest could have been avoided. I clenched my fist at the thought.

Chloe had cookies waiting for me, and somehow that fixed everything. She replaced the trash bag without saying a word. Everyone around me kept phasing in and out like ghosts.

"Hey," Jed put a hand on his hip, "you wanna call Maria over here? She's back at her place, but you look like you're getting tense."

"My being tense is not her concern, nor should it have to be."

Chloe and Jed looked at each other warily, silently agreeing that I wasn't making much sense.

"Anything you wanna talk about?" Every now and then, Jed was a true friend.

"No. I'm okay." Then I thought about it. I was not, in fact, okay. I said, "I keep being okay, then feeling guilty and embarrassed, and depressed, and then I cry more. I'm not saying I feel guilt about anything. It's not even a yearning. It feels like I brutally murdered someone's dog with a crowbar for no discernible reason.

"Graphic," said Chloe.

I snapped my fingers, "Figured it out. I feel like I wasted everyone's time."

"You haven't wasted anybody's time," Jed stepped forward.

I instinctively stepped back, farther toward the box, as though I was worried he might steal it.

Jed reached his hand toward me, "Listen man, you gotta talk this shit out, okay?"

I laughed cruelly, "Like you do any talking? All you do is drink and hope your problems go away." Depression had turned to anger. Jed knew what was going on better than I did, and so simply waited for me to catch up. I had stunned myself enough that I whispered, "Wait until I get to acceptance for me to try that again, yeah?"

"Well, how about you take a nap for now, Buddy? Or a shower?" Jed gave me a solid pat on the back. "We'll sort things out a bit more here."

"No, I can do it..." I was like a zombie, saying words that once had meaning as I picked up the putrid stack of what was probably all copies of something cleaner anyway, and headed to my room. Jed put his hand on my shoulder to stop me.

"Seriously," he pointed to the box. "Put the box down, and take a shower. I'm gonna call Maria. Liz is downstairs making food, and she's gonna want her here anyway."

I stood in the shower feeling nothing. I tried to meditate on the water. Each drop was a part of the greater whole. It poured down my back and dripped down my chest. I let the water penetrate every pore and scald whatever it wanted. I turned around to face the blast, alone in deafness, water rushing all around my ears, then around again. I stood there until a pale, faint blue trickled down, through and past me into and down the drain. The longer I stood, the more my leg hurt.

Stepping out into the steam filled room, I wiped a spot to look into the bathroom mirror and tried to twist myself to see the whole bruise that had formed. I reckoned it was from a tumble, but I couldn't remember. It was impressive. It covered my entire shoulder and was greens, purples, grays and all manner of other colors. Gross yet pretty in an odd way. I noticed that empty feeling again. It wasn't sadness. There was no reason for it.

I had survived, but it didn't feel like I had. There was no Black. It wasn't a sinking 'war's not over' or waiting for the other shoe to drop sensation either. No. This was altogether different. Almost exotic and exciting if it weren't so gut wrenching. It was as though pieces of me were falling off. Hunks of flesh crumbling away. Not vital pieces mind you, but still ones to be missed. There was a feeling like I had forgotten something important that I couldn't place. Something I needed to get done never would, and that awful sensation trickled down my spine and upset my stomach like bad seafood. If I had been art, I didn't want to need an interpretation. I wanted to be simple. My friends felt the same about themselves.

Maria was thankful when Jed called. She needed a moment of laying on her couch with tears welling up in her eyes before she could drive over though.

She had just had a panic attack after another phone call from her mother, and bottling up everything else in her life for so long meant something had to give. The realization of how often I was in and out of a hospital shook her even more, and knowing I was holed up in Liz's parents farmhouse didn't help the situation. I wasn't great at telling her when I was half-dead, and she was worse at telling anyone when she needed emotional support. She was worried about telling Liz just as much as she was afraid to ever see Liz half-dead.

Maria was raised to believe having emotions made her less loveable. She was wrong, and maybe some part of her knew that, but it left her lonely and pushing away the people she needed the most. Let's face it, I was never the best option for such a thing, and yet, she told Jed that she wanted me there.

"Go over," Jed said to me. "Help Maria pack, and then she'll stay with all of us for a while."

"I don't know if that feels like the right thing to do," I said.

"I'm gonna be your ride. Get her to come stay here, okay? I wanna live with everybody."

Hudson called while Jed and I were driving over to say, "Rayne is conscious and seems ready to talk. I hate to do this to you, but do you think you could stop by the hospital tomorrow to do this? None of us are having any luck."

I was so very tired, "Why on Earth do you think I would?"

"He says he likes you."

Jed chuckled at the face I made. I hung up, explained the situation, and got out of the car at Maria's.

"She'll bring you back with her," said Jed.

Maria dabbed the tears from her eyes and reapplied her eyeliner in the mirror in her front hallway. She did it for herself, to feel more put together. To feel a quick sense of control.

She opened the door seconds after my knock. She, for once, was not in a robe or a dress. She was wearing comic book sleep shorts and an oversized band T-shirt. Her hair was spiked about in every way it pleased to be. She was absolutely strikingly beautiful.

I kissed her face, then wrapped my arms around her waist. She sighed into my armpit.

Maria looked up at me, "I'm glad you came over. I know I should have just gone to where you already were, but I don't know that I can do that just this second."

"Are you okay?"

"Not particularly."

I kissed her head and asked, "Is there a reason you couldn't get Liz?"

"I didn't ask."

"That would make it difficult to get her, I guess."

She chuckled and hugged me tighter before I asked if she wanted to talk about anything. She said no.

"What about you?" she asked.

"I'm fine," I said smiling, as I started to break away.

Something had been bubbling and brewing inside of her, like there was something important she wasn't letting on about.

I had fallen back into the idea of keeping her out of the mess of it. The problem was that the "mess of it" was my entire life, and now her other love interest was involved. At least, I assumed Liz was involved. None of this was my job anymore. The proper people were leading the Black/Bomber case. I took in a deep breath to remember that I actually had the time to spend with Maria, I just didn't know what to do with it.

I removed my hat. Her little smirk became a relived grin. She was too nice and I was too dumb not to take advantage of that fact.

I asked again, "You said you're not okay. Will you tell me what's going on?"

"Oh. I hate that I feel the way I do about my mother. I hate the way she makes me feel. I hate that I don't get to be an adult, and just revert to the scared little girl hiding in her closet, waiting for her mother to scream about whatever it was I was supposed to be doing for her, and I hate-" She stopped short, breathing heavily.

"I remember her being horrendous, the few times I'd come in contact with her. Did you see your mom recently?"

"She's called a few times this month. I'm not sure why. Did you know I had to call her for my birthday?" She hugged me tighter.

"You had to call her?"

"I had to call her!" Maria sobbed for a minute against my chest before taking in a deep breath, sighing, and wiping her eyes.

"Okay. I feel better now," she said.

"Are you sure?"

"Yes. So. Tell me what's horribly wrong with you. You were limping a little when you got inside. Are you hurting?" She backed away to get a better view of me.

I looked her in the eyes and said, "Outside, everything is fine. On the inside, I am screaming. So, you're right. I thought you should know."

She frowned, "Is being here with me helping or harming?"

"No! You are never the problem. Ever. You understand?"

She nodded, still unsure of what to make of me. When I was direct, it seemed awkward and out of place.

I gently brushed her hair out of her eyes with my left hand, still clinging to my hat with my right. "Why did it take so long for us to reconnect? I mean, besides me being an idiot."

"No. It wasn't all your fault. I mean, it was mostly your fault, yes, but I remember the times you wanted to see me." She held my hand against her face with hers, then let go and spouted some honesty, "After a while, I drifted away because I couldn't do it anymore. It hurt too much. I wanted to sit there and smile for you and spend time with you, but I'd always question why those other girls were good enough for a relationship and I wasn't. Neither of us were willing to just be friends, and I felt like I was taking off pieces of myself to make you happy."

I shook my head, "It wasn't that you weren't good enough. It was the opposite. You deserved better and I knew it, so I let you go."

After swallowing, I said, "Wow. That sounds really crappy out loud."

She took my hat and placed it on the rack, followed by my jacket, "You wanted other women and you made me watch. I should have closed my eyes, right?" She chuckled, as though that had been a funny thing to say. "I wanted to spare myself, and it seemed better to walk away in case my feelings for you ever dropped off."

She walked toward a bottle of wine and refilled a glass, "I was hoping that when I saw you again, you'd be less attractive, or your voice wouldn't send my head spinning so easily, or your eyes wouldn't drown me, but it was worse. It doesn't matter anymore. I have you now, right? In a way." She took a sip through her sarcasm. Then she looked at the glass and said, "You'll drive us to Liz in my car, right?"

"Yeah. Hey, why am I here instead of her?" I asked. Maria kept smiling as she put the glass down, walked back over to me, and placed her arms around my neck. I put my arms back around her waist, as though we'd slow dance.

She shrugged, "I'd finally given up."

"Given up?" That sounded less than good.

"Given up pretending I didn't miss you. Given up waiting for the right moment to tell Liz my life story. Everything. Gave up on you both." She sucked in a deep breath, "She wants to shop around a bit, and you know what? I was worried how awful it would be if I ran and you didn't chase after me this time."

"I'm sorry about that." I brought my lips to hers, but

she spoke over my kiss.

"Don't be," she said. "I finally got the courage to do it while you were using me to solve your wrap around mystery. I realized then that you were no hero. You're a regular man."

"Is that good or bad?"

"I wanted so much to be with someone who had feelings for me. I wanted to love them back. You when you weren't ready, and Liz now when she's decided she's not ready for me."

I needed to start being clear, "She should be here instead of me. You weren't kidding. You really didn't call her, did you?"

"No. I didn't. She doesn't know specifics about me yet and I'm not ready to tell her. I think she kind of knows. We aren't... I mean, we make out, we go on dates, we have sex. We do all the things you and I do, but Liz is about as great with commitment as you are."

I said, "You love her though."

"Yeah. I do. I don't know if she loves me, and we aren't even really together. Same with you, right? And I know you love me. At least, I think you do. You love me until you get bored." She dropped her hands from my shoulders, but I didn't let her go. I wanted her to keep her arms on me, even on my busted shoulder. I didn't care. In fact, I wanted her to beat the crap out of me, physically or verbally.

My eyebrows scrunched, but I was more confused than hurt. "That's pretty morbid. Haven't I proven myself at this point? And Liz seems like a pretty solid force for you these-"

"Do you want me to drop you off there and bring her back here? Why'd you come straight here and not back to endless research? Do you even want to be here with me?"

My mouth agape, it took me a second before the words came back, "Look, I've got to go talk to Rayne tomorrow, but right now, I want you to be standing here with whichever one of us is going to make you feel better."

"I don't want to put all this on her. I don't want to talk to you about it either, but I want to be here with you right now. You are the one I thought of because I already know you'll understand and..." Her eyes got wide as she realized, "I don't want kid gloves right now. I don't want to have pity or have someone mother me or hold me while I cry, and I know you would, and I know you literally just did, and I know Liz WILL if given the chance, and I don't want that right now at all."

I blinked at her, "Okay."

"As for proving yourself, no. It's been a long time since you've been here with me, and longer since it wasn't for a case."

I couldn't argue what was true.

She bit her lip, "And before then, you loved me because I was aloof. You loved me because you had to save me, with bullets flying around you like an action movie. You loved me because of the excitement and the fact that I was just out of your reach. One fight with me, and you would leave for some other girl. Even if you felt awful about it later, I bet you would do it for the drama even now. If that is what it takes to keep you, maybe I could give you that, but maybe I don't want to. I don't know if I could make up some soap opera for Sir Gabe Gekman's royal entertainment." She waved her hand in my face, as if dismissing me.

I took her hand in mine and held her body firmly with my other arm, "Please. I know I'm going to screw up on some level again and again until I get used to this, but please, please let me try. I want to be your friend. I want to be here for you. I want you to call me even when I'm too screwed up to call first. Romantically, I'd be happy for another chance, but I'll be happy if you move on to someone else too. You know? You deserve better and I want to *be* better. Both are true. When I let us just be together, I am absolutely happy and relaxed, and I'm scared. That's all that comes down to. I'm scared. I don't know why."

She breathed in through her nose, then let out a sigh through pursed lips. "It's the devil we know. And... To tell you the truth, Chloe keeps saying that Liz pulled away because I did to her what you did to me, and refused to tell her anything about myself."

She giggled, as if to ward off everything she had just said, and kissed me on the cheek, "So let's go hang out with everyone!"

I laughed and didn't move. Her face was one of stunned shock.

"I want to show you something," I said as I unbuttoned my shirt. Her coy smile turned to a slightly open-mouthed sadness when she saw the bruise. It had swelled into a grey and purple mass covering the deltoid, seeping up to my clavicle and around to the trapezius. In other words, ow. I felt a little like a pirate on the cover of a bad romance novel because my cuffs were still buttoned, attaching the cape my shirt had become to my body. I took her hands in mine again and she kissed me. I brought her hands back up around my neck.

She unbuttoned my cuffs and moved my shirt down farther. She held my shirt by my wrists. She looked at my bruise and gently kissed it, letting me go. When she asked what it was from, I told her that I wasn't really sure, and the fact that I wasn't sleeping. I had to explain why I hadn't said anything before. I had no valid reasons. I wound up rambling on until I had told her every last detail of the case up to that point, and which parts haunted me the most.

Once we'd made it to the couch, I flopped my shirt over the back. She grazed her fingertips against my flesh over the bruise and over old scars on my chest and stomach as I spoke, nodding on occasion. She had seen most of them a million times, but in a way, she had never really *seen* them before. She had never truly felt how they affected me.

Then she looked me right in the eyes and said, "I need you to leave."

"What?"

"I need you to go to Rayne and see if he'll talk to you. I think he still has some sense of humanity in him. Appeal to that. Find that and use it. That'll help you find Black."

I nodded, but cupped her chin with my curved index finger and thumb to tilt her head for a gentle, tender kiss.

I told her, "I will. Tomorrow. I was told to go see him tomorrow, and I will, but not yet."

"You promise?"

"I can stay here tonight. Only if you truly want this. Otherwise, I'll call Liz for you. Don't be afraid of what you want, okay?"

"You promise you're seeing Rayne tomorrow?"

"I promise. You're gonna drop me off to see Rayne, and then you're going to the farmhouse. In fact, if I spend the night here, that means I'm gonna go to Rayne pretty much immediately after whatever we do. I have time."

She kissed me again. It felt like I got permission for something I didn't even know I needed. Companionship. The thing I needed so desperately from Maria was her friendship, and to show her that I could give her mine, but for that moment, we couldn't quite slip off this physical intensity. We weren't sure how to speak the language of love with any other words.

"Does being with me still scare you?" she grinned playfully.

It was such a joy to see her smile, and I wanted her to know the truth, "You make me happy and I don't know what to do with that. My default is to mess it up beyond all recognition, as you know."

She smiled again, "Good. We're on the same team then." She took off her shirt.

It didn't take long before my pants were in a heap on the floor by thrown shoes and gleefully discarded panties, sleep wear, and boxer-briefs. She took a good long look at the bruises and horrendous scars that decorated my legs and lower back.

"Gabe. For fuck's sake."

"What? Not sexy?"

She stopped me on the way down the hallway to the bedroom to gently push me so she could see every inch of my torso that was bruised and hurting.

Maria let out a little gasp, "Seriously. Are you okay? I have ice! I can-"

I grabbed her from her thighs and stood up with her. My attempt was to move us to the bed, but she grabbed onto the window ledge in that hallway, and guided me against the wall until we were back in the living room instead. She wrapped her legs tightly around me like a hug for the whole body. An embrace for every last inch of me.

A comforting rush. Ever sit in a plane during takeoff? That vibration beneath you, everything pushing your whole body back, and then, for a slight second, you are weightless. This was like that. Everything was far away, but for her. Warm in every conceivable way.

The lavender paint of the walls felt like the outside of an ostrich eggshell against my palm. I used the other hand and arm to hoist her up and down as best as I could, though she was doing a good job of that herself. Using the wall against her back as support, I became little more than a jungle gym and I absolutely accepted that freely.

After a while, we were rocking into each other. It was nice and soothing. She gestured to the couch. I sat down with her still straddling me. She continued to rock into me, lifting a bit more now and then before gliding back down.

Something hit me in a wave and I started to tear up. Not crying outright, but enough to clench my jaw, showing some teeth and furrow my brow with my eyes tightly closed as I moved my hands from her hips to wrapping my arms tightly around her torso, just under her arms. She held me back, and whispered a question of whether or not I was all right. I said I was, so she continued, even slower, then pressed against my chest with one hand, guiding my surrender until we were laying down, with her on top of me. She slammed herself down a little too fast and stumbled for a moment, but landing on me wasn't going to do any damage. I was never the tallest guy in the world, but she was not the largest woman either.

When I made another huff noise and let a tear fall down my temple to my ear, she asked, "Would you like to stop? It's okay. We could take a break or something." She put her hand on my face and wiped the lone tear away with her thumb.

Her lips came painfully close to mine as she said, "It's okay. You've been through so much mentally, physically, emotionally. I know firsthand that it isn't healthy to keep going forever without any breaks."

Gruffly, I smiled and said, "This is my break. You. You are my escape, so no. Don't stop. I'm just gonna lay here and let you do your magic, and I'm sorry about that. I am. I just want to be here with you." I pulled her in again tightly, smooshing our noses together, "I like this."

She said, "You're sure? You've been through so much."

"I'm sure. And thank God for you."

She titled her head down a little, but maintained eye contact as she said, "For me, huh?"

"Yeah. What other woman would be crazy enough to keep doing a guy who cries in bed?" She brought her arms down to cradle me more, and I did the same back, biting my smiling bottom lip and remaining inside of her. The rest was peaceful and very much needed.

In the morning we took a shower, ate breakfast naked, and then we lay still for a long time on the couch before I mumbled half to myself, "You know, maybe I should quit after this case."

"This again? Quit what? Being a PI? Or like... being any kind of detective?" Maria rested her lips against my neck.

I sucked in my cheek and my brow furrowed into a deep face of confusion, "I'm not even sure, but I could put more effort into us if I did quit. I could take a desk job, like I've said a million times before, but... Really. There are plenty out there for me. Jed could finally get put into some good therapy and we could be done. He'd be pissed of course, but-"

Maria sighed and lowered herself to put her chin on her hands, layered on my chest. She said, "I can't hope for something so romantic. I can't. I trust you for a lot of things, and I know you at least half as well as Jed does, but I don't want you to make promises for me. I want to enjoy being with you, and be here when you need me, no matter what you decide to do."

"I don't wanna be that person anymore. I'm tired of it." I sounded irritated and I guess I was. Still, I toned it down enough to say, "If I want to chill out on the actual field work, I can choose to do that, I realize. I'm not asking for permission, but you're smart and I'd love your opinion. Plus, you know, I want to make us something official. If you're into that." I laughed, trying to make light of it.

She returned the forced laugh and moved her hair out of her face but it flopped right back, "Okay, so let's go by what I know about you. Why would I ever let you give everything up just to slump over a desk like an average person? You and me, Gabe, we're not particularly average people. Besides, you seem pretty convinced that Liz is the love of my life."

"I'm right." I smiled, "What if I've found someone worth more to me than my career? What if that person is you, or even Jed?" She kissed me more as a way to shut me up before I made any more promises than as an act of affection.

"I'm in love with your lips, not so much your mouth," then she got up to find some clothes and pack a bag.

I put myself back together and kissed her again as I stepped out of the doorway. She put the hat I almost forgot onto my head, then stopped me with a pull to my coat.

"Wait," she said. "Jed dropped you off here! I almost forgot. I'll drive you to the hospital. You can take your precious bus after that, but I can at least get you to where you're headed. You *are* seeing Rayne, aren't you?"

Maria questioned if she should call Jed for this visit, but I decided to leave him be for now. It was the right call, as Jed was busy putting his arm around Chloe on the couch.

"Oh, showing me affection now?" said Chloe.

Jed inched closer to her and said, "The way I see it, if you're willing to stick around even though I'm a huge mess of a person, you can't be SO bad."

She titled her head up at him, smiling close to his face, "Even if I stab you?"

He chuckled, "Maybe even if you stab me."

CHAPTER 21
Got the Blues

Once we got to the hospital, Maria drove off, waving to me like concerned parents might wave to their son on his first day of school. I tried to collect my wandering thoughts, tried to slow my heartbeat, tried to tell myself that I just needed to ask some questions about Black. That was all. Nice and easy.

A lone bird fluttered above my head as I walked towards the building. It danced to unhearable music and I found myself jealous of that bird's flying moment. I did not want to go in, and my leg didn't make it any better. It started to throb. I leaned against the siding and fumbled with my pockets. The pill jar was empty. I had another at the farmhouse, but for now, I'd need to power through.

The clouds were a backdrop of white powered finger prints on blue, with fluffy cotton lumps drifting far in front. There was something poetic about the gaggle of nurses smoking and coughing outside. I tried sitting at the park bench to massage my leg for a moment, but there were more cigarette butts than grass, and more gnats than oxygen. I gave up and attempted to walked through the automatic doors. People in the waiting room stank of stale perfume and self-loathing. The woman at the front desk realized who I was and rushed me through the doors to the right. I wanted to take my time, grab a cup of water, and see if someone had a pill I could take for the pain, but she was not having that.

The thing about stains on hospital carpet is that you've gotta wonder if it was a chemical or from some leaking person. I took a sharp left to the bathroom, still avoiding Rayne.

His history didn't match his criminal profile, according to the Psychologist's notes. I was amazed that the department actually complied with my request to send those to me anyway. A tightness in my gut started as I thought of all the ways I wouldn't be able to predict his next moves, and a worry that I felt sorry for him. What would that do to my ability to interrogate him? I was afraid of him. Surely nothing more.

The tile in the bathroom was a strange brown-green, like a color guide for what your crap might look like when you need to go to the hospital in the first place. I was thankful for the tiny slit of window and the thin, cool air slowly seeping through. I took in a few deep breaths, and then finally made my way to Rayne.

The curtain separating him from an empty cot on the other side of his room creaked as I pushed it to the side.

"Do you remember me?" I asked.

He gave a half smile and whispered, "Sure. We have the same hair stylist."

I chuckled at that. He didn't seem so monstrous now.

"I'll cut to the chase here. How long were you working with Black?"

"Eh. I do not know. It did not start with bombs. She was with that company, and I only did the toxins because they made sense in a puzzle way, but I did not understand the point. Still do not. I left her then."

"But then you got back together with her?"

"Yeah. I was not strong enough to avoid as such. I did not speak up and stop anything she did, though I could have. Changed to bombing with her, which actually fit better, since I am a tinkerer." He put his hand to his throat and let out a little cough.

"A tinkerer?"

"Yes. I thought she wanted the machines. She did not... But I was proud of them. The blueprints were like my children, yet I sold them. My prototypes too. I sold it all to a nice woman who repurposed my work. Mine were like tanks that could dig underground. Tunnel makers. Now, the lady makes them for science, building, repair work.

They collect Hi-En, which is good. It is better, I think, but I missed tinkering with the mechanics."

The lady in question was Chloe's mother. She bought his blueprints, but he still had the design inside his head. That was enough for him to ask Liz to make those small gear-like parts.

I asked, "Did Black promise you your machines again?"

"Yes, but I should have known better. I did horrible things for her. Maybe I just liked having someone to talk to." He closed his eyes, clearly in a deep pain he wished to hide.

"On the roof, you were working on a bomb. Can you tell me where the detonator is?"

Rayne clicked his tongue, "Did not make one yet." Raspy and taught, his voice struggled to keep it all together and stoic, "They are going to take me to prison, yeah? Ship me off to lock me up and maybe kill me later."

One bruised purple eyelid opened enough to glare at me as he said, "It will not matter. There will not be a trial. No need. I will go. I will go and maybe die."

"Look, it doesn't have to be like that." I put up a hand, but he put up his to stop me from talking. For a moment, it looked as though we might high five.

Both eyes opened, and he raised his eyebrows as he said, "It does not matter."

He seemed older in that moment, tired like an old man on his death bed, telling his grandson the ways of the world.

"And you are not going to get anything from me while I am like this. I cannot see straight. I can barely talk because of her." He chuckled, "Take that as you will."

"You sound cooperative though. Does that mean you might help me out later?"

"Perhaps. I have learned things about myself. She taught me."

"Black?"

"No. The doctor. Actually, I think she was not a doctor. Counselor? Either way, she was very smart, and very kind. Kindness is a rare trait in this world." He laced his fingers together on his lap.

I pushed out the words as though worried he'd wander off before I got to say it, "Really, if you know anything about where Black might be going next, please tell me."

He tried and mostly failed to prop himself up, so I handed him the little remote to tip his bed at an angle.

"What makes you think she told me anything?" The bed hummed and clicked as it sat him up a bit more. He took a big breath in through his nose and said, "What makes you think I remember anything she had said?"

"Well..." I didn't know how to continue, so I trailed off for a moment. I took off my hat as though I might stay awhile, "She seemed pretty important to you. You did a lot because of her."

Rayne clutched his throat as if he did not trust the bandage to stay in place. He croaked and grunted, "You think she is the only woman who ever stabbed me in the back? I am not stupid enough to think they are all like that, but any woman who goes after me for romance has some ulterior motive. Look at me. Big, hulking monster pretending to be a man." Bitterly, he added, "I do not mind. Makes it all more exciting."

Exciting. Crap. Was Maria right? Did I think like that too? I stepped towards Rayne. He shrugged one shoulder like he was trying to pop something and showed his teeth in somewhere between a smile and a grimace.

"Romance tends to get even the greatest men in trouble." Rayne laughed when I said it, and then I added, "And I'm not a great man." It was in an effort to show I wasn't full of myself, but his chuckle stopped short.

Stern and with the clearest articulation I had yet

heard him utter, "Romance is not the same thing as love."

Without thinking, I responded, "Love is terrifying. Easy to screw up. Romance at least leaves a story. Love is that empty feeling. It needs romance to get anything done."

Oh dear lord. Was I having this conversation with Rayne? What was wrong with me?

He laughed a real laugh this time and spoke to me like we were old buddies at a bar, "Is that the logic you use to screw things up when you get scared? No risks, right? I bet that is what you do. Ha! You ever let yourself love, or are you in it for the dramatics of your so-called romance?" He looked like he wanted to pat me on the back.

We both ignored the situation we were in. This made him all the more horrifying. However, that was a brilliant question. I looked to the side with my mouth slightly hanging open, moving my jaw as I gave it too much thought.

Rayne took it upon himself to finish the thought for me, "Your strategy is boring and cowardly. Mine is ignorant and impulsive. Both are selfish." He leaned forward, almost pulling the IV from his arm as he pointed at me, "I have read about you. I know people who know you. I know you are a greater man than that. Stop being foolish."

"That's oddly fair, actually." I shook my head, "But not why I'm here."

"I do not know what information I have yet to give you."

"What about older information?"

"Older? Ah. Before Candice, there was someone good in my life. After she left, the soil went dry. The vineyard still stands, but it is empty. The winery holds barrels of sour, undrinkable wine underground in a cellar."

"That sounds like a metaphor." He laughed at my comment, and I tried again, "What went wrong with the MOTH company? They're still around, but to what capacity?"

"Rayne scratched his head, "Oh, they still have

feelers in politics, but they used to be untouchable, and have a lot of money as a company. Very recently, years wise, it all fucked up."

"Okay. How?"

"They threw up a bulwark against a changing world and got plowed under. What can I say? Their patents expired, new technology emerged, and big gambles did not pay off. It is not so complicated."

"I've heard whoever was in charge almost got caught for money laundering, but the last guys out the door took all the rainy-day cash. They were broke, and there was no proof of doing anything wrong. That about right?"

"No. Not really." He put up a finger for emphasis, "One. One man got caught for the crimes, and he fell for no other reason than his job was to take the hit. But no one worth 7 figures went down. The head of the R&D division, the PR person. Eh. Which one he was depended on who you asked."

"A fall guy. Who was he then?"

"Old papers would tell you, but his old name would not help you find him. He is out now, with a new just-as-seedy identity as a used car salesman, closer to Cornsbrook. Does not own the lot, but he is an employee. That I know. I cannot imagine what information he could give you though. I do not think anything. Lost everything. He did not even know until after the news hit, but he still lied about it because that is what PR guys do, you know?"

I scribbled out what little I had written in a frustrated rush. Rayne chuckled in response.

"This is funny to you, eh?" I asked. "The fact that I keep running in circles."

"No," he coughed and wheezed for a moment, so I handed him the glass of water from the counter.

"Thank you," He took a sip. "No, the circles your villains run in. That is what I find funny. Neither of you are particularly useful at what you do. It is not just you."

"Gee. Thanks." I sighed, "So here we are, in a world where this once monolithic organization is now somehow involved in underground drugs, a possibly still unrelated dead college student, an absolutely-related dead child from decades ago, and I'm pretty sure human trafficking under the club of my ex-girlfriend, but I don't have enough to go on to get in where they fled to in order to find out."

He looked away for a moment to contemplate something before coming back with, "What else can I tell you? One class action lawsuit for testing on hospital patients without consent drained them between the legal and civil cases. That did happen."

My jaw clenched hard and I swallowed nothing. Rayne noticed and asked, "Was that the absolutely-related child? Ah. This is not a case to you. This is something personal. Something old. There were a few children from my understanding. Which one did you know?"

"Shut up."

"You wanted me to talk."

"I did. It was a mistake. You aren't helpful." I started to walk away, and Rayne made a humming sound. I looked back and he had his finger up again. "What is it?"

"I want to know." He sounded eager to keep me there as he said, "I do not know what else about Candice I can say, but I will tell you what I can about other things in question. I just want to know what this is to you."

I looked to the ugly Styrofoam drop ceiling, then cracked my neck back and forth before walking back over to Rayne. "Fine. You start."

He adjusted and took another sip of water while kind of smiling like he just thought of something fantastic and exciting he wanted to tell me, "Like I said, not everyone escaped prison. The doctor doing the injections was convicted. He said he did not know it was not sanctioned, but he was paid you know? So, no one would believe he did

302

not know."

He scratched his nose, "I do not remember his name, but you could find it. My point is that the things you are probably maddest about were already paid for by the company. You know that, I bet."

"Yes, but that isn't what this is about. Michael Crown, the college student-"

"Ah, might have something to do with the company, but might not. Yeah?"

"He knew Denny. They were roommates."

Rayne waved the idea away, "Everyone knows Denny. He is a parasite who views himself a king. Gets his grubby hands in everything because he thinks he deserves it. He deserves nothing." He gingerly touched his throat. "Let me see. The old CEOs are not publicly recognized figures anymore, you know. They live richly but quietly by donating to the right politicians. That part is still true. Let us get to the point. Who are you after? Who specifically hurt you, do you think?"

"Your Candy girl." I could feel the air stop. Rayne didn't expect that, I suppose.

"Hmm. And why is that? Why pick her out of the crowd, hmm?"

"Hardly a crowd. You said it yourself. There's only a few higher ups. Denny mentioned a woman as THE highest of higher ups. Logically, it's her."

"And taking her down will fix your broken soul?"

I bit the inside of my cheek, "No. I don't expect it to."

Rayne nodded in a way that made me feel like we were in group counseling together, "What will it do?"

"Closure. Everyone thinks I'm crazy. Everyone always has. Yet, people knew. My parents were in denial, but it's obvious my sister was a victim of all this."

Rayne's eyes became like dinner plates as he processed what I was saying. He leaned forward a bit, curious to hear the rest.

I continued, "Yeah, it's been taken care of, but I've always known the higher ups were still out there, and now I've got names. It's a generation later, but it's gotta end, Rayne. It all needs to end."

"Believe me, I understand," The whirring buzzing of the bed motors echoed as he laid himself back down. "Talk to me again some time. I have nothing else to say about Candice right now, but I will help you if I can. I remember nothing else. Too much pumping through my system." I believed him and I didn't have the right questions for him anyway.

To be honest with myself, it was good to know he was all right.

He added, "Go to your friends. The big one seems nice, from what I have gathered." He smiled with one side of his face, yet it wasn't quite a smirk. It was a satisfied, honest smile a man might give a punk kid he's just taught a lesson.

It wasn't until I began to leave that I noticed the ripped straps dangling from the bed. Rayne must have been securely strapped down at some point, but broke out. Why didn't he leave? ...Or pummel me to death?

CHAPTER 22
Dead Men and Their Tales

Texting Jed what had gone down with Rayne meant that I was barred from taking the bus back to the farmhouse. Instead, he picked me up to have an in-person chat.

"Maria, Liz, and Chloe are all back there now, so that's cool. I wanna do a big family dinner tonight. Gonna have mac and cheese. Other stuff too, but that's a must." I hadn't seen Jed so excited in years.

"I spent the night with Maria," I said. "I'm honestly hoping Liz comes around soon. I don't think we're good for each other. Not as this."

"That's big of you, Man. I'm like, weirdly proud. Not of you getting laid, but of the other thing you said. Letting Maria go is cool."

With a nod, I asked, "So, what's going on with you and Chloe these days? Are you two an official item now or what?"

"I ain't gonna make her walk." This was the nearest approximation of getting close to a woman Jed had experienced in a long time. He shrugged and continued with, "If anyone is willing to stick around through the Hell I put people through, I ain't gonna push 'em away."

"Guess that's why you keep me around, huh?" He smiled. It was good to see that.

"You blue-brained son of a bitch." He put a hand on my shoulder. "You know I'm keepin' you around forever."

Dinners and days had gone by in a pleasantly uneventful way, though the version of me glaring from the bathroom mirror was an absolute horror show. My hair had become a shade of mold as the blue began to look as worn out as the rest of me felt. My feeling sorry for myself was interrupted when my phone rang.

Stanley Addams was sober when he called me, trying to remember my real name. Eventually he gave up and went with the code names from when we met.

"I've got information on my family you might want," he said. He told me where to go, and I cleaned up quick to head out.

I caught a glimpse of Jed and Liz playing cards in the kitchen, so I poked my head in to say, "I'm going to go talk to Stanley. I'll call if I need anything."

Jed gave me a nod. I took a pill, and got on my bike.

The walkway up to the house was made of an orange-brown stone and jutted off from the driveway itself. Pretty, but had it been winter, the house was far enough from where I could park my bike that I would have certainly found a gripe with its placement. The house was an off white. It was a cute little place. Pink and yellow flowers in terracotta pots lined the right side of the steps up to the porch. A crooked, but still-holding-up bench lazily creaked in the breeze.

Stanley greeted me with, "Hey! When did you dye your hair blue? Looks good. Oh! I made coffee!" and guided me inside. The first room of the house after the overly furnished front foyer was the kitchen. A wooden chair gave a little puff sound as I sat down. The walls were mostly an avocado green, with one oddly placed brown accent wall. The kitchen table was a dark brown, matching the old and near stylishly outdated cabinets, but clashing with the pinkish refrigerator. Magnets sporting generic cutesy photos and nonspecific, faux snarky sayings cluttered and clung to its surface.

A woman with wavy brown hair and a green pant suit

came out from a hallway to kiss Stanley. She pointed at me and looked at him.

He looked to me and said, "Oh! Gekman, this is my girlfriend, Ginger."

She gave a wave and a smile as she grabbed her purse, "And this is his girlfriend going to work! It was nice meeting you, Detective Gekman."

"Oh, I'm a PI, actually" came out of my mouth, but she was already through the door.

We heard some unintelligible arguing outside, followed by a slam.

Carl Addams ran up to Stanley, "You brought the cops into your fucking house?"

"I-I just made a friend, is all." Stanley's shoulders were to his ears, hands outstretched.

His taller brother turned to me, "You stay out of my business."

I stood up, "I don't know what your business even is. You're making yourself seem suspicious with every word you say. He obviously wasn't expecting you, so what brought you by, Carl?"

"I've got his phone tapped. I know every call he makes." He reached around Stanley to put him in a headlock, "Figured if you were going to be here, I could just stop on by for a visit and let you know in person that you don't go near this family again, if you're nearly as smart as you think you are."

Stanley mumbled out from armpit, "Don't threaten him! Leave us alone!"

Carl let him go, but in a flash grabbed the back of his shorter brother's head and slammed him into the kitchen table.

"Hey! Back off or I call reinforcements," I took a measured step forward with a hand by my inner coat pocket, as though reaching for a gun I did not have on me, "You wanna make this bad? I'm willing."

With that, Carl pushed off of his brother's head, and spit the ground, "I'm watching, listening, all the time. I want you both to know that. I got eyes everywhere." He left.

I lurched forward on the table, "Are you okay? What was that about? Do you need a hospital?" Stanley sat up slowly and wiped the blood from his lips, but a smear stayed plastered to the side of his nose and his cheek.

Another trickle traveled down his chin as he said, "Carl's a monster." He licked the inside of his mouth, wincing at the wound in his cheek, "My teeth are all where they belong. Next time, just meet me at my dad's old place. I'll write it down." He got a pen from a drawer and went to find some paper when we heard the bang outside.

I nodded to him, "I'll go check that out. You wait here."

My bike lay sideways on the pavement, tires slashed. Carl gave me the finger from his open window as he drove away in his oddly cheery looking yellow car.

"I'm so sorry about all of this!" Stanley's voice was cracking and harsh as tears streamed down his face from the doorway, "You're only trying to help me, and look what I got you into! I'll pay for your tires."

His nose was near sideways on his face. I hadn't noticed the damage his brother had done with all the blood coating him before.

"No, no. Don't worry about it, please. I'm okay." I wasn't happy, but there was no reason to take it out on poor Stanley. "I'm just gonna call my buddy for a ride, and maybe we can get you to a doctor to set your nose?"

"Oh, I could at least drive you wherever you've gotta go."

He couldn't know about the farmhouse, "No, really. It's okay. How about we go back inside and have some coffee?"

I texted Jed to let him know the situation, and he was

quick to text back that Chloe would be there to collect me and my, "bike's corpse" soon.

I sat at the table and we both pretended to ignore the tiny blood stain left from where Stanley's cheek was sandwiched between teeth and wood. He looked into a few mugs from his cabinet before he found one clean enough for a guest, then poured me a mug of cold coffee before scrambling to get the sugar and cream.

I took the piece of paper with his father's old address on it, and folded it up to place in my back pocket. We sat with our coffee for a moment.

"So, what's at your dad's place?" I asked.

"There's a box of old files about my step mom, her company, a bunch of stuff. I figured you could see for yourself and pick out whatever might be useful. Might be things you already know, I don't know."

"Fair enough," my thoughts were interrupted by a knock at the door. That was quick.

"Ah! You must be Detective Gekman's ride." Stanley led Liz and Chloe inside.

Chloe grabbed Stanley's chin with one hand to get a better look at him, "Yeah. You know what? We're gonna leave Liz's car with Gekman, and you're gonna come with us and the bike in my vehicle. We'll get you and the bike patched up in no time."

He had no time to disagree as Liz tossed me her keys, and Chloe led him by the arm like he was a delicate elderly grandfather.

Stanley called over his shoulder, "The keys to my dad's place are on the counter there, if you wanna go on without me! I can meet you!"

I took the keys, told Jed where I was going, and got into Liz's car. At the time, I had no concept of what had gone down.

Driving along until a rush of color, bright yellows,

and a blur of the sky and road and the whole world around me spun, alive and lifeless all at once. I saw nothing and felt nothing except that confusing haze ahead of me. The blur found its way inside my skull and inside my stomach and then I wasn't breathing. After a moment, I finally caught up to the pain and hyperventilated, afraid to move.

I tried to piece things together haphazardly from shards of memory mixed with shards of glass and chunks, hunks of car spread crookedly and pained like the side of my body. Everything pulsated and heated itself from an invisible source. I was passing the station when it happened. Being that my light was green, it never occurred to me that I might get hit. I was driving along. I vaguely remember seeing that yellow car, but the assumption was that it was going to slow down at the red light. I didn't think about who could have been driving it. I was still cautious, of course, but then the other car sped up.

A slam. My car jutted to the right. I think I spun. I wasn't sure at that point. Yes. Yes, I must have spun around. The car was turning fast once we had impact. Not quite aware of it all, the airbag punched me angrily in the side, bashing me into the center console. No, I was thrown into the center console, and then to the other side of the vehicle, bouncing around like a rubber ball, or a boneless rag doll. Luckily, I had unbuckled my seat belt while stopped at the previous light, to bend and find my pen.

In a different car, I would have been dead. Crushed. Instead, I was only left thinking I had been crushed. Thankfully, Liz cared about safety over style. I started wheezing. It was a labor to desperately suck in each breath. Winded, my chest felt tight. My ribs expanding to breathe felt like fire in my lungs, as though I had run five miles without stretching. However, this was from having the wind knocked out of me, not from my lungs collapsing nor from the bottom half of my body being severed. I blamed the air bag. I hoped and prayed it was only that. All of these thoughts shot through my head. No. My foot was broken, or shattered, or gone completely. I wasn't sure. A couple ribs were certainly out of commission though. Had anything run me through? I pat myself like I would if checking my pockets for my wallet, but my wrists and shoulders hurt. My eyes closed.

Lights above my eyes blared down as I lay on paper and metal. I had no memory of getting to the hospital, but Jed was there with the note from Stanley in his hand. I mumbled that he should go without me. He shook his head.

Hours later, I opened my eyes to see the ceiling above a hospital bed. I instinctively clicked the button to send a rush of morphine through tubes into my veins. I thought the doctors would need to put my foot back together like some gruesome jigsaw puzzle. Honestly, I assumed I would need a prosthetic. However, my foot wasn't more than badly bruised.

A nurse explained, "You were probably having a panic attack during the incident, especially when you got the wind knocked out of you. The whiplash is real though, and cracked ribs, and when you bashed against something with your foot, your brain decided the worst."

I was thrilled that I was crazy, and found myself stuck on the joyous thought that I'd one day be crunching fallen leaves beneath my feet again. My ribs needed some patching up, but I'd been through that dance before.

Jed was quick to point out, "For once, your car got totaled and it wasn't my fault!"

I was so drugged and immeasurably befuddled that answering him was strictly out of the question. He put his cabbie cap on my head and I felt like I might melt into the bed.

"We got info on the maniac who crashed into you," said Jed.

My eyes rolled in his direction as I mumbled out, "It

was Stanley's brother. Where is he now?"

"He's dead." The nurse took this as her cue to leave the room, and Jed continued, "Carl Addams, brother of Stanley, and son of Eli, like you said. That was all figured out from his license plate. When I found out Liz and Chloe had brought Stanley here to fix his face, I asked him what might have gone down. He told me to find the paper, so I did that."

The back of my hand ached from the IV. I twitched my fingers and said, "Is Stanley still here then?"

"Nah. Liz and Chloe made sure he got his nose lined up, and then dropped him off back home. He wants us to text him when we're going to Eli's place."

"What was Carl's connection to the case at hand? Unfinished business? What's he so afraid of?" Jed shrugged at my questions, and we sat together while I tried my best to take in a few deep breaths.

Once enough of the drugs wore off, I blinked a few times and thanked Maria for coming. Jed had called her while the doctors were looking at me, and she had been there for a couple of hours. I had no memory of any of that.

She made quick work of taking out the day planner from her purse and jotting down a future friend-date with me before she went home. Jed wrote the information on his arm, because he apparently evolved into a human calendar when I wasn't looking. Perhaps he wanted to play secretary.

"Wait, wait," I grabbed Jed's hand, "she's going home? Or the farmhouse?"

"Gekman, Liz is in danger now too. That was her car that got totaled, remember? We don't want any chance of her information getting out. Besides, if more people wanted you dead, you would be. This is not the most secure hospital in the world."

"I don't understand. It's only been like a day?"

Jed shook his head, "Chloe has taken care of the car, and I'm gonna take care of you. We're going to Eli Addams' place later, okay?"

"I can't. I need to stay here."

Jed raised an eyebrow, "It hasn't been a day. It's been many days. You don't have any fucking idea because you kept hitting for that morphine even when the timer was on. It doesn't let you over do it, you know? I got all your new prescriptions and shit. Let's get you on your feet."

He took out my old leg braces from somewhere I couldn't see, stood by the bed, flopped my blanket away, and began to strap in my knee and ankle where they belonged.

Jed gave my leg a gentle pat, "Let's get you dressed, something to eat, and then give Stanley a call. He wants to know how you are after almost going splat." My head was still spinning.

On our way over, we stopped at a new restaurant that was handing out samples of fried chicken. Only a drumstick or so per person, but I wanted it. I wanted that delicious smelling, grease laden poultry with every fiber of my being.

The line was incredibly long, almost going back out the door, and so I looked at the egg-shaped clock on the wall and realized, "I don't have time..."

That smell haunted me, but I had that meeting with Stanley planned. I picked up the phone to call him, but Jed pushed my hand back down.

"Line ain't that long, man. Just chill for a second. How about you sit down over in that booth, and I'm gonna get you something. I'm gonna get you more than a free piece too, cause I treat my dates well, okay?"

The Chicken Palace mascot looked thrilled to be chowing down on his brethren. The glare of the lights bounced from the yellow and white checkered tile floor.

Covers of pop music with the lyrics changed to chicken-related topics blared from tiny speakers from the corners of the ceiling. Behind Jed in line two gentlemen were complaining that it was not yet Winter. One man even sang, "I'm dreaming of a white New Year's... One where I doooooon't have to work tomorrow..."

Something swam inside my skull as I sat down. Food was a good idea. Jed and I were no good at taking care of ourselves, but we were always there for each other.

Poultry was consumed, so number was dialed. I let Stanley know what was going on, and asked if we could still have our chat.

"I'm so glad you're okay."

I could hear him choke back a few shocked tears as I asked, "So you don't know anything about this? Why he did this?"

"I don't. I know he and our step mom had a really disgusting relationship, but I don't think he'd try to kill someone over her. Maybe he would. I don't know, I'm sorry."

"How you feeling about him not making it?" Smooth, Gabe.

"Uh. A lot. I'm feeling a lot of things, including sick. I feel heavy in a weird way. Sometimes I feel nothing. Listen, I can meet you at Dad's old place now."

"We'll be right there." Having failed to chug the rest of my comically large soda, Jed grabbed it to take for the ride.

Jed popped open the glove box to hand me a small flashlight, "Looks like this place is condemned."

"Ah. So, let's not assume electricity. Good call."
He stuck the second flashlight into his pocket.

I snuck a pill from my new prescription and took another gulp of soda from the cup before limping out of the car.

The house was tall and a faint green. The yard was wild, and dotted with roof shingles that had blown off during a heavy storm. Small particles of rot in the old wood plank siding allowed us little glimpses of the inside as we approached. A fearless nest of mice had made a home in a hole in the foundation. Stanley creaked open the heavy wooden door.

"Seriously though, are you okay?" I asked.

Stanley shrugged, looking a little shell shocked, "I don't know. I'm gonna be fine. It's all weird. I keep thinking he's gonna call, but he only ever did that to threaten me anyway. I should be relieved, right?"

"He was still your brother."

"I used to wish almost every night that he wouldn't wake up the next day. I know he did it to himself, but some part of me wonders if I could have saved him."

"There was nothing you could have done differently to change a guy like that."

Stanley nodded as we continued inside. Large windows paved the way for the bright sunlight to illuminate our journey, so there was no need for the flashlights Jed and I had brought. The hallways were lined with photographs each in ornate gold and copper frames. Jed peered behind each one. I'd say that was excessive, but this was a sneaky family. It was a lot of work for him, as the hallway seemed to go on forever. At least it was a reasonably comfortable temperature. Insulation didn't care what the weather was outside in either direction. Then we creaked open the door to the basement.

Stone and cement offered no warmth, and the chill up my spine made me question if the place was haunted as we made our way down the rickety steps.

Our guide found the light switch. When the bare light hanging from the ceiling turned on, Jed looked in the direction of whatever too-many-legged things had scattered.

He said, "So did you guys build this to specifically look like fucking serial killers lived here or what?"

Stanley shrugged and titled his head like it was a distinct possibility.

I asked, "Wait. Why does that light still work?"

"Battery," replied Stanley frankly. "Even without paying for electric, parts of this house will still turn on for a bit. Probably not long though. Who knows when that light was replaced. Didn't matter upstairs, right? Had plenty of daylight. Here, not so much."

There were tiny flat windows close to the ceiling, and little light got through them and the overgrown shrubs outside. The basement air was cold and damp enough to chill my bones. There were square patches of brown rugs now and then, half buried under cardboard boxes, and plastic shelves overloaded with records, VHS tapes, and more boxes. The rugs were clearly meant for standing on with bare feet, but I reckoned that was back when there was any heat in the house. A once white washer and dryer could be found off in a corner, both dented like they'd been thrown into place. More boxes leaned precariously in piles nearby. There was a drain off in the far corner that may have been there to prevent flooding, and clearly hadn't helped much in the past. Cobwebs like intricate, dusty lace took up the upper corners of the room. Spiders, silverfish, and house centipedes ruled this place, occasionally becoming curious enough for a lean-in and peek, then scurrying away again.

"So, where's that box of files, Stanley?" I asked, realizing we hadn't had much conversation since our arrival.

His eyes glazed over as he pointed to a square of floor devoid of dust, "It would have been right there. The fuck did Carl do? Well, there might be other stuff my brother might have left, right?"

"I don't know. What else do you think is down here?"

"Uh, we used to get bored and mess with company stuff as kids. He was in the basement for a long time, so I don't know if he hid anything. The only thing I knew for sure about was that box, and now that's gone. I'm so sorry."

I pursed my lips, then asked, "Was he stuck down here?"

Stanley shrugged again like it was nothing, "Dad was a little intense with his punishments sometimes, yeah."

"You said the box was of stuff about your stepmother, right?"

"Well, about the company. It was a lot of hospital records." Jed froze and didn't move again until I took another obvious breath, at which point, he resumed his search. He started looking through mildewed papers and photo albums when he noticed a torn piece of cardboard seemingly hovering slightly over the floor. The end of it was tucked into where the concrete floor separated from the stone wall, causing it to stick out straight to the side. Partially stuck-melted into it was a small wax mold.

"What's this key?" Jed asked, holding up his finding. It was indeed an outline of a key.

"Oh shit." Stanley said it quietly, though he may have been screaming inside his head. "That would have been the key to the files room. All the keys were buried or destroyed, I think. Why would Dad have that thing?"

I said, "He might have had it as a backup plan, especially if this is the key to something that could have been used as blackmail."

"It's an imprint of the key? What's it for?"

Jed walked up to us with the cardboard held aloft, "It's a mold! A locksmith can take this and make a key. Look, it's even got the indents and shit. This is detailed."

Stanley slowly moved toward Jed, "You call me

when you've got that made. Or... Or don't, actually. Oh Jesus. I don't think I can do this anymore, you know?"

"Hey," I put my hand on his shoulder, "It's okay. Can you tell us where the filing room is? Once we know that, we can get out of your hair."

"It's written somewhere at my house. I can't... I don't know. I can't think anymore today. I'm sorry I can't help you more tonight."

"You've done plenty. You go on home, okay? Don't worry about any of this."

"I'll find that address for you. I have to. I'm still complicit."

"What do you mean?" asked Jed.

"I knew. I knew what everyone was doing. I always knew. I was just too much of a coward to do anything." Stanley sniffed and turned to leave.

We followed, and Jed called for his favorite locksmith. He was in, and it would be a while to get the key from this piece of wax. Jed left it with the locksmith, then went back to my place.

Jed was quick to fall asleep on my couch in the living room, while I took the longest, hottest bath of my life. I wanted to bake away the intensity of my day. Or life, I don't know. When I was done, I took a pill, wrapped myself in my bathrobe, waddled to the bedroom, and then lay under the covers naked, staring at the ceiling. I may have slept for a couple hours total that night.

The kitchen tile was a biting cold against my bare feet in the morning. I was never a fan of its randomly placed flower pattern growing up. As an adult I found myself counting the few watercolor violets scattered among the floor in the dim daylight for comfort.

The sunrise lazily trickled in from beyond my new magenta curtains. I had opened the window above the sink just enough for gentle gusts of wind to dance gracefully with the lacy trim.

My eyelids felt heavy as I turned my head to the stove clock and tried to make out how few hours I'd actually slept through the night.

Jed yawned in the doorway and held up his phone, "Locksmith. Guy has it. Let's get you dressed and we'll go to Stanley for more info on what the fuck file-room-whatever this is for."

Every breeze reminded me of how much I looked forward to Summer. While I thrived in the sweltering heat, Jed complained of "swamp ass" and I avoiding asking what that meant.

On the way to our meet up with Stanley, I complained of wanting more fried chicken. I had never stopped being in the mood for it. I wanted the grease to line my veins. Jed pulled up to the drive through window, gave our clear chicken-related orders, had them repeated back to us to be sure, and then went around to the next window to pay, and collect said food. Simple enough.

Jed opened his bag and was pleased to find exactly what he was expecting. I opened my bag and peered inside.

"What is this?" I was flabbergasted.

With a mouthful of God-knows-what, Jed pointed knowingly at the bag as he expressed, "The Tiki Taco fun pack. Hmm. That wasn't what I ordered."

I stared into the bag as I said, "How did this even happen?" We didn't have time to complain, so I ate my taco in silence and we were off.

The walkway up to the house looked the same as before, but now-dead flowers in cracked terracotta pots lined the right side of the steps up to the porch.

Ginger's cheeks were still stained with mascara tears when she answered the door, "Oh, you're the detective, right?" Her flushed and goose-bumped skin made a pattern not unlike that of fancy hotel toilet paper on her shoulders and upper arms. It was clear she was coming down from giving herself stress hives.

"Are you all right? May I speak with Stanley?"

"He's dead. He fucking killed himself! He told me his asshole brother went after you. He started falling apart right after Carl died." She broke off into more sobs and mumbling that must have been words, but I couldn't understand any of it. After some time of letting her cry, she finally became coherent once again.

She said, "I'll give you whatever you need, but then I never want to see you again, okay? Come in."

The first room of the house after the garishly bare front foyer was the kitchen. A wooden chair gave a sad sort of squeak as I sat down. The refrigerator was a dirty pinkish beige. I wasn't sure if that was supposed to be its color and I simply hadn't noticed before, or if something had managed to spill all over the poor appliance.

The can of tomato soup was no longer within the pantry. Instead, there were papers crumpled and crammed in among books. The kitchen table was the same, though still placed dead center in that kitchen, now acting as both eating apparatus and preparation dock. Its thin, fancy legs seemed to buckle under the weight of the sheer amount of useless crap perched upon its scratched up back. Old school papers, empty shoe boxes, tissues, both used and not, food waiting to be found and thrown out, wrappers, empty cans, light bulbs, empty cups, dusty fabric flowers, something that may have been a wooden sculpture of a squirrel, and a small scrap of leather all sat upon this poor, defenseless piece of furniture.

"Stanley had been going through things like an animal, tearing everything up trying to find something for you," Ginger didn't look me in the eye. "Any idea what it was?"

"An address," I kept my voice quiet and calm. "He said there was an address for a family filing room. I don't know where it would have been."

She flipped through a few things on the table, then moved to the cabinet.

She sighed and said, "He blamed himself for your bike, for Carl's death, for everything. He went down and dragged our home down along with him."

Barely above a whisper, she said, "I'm still here."

We didn't stay in the kitchen long. We were herded into a much more pleasant living room, onto a couch set of brown leather.

She put her hands out as through ready to catch one of us running, "Just hang out here for a second. I have an idea where the stupid paper might be. The album may have other things you want to know too."

She turned, then came back to add, "I'm sorry I was rude before. I've been under a lot of stress. Please make yourselves comfortable. Those seats recline." She left to go upstairs before I could tell her it was okay.

Jed quickly set about reclining the end seat. I attempted and failed to do the same, then folded my hands in my lap as though the ridiculous show of a struggle hadn't happened, like a cat missing the jump to a counter. After one try, I should have stopped trying. The same went for Jed. He managed to succeed, in his own way. He may have clumsily broken it, as witnessed by the audible snap, but the seat reclined none the less.

Ginger came back down the stairs and sat down across from us to sprawl the evidence around the octagon coffee table. Beneath the glass surface sat a metal sculpture of the title character from Fiddler on the Roof, and a copy of "Edgar Allan Poe Classic Tales of Terror".

Jed and I each took sheets as she handed them to us,

continually looking down at the album. We began to furrow our brows as we saw more and more horrendous things. We looked through photos and read journal entries. Soon, one glaring, repeating thing poked through into our conscious minds.

"Black and Carl were fucking? He was her stepson! What the fuck?" Jed was the first to say it out loud, but we all had gathered this information.

Ginger sighed and said, "After she killed Eli... Well, Stanley and Carl both knew. The difference was that Stanley hated her for it and wanted her taken down. Carl wanted her for himself. Then when Stanley was finally getting close to finding out where she was, Carl started threatening him. Fuck... The bastard kind of won, huh?" She started to cry again. I reached out a hand to put on her shoulder but Jed pushed my hand down. I didn't know her well enough for that.

She almost handed me a crumpled piece of paper, but snatched it back to rub it against the table in an attempt to flatten it out, then folded it neatly before handing it to me.

"This should be it," she said, "at least, I think so. The filing room. Do you want to just keep this album, actually? I kind of hate it."

"How did you know it would be in here?" I asked.

"I didn't know. I'm not even sure what I handed you was right. I just know this album has stuff specific to his step mom. If I'd known what he was looking for, I could have helped him. He wouldn't tell me."

Jed leaned forward and took the album, noting a photo of a house we hadn't seen before.

"Oh," said Ginger, "that was her place before she met Eli. It's been converted into a little shop now." She rubbed her palm with her other hand's thumb and said, "Could you guys, like, leave now? I'm sorry, but I just can't do this anymore."

"That's okay," I said. "Thank you for all your help."

Jed and I left for the car with few words between us. My back below my right shoulder blade was throbbing and stabbing, as though part of my ribcage was trying to escape. Was this a heart attack? I took a pill.

"You're not having a heart attack. You're just all stressed out," Jed replied to the question I had not said out loud. I guess he knew me pretty well.

"Okay. So how do I de-stress before I die?"

He started the car and began to drive as he said in a drone, "You call Hudson. You give him the addresses, the key, all of it. You walk the fuck away before I have to bury my best fucking friend. Let him do his job."

I did as instructed on the way to my place, which meant Jed doing a U-turn to meet up with Hudson instead. I could feel my veins twitch. My blood felt thick.

Hudson's office was stuffy and warm. The hum of his computer acted as a white noise machine while I zoned out in a chair. He painstakingly went over every piece of information before glancing in my direction.

"Gabe? Gekman, you okay over there?" I didn't answer, but I opened my eyes to look at him. He nodded, then turned his computer screen to face me.

Jed said, "So, you figured out what this address is?"

"Yeah, and the way this building is laid out," he pointed to a blueprint, "I think this could very well be your filing room."

I lifted myself to standing and said, "So that's where we go."

"Only because your boys in blue won't do shit," said Jed.

Hudson turned to face Jed, "What was that?"

"If the guys who actually still work here did their fucking jobs, Gekman could move on with his damn life."

"Well, I won't argue with that."

I looked back and forth between the two of them, "Wait, what?"

The drive was quiet. Jed and I were in our usual positions, this time trailing behind Hudson's lead. I didn't feel like talking.

Once we found our destination, Hudson got out of his vehicle and stood in front of the dilapidated building, arms crossed, but with a calm smile on his face. Stern yet comforting.

The key weighed heavy in my hand. Would answers about Abby reside inside whatever this key fit? Yet another door left unopened, at least for me. Forever closed in every sense, but it needed to be, for my sake. What would happen if I let that dam break? Not the end of the world, but the end of mine. The end of my everything, it felt.

I tugged on Hudson's sleeve like a child desperately trying to get his mother's attention at a crowded party.

He turned with scrunched confusion in his eyebrows but accepted with little choice as I grabbed his hands and shoved the key into his palm half-frantic, attempting to bury it, make it disappear, make my memory of my life without my sister go away forever so I could pretend that I listened sooner and saved her.

Hot tears streamed down from my burning, salted eyes. I let out no sound. Hudson managed to pry a hand away from my vice grip to put an arm around my shoulder.

"It's okay, Gabe. Son? You listen to me. This isn't your problem anymore. You're done. Everything is over now. We'll take it from here. I'll take it. It's okay."

I took a pill as soon as we got back into the car. Jed had been buried in his phone for a bit with the car still parked before he announced we were to visit Chloe's garage. More errands to run. He was set on distracting me when all I wanted to do was crawl up in a sad little ball on my bathroom tile. A day of mindless chores to fill my empty head seemed better than wallowing, though it would amount to about the same.

Chloe had what was left of Liz' car splayed out like an autopsy on the lift.

"Yeah," she said to Nick, ex-Denny-goon, more than me, "this is dead. There's no bringing this car back."

He gestured loosely to the car, "We scrapping any of this?"

"Yep! Franken-mobile it is." She turned to face me, "Liz already knows she's getting paid for the parts, of course."

"She must hate me," I said.

"She doesn't. I'm surprised this wasn't a total loss, actually. It's not like you were on her insurance."

"Well, I would hate me."

"You know, you wouldn't need a car if you lived in Cornsbrook."

I sucked in gas-flavored air, "Why would I ever live in Cornsbrook?"

Nick answered meekly as he casually gathered his long, thin dreadlocks into a neat ponytail, "So you wouldn't need a car?" I was a touch jealous of his hair, but not enough to fully distract from my ribcage, Liz's car, unanswered questions about my sister, my leg acting up, and my general being-surrounded-by-death. Also, Nick hanging out with Chloe put me on edge whenever the back of my mind brought up how he shot at me when we first met.

I placed my forehead against Jed's enormous

shoulder in exasperation.

It was two days later and I'd been careful to send every scrap of information I had to Hudson and his team.

We stepped out of Jed's car. The trees leading up to the office looked as though their branches were long fingers holding flowering rings as the wind bristled throughout the leaves. Shadows danced on the brick face of our establishment. Jed let me go in first, citing that he had to get something from the car.

Moving felt like floating in the least pleasant way. Sitting at my desk was worse. God, my back hurt. It was sort of a cold pain, starting at the back of my neck going upward into the underside of my skull, then back down my spine, curling under my shoulder blade. I tried stretching out my shoulders to alleviate it, only to clench my jaw, causing the pain to travel there instead, like a beacon, spreading within my cheekbone. It was like I had been chewing my own teeth. How much was from the wreck, and how much was from the case? I took a pill.

Ghostly afterthoughts danced behind my eyes too fast to catch and hold one. I was having trouble moving forward in every conceivable sense. I wanted to function. I did, yet there was nothing but the ability to sit in that chair and have thoughts without thinking. The dissolving pill pushed the pain down.

"Have you tried yoga?" Jed asked me as he opened the door to come in.

"What?"

"Look I get that you're tense for good reasons, but like, you're always tense."

I was flabbergasted, "This coming from you."

He handed me a CD with the words, "Morning Meditation" written in marker, and took a seat on the old, peeling wooden chair after he swung it over, closer to me.

"I've been trying everything," he said. "But this shit is good. It's not fucking curing me, but it's really good for my back and shoulders."

I said nothing as my eyebrow twitched in response.

"It's relaxing. Like you fucking need, you living blue raspberry." He smiled, patting me on the back.

He was right, of course. As much as I hated to admit it. He was there for my calm in high school, and now it was only storm, with me drowning on a ship I had shoddily built on my own. I felt like my life was going by too fast, and too much was happening. Black, Abby, my love life, the pain, my memories.

I wanted a pause button on the world, even when we had nothing left to do. I felt my life ticking down a day at a time, then suddenly a week, three months, five years. I wanted it all to stop, but the fear of everything stopping was crippling. I didn't want to die, and I missed thinking there was something after. I believed in such a thing as a child, and I wanted to know my sister was safe somewhere, even when my faith had been stripped away long ago. I felt my heartbeat thumping unsteadily inside my right ear.

My eyes glazed over and I forced myself to blink out of it.

"Yeah," said Jed. "We both need some help, eh?"

He laughed awkwardly, "Darcy joked that she was gonna get Chloe to put a tracker on my car, just to make sure I don't go to as many bars! Like I wouldn't immediately bitch about that forever. Besides, you're always gonna be with me wherever we go, bar or not. I know you ain't gonna do therapy any more than I am. We're both too stubborn for that."

He pointed at the CD case in my hand. I'd officially worried Jed to this point. That wasn't a good sign.

"You really want me to try this out, huh?"

Jed nodded slowly, almost glaring into my eyes, "At home. We got no reason to still be here, Gekman. Case is closed, far as we're concerned. Let's get you home. I don't know why you even wanted to come into the office again. Hudson's got it covered, you're just still obsessed. It's ain't healthy."

"I thought I needed to solve the case."

"You're solving a bunch of ca-"

"I want Abby back."

"Oh." Jed leaned against my desk and we were quiet like that for a moment.

I placed the CD inside the black leather briefcase I could use again, now that any files I'd need to take back and forth from the office were no longer only in big carboard boxes.

My phone rang, so I said to Jed, "Speak of the devil, right?" and answered the phone, "Hey, Hudson."

"I'm sorry to bother you like this, but any chance you could come to the station to answer a few questions? Nothing serious, it's just that you've talked to all these people already, and I'm having trouble making heads or tails outta your notes."

"Because he scrawled it all down like a fucking lunatic writing with his own shit on the walls, right?" said Jed. Hudson chuckled, didn't disagree.

"Our young Officer Kells could use a hand." I wasn't sure what Hudson was asking of me, but we left to go back to work once again.

I opened Jed's passenger side door to a cascade of tumbling aluminum cans spilling from within.

I looked at him through the car, "You're not driving while drinking, are you?"

"Yeah I- Wait, no. Not beer. That's all iced tea."

I picked up a can and tilted it to get a look inside with the sunlight, "It's... very purple."

"Yeah there's cactus in it. Anyway, get in the car. We'll do the recycling later."

A kind of punk-pop song played from the radio, and some of the dirtier lyrics made me think of Maria. Somehow, that didn't bring the usual smile to my face. Nothing seemed to anymore.

We walked briskly down the corridor as men with a mission. A maybe college-aged kid came out of one of the rooms, probably there for something minor, and he stopped in front of me. He fingered his hat and shouted, "See, I got a fedora too, Hot Shot!"

"First of all, that's a trilby, not a fedora. Second, what the Hell are you doing wearing even that atrocity without a proper shirt? You look like an idiot." I kept walking, trying to keep my cool, regardless of the fact that I was clearly not-cool.

Jed noticed that I was incensed and laughed at me.

I said to Jed, "My hat is wool, and has a wide brim similar to something a classic detective from the old movies might wear. This is *not* to be confused with a pork pie hat or a homburg or even a trilby. Such a thing is a perversion of a fedora that is shorter brimmed, less classy and generally worn by awful men, such as the one worn by *that* jerk."

Jed continued to laugh. I suppose mine was shaped more like what you might call a "mountain fedora" anyway. Not the point.

There was always a package of donuts outside the courtroom on a little table.

"Way to live up to the stereotype," said Jed as he heartily patted officer Oliver Kells on the back. Kells was a thin enough man that he could've used a donut. He was shoving them into his face as though he hadn't eaten in days, and by how lanky he was, that was believable.

Kells bent down and rubbed his knee before taking another donut.

"Are you okay?" I asked.

"Minor surgery. I mean, I'm fine. People blow it out of proportion." It seemed he was determined to prove himself as more than just the new guy. It had already been a year, but he was going to be the "new guy" until a newer new guy or gal joined the force.

Hudson entered the scene from around the corner and swooped up a donut like a hawk grabs a field mouse.

"Hey!" Kells pointed at me, "You guys wanna come to the bar with the guys and me tomorrow night? It'll be fun!"

Jed tapped me on the shoulder and said, "Nah man. You got a playdate with Maria. This is technically the make-up date, remember?"

I had not, in fact, remembered. He went on to explain that I had outright ditched her a couple months back, after making a big deal about a date with her. I had no recollection of this at all, but I believed him.

As we followed Hudson into a conference room, we could hear the other cops explaining that they don't really invite me places and for Kells not to do it again. They were laughing, and this was clearly meant for me to hear as a joke, but I still felt the sting of it. They hurried up to join us in the too small room with a too large table. We crammed in around it and spent the next few hours going over everything that had happened.

"So, you got into a wreck and then got right up again to tell us this stuff about Black and Carl Addams. You must have been working off straight adrenaline, right?" Kells wiped some crumbs from his pointy chin and raised his eyebrows.

"Yeah, I'm fine. Exhausted. I mean, there was time spent in a hospital in between."

A woman I didn't recognize said, "Gekman, you're not on this case anymore, right? Or is it different with you being a PI?" I couldn't tell if that was sarcasm, so I shrugged.

Jed piped up, "We're already in it from a previous case, so it's easy for us to get information you don't have access to. Then we pass it along to you guys, who can't even call in a bomb squad when we need one."

Her lips tightened and nearly disappeared like she had tasted something sour. No one defended that lack of help, but no one said things would change either.

"He's not wrong," said Hudson. "Plus, I like keeping Gabe close to make his return go smoothly." I wanted to interrupt, but he continued, "Besides, Kells could use a new mentor when I retire."

Oh. Kells and I shared a concerned look. Neither of us signed up for that.

The rest of that day and well into the next night was spent trying to inform everyone of what we could.

Groggy and exhausted, everyone began to file out of the room to go home. Once Jed, Hudson, and I were the only ones left, I took a pill, then got up to use the bathroom.

"Wait a second," said Jed. "How many did you take today?"

"How many what?"

"How many pills?"

"I'm okay," I continued my way to the bathroom, fully aware that I'd have to take care of the pain away from prying eyes from then on.

I heard yelling echoing through the hallway upon my return, and caught Jed stomping away from Hudson.

"What was that about?" I asked.

"Just shut up and get in the car."

CHAPTER 23
Mistakes Were Made

Another day was spent pouring over files with Hudson, trying to decipher my own notes, and coming up with a terrible plan to move forward with a case that was stuck in concrete.

I crawled back to my house and found Maria in her car outside. I had forgotten about a date with her, and then forgotten about the make-up date. This meant that I effectively stood her up twice.

She rolled down her window, and I said, "I've got a lot going on."

Sitting with her arms folded, she looked away from me, "Yeah. I get that. We've been through that."

I opened up her car door and she continued to sit still. "Please come inside?" I gestured to my front door. She didn't move.

I got into the passenger seat and immediately started talking, "It's just a lot to also be thinking of ways to see you on top of a case." Who was I kidding? There was no case. The case was me lingering at the police station, thinking about my sister, although I was too afraid to say so.

Maria, still physically balled up, said, "You're busy, and so you don't want to care about me, or are you saying you don't have the capacity to do so?"

"I care, and you said we're not a couple. Right? Isn't this why?" This was exactly the wrong thing to say.

She turned to me and if her arms hadn't still been folded, chances were that she would have been strangling me. "Yeah, but I still need consistency and support and fucking friendship."

I dug my arm under hers so we'd be arm-in-arm, "You're still my friend, even if I can't always be around for the support part."

"Then don't call me your friend!" She tore her arm away from mine, reached over me to open the door, and pushed me out. I got up, closed the passenger door for her, and she drove off.

I sat on my porch to call Jed.

"How'd your date go?" he asked before giving a hello.

"Yeah. About that."

"You forgot."

"I forgot."

"Have you spoken to her yet?"

"She's mad."

Jed sighed with his whole chest, "Okay. Let's assume you're single forever and should be out drinking." He was sort of understanding to a point. He could tell I was upset, at least.

"I can't drink if I'm taking pain killers. Should I go after her?"

"Stop taking the pills." Jed sighed, "If she's gone this time, she's gone. You weren't great for her anyway. I mean, I love you man, but I wouldn't fucking date you. You're kind of a prick to girlfriends."

"Thanks." I let my shoulders glide up to my ears.

"No, seriously. She is way too good for you. I love you though."

"Right."

"I'm gonna go to your place."

I shook my head, "Nah. We'd plop ourselves down at my kitchen table as we would waiting like bait in the water in any bar, but there's no fish poking around in my house."

"You're thinking of getting laid right now? The fuck is wrong with you?"

"I'm just lonely."

"Gekman, I already screamed at Hudson to let you the fuck go. I'll do the same to anyone who enables you with this bullshit."

"What did you say to Hudson?"

"The truth, but if you were there all day enough to forget your date, he obviously didn't fucking listen to me. He wants you back as a cop, and he'll keep you stuck to Black and all this horseshit until you give in."

"You make Hudson sound really callus, Jed."

"He's not. He thinks he's doing good by you, but I know you. I know it ain't right."

I took in a breath, "I want to call Maria."

"Get your bike. Chloe said it's all good to go. It's back in front of your garage, right? Get on that, get to Maria's place, say you're sorry. But do not go back to dating. Christ. I don't like being the rational one, man. Don't make me be this."

"Okay." I half listened.

Instead, I called Maria and said, "I'm sorry. Please meet me at our usual spot. I swear to God I'll show up. I'm leaving now."

I didn't give her time to answer before I hung up. It was a dick move on my part, and I wasn't going to be angry if she left me hanging. It would have been only right. I hummed songs of drowning, and I hopped on my bike. It felt like forever to the restaurant.

I adjusted my tie as I entered, and to my amazement, there she was at our booth. The conversation went back and forth through heavy waters and light fluffy passes. I was beginning to get sea sick. We discussed the matter of whether or not I could call her mine again.

She responded with her arms folded, "I'd rather not."

"I understand. I know I'm a mess." This got a laugh out of her, but she was still clearly unhappy with me.

It was a bitter, cold laugh, without pity.

She laced her fingers together on the table, "Well, if we're going to be only friends, at least that makes it easier for me to also help you in your work, right?"

I was quick with information I hadn't told Jed about yet, "Fact is, I'm about to leave for Newsburg again, to gather up some missed pieces connecting Rayne and Black. It's only an hour or so away, but you aren't going to be joining us, if I have any say in the matter. Too dangerous."

That fact made her even more upset.

Calmly, direct and stern, she stated, "I'm going to the bathroom and I'm going to stay there until I cool down enough not to hate you with every fiber of my being." The door to the restroom acted more like the door to an old saloon, swinging loosely back and forth.

The toilet paper holder squeaked like a mouse caught in a trap. Maria winced at this, then played games as she sat there, making up stories about the graffiti. "Clearly, Mindy loves David because of that one night in Soho," and so on. It only took her about eight minutes before she became bored enough to come back to the table. Over the years, I'd found that Maria was actually easy to please. She had simple needs and she was direct about them. I was just an idiot.

"I'm sorry," I said again.

"I'm sorry I came here. Are we going to order food, or can I leave?"

I bit my lip, "I'm going to leave a tip whether we have more than water or not."

She took a seat, "Go talk to Rayne again before shuffling off on a wild goose chase fueled by family drama."

"Call Liz," I answered.

"I'm going to, but understand that I've made my choice. She's kind to me, and she makes me happy."

I nodded while making a job out of folding a napkin into a frog. Maria reached over to tilt my chin with her finger so that I'd look her in the eyes, "She's grateful when I do things for her, and she's everything I wanted you to be. You could have been all of that, and you chose not to, and you know? That's fine. Be my friend."

"I will."

She dropped her hand when I stood at attention, "I think you could be a good friend if I'm not delegated to girlfriend. We can't sleep together ever again. Okay?"

She smiled, and I tried to mimic that. Mine was more of a grimace. I was thankful that she didn't hate me.

"Hey," I held her hand. "Rayne knew Denny. Did you know Rayne?"

"Kind of. Not enough to be helpful, but that's why I'm pushing you to talk to him, yeah."

"Fair enough."

I got home and called Jed to tell him about the plan I'd made with Hudson earlier that day.

"So, you're heading to Newsburg to go to the prison?" he said.

"Well, we are, right?"

"I'm not. You and Rayne have a whatever-the-fuck with each other. You go, but take my car. It's still afternoon, but if you're there late enough, you'll be safer if you're driving a car than if you're riding a bike."

"You've been extremely calm lately. Are you okay?"

"I'm trying to drink less, and I'm bad at it. Take your bike here, trade it for my car, stop asking me questions."

Since we hadn't ordered any food, I made myself some twice baked potatoes before heading out.

Jed's car smelled fruity, like citrus. I did my best to concentrate on the smell and not my racing heart.

After a series of additional psychological tests, Rayne had not been considered sick enough in a clinical sense to be an inmate at Cornsbrook Asylum. Instead, he had been shipped off to Newsburg Penitentiary, which made him nice and close to me. He would be behind bars, and I had already spoken to him with nothing to hold him back, so why did this feel so much more gruesome? I took a pill.

The prison was a brutalist concrete block on a hill surrounded by marshland. Some part of me wondered if it was possible for a visitor to get lost inside and never escape. Gates led to more gates, and finally an officer waved me in from his little security booth. Our eyes met through smudged and fingerprinted bullet proof glass. I saw the bitter silhouette of faces along the walls where cobwebs cast their shadows from the LED light inside.

After a series of metal detectors, doors, and glares from hundreds of prisoners stacked in barred boxes up three stories, high windows meant light dipped its way through the otherwise grungy darkness of the prison. The illumination gently touched all it could, which was not much, caressing the cells as it went by. The shining, silver gleam of the bars sparkled in a way to make the whole place less daunting, like an angler fish. I knew what teeth sat in waiting beyond that light. Each step forward felt heavy, like pushing through mud. Shaking it off, I sucked in a breath, pulling my shoulders back until my steps were sure and weightless.

My spine filled with cement. In what way was he more intimidating behind bars? Different context, and more jeering and howling. The men there could smell my fear, and their animosity toward me was palpable. My hat and coat had been removed at the entry point. I felt naked and exposed. His energy felt more malicious than ever.

Rayne had his own too-small sink next to the toilet. He was awkwardly bent over it and washing his face, then stopped, sensing me behind him. He used his undershirt to dry off before peeling away the shirt entirely. It was tight on him anyway. Rayne didn't say anything to me, but sat down on his cot and looked at me with no expectations of anything in his face.

After all our previous interactions, I started with all I could think of, "Did you know Black's step son killed himself recently? Apparently, Stanley was too overcome with everything his family had done. And his brother Carl tried to kill me with a car before that. He died in that crash. I obviously survived. I'm wondering how much of what Black was doing you even knew about." This piqued his interest.

After lifting himself from his cot and sauntering over to the bars, he grinned. The intimidating spell broke despite the hulking way he held himself.

"You have survived much, have you not?" Rayne's voice sounded like his throat was feeling better, "I find myself impressed. How did you endure this crash?"

"I was driving Liz's car. You know, the person you get those little machine parts from."

"You destroyed that nice young lady's car?" He laughed, "What did she ever do to you? Oh, but tell me she is all right." He listened intently like a psychologist who was honestly interested in a client's tale.

"She wasn't in the car at the time, and it got all handled by a friend. No long-term harm done, except to Carl. I spent some time in a hospital for it, but I'm mostly put back together now."

"Ah. I am thankful for that." His eyes showed more concern than I expected.

My training left me with the often-distracting ability to notice a myriad of facts and features about an individual, physical and otherwise, while speaking to that person. On some level, this may have been what left me so jittery with Maria. She was harder to read.

Rayne held his whole life on his sleeve, yet said nothing about it. He accepted it all in a sad way. It's not that he had given up, but more that he did not seem to know that there was any other choice for him. It was as though he thought his life was being written, directed, and decided for him. His old wound along the left side of his face went along with a very faint scar I hadn't noticed before on the right side of his forehead. His shaggy blue hair hid dark sideburns and was far dingier than mine in color, not as kept up. This was saying something considering what mine had become. His black roots showed through. I knew blue was not an easy color to keep on one's head, and I wondered how long this had been a hairstyle for him, but this was not going to be part of the conversation. His eyes were dark like Maria's.

I noticed a recent wound on his upper left arm and asked, "Where did you get that?" It looked like a claw mark, and by how Rayne kept his nails, it could have been his own doing.

He turned his head towards that shoulder, not really looking at it as he grumbled, "Does not matter." Then he looked at me again to ask, "Do you know why Carl tried to kill you?"

"Not really. He was sleeping with Candice Black at some point, so prevailing theory is that I pose a threat to her. I was only talking to Stanley at all because he had an idea of where she might be, or where some of her files would be. We also found an album with some photos of an old house of hers, which the police I'm working with might go check out for clues of some kind, but who knows?" Rayne tilted his head back in thought, though the pain from his throat showed in his tightly closed eyes and tense cheeks as he did so.

He said gruffly, "I would tell you where she was if I knew, though I will admit, if she told me to kill you, I probably would."

"Oh, come on," I tried to laugh it off, "we've got a rapport going on here, don't we?"

"I am not joking; I do like you. Truly I do, but I would without question. I am sorry." He rubbed his chin with two fingers, "And I think if Stanley knew where she was, chances are pretty good that Candice knows he knew. The fact that you found all that shit out about Carl and Candice is also pretty interesting, so I am assuming the wrong people were talking to you. That, or whoever decided to let you in on it was stupid."

He cocked his head to the side, head down enough to be looking up at me under his almost always furrowed brow. "Perhaps they thought *you* were stupid." He lifted his eyebrow in a fairly sassy fashion. Was he being funny? He looked like he was waiting for me to say something clever, but I had nothing.

I looked at that recent wound on his upper left arm again. He put his other hand over it, then sort of rolled back to his cot and sat down with that arm away from me, as though I'd forget what I had already seen.

He sat propped up with his back to me. "You should not worry about me, detective." He took in a deep breath and then said, "I will not be here much longer." He curled up, as though trying to physically hold himself together.

I mumbled something about staying safe and turned to go. Rayne's expression changed as though no one in the world had ever voiced concern for him before.

He blurted out, "She is not there anymore. Your officers would be looking in the wrong place." He resembled a little boy trying to explain that it was the neighbor's kid who broke the window instead of him. "She had a lot of places, and that one is not even a house anymore. You will see."

He took in a breath to collect himself back inside his cool exterior, "Do not waste the time."

I nodded and thanked him and almost left. Something kept me there for a moment.

"What do you see in her anyway?" I asked.

Rayne's right eyebrow shot up as though it was the only part of his face I had startled. Then he laughed heartily while clutching his throat.

"You never had a girl who was bad for you?"

I shrugged and said, "My girl was far too good for me. I felt guilty even having her, and eventually she got tired of my bullshit and left." I don't know why I told him that.

Maria was hardly ever mine. Most people who dealt with me on a regular basis got tired of me after a while, save for Jed.

Rayne laughed again. It was a knowing laugh this time.

"Well, I do not have that with Candice," He slumped a bit on his cot, turning to have his legs swing over the edge and grabbing the cot cushion with his hands on either side. He looked at me again, "But I did have it with someone. Once, a long time ago." He looked at the wall opposite him as if staring into a mirror, but there wasn't one there.

"What happened?" I stepped forward again, wanting to go into the cell.

I couldn't tell if he was answering me or muttering to himself as he said, "I wanted her to tell me to come home."

"Who was she? Someone you lived with?"

"It does not matter now, but no. We were living together in the sense that she was in my heart, a part of me," he put his fingertips against his chest, then curled them into a fist, "but no. We did not share a lease. It did not matter where she lived. Whatever street she walked, wherever she had her coffee in the morning, that was my home. She was my home."

His hand fell to his lap as his already protruding jaw went out a little more in a pout, "I wanted her to tell me to come home. I wanted her to ask me to be with her again, where I belonged. I waited. It was a mistake to wait, but she did not want me anymore. I changed for her and became this monster, you know? And then she did not want me once I was broken like this. Now she is gone from my life, and so there is something missing that I will never get back." He sniffed without tears, letting his head hang down away from me. "At least I know she is safe. In the end of it, all I wanted was for her to be safe."

I didn't know what else to say besides, "I'm sorry."

His eyes dragged along the floor, his head slowly following suit up the wall and finally towards me, then back at the wall again, "Candice. She is not too good for me. She is not good at all, and I know that, but it is company. I know what I am." Then he once again pointed his gaze at me and said sharply, "Sounds like you know what you are too."

There wasn't much else to say at that point when I saw him getting up again.

He walked back over to the bars and put his arm up to brace himself as he said, "What do you do for this girl of yours? This woman. What would you do? Would you die for her?"

I felt my stomach make a run for my throat as I answered, "Do you do anything out of love anymore, or are you just lonely?"

He did not respond the way I thought he would. He looked deep in contemplation and sad. His eyes were focused on a crack in the floor and I got as close as I could, my face twisted with some strange worry. I put a hand on the bars, as if trying to comfort the metal, and then shot backwards into a rigid standing position when Rayne snapped into a growl.

His fist clenched above his head, the bar leaving a mark in his forearm as he pressed hard against it, putting all his weight into it. Through gritted teeth and a snarl he spat out, "Say it. Come on!"

Not knowing what he wanted me to say, I stood my ground and waited for him to fill in his own blanks. He didn't seem to be asking about my love life anymore. I wanted to put my hands in my pockets to find a toothpick, but the guards had taken my coat along with anything pointy. I didn't want to come across as flippant anyway. Instead, I stood in silence, thumbs hooked, resting on the edge of my pants pockets. Rayne's Romanesque face softened at my complete lack of outward response, then hardened again in a confused anger, perhaps even a mock anger in an effort to intimidate me. It was working, but I couldn't let him know that. He took in a deep breath through his nose, rolling his shoulders as he did so, then cracked his neck as much as he could without hurting himself.

He spoke again, "I am a clot in the blood flow of society, right?"

I didn't nod. I didn't even blink, but my eyebrows gently pulled together as I questioned what the heck he was thinking. Had someone called him that once before?

He continued with only, "And you think you can thin me out. Save the heart of this stupid place."

He used his arm to push himself off from the bars. Standing before me with arms down and out, he held his head up. All of his physical scars were on display for the world to see, and to judge. His emotional scars were poorly hidden too. Rayne was not unattractive, but he obviously didn't think highly of himself. I searched his face with rapid firing thoughts, trying in fruitless desperation to discern what he wanted from me or from anyone. He puffed out his chest and standing up straight he was beautifully massive and frightening. As he was usually so hunched over, I had misinterpreted his stature and his build.

The man was a six-foot seven brick of muscle. There was nothing else too him. He could have killed me a thousand times over with one finger. My stomach tightened and I swallowed my fear and awe. He was standing there, as though asking me to shoot him right in the chest. Maybe stab him. What would he have preferred?

Looking down at me past his nose, yet not condescending, he said plainly and quietly, begging for nothing, "Good luck."

I waited for him to sit down again before walking away for good.

As I was leaving, I asked a guard to keep an eye on Rayne with a message to escalate it to management. Rayne may not have been much use to me, but I absolutely did not want him to kill himself either, and I had cause for concern. The eyes I saw were those of a man who wished he had died years ago. That new wound on his arm was more than suspicious.

Officer Oliver Kells went out to see if Rayne had been telling the truth about Black's old place. He was. The address had been a store front, and then was nothing more than rubble. Perhaps Rayne himself had blown it to smithereens. Hudson related this information to me via text, and I went to meet Jed at a Freaky Fowl.

"Sorry," said the man behind the counter, "but we're all out of chicken."

"How is that possible? You're a fried chicken place."

Jed laughed and patted me on the back saying, "Cotton candy coated cock-sucker!" Sometimes I wondered if Jed even remembered my name, and how panicked he would be if my hair were my natural brown again for more than a costume.

I had been craving that bird so badly, it was a miracle we didn't have a shoot-out.

My phone started to vibrate.

"You're not mad at me?" I asked Maria.

"No, I'm used to you. Are you with Jed right now?"

"Yes, and failing to get any chicken, which is an atrocity. This is a fried chicken place. Like, that's literally what they do for a living, and there is no chicken. Can you believe it?"

"Okay, well… Per your case, there's nothing you can do right now, right? You're waiting for more information?"

I nodded, and then realized that she couldn't hear the gesture over the phone, so I answered, "Yes. Right. I don't know what to do with my time while I wait."

"I have an idea," she said slyly. We were to meet the girls at a club nearby. Maria said it was a haunt for some of the older generation MOTH people years ago, and Chloe had the idea to check it out. Maria was pretty convinced no one would still be hanging around, so best case would mean a step closer to the villains, and worst would be a fun time for us.

"Technically a business expense," I said.

"Yeah! My points all still stand though."

"Understood."

"Stop fucking up so much."

"I gotcha."

The club was dark in a gothic way and so Maria fit in perfectly with the newly clipped in purple streaks in her hair, and her heavy black eyeliner, all above a tightly bound waist cincher, a short skirt which lay beneath it, covered in chains, and a black and white striped fishnet top beneath it all. Her black bra showed directly through the 'shirt' but no one minded. I thought about how out of place two men dressed as Jed and I did must look, and wondered if I should buy a spiked collar from a vendor sitting beyond the entrance.

Before we could go through the heavy metal doors, a man I recognized from my childhood, beyond the raccoon-esque eye makeup came up to me to shake my hand excitedly.

He was extremely wordy and yet said very little. Thankfully, the exchange was brief, before he ran inside, promising we'd meet up again.

"So, who was he?" asked Maria.

I closed my eyes for a moment, then said, "I didn't remember the guy's name at first, but it's Jacob. Honestly, I'm not really positive we ever spoke before today, but I know I technically met him at a Jewish Summer camp when we were kids."

"Yeah," said Jed, then paused before, "I wanna make a Jew-camp joke but they'd all be really horrible."

Maria hit him, then opened the door for us.

"I didn't say it!" said Jed.

The music was so thumping and preposterously loud that I could feel it in my neck. Any attempt to speak in an audible fashion left me light headed and nauseous. Still, there were girls dancing in belts they called skirts, so it was worth the stay. I decided I liked the music when it switched to a gothic remix of a song I knew. Chloe plucked Jed away to a small booth over to the side. Maria had been wandering about, shmoozing, but stood by my side soon after. As she looked around, I thought of how badly I wanted her to move against me like the dancers all around us did each other, soaked with sweat. I thought of this as I turned to watch her stroke Liz's spine with one hand and tilt her chin upwards for a kiss with the other. Liz was all in green, right down to her knee-high boots. They disappeared into the crowd.

Childhood-Friend-Jacob appeared before me like a spectre of Death, and from out behind him danced Kirsten, the sexy bartender from the Platinum Spoon I had never called months before. Whoops. She put her arm around my shoulders as Jacob slipped away, job done.

"Jacob is my brother! Small world, right? He said you came with a few people. Where'd they all go?"

"Off having a good time, I suppose," we swayed to the beat, "like we should be. It's good to see you again."

I attempted to tell her I was sorry that I'd never called, but she interrupted me with a kiss. No hard feelings. Perhaps she could read my thoughts. That, or she was bored and easy to arouse.

She got a hold of my tie and yanked. My body followed like a rag doll into the ladies' room, and then into the stall. My belt, pants and underwear were fairly unceremoniously loosened, and dropped to the no doubt soiled floor by my ankles. She then pushed on my shoulders to let me know where to go. I slammed down on the toilet. Generally speaking, I hate public restrooms. They are vile and we can't possibly know what herpes-laden monstrosity sat there previously. At that moment, however, germs were the last thing on my mind. She handed me a condom from nowhere, and I made quick work of it. She moved to the still-too-loud music as she delicately lifted her dress and placed herself on top of me. In that moment, an old industrial song I remembered from high school came on and became somewhat muffled into the background of what was happening.

Like any good exotic dance, there was a smooth gyration, a few dips and turns, and a steady, pounding beat. Quick but successful. I removed her after we had both finished, but this was not in an attempt to stop the show. Far from it. Simply put, I wanted to devour her. All of her, but I'd would settle for one part at a time. I bent over, effectively folded in half, and held her soft thigh to my shoulder. Somewhat appropriately, a song screaming about stardom and porn stars was playing by then.

We spent about ten minutes in that dimly lit slime

hole of a bathroom. I didn't care. I very rarely ever felt a sense of control anymore, and certainly didn't anytime our hips collided and she reeled in ecstasy. The overpowering comfort she instilled in my chest made up for my generally not knowing what I was doing with my life anymore. Honestly, with a body like hers, I would be whatever the Hell she wanted.

She hurriedly cleaned herself up, as though we were suddenly short on time. I let myself lean back to take it all in before I noticed that music was, in fact, still playing. We left the toilet.

My bartender had gone back to wandering through the crowd. I watched her laugh with her brother, and lean with great emphasis on a nearby man I didn't know. She reminded me enough of Maria that I knew I shouldn't make a habit of this.

I couldn't hear the words trailing on shrill voices of the young women coming in on either side of me. They were nice to look at, but their eyes all seemed so vacant and soulless. Maria kissed Liz a booth down. Jacob winked at me from somewhere over Liz's shoulder. Kirsten was nowhere to be found.

I shrugged and plopped myself down into the booth at the stranger-girls' simultaneous gesture. I could have had them both at once if I wanted. I didn't. Thinking nothing of it, I placed my arms crossed on the table, and then put my head down on my arms like the sad sack I had become. I hummed along to the song. Within minutes, the girls were gone, having gotten bored with my charms.

Chloe caught a glimpse of me, and ran to the bar where Jed sat, and the two then ran together to gather Maria and Liz. I moved from my face-down position to catch a breath of stale air.

"Hey, do you want to go home, Honey?" Chloe

handed me a napkin to wipe off whatever drool I may have had on my face.

Jed reminded me that we had nothing to do, so I was totally in charge of where we'd go next.

My eyes got wide, "You'll drive me home?" I meant to ask that with a 'please' but Jed understood.

He pat me on the shoulder, "Come on, Kiddo. I think we're done for the night."

CHAPTER 24
The Walls Came Down

Jed got out of the car to walk with me to my house, and it was only then that I realized Chloe, Liz, and Maria had followed in a car behind us. Sleepover at my place, I guessed.

Once everyone had filed inside, Maria got to getting everyone water, coffee, and so on. Liz found a blanket on a chair and put it on the couch. Chloe lit the fire place. It was all cozy and nice in a way that I didn't know I needed.

"You're gonna lie down now, right?" asked Liz.

I shook my head, "No, I have something on my mind."

"What's up?" asked Chloe.

"Well, I just have to get something. I'll feel better once I do. Hold on."

Everyone sat down on the couch and chairs, waiting patiently for me to return. A few minutes later, I limped while dragging the same boxes of papers to the living room.

Maria marched up to me, "Why now? Nothing has changed. You need rest! You keep doing this, Gabe."

She was right. Over and over I'd pour through this information, desperate to find something new. I couldn't help myself.

"Nothing makes me feel better," I said as I sat by the box on the floor.

Jed squat down by me, "Dude. There's nothing useful in any of this shit. We're waiting for our next step. We're waiting to hear if and when Hudson finds Black, right?"

I ignored him and continued looking and searching for nothing, trying to focus on anything other than the pain, which at that point was mostly in my head. I got up, which prompted a collective sigh of relief before I reached for my pills.

Maria snatched them from me, "We need to talk about what's happening here. You need a clear head for it."

Noticing the gleam in my eye and seeing what a shell of a human being I was about to become, Maria spoke up again, "This collection of information isn't doing anything for you anymore. There is nothing in here you haven't memorized. Nothing new to find that will magically end all this. You've already said a thousand times that none of it will help book her."

I meekly stammered, "I know but-"

Jed bellowed, "Toss them into the fire place! Let's get this shit out of here."

"What? No!" I let out a yelp and grabbed the end of the box when Chloe grabbed the other side. I sat with a slam, hugging the box, "What if I missed something? I need it! I have to check again. I have to keep trying!"

I looked to my left to see Maria reading the label on the bottle of pills, and I shrieked, "Give them to me! Okay? I'm in pain!"

"Gabe," Maria took my hand and sat with me, "What hurts? Your leg?"

"No. I don't know."

"Gabe, please think for a minute. What hurts right now?"

My vision blurred completely from the wall of tears. My jaw clenched into a grimace, and I wailed. Then, I wiped my tears away with my hands on my face, stood up, and nodded to no one in particular.

Chloe let go of the box. Maria stood to put the pills on the counter. Jed sat down on the couch. Liz hadn't moved throughout this scene.

Silently, I started tossing handfuls of papers into the fire. There was nothing to be done. The paper turned to gray bark, and finally, to ash. Maria poured healing, glistening water over the pile of forever lost knowledge...

Only, it wasn't lost, was it? Just copies. Jed got up to grip his arms around my entire body, as if holding me back from myself. We sat down on the floor. Frustration and anger had turned to desperation, and now- in the stillness -an overwhelming sense of relief. It was done, and I couldn't look over those notes and hum what ifs and maybes, even if I wanted to with every cell in my body. I couldn't. I had to let it go.

"Gabe," Maria's voice was soft and reassuring.

I said, "I knew these were copies of copies. I knew that. They aren't even the ones I have organized all over my office. I'm obsessed, just like you've said." I started to shake and the tears followed soon after.

Maria kneeled down to hold me with Jed as she asked, "Please. Let us help you." Struggling to breathe through my left nostril produced a sound not unlike that of a large zipper.

I didn't ask for the pills, but I didn't throw them out either.

An hour went by before I turned to Liz and said, "I'm sorry."

"For what?" she asked.

"For my breakdown. You didn't sign up for that."

Jed laughed, "You think I signed up for that shit? Yeah, I guess I did."

"We all did," said Liz. "We're friends." She shrugged and sipped the rest of her tea.

The ladies didn't spend the night, but Jed had no intention of leaving my side. He leaned against my front door and waved to them as they drove away.

Then he turned to me to say, "Hey, I gotta say

something to you." He closed the door.

"You okay?" I asked. "If it's about earlier-"

Jed's words tumbled forward as we made our way up the three little steps back to the living room, "I need help too, Gabe."

"...Pardon?" I gestured to the couch for us to sit.

Jed took in a breath, "I've gone way past the point of functioning alcoholic and straight into the regular kind, and I know I gotta stop, but what the fuck do I do if I don't go to bars and shit? Where the fuck do I go? I'm fucking scared. I don't wanna fuck this up."

"You've already been drinking less, haven't you?"

"Sure, but I still want that third, fourth, fifth on and on forever drink. I don't even really want to quit. I wanna not be running forever from whatever it is that makes me prefer being drunk off my ass."

"Well, you aren't alone. We'll find other places to regroup and hang out. It's okay. And hey, I know it's not the same, but I don't have to drink if that's gonna make it a little easier for you, okay?"

"Yeah. Honestly, you on pills is shitty, but you not drinking has made it a little less hard for me. I'm so scared, man. I talked to Darcy on the phone. I found an old message I had ignored and I left the club for a second to fucking call her because I couldn't look at Chloe while I talked about this shit."

"How's Darcy?"

"She's happy, and like, I know we ain't gonna get back together. Neither of us want that. I wanna have her in my life again. Her husband is cool too." He let out a huff, "And I don't wanna do a program! And I know it's gotta be cold turkey, and that stuff is gonna happen to me, and I'm fucking scared, you know? I know I'm not alone, but I feel really fucking alone."

"I know. It's going to be okay, Jed." I stretched up to put an arm around his shoulder. He quietly shook and clenched his jaw. When I gave him a tug for a one-armed hug, he loosened up enough to let it all out.

After sobbing for a minute, he wiped his eyes and sat up straight, "Kells and Hudson find anything else on Rayne? We should see if anything happened after that old hideout was a bust."

I kept my arm around him, "Just like that, huh?"

"I got it out of my system, you know what's going on now, I'm good. It's whatever."

I sent general inquiry texts to Officer Kells and Hudson. It was late enough that I didn't expect to hear much until the morning one way or another.

Once Jed fell asleep on the couch, I snuck away to get a blanket, then tucked him in.

Morning was silence over coffee until Jed got up to make a phone call. I assumed it was to Darcy again, but I was evidently wrong. He was on my phone.

"Hudson sent you the number for Newsburg Penitentiary, so I called them."

"What's up?"

"You told someone to keep an eye on Rayne right?"

I put my mug down and stood up, "Yeah. Why?"

"They didn't. The guy I just spoke to said Rayne's dead. Hudson and Kells are gonna meet us at the prison whenever you're ready."

"Rayne's dead? Did they say how?"

"His face had been so pummeled in that Hudson said he was barely recognizable."

"Well, that's not the way I had anticipated he might go."

As I finished getting dressed, Jed went on to say,

"Hudson said it was a good thing he had that hair and size. The hair I get. He looked like a freak like you do."

"If his face was pulverized, his dental records would have been useless. Of course, it must have happened in his cell, right?"

"Yep. Door was locked up and everything."

We got into the car. A song about the open road was playing, and Jed turned down the radio so I could say, "Then how did the perpetrator get in to kill him? This was clearly not a suicide, right?"

"Through the wall."

We got to our destination and made it through security in record time.

Hudson welcomed us with, "Wait until you see the three-foot-wide hole in the wall which leads to an even wider in diameter tunnel underground."

Kells was with him, and he handed me a pair of rubber gloves in silence.

I walked faster than I could think to the cell. Hudson pointed to the body, "Like I said to Jed, Rayne's unique size would have been helpful for identifying him even if he wasn't locked in here. Six foot three is not an average man."

"Wait." I put on the rubber gloves and squat down to get a closer look. Rayne's "unique size" was closer to six foot seven, not six foot three, and his shoulders seemed to have shrunk as well. Had more happened to his body than we could see? I took a closer look at the rest of the scene, because this did not seem right to me.

The cot was all but gone, crushed to the wall and shredded from the force of whatever it was that had burrowed its way in there.

"The cot is upside down," I said.

"Upside down?" Hudson titled his head.

"It's been spun around, like crushed but on a giant drill. This was done by one of those digging machines."

"Like what Chloe's mom makes?" asked Jed.

"Yeah, but maybe an older model. Look at this," I pointed to long, thin scrapes in the floor. "It's like something dragged itself in, and didn't dig so much as drilled as it went.

Kells spoke up, "The tunnel leads outside the prison grounds." Any trace of the machine was gone beyond a cave entrance in the dirt.

I nodded to Kells, then turned to Hudson to ask, "Did anyone hear anything? These machines are loud. Even with concrete walls, someone would have heard something before the smash." Hudson scratched his chin.

Kells took out a notebook, "Yes, actually. I apologize for not mentioning before, Sir."

"Let me see that, Ollie," Hudson took the notebook and flipped through, until he let out a grunt in my direction. "A couple prisoners told Officer Kells here that they heard a rumbling, some scraping, and a guard mentioned a small earth quake."

"Yeah," said Kells. "He said he didn't think anything of it, but I grew up around this area. We never got any quakes or tremors. That doesn't mean they knew what direction it was coming from though. The prisoners both said they thought they heard it coming from below them, and the sounds didn't take long before the loud boom. By that point, everything went by really fast. We figure something smashed in, smashed Rayne's face in the process, then just turned around and left the scene."

"Who was driving?" I asked. I took my squat position again, "This is all wrong."

"What's all wrong?" asked Jed.

"The hair is the same blue hue, but looks dyed that way."

Hudson chuckled, "Did you think his hair was natural? Is yours?"

"No, I mean, rather than pale over time and washing. This was recently dyed to look older. Even the scars on the throat and hand are present, but also look newer. This guy is too short and look, there's nothing on his left arm. There's also a scar on his stomach that I can't explain. It goes straight across the torso, but I never saw it before."

"What was that about his left arm?" Hudson came closer to get a better look.

"Rayne hurt himself, I think to let me or someone else know he was still alive out there. Did he want to screw this plan up?"

"Maybe, but then who was this poor sap, if not the Blue Bastard Bomber? Also, how do you explain the machine smashing his face in then? You think Rayne had time to get up, get this guy out of it, get into it himself, and then use it to kill whoever this was?"

"No," I pointed to the sink on the ground, "Look at where this landed. It's the wrong place, given the trajectory of the machine coming in this way. I think Rayne was untouched, got the guy to come out to talk to him, ripped the sink off the wall, and sandwiched the head of whoever this was between the sink and the wall." I got up and coaxed Kells into seeing what I was seeing, "Look at the blood on the sink here, and the wall over there."

"I hadn't even noticed that!" said Kells. "I thought it was just splatter from the mess itself. You're saying that was there before the body hit the ground."

"That's exactly what I'm saying. Now we need to find that machine, and find Rayne."

We asked the forensic team to collect and send some DNA evidence off to the labs to search for a match. Hopefully, this man was a criminal already in the system.

Hudson waved the notebook above his head, "All right. You three set out to find him, and call me if you see any clues. I'm going to relate everything you figured out here to the rest of the team. Now get going."

So, the three of us followed what little tracks were left by the thing that dug into Rayne's cell, and then stood above that big half-caved in hole in the ground.

"I'm not gonna fit down there," said Jed.

"Sure you could, but then how would you get back out anyway?" asked Kells.

I began to walk alongside the strip of broken ground leading away from the prison, "It's too dangerous to go inside the hole. Let's go this way, see how far we get before we loose the trail, then call for back up. Maybe we'll find an exit wound for this thing. He had to come back out at some point, right?"

By the time we lost track of freshly upturned dirt, Jed, Kells, and I were in the middle of a field a mile or so away from the prison itself.

"You wanna hear something fun?" Kells pointed at a few small buildings nearby, "You see that little blue house between the white one and the old school house? I lived there until I was nine. My older brother and I used to walk down to the lake and skip rocks."

We felt a rumble beneath our feet every now and then, and we'd brace for whatever impact, be it the ground falling away from our feet, or a nearby tree shaking down on top of us. We continued in the same direction for another half of a mile before I put up a hand.

"I think this is where we stop. Let's all head home, and send out a better equipped team to this general spot." I nearly tripped over it at first. This strange metallic device, shaped like a large arm of a human skeleton, was poking out of the ground like a sad Charlie Brown tree.

"Is this a piece of the machine, broken off?" Jed prodded it with his foot. That seemed to piss it off. The shiny silvery fingers grabbed out at him, and so he lunged backwards. Another hand emerged from the dirt and within seconds they were digging, pulling the machine they were attached to from the ground.

"Told you I would not be there long." Rayne's voice was muffled, but close by.

"Oh God," said Kells, "he's still in the ground."

Like some monstrous metal insect, it came forth from the ground roaring and ready to destroy us, along with anything else in its path. It looked like a tubular tank with those two skeletal arms and a drill on the front, and an even larger drill in the back.

From the top, a latch unlocked and Rayne showed himself. He casually leaned forward with an elbow on the rim of his pod like a greaser showing off his new car.

"You better run," he said with a calm demeanor.

We complied. We ran. Metallic mayhem thundered behind us in a magnificent clamor.

"You don't have to do this, Rayne!" I shouted above the din, "She's using you!"

"Yeah," chimed in a desperate sounding Jed, "that bitch is gonna kill you!"

Rayne responded with a maniacal cackle, followed by, "I am sorry, Gekman! You should not have saved me, but I still did enjoy our conversations! No hard feelings!"

Jed turned around long enough to let out, "What about me, Fuckhead?" Then, he realized that running backwards would only slow him down.

Meanwhile, I was working on pure fear.

Kells was moving too slowly. I could see he was still in pain from his surgery and trying to hide it, wincing with a sharp inhale. I tried to reach a hand out to him. One of the thing's arms with its spindly metal, spider-like fingers swiped in front of Kells legs and grabbed hold of him around a knee. He slammed to the ground as it dragged him backwards toward the drill and crushing treads of the machine. He repeated a quiet, out of breath "no" over and over to himself, scrambling, fingers grabbing dirt and grass. I fell forward, ignoring the crack in my leg as I tried to reach for him. His bloody puree splashed my hand, and I said nothing as Jed grabbed me by the waist back to standing so that we could run again. It was no time to mourn.

The machine started to slow down. Kells was gumming up the gears. It was still trudging along, though the new speed allowed us to get a step ahead. We hit a somewhat populated fishing town where tourist business would boom in the summer, and would otherwise be quiet. We hoped Rayne would avoid the few people working as we dodged through alleyways in an attempt to slow him down. Rayne's machine bashed into brick walls, crushed cars, and sent some people screaming away.

We had run on and off for almost two miles, panting, hiding, and in pain between bursts of running more, when we got to the lake.

We stood on the tiny dock, and Jed motioned to go into the water, "The machine won't be able to make it, but we can."

"You can! I'll drown!"

"I'll drag you!"

Jed's mouth went agape and I felt a rib crack, my feet dangling in the air. I slammed my fists down on the metal hands around my torso in an effort to make it let go, but all I did was slice the side of my hand open. The machine smelled like a dead sea creature, salty and stale on concrete.

Rayne opened his pod to say, "I am sure this could have gone better for you, but I have already told you what I would do to you if I had to. Again, this is nothing personal."

A thunderous bang vibrated my ears. Jed had found a rebar to whack Rayne on the head. Rayne and his monstrous metal body began to go down, releasing the fingers around me, slamming me into the lake.

My tailbone smacked against a rock, sending a jolt of pain into my legs and back, forcing the precious air from my lungs. I panicked, splashing about awkwardly, unable to breathe. Green spots and haze overtook my vision as I desperately tried to keep my mouth closed and avoid a gasp. I failed and took in gulps of water. Intense pain shot through my lungs. I grabbed upward, outward, searching for some way to climb up and out of that lake as my vision began to go dark, creeping blackness at the sides of my eyes.

An arm hooked around me and managed to pull me upward while I threw up water. He tossed me onto the muddy ground by patches of grass, and Jed's silhouette blocked the high sun above me.

"Told you I'd drag ya," said Jed. He let out a howl as he took of his shoe. His foot was swollen, though it didn't look broken.

Rayne's vehicle remained jammed halfway underwater, looking dejected. The cockpit was empty. Jed hadn't seen where Rayne had gone.

Time sped up again. I was in and out for a while. Paramedics, Jed being oddly somber, Maria's voice inside my head when she wasn't even there. By the time I caught up to the world again, I found myself breathing rapidly. It wasn't quite hyperventilation, but I was having a hard time slowing down. A chill permeated every molecule. I questioned if the whole darn hospital might be a morgue, cold, dead, forgotten.

To help organize my thoughts, I had written to my father to tell him everything we had learned, since I was stuck in the hospital overnight. Only when I tried to locate the note, I found it had never been written at all.

There were three empty beds in the room with me. I wondered if they were going to be filled by strangers soon, or if I had somehow forgotten that they were already filled before.

Jed wandered into my other-than-me empty quad hospital room soon after.

I absentmindedly grabbed his hand and asked, "You're sober. How are you feeling? You doing okay?"

"I put fries on my cheeseburger this morning like they were just another fucking condiment."

I couldn't hide the grimace peeling my face to the sides, "I'm not sure if that means you're feeling better, or much worse."

He shrugged, "It was delicious, so I guess I felt better after I did it. You're the one who fell off the planet. You shattered your fucking tailbone and nearly drowned. Why are you even asking if I'm okay?"

I didn't hear his question, having fallen asleep.

CHAPTER 25
White Hot Black Out

I assumed it was Jed to Chloe who then alerted Maria.

After the hospital, I found myself on Maria's couch. At least, I thought I was on her couch. It was tough discerning the reality from the dream. Liz said nothing as she put a cold compress on my forehead and occasionally brought me things to eat and drink. She had left the room to refill the icepack when I fully woke up for the first time since the fall. Shirtless, blood had coagulated in stripes. The purple towels were uniquely soft beneath me, even with all the dried blood. Why was I still bleeding after the hospital? I felt pangs of guilt at ruining Maria's nice towels.

My tailbone, or what was left of it, rendered most of my body useless and pained as any pressure from anything beyond the damp, circular ice pack beneath my rear sent razor blades shooting up and down my spine, my limbs, and into my neck and my head. Sharp, stabbing pains screamed about old wounds as though worried I might forget them in favor of the newly implemented suffering. I was pleased as punch that I could feel my legs at all, so they could do whatever they wanted, as far as I was concerned. I couldn't prop myself up too much, as being on my back meant a harder time getting air in, but anything else was agony.

I caught Maria to ask why I was there and not the hospital.

She sighed, "Broken ribs, compression fracture of the back, and shattered tailbone seem to be the things doctors aren't terribly concerned about. The doctor's advice was to breathe less. Luckily your lungs weren't punctured, and you didn't suffer any brain damage from, you know, drowning."

She had a strange, lipless smile before adding, "We've got a whole list of stuff to do to help you through this, and we're not going to let you suffer alone, no matter how much you bitch about it. You will be literally surrounded by people who care about you at all times, and that's the end of the story."

Had I been arguing? Ringing, humming, feedback and white noise surrounded my head and invaded my brain until my neck began to vibrate. Television. Television would plug the noise. Drown it out with flashing pictures and structured noise around my floundering din.

"Wait," I said, "Am I still bleeding?"

"Oh, it looks worse than it is. You did have a pretty bad gash that got stitched up, and then something opened up again, but we were told to just replace the dressing once in a while. The sweat is making it look like more blood than it is."

"The sweat?"

She pet my head, "Just keep laying down and rest, okay?"

It felt like I was too close to the window and that I would hit my head, but there was a couch cushion, a regular pillow, and a spare blanket between my noggin and the left arm of the couch, as well as at least another six inches between the arm of the couch and the pane of glass. Attempting to roll onto my left side to get my back to the back of the couch and be facing the television served to only tangle me in a sheet covered in a print of watercolor birds. Literally a captive audience.

Every now and then, the blackness filling my eyes would let up and part fuzzily, enough to let me glimpse a passing moment of Liz holding a pill. Sometimes it was Maria, and sometimes it was Jed. I never questioned what the pill was. It came from an orange bottle that had my name printed on a cold and distant label. The pill tasted like an old fish tank and slid down my throat on a water slide from the kitchen sink, poured into a wine glass. Of course. Of course, Maria didn't have any tumblers.

"You look good with a little stubble," She said.

"I feel unclean."

Jed said, "I always have some hair on my chin."

I didn't turn around, "You look unclean."

Maria laughed at my drugged remark, and Jed thankfully didn't take it too personally, "Yeah well, we'll get you cleaned up and back to looking like a suffocated naked mole rat soon enough."

I tuned out for about an hour. Liz handed me another wine glass of water when I came back to realty again. My thumb pressed against the glass and emphasized my irregular heartbeat. My hands felt fat, swollen with blood maybe, like what little I still had was struggling and rushing all to the same areas at once, unsure what to do with itself. My feet were ice and floating, sometimes on fire and made of lead. My thighs were always bricks of clumped concrete in a flimsy burlap sack of skin. I was but a former human.

Somewhere in that mess, the television had been turned on, and the remote had been placed into my hand. "Infrastructure" became... Not a word. It was eventually replaced by "roots" and "skeleton" until I completely forgot what I had been trying to say to begin with. My right cheekbone had stopped throbbing and instead felt like the hunk of bone had detached itself and was flopping around under the skin. To my surprise, it only felt bruised, not loose when touched.

My head rolled to show me the window. I was tired of the droning television anyway. All the passing cars were silver. All the cars were gray. Jelly people waddled down the street. Balding pretenders stopped off to be groomed. A balding, mustached jelly man started following a too young, too attractive woman. Too smart too. Her words cut through his jelly head. A jelly woman caught his eye before long. She ignored him outright. You go, Jelly Girl.

I reached for the remote on the side table forgetting that I had placed it back there at some point, but I couldn't quite reach it. I let out a, "HEP!" as though that would help me heave ho to it, immediately followed by, "Fu-" as I fell off the couch.

The floor was cold in patches, reasonable where her

rich blue carpet lay. I noticed then the newspaper and saran-wrap lining the couch and rug surrounding that piece of cherry brown leather and wood. No other towels were strewn about but what was on the couch itself. How much was I really bleeding? Maybe she was worried I would pee myself. Oh no. Had I done that already?

Oh God. Was that blood caked under my nails? I needed a bath or I felt I would die. Christ. And Maria had seen me like this. Perhaps the paper then was to catch the poor woman's vomit. Everything was too tiring, too heavy to move and that created a unique type of frustration that I imagined would lead to an even more unique kind of insanity.

The swinging kitchen door made a suctioned, rubber sound. Nothing echoed.

"Always falling, huh?" Maria stood, ice pack in hand, chuckling for a bit before deciding to help me up. I asked her if I had peed myself. She didn't answer as she laughed again and turned off the television. I asked her if Liz had seen me pee myself, and again she smiled and didn't otherwise respond. I asked her if she dumbs herself down when guys like me are like this.

"How many guys like you do you think there are?" She sat down by me on the couch.

"I mean, when you're in the club, you talk more... fancy. I feel like you speak differently to me."

I could hear Liz chuckle from somewhere.

Maria raised a hand to my face to wipe off my sweat as she said in a motherly tone, "First of all, you do the same thing. We perk up and speak differently when we want to impress or talk down to someone. Second of all, we can speak like intellectuals and feel very smart and have no one learn a thing or be able to understand us. We could do that, or we could speak in a way people can follow what we say, and actually be more respectful that way. Right now, you are on pain killers that could subdue an elephant. I don't want to fancy-talk you too much. It's as simple as that."

I nodded, then found myself laying down again as she stroked my hair and kissed my cheek. I don't remember Maria becoming Liz, but it was Liz who then held my hand and hummed a little song until I fell asleep.

The nightmare that followed swallowed me whole.

I was on a case, called in by a family to get rid of a little girl who was stuck in their house. The little girl turned out to be Abby, with eyes blacked out, white and peeling skin, and an expression of dissatisfaction. Every time someone tried to kill my little zombie sister, she simply would not stay dead. I tried another tactic, by giving her toys and candy, but she gave them back, bones exposed at her wrists. This filled me with dread in the dream, because I knew that it meant she was not happy; she had become vengeful, and would never move on. I could not figure out why she was so angry. I had done all I could do, right?

Liz was still sitting by me when I woke up, so I couldn't have been out too long.

"Do you have a fever?" She put her hand on my forehead and then grabbed a tissue to dab away my sweat.

"No. No, I'm okay. I'm okay, right?"

She nodded.

Then I was in the bathroom. I woke up to my own voice shouting out, "Oh God, it's just liquid with bits and chunks of green and grey sludge in it. I'm shivering. Is it cold, or is this part of whatever sickness has latched onto my innards?"

Jed barged in, not minding my pants down, to hand me a robe. "Put it on backwards," he said. "It'll keep you cozy as shit without blocking anything. Like a blanket with sleeves."

I could hear Liz ask if I needed water, and Maria answer that I would as soon as I was done on the frozen throne.

When I was back on the couch buried in blankets and wearing the robe correctly, I realized I wasn't wearing pants. At some point I must have stripped down to my boxer-briefs. My fingers felt like they were coated in chalk, soft and slightly numbed to the touch.

"Where's Jed?" I asked no one in particular.

Maria leaned in from a doorway to say, "He said he was going to talk to Hudson for you. He had questions, apparently. I don't know what that means." I wasn't sure what that meant either. I looked at the ceiling, trying to psychically connect with Jed.

Maria and Liz came into the room with a tray of fruit and cheese squares. I was perhaps overly thrilled and immediately sad when I couldn't get myself to sit up to eat. Liz fed me. An angel. That's what she was.

I mumbled, "Liz! Liz where you come from? Wait. Where did you live?"

Liz turned to Maria, then back to me once she processed what I was trying to ask, "Oh! Okay, you live in your childhood home, right? Well, remember the farm Michael Crown protested at? The one we all stayed in for a bit when you needed a hide out? I'm actually from that farm, so not far from here. I really did grow up there, and now I'm living in a little apartment close to here."

I waved at nothing, "Wait no, I knew that. And we found Maria somewhere! Where the Hell did we go to school? Newsburg?"

"What is he saying?" asked Liz.

Maria spoke through at least three grapes in her mouth, "Oh, he's all confused. I'm from a little past Cornsbrook. I'm not from around here. Not originally. Gabe and Jed met me when they came to my hometown for college. Then I followed them back here years ago and the rest is history. Like, I realize I'm not from that far away, but the other side of Cornsbrook is years away when you don't know what's going on in the outside world. Anyway, still Auburn County. So, it's here, then Newsburg, then Auburn county starts, then Cornsbrook, and then where I'm from."

Liz said, "It's funny, even growing up around here, I'm still trying to understand which area is which."

Maria fed Liz a piece of cheese, "Cornsbrook has the beach, some old town houses, and a giant asylum that I think controls the town with an almost supernatural aura. So that's how to remember Cornsbrook. Newsburg has a lot of woods and farmland surrounded by an old cityscape, with bridges connecting the tall buildings with glass walkways and makes me think of how people in the 1950s probably viewed the future. Bellevue has Gabe within this fairly suburban area, bits of a newer city crawling in about ten miles South, and more than a reasonable number of bars."

"I'll pretend to remember all that," Liz laughed. "I like Bellevue. It's easy enough to get into the city proper where most of the apartments stand, like where Jed is, right? So that's probably good for Gabe." She turned to me then as if I'd have an opinion. I had no such thing. I wanted to listen forever, until I suddenly wanted to be involved.

I asked Maria a little about Moth, trying to keep the conversation to the club itself, but I wasn't making much sense.

I fell asleep again for a moment and woke up to Liz bringing a tray of Chloe's cookies and a tea kettle from the kitchen as Maria said, "You know, you asked me before if I knew Rayne. I told you I kind of did, but I didn't really tell you anything, did I? I met him a few years ago. I knew there was a woman in charge back then, but I had no idea who Candice or whoever was. Him though... I had met Rayne." She poured a third cup of tea.

I tried and immediately failed to sit up, "And? What was he like? Did he hurt you?"

"No. He was clingy, I guess. He was sweet and quiet for the most part. I think he wanted someone to like him. And big and scary as he is, he was always kind of introspective and sad. He'd pick a woman and be her lap dog until she pushed him away. And when she did, he wouldn't fight it. ...Unlike Denny."

"I hate Denny." I sounded like a small child.

"I know, Dear." She smirked and sipped her tea, then laughed, "They almost killed each other once, actually."

Liz perked up at that with curiosity, but Maria moved on, "Anyway, He would talk to me and not really to anyone else, but we didn't hang out."

"You're nice to talk to!" said Liz. "What kinds of stuff did a guy like that want to talk about though?"

"There was a vineyard he liked. He knew the woman who ran it, and I think they were a couple once. She left, and the vineyard changed hands a few times, but no one could keep it running. According to him, the grapes went sour because she left. It's a romantic thought but I'm sure it shut down for other reasons."

I managed to steal a grape, "And after that, he found Black?"

Maria refilled her tea cup, "Well, Rayne was one of the original members, before it was a corporation, back when they were normal dealers. From what I gather, he got bored of it pretty fast, but he didn't leave until Black rose up and got kids involved for testing. Rayne thought it was wrong, and took his knowledge of these ridiculous contraptions with him. He wound up selling the patent of said contraptions to Chloe's mom, which makes this a very small world." She stirred in too much sugar, "So, as far as I know, he and Black hadn't really interacted before that. More than anything, it was probably because he simply had no interest in her at the time and was focused on someone else. Thinking about it, I don't know where the bomb thing came into play. That seems odd for him. I wonder if he remembers me?"

"I'm sure he does, and as much as I'm intensely

curious about you knowing Rayne," I tried and failed once again to sit up, "I'm more curious about you and Denny. I don't want you getting hurt again. How did you even get involved with him? Through the club?"

She chuckled, "Other way around." Then she sighed into her cup, "I'll admit, it's sort of my fault. I mean, I used him. I was awful to him. It doesn't mean he never deserved it, but I really did use him to get to where I wanted to go. Not that it entirely worked, but still."

She noticed with a side glance how I was squinting at her, and so she went on, "Once upon a time, I liked him, but the moment he became a jackass, I dropped him."

"I'm amazed by that."

"Hey! I used to be a very good judge of character. Then you happened." She and Liz shared an awkward laugh.

I gestured loosely at Liz, "Your judgment got better again."

"Thank you," said Liz as she adjusted on an uncomfortable kitchen chair she'd dragged into the room. The added flower printed cushion didn't help much.

Maria nodded and said, "In retrospect, he thought he was in love and very possessive. See, Denny had actually been a client of mine. It was very much business only, but with him sometimes getting off. No touching on my part. I got paid. It was a win-win situation until it wasn't. It was such a weird set up. If I was a doctor, it would have been outright illegal."

I tried my best to lean in. She noticed, "Okay, okay. So, it started back when I was still in my hometown. That's where he was my client. He was from around here though. Then when I came here with you, he kind of took that as a cue. I thought he was going to hire me for the other stuff, but he started dragging me to dates instead. I didn't like it, but he wasn't ugly and he didn't seem like the lunatic he turned out to be. I also wasn't in a great place financially at the time, so I'd take what I could get, so long as it still stayed within my boundaries. It was a bad set of decisions on my part."

I was having trouble keeping my eyes open, "What were you getting out of it?"

"He offered me assistance in getting the one thing I had always wanted. The club. I could do whatever I wanted with it, so long as I let them do their work downstairs. That was it. It seemed so simple. I didn't realize Denny would want me to be his pet. It's like he wanted vengeance for everything he had initially hired me to do. Like it was the other half of a game I didn't even know I was playing."

I cringed at that, "He was your in at the club, you guys broke off your deal... relationship... thing, and then he tried to, what? Take it all back?"

"Then it all went to shit. Denny was jealous because I had feelings for you. It had nothing to do with MOTH or your case. He wanted to kill you in front of me so that I would see Denny as the Alpha Male. Evidently, that didn't end well for Denny."

Liz laughed at that.

The kitchen tiles found themselves against my feet, then left again when I awoke once more on the bathroom floor.

Liz was standing above me as she said, "You have a guest."

She and Maria attempted to get me to the couch, but I wound up sitting on the floor again, leaning into the sofa like it was one big pillow. I could see the door from there as Jed took his hat off. It was a solemn and weirdly respectful gesture.

"I'm really sorry, man," he said. I checked to make sure I still had legs. Yep. So, what was he sorry about? Oh.

I reached at him, thinking he was closer than he was. Jed stepped forward as I asked, "The cops found Rayne,

372

right? I saw them, I thought."

He didn't answer. I said, "There were police officers everywhere. Hudson was behind us. Hudson knew we were there. They got Rayne after I got broken."

Jed shook his head.

"Why not?" My voice almost cracked, getting higher and more tense with every word that crawled out from between my lips.

Jed sucked in a deep breath and said, "After that kid-cop died-"

"Kells. Officer Oliver Kells."

"Yeah. After Kells died, another cop got caught as being a plant. Thing is, nothing really happened with that. Some douche-bag cop was one of them, and it was like no one fucking cared about what we were doing. It all got lost in the shuffle of shit."

"Who was it?"

"I don't know, man. Nobody tells me shit. The point is, there are others, and nobody is sure who is under the bitch's thumb. But that's why no one came to help us with the bomb squad too." Jed put his massive arms under my legs and around my shoulders to hoist me onto the couch where I belonged.

I shivered, "Why would... Why?"

"Blackmail, it sounds like. I don't know much more than that, but from what we've heard, Black has dirt on every fucking cop in the area. Probably you too, though fuck knows what, ya squeaky clean bast-"

"What do we do?"

Jed leaned back with wide eyes. He had never seen me beg before. Even with everything we'd been through, and everything he had done to me directly, Jed Dean had never seen me beg.

"I don't know, Gabe. The regular cops ain't doing shit now. She's scared them all somehow. No one wants to make a move in case no one else does. No one wants to be the target as that one guy, you know? Dude, we've been alone in this one from the get go."

Liz folded her arms and said, "A bystander effect isn't supposed to affect cops."

Maria handed me another pill when I began to wince once more, but I reached over and put the pill away, back into the orange bottle. I glanced out the window. Autumn had shoved summer away with orange leaves and a chill in the air.

"How many days have I been here?" I asked.

Jed shrugged, "You were in the hospital for like two days before they sent you away. Then we shipped you here and it's been about two and a half weeks here, I think."

After a shower with Jed's surprisingly nonchalant assistance, and a change into a clean suit, I pocketed the pills and limped on my way. None us had any idea where I was going, but I had to go somewhere, anywhere closer to finding that ever elusive closure. Back to square one.

Liz grabbed my arm, trying in vain to stop me from storming off to nowhere.

Then I was on my own bed, still fully dressed, and having no idea how long I'd been there. Everything felt knotted up and stiff, like cement had been poured into all of my organs, or a metal rod had pierced through my whole body the long way, ass to head.

Maria walked into the room and placed a lap desk on me, complete with pen and paper.

"Write a letter to your parents," she said. "Then, you can call Hudson and see if anything has changed."

I didn't quite manage that phone call. Maria put her black jacket on to mail out the finished letter for me, and managed to get me undressed, then into pajamas after checking on some wounds, all without taking her jacket or shoes back off. I had never felt so entirely loved and taken care of.

"Why?" I asked, sitting on the edge of the bed as she stood in the doorway.

"Why what?"

"You're here. I mean, I'm glad it's you. I don't want you to go. I want to know why? Why be here with me through all this?"

Maria's cheeks went pink, "Well, I love you. You're basically my best friend, sick as that is. I'm sorry if that makes things weird but-" She looked a little scared when I stood up and put a hand on either side of her face. I'm not sure what she thought I was going to do, but her shoulders went down again once I smiled.

"It's not weird," I said. "I'm just lucky."

Maria opened her jacket to reveal a soft, fuzzy lining. I put my arms around her. It was like I had been engulfed by a teddy bear. My temples stopped throbbing, I took a deep breath in through my nose, and then put my chin on her cashmere-clad shoulder. We stood like that for a moment until she put me back to bed.

She nuzzled up against my armpit for a moment in a half-hug. I didn't feel like rushing anywhere anymore. It was for the best. She left once I fell asleep.

A few days later, Dad responded with a detailed letter stating that we shouldn't tell my mom about any new information or progress in our case until it was all over. That way, if I never found Black, her heart wouldn't break all over again. Also, Dad was happy I hadn't woken up paralyzed.

I had to find Black. Even if it meant dying in the process, I'd take her with me.

CHAPTER 26
Ripping Like a Bandage

Maria and Jed showed up at my place the next morning with fancy-flavored coffee.

"Aw, thanks guys! You didn't have do all this," I was swaying a little as I said it.

Maria held my face in her hands a little harder than necessary, "We're helping you. Now sit down."

Jed asked, "Do you remember sending a text to me last night?"

I didn't. I checked my phone. I had sent only, "Kells" and nothing else.

Reading the name did something horrible in my brain. I burst into sobs as Maria guided me to a kitchen chair, and put her purse on the table.

"He was so young," I said. "You remember he talked about his brother? Does his brother know he's dead? He had family."

Maria looked at Jed, who nodded, "Yeah, he told us that right before we lost him."

"Oh," said Maria.

Jed took a seat next to me and held me close as I stammered out, "He was right there. I saw him and he was so close but I couldn't get him in time! I couldn't grab him and then he was just shredded like paper."

Maria said nothing but reached out to hold my hand.

When I whispered, "He was torn and blended. There was so much blood" Maria squeezed my hand, and Jed hugged my shoulders harder.

After a few minutes, I was feeling better, but still not quite functioning. My head felt like it was floating, full of air.

I noticed an envelope sticking out of Maria's purse

and asked, "What's that?"

"You wanna show him what you brought?" Jed asked Maria.

"No," she folded her arms. The envelope had my name on it.

Jed handed me the envelope.

After I picked it up and asked half of "What is this?" Maria snatched it from my hand.

"It's something I wrote for you months ago," she said. Her pupils shrank as though the paper in her hand was growing tentacles and blood-filled mouths.

"If it's how you felt then, I'd like to read it."

She narrowed her eyes and frowned, "Why?"

"Because if your reaction is that strong, clearly it was important. I mean, you brought it here specifically to show me."

"Yeah, but you're feeling delicate right now. I should wait until things are less," she gestured to the air in general.

"I'll read it later then, and I'll do it with a pinch of salt, okay? Just let me have it."

Begrudgingly, she handed the letter back to me. I put it in my briefcase for safekeeping.

Ripples in the window were only tricks of the light from the rain outside. I lit a candle that smelled like pumpkin pie in an effort to drown out that of my own rotting, healing flesh.

A knock at the door was Liz. Her eyes brightened with a smile at the sight of Maria.

They sat on the couch and chatted about Liz going to get groceries for Maria, while Jed and I sipped our coffee. They made a deal for Liz to pick up more tea and Maria would in turn buy pads for them both. It was a surprisingly bland conversation to listen in on, given how giddy the two looked. Of course, Liz had the kind of mouth where the corners were always curled to smile.

As soon as Liz left the apartment, Maria turned to me, arms folded.

"The Hell was that?" she said.

"What was what?"

"You got all quiet! You can talk to Liz too, you know." OH. She was kidding around. Jed hadn't said much either, but that didn't occur to me at the time.

The sound my face made was more of a snort than a laugh. "Everybody takes good care of me. I wanna return the favor but I don't want anyone to have to get injured for it." I thought for a second, "Do I have any more antibiotics?"

"Nope! You were a good boy and finished them yesterday. She sat on the couch, putting her hand where Liz had been sitting. "How are you feeling?"

"I took a pain killer this morning, but I wasn't happy about it. Also, I keep thinking I'm going to throw up in waves. I want to do something other than sit around."

Maria took a small paper ad from her purse. It was for a roller derby match.

"You wanna go? Liz plays. I haven't seen her do it yet. Race? Or is it fight?" She laughed so much louder than I'd ever heard from her before, "I don't know anything about roller derby!" Maria was the kind of person who would put on eyeliner to go to the dentist, so I was more than interested to see her at that kind of sporting event.

"Sure! You just tell me when."

"For now, I've got to go get ready for a date with Liz, and I know Jed's been wanting to go somewhere with you."

She pointed to Jed who let out a raucous, "FINALLY! Let's go. Get some shoes on." Sinister moving creatures found my eyes but were only shadows. Nothing more. I questioned if I was okay to go out, but shook it off when I put my coat and hat on.

Jed ran to his car, then leaned over and popped open the passenger side door, "Get in!"

"What is happening right now?" I asked as I buckled the seat belt.

"I wanna spend a minute with you outside of your house. I know we've been goin' through some shit."

I looked at nothing in particular in front of me, then back to him, "Thanks."

"You hungry?"

"Yeah, actually. Think there's a chicken place open now?"

Jed grinned, "Seriously. Are you pregnant? It's been like months. What's your obsession with the fried cock in your mouth?"

I laughed, "It's become my go-to comfort food. I just want something warm, I think."

"Ah. That's fair. We both could use a little comfort, eh?" He found us a roadside diner.

The air was greasy. Not that it smelled of grease, but that it felt dingy. Still, it was a quaint little joint. Green and blue, bell-shaped lamps hung over each table and the counter. The floor was clean, glittering teal tiles. The waitress was a pretty woman in her forties, and the man behind the grill was her husband, according to Jed. We took our seats at the counter, the same way we would at any bar.

"Hey, April," Jed said.

"The usual, sweetheart?"

Jed nodded to April, then pointed at the Ruben on the laminated menu she placed in front of me.

"Oh! I'll have a Ruben please," I said.

The fries were endless and covered in cheese. It was like Heaven before I effectively threw half of my iced tea onto myself.

"It goes IN your mouth," said Jed. "Jeez, and I thought I was the one with the drinking problem!" I laughed as I dabbed a pile of napkins against my chest. He smiled wide, "Wow. I'm hilarious when you're on pain killers."

I stopped laughing. Bugs. I felt insects in my skin,

but it was only the breeze from a closed and sealed window nearby.

"I'm not okay," I said.

"I know." Jed put another fist of fries into his mouth, then mumbled, "That's why we're not gonna let you be alone for a while."

Awkward plastic pretending to be lumbar support jabbed menacingly into my lower back. The squishy, yet somehow flat cushion beneath my bum fared no better. There was a thing on a shelf in front of me. I was unsure if it was a snowman or some form of Santa or what, but I hated it. Lumpy, round, tilted and red and white, with a pointed hat and beady eyes, perhaps it was meant to be an elf. I had become acutely aware of the veins in my hand and forearm in that moment. Blue and purple and strained, I was reminded of the blurry flashes of color and the pounding sea of blood inside my head as sharp water flooded my lungs... And a moment later, that event was not nearly so very close anymore.

CHAPTER 27
Darkness

Three nights later, I woke to Jed gently pushing my shoulder, "Your phone is ringing."

The number wasn't one I recognized, and I answered with a slow, "Hello?"

Rayne cleared his throat, "I am glad you are not dead. I do not like my fault in how you got hurt. I am sorry."

"You murdered Kells, but care that I nearly drowned and broke my ass when you dropped me? You understand that you murdered a cop, right? And who the Hell did you kill in the prison? No one could tell who that was because of how you bashed his damn face in!"

Jed looked ready to fight Rayne through the phone.

Rayne said, "I do not say it makes sense, but you are the one I have affection for, in my own way. The man I killed was one of Denny's muscle. His name was Rex, and he did not know he was to die, I do not think. Anyhow, Candace told me to tell you she is meeting up with Zeke and Denny somewhere, but it is a trap."

"Why are you telling me at all then?"

"Denny and Zeke will still be there. It is a trap for them too."

"I don't know what that means," I looked to Jed as he shrugged.

Rayne took a breath, "Zeke and Denny know things, and the two of you keep asking things, and Candice is hoping none of you get out alive. She is betting on a shoot-out. My suggestion is to get your police friends to take care of it."

"How did Black convince Denny to go along with this?"

"Ah. Candice had said to Denny she is handing an

off-the-books asset of her legitimate business in exchange for transport out of the country. I do not know what this legitimate business version of things would have been, but I know it has been the talk of the under-town, if you understand."

"Do you have an idea of what I'm looking for?"

"I do not think you should be the one looking. You are hurt, are you not? However, I know it would be on borrowed land. She tends to pick run down, empty places for making deals, but keeps anything important in nice big cars, trucks, whatever. It is her thing. She would have gotten something to park for it to look real."

Jed had a few vague ideas, enough for us to ride around and see what we could find. I took the pain pills from his hand, and got myself dressed for a drive, complete with side arm.

Once on the road, I called Hudson to let him know the situation, and his response was quick, "You call me for back up if you find anything, but it sounds like Rayne wasn't expecting you to go at all. I'm guessing this is a wild goose chase. You give me that number he called from. I'll see if I can track our Mad Bomber down." I said my thank yous and hung up before we continued driving.

We stopped for snacks a while later, so I called Hudson to find that the number Rayne called from had already been disconnected. We got back in the car for another stretch of time.

We had gotten to empty land far from any kind of city. Headlights reflected off day glow signs to nowhere in the night.

I rolled my head back, "It's getting late. Would anyone even be around now? Nothing good ever happens after 2:30 in the morning."

Jed pointed out in front of us, "That's a $75,000 RV parked in front of a barn that should be set on fire."

"Our best bet yet."

We parked the car a few blocks away, and got out to slowly creep toward the RV. Beyond it was a metal storage unit. We squatted down to take in any sounds we could, then peeped a look at Denny yelling at Zeke inside the RV.

Denny was standing, gesturing wildly with his right arm, the left in a sling. I remembered then that he was shot in his left shoulder before hiding behind the ill-fated crates. He had no more bandages covering his face, but his left ear was gone, as was chunks of hair, and from the look of him, so was the use of his left eye. It was still sitting in its socket, but the flesh that had once been two separate eyelids had welded themselves mostly together. If he could see out that eye, it was through a pin hole.

We watched him remove the sling as though he was making an angry point to Zeke. His arm hung down, clearly unable to be lifted before Zeke hurriedly grabbed the sling and put it back on Denny's body, crying and begging as he did so.

We ducked back down so I could call Hudson but there was no service. Not even for emergency calls. A complete dead zone. I showed Jed, who nodded in response before I put my phone back into my jacket, happy to feel my pocket flashlight still there. It was a small comfort, considering it wouldn't help me in a fight, and didn't have much battery left, but I was clinging to anything by then.

Jed squinted like an Old West cowboy, "Spin me around three times and shove. Whoever I shoot, oh well." It was nice to know his personality was still intact, despite the obvious emotional trauma we'd survived by then.

"I don't know. This feels like the last tap before a shatter. Something isn't right." Then we heard the sickening crack to my left, followed by the sound not unlike a fizzy soda crackling open. The noxious flume enveloped us. I imaged myself getting up, grabbing Jed's arm, and the two of us sprinting off together. I wanted to do that. I willed myself to stand, but we hit the ground instead.

We awoke to darkness. The air was cold with dizzying
odors of old oil and standing water. I stood up, feeling a
metal floor beneath me. This wasn't the barn. Where were
we? I pat myself down to see what I still had on me. No
gun, but they'd left the flashlight. Almost kind of them. I
heard Jed's familiar gait as he crept by me, and I wondered
why they hadn't killed us. I clicked on the flashlight to see
him lightly drag his hands against the wall that had a large
knob-less door, looking for anything strange. The metal slab
remained unyielding.

"There's rust here, toward the bottom," said Jed
before he began to smash his fist against the abrasive area.
"Those dinky flashlights don't have much juice, so keep it
off for as much as we can, yeah?" I concurred. In the
darkness, I could only hear the thuds and strange echoing
vibration of the walls from the impact. Jed groped the
flashlight away from me, and turned it on again to inspect
his now scrapped up hand. "Didn't work," said Jed as he
clicked the flashlight off and handed it back. My head was
still swimming from whatever that gas had been. I squeezed
my eyes tight shut to remind myself that it was only
darkness and not blindness.

It was difficult to tell how much more time had
passed, but we had each already found a designated corner to
pee in. A grating, repetitive noise gnawed at the back of my
head the way a wild animal might rip at a newly found piece
of meat. I wondered how long I had before I went mad like
a starved dog. I fondled my coat pocket for my pills, but
someone must have taken them with the gun. I could have
used about five. I decided it was for the best. I had to keep

my wits about me anyway.

"How you doin' over there, Jed?"

"I'm thinking. Thinkin' about getting out of here, thinkin' about how hard it is not drinking, and thinking myself to death."

"I realize we're in a box, but is there anything I can do?"

"You've been helping. So has Chloe. I just want her to stop shoving brochures for weird groups at me and like, reminding me that I'm an alcoholic even when I ain't doing anything, you know? There's a pressure at the back of my very soul, pushing it out and over my ribs every time she talks about it." That didn't sound healthy, but I wasn't about to question it then and there. It was a weird time for him to bring it up, and a weirder time for me to play counselor.

After a moment, I couldn't see it in the blackness but I knew the familiar rapid drumming of Jed's fingers when his eyes went wide, "Oh shit. Sober-me sounds like every-fucking-day you. I hate this."

He wasn't wrong.

A throbbing in my foot reminded me that it at least still had feeling. Every now and then I'd smell something strange like plastic burning, or vanilla, and with no knowledge of from whence or from whom it came, I would question if I was having some sort of a stroke. My tailbone felt like it was never going to heal, but that was probably my own fault. Lines danced across my otherwise blackened vision like vines, like snakes, like worms, like maggots. Where was I? Right.

"You okay?" I heard Jed ask.

"No," I said, "I wear a mask. It is cheap and not very convincing. Still, no one ever questions it. Maybe they're too embarrassed to do so. Embarrassed for me and what they feel about me."

I heard him pull up a crate-seat as I continued to softly rant, "No one ever thinks to peek behind the mask.

No one would ever want to. I figure, so long as I project this sense of successful, punk-detective bachelor, I'm protected. The moment my guard goes down, people can see the botched, haphazardly stitched together sham I really am. So, they leave the mask on, knowing that what lies beneath is so much worse." After a beat, I sat on the floor and said, "Except you. You know me."

"Yeah," said Jed. Okay, so now we both played counselor.

We heard a familiar hiss, and then nothing.

When I awoke, I couldn't hear Jed. I flicked on the light, and found that I was alone. I clicked the flashlight off again, leaving me alone to hyperventilate in darkness.

Jed must have been knocked out, though he didn't remember that happening. All he knew was that he had a headache, and he appeared to be in a tall, but otherwise small container. Jed could slouch, but not enough to really put his legs out. Strangely shaped shadows formed from a tiny bit of light draining in from above. He looked up to see holes, as though he was a rodent being kept for later.

He heard Denny clearly yell, "Just remember who set this up for you. Be sure Gekman hears this bitch scream."

"Thank you," said Zeke.

Jed spoke up, "You two are partners then? Is that what you think? You're just his goon. After he gets whatever the fuck he wants from Gekman, he's gonna drop you, Zeke."

"You don't know what you're talking about. I'm the last man standing!"

"Denny is! Not you! He's gonna leave you out to

dry! You that fucking dense?"

Jed couldn't tell if Denny had walked away or if he was still nearby, but he could hear Zeke mumbling above him, "Gonna set you on fire, you worthless piece of shit."

Liquid began pouring in through those holes, a glopping sound slapping against the floor, his shoulders, too close to his face. The smell, that acrid chemical skunk-stink of gasoline. Panicked, Jed slammed the whole of his body weight to smash against the side, desperate to knock whatever container he was in over, but it wouldn't budge.

"What the fuck!?" Jed was scared more than he was furious, but anger was easier to contend with in such a situation.

"You blew up my house, Jed." Zeke's voice bounced off the metal walls, thundering into Jed's ear drums.

"You hit our car and ran away like a fucking coward! After what you did to Darcy, you deserve everything I've done to you and more, you little shit!" Jed spat out the bit of gasoline that had seeped between his lips, "Do you even know what you did?"

Zeke swatted at an imaginary fly in front of his face, "You think I don't remember her face? I watched her fly out in the rearview mirror."

"So, you run unless Denny tells you to stay? Is that what you're saying?"

"There was nothing I could do! I knew she was dead, so I fucking ran."

"Naw! She's alive, dipshit!"

"LIAR!"

"Why don't I try to break out, like in the movies?" I asked myself like a lunatic. I answered, "I have no weapons."

I heard Jed's muffled screaming. I turned the flashlight on again and trailed the beam over the now familiar boxes, "Bullshit. I just gotta put them together like a puzzle. Like Jed would do. God. They'll blast us to Hell the moment I try anything. I don't care."

I put my ear up against the wall of the storage unit, "There will be guards," I whispered, and with a smile, I said, "I'll come out roaring."

I needed both of my hands, so with a grimace, the flashlight went into my mouth. I made quick work of dragging and rearranging some crates against each other, between the wall of the unit and my body. I then sat on the floor once I was convinced that I could easily scrunch up, a little crunched between those crates and the one directly in front of me, braced by the other side of the unit. Then, I kicked. I kicked again. I twisted my ankle and was too high on adrenaline to care as I drove my foot into the crate, finally forcing two of the planks to shatter with a satisfying splinter. The newly sharpened wood sliced into my hand as I plunged both of my arms into the crate, rummaging around to find something, anything to help me.

Blankets. The crate was full of soft, comforting, fleece. An unhinged laugh broke through my shock, but I was still determined. I stumbled my way back to the possible front of the storage unit. Where was that rust? Could I kick through? I'd have no feet left then.

The flashlight wasn't doing me much good in my mouth, too close to see anything, so I put it in my pocket. I climbed enough to grope around the edge, and found how the storage locker door was attached. It was a roll down front from tracks on the ceiling like garage doors. These units were not built to take much more weight than the door itself. I piled up the crates, wobbling, but sturdy enough to climb. Once high enough, I grabbed a railing and jumped down. Light cascaded inward from the wound that was once the storage unit door, as my skin peeled just a little too far back on my palms, my own wound too deep, too slick with blood. The track fell down, slamming onto my upper back, and my landing on the ground of the unit was awkward on my already twisted ankle.

Success none the less! I had torn the top of the door away from the opening, and was able to crawl over the remaining metal panels to the outside, slicing my suit and a little flesh as I went. Whatever. I was fine.

I patted myself off as best as I could among the sticky viscera of my own crimson mash, then looked up to see my surroundings. I was in a kind of wooden-box alleyway under a makeshift metal ceiling leading to the rest of the interior of the dilapidated barn.

Denny was standing before me, as he had just turned the corner to see what all the noise was about. He stood still with the one eye that-could-be-wide and the eyebrow-that-could-look-angry doing so, watching the gruesome red and orange tie-dye streaming down in front of me, trying to piece together how I got out the way I had.

I launched from my good foot to lunge forward, grabbing Denny's splint, pulled down hard, and kneed him in the nose as he came down. His still screwed up arm flopped down to his side, and I effectively climbed over him, scrambled over his head and shoulders, pushing his body behind me as I went.

He shrieked as he smooshed into the ground, and Jed screamed from somewhere in front of me, and Zeke was sitting on what looked like a mini silo up ahead. I took the small flashlight from my pocket, and chucked it at Zeke's head. He flailed about a bit like a penguin before slipping off of his perch, missing the ladder up.

Denny ran in from behind me, blood pouring from his nose, and I dashed around the room-within-a-room as though I was wearing socks on smooth tile. I found a door held shut by an easily lifted bar. Jed collapsed out of it, soaked and stinky.

Denny didn't spend any time nursing Zeke's broken ankle, despite Zeke's wailing. We all stopped short when we heard the humming sound from outside. The exterior low crack and loud snap of a giant locking mechanism was frightening enough by itself, made worse when we realized what wall the machine would be crashing through.

Jed would have cocked his gun had he had one, instead he shot me a knowing look as he said, "Gekman, do me a favor, you blue haired, lovable tart."

"Yeah, Jed?"

"Remember the Rusty Clam."

"We do the same thing now, huh?"

"We've gotta."

I nodded in response. And so, we ran right back into the storage unit. Jed snatched Zeke up in a fireman's carry, bringing him along for the ride. We ran away, desperate to hide and hopeful we wouldn't be crushed as the barn came crashing down. None of us cared about Denny.

Zeke panted on the metal floor, "Why would you save me?"

"I don't know." Jed shrugged, "Eh. I realized you're a fuck up like me. We still ain't friends though."

We could see two things from the bloody opening of the storage unit. First, that I should be damn thankful I got that tetanus booster shot and second, that the monstrosity coming in had a drill on the front. Was it Rayne, back to claim his stake? Who else had a digging machine that might know where we were?

As it pierced the wooden wall, the building splintered. Shards of wood fell from the roof, tossing chunks and pieces of ceiling, walls, and support beams down into the stomach of the barn. Denny let out a howl from wherever he still was beyond the dust.

This machine was different than any we'd seen before, bigger, like a dark and armored bus. For now, it seemed the machine was lodged in enough to act as a makeshift support wall, keeping the whole barn from crashing down.

A bright orange flash of light sliced through the metal of our hiding place, making a much larger opening. Chloe stood on the other side when the door fell, holding what looked like a large welding torch. Beyond her, we saw the machine had an open sliding door in the side, and Maria was taking her time getting out. She was dwarfed by the massive vehicle they had left. Close behind them was Darcy in an interesting chair that let out its own ramp and track, like the wheels of a tank combined with a roller coaster. Once she reached the floor, it retracted back into her chair.

Zeke sat up as much as he could muster to get a better look at the three women moving in our direction. He recognized Chloe and Maria immediately, but then there was that third member of their party.

"Who's the chick in the chair? Wait," His eyes focused in stark confusion, fear, and joy, as though seeing the face of a god, "It's you. You're alive?" Darcy's chair made a whirring noise as it lifted up and forward into the storage unit.

Bullets rang out from where Denny was otherwise pinned by a beam. He shot three times before he ran out of bullets with no damage done. The rest of us went about our conversations.

"I told you!" said Jed to Zeke.

Zeke responded, "I should have set you on fire when I had the chance!"

Darcy asked me, "Should I know what's going on?"

I replied with a casual point, "That's Zeke. I'm sure Jed's told you about him, and now he's tried to kill my best friend."

"I'll grant you that, but they're both acting like children, but now is not the time." Darcy crossed her arms and looked to Zeke, "So you were the driver then? Can Jed let this go now? The building is coming down, and we need to go right now."

Zeke shook his head, "…but I did this to you! I crippled you!"

"No. I'm fine. I don't know you, I haven't thought about you, and you don't matter to me."

In a sweet tone, she ended the subject with, "I've moved on, and now I need you two to do the same, okay? Let's go!" Zeke and Jed looked at each other but said nothing.

Chloe pipped up, "Good thing we got here to sort all

this nonsense out, huh?"

"How?" Jed's left eye went wide while his right lower lid tried to twitch closed as he looked at Chloe but pointed at Darcy, who began to pull him toward the machine.

Maria responded flatly, "We were all worried about you, and Gabe had already coughed up Chloe's number for Darcy's new ride. We figured she was part of the team now."

Chloe let out a gasp, "I asked you not to tell him!"

Maria pointed at Darcy, "She's physically here. In front of him. Like, he knows."

Jed wanted everyone to focus as he ran back to heave Zeke over his shoulder again, "What the fuck ever! How'd you find us?"

"I told you," said Darcy as the rest of us ran to catch up. "I had Chloe put a tracker on your car, and then she gave me fancy new robot stuff for my chair."

Jed, for perhaps the first time in his life, was dumbfounded.

Denny wailed from among the rubble, "Zeke, you idiot! Do something! Help me!"

Zeke screamed, "No! No, I did everything for you. For years, I've been your goddamn lap dog and you've treated me like shit for it! You let me be homeless. You let me be miserable, and you never even asked if I was okay. You knew what was going on with me, but only because I told you, and even then, you didn't care." Jed lowed Zeke into Maria's arms, who helped him scoot the rest of the way into the vehicle.

The door closed once we were all inside. Zeke looked around until he found a round window. He struggled, obviously trying to open it before Chloe pushed a button on her way to the driver's cabin.

The window opened, and Zeke leaned his head out, "Fuck you! I loved you, and got NOTHING in return!" He then gestured wildly with a grabbing motion in my direction,

"You're looking for Candice, right? Or whatever the fuck she's calling herself now."

He responded to Denny's angry shriek with, "I'm gonna tell them!"

I took my phone out to type out what he was screaming.

Once we got the address, Zeke calmed down, looking down at his sideways foot, "She's expecting us to meet her to tell her you're dead. Be there instead." I couldn't help but smile in my relief as I sent the text to Hudson, which would automatically send whenever we stumbled back into an area with reception.

We drove out, leaving a collapsed barn in our wake.

"Hey Chloe," I walked up to her like one would walk through any normal moving bus, "How did you know we wouldn't get crushed too?"

"Oh, honestly I wasn't even thinking about it."

I laughed, but she didn't.

Chapter 28
Let Go

It didn't take long before Hudson was giving me a nod as he and a small handful of firefighters, EMTs, and police officers passed us walking out. Zeke was on a stretcher laughing to himself. The girls left in the machine. Jed and I found his car. As I turned my head back toward the road, I swooped to grab Hudson's arm.

"No one has checked the RV, right?"

"We will. Go check out your leg, Gekman. You're limping. ...And you're bleeding from everywhere."

I said nothing.

"You're not going to let this go, huh?" Hudson signaled to the beautiful Amazonian cop I'd met once before, and then to the door of the RV. Still without introducing herself, she jimmied it open and let me go on inside.

We looked around a bit before I started to get dizzy.

"When's the last time you ate anything? Seems to me you've just been through Hell," she was right, but I didn't want to hear it. Still, I took my leave, using the hospital as an excuse. Not for me, of course. Well, maybe I could've used a checkup too.

Maria, Liz, and Chloe met us at the hospital. Maria had changed out of the soot covered black dress she had worn to the barn, and was wearing a dress that was green, then blue, then purple on the end, with little cherry blossoms on pale branches. This was odd, though nice to see some color in her life. Her hair, dark waves cascading down by her cheeks. Her dark eyes hid beneath heavy eyelids lined in black. Her skin was soft and sun-touched. When she laughed, her brown eyes held glimmering gold. Sure, sometimes her smile was still because of something I did, but her real smile was reserved for Liz. Liz was wearing pink shorts and a black top she had borrowed from Maria's closet.

They pressed their noses together like they were posing for a greeting card. I could feel her breath on my face when Maria slammed into me for a hug. My friend.

Jed pulled Chloe in, "I missed you," he said, holding her in his arms.

"I don't believe you," she answered plainly, not quite smiling, "it's only been like a couple hours, but okay."

"You don't believe that I missed you?" I was appalled that he had to say it. What horrible thing had I inadvertently taught him?

"You really have changed over a few months, huh?" she kissed him and smiled.

Maria handed us their purses and said, "Love is effortless. Relationships take effort."

Jed shrugged, then made Chloe laugh with, "It's only so long you can go, pulling a heavy thing like you and me alone. I'll try even harder."

"Oh, Honey. Be here with me. That's all I need."

Hudson met us as we were exiting the hospital grounds.

"You missed visiting hours," I said.

He got straight to the point, "We went to where Zeke told us to go, but Black was nowhere to be found. Either he was wrong, or he lied to you."

"Or," said Jed, "she knew we were coming because Denny snitched."

Hudson ignored Jed, "We still have Rayne. He's more likely

to know where Black is, right? I know he's been a help, but we've still got to put him back where he belongs, and we can question him then. He's clearly been calling you from a burner phone, and I don't know where he's gone. Maybe you'll have more luck."

"You're right that we won't find Black without him," I said. "Going in with guns blazing will just chase him farther into hiding though."

"Either way, we want you to come with us to get Rayne. He might listen to you. You figure out where he might be, and then we'll follow your lead."

"May I come?" asked Maria.

Hudson made a face like a fly had just landed on his nose, "Why would you-"

She stepped forward, "I knew him! Also, I think I know where to find him."

Maria explained about her time with Moth, the battle to get out of it, and the struggle she knew Rayne had as well.

Hudson had a glazed-over look in his eyes, "Well then, I suppose you should come."

Maria turned to Chloe, "Will you take Liz home?"

Liz frowned, "You're about to go talk to a serial killer and I'm supposed to just leave?"

"I'm not lying about where I'm going. I want to keep you safe."

"I want you to be safe too," tears began welling up in Liz's eyes. She was right to be afraid. Maria was always right to be afraid for me too.

They kissed, and Liz admitted defeat, leaving with Chloe.

CHAPTER 29
The Oubliette

Barrels stacked precariously on their sides acted as walls in the old distillery. Cold and damp, the place smelled of rot more than fine wine. Rayne bent his massive self down enough to strike a match and hold his hand cupped behind a lone candle placed upon a crate. He continued to cup his left hand around the flame as he shook the match quiet, as though a gust of wind would otherwise come and whisk the fire away. There was no such breeze in his seclusion. He lifted a familiar panel, revealing stairs into darkness, and took the candle with him into the underbelly of the vineyard.

It was miles away in a direction I'd never thought to travel before. The remaining trees were bare, the trellises which once supported vines were empty, the ground was the color of cold death. Jed and I stepped out of our car first, followed by a hesitant Maria.

We heard a noise come from inside. Maria turned and so I turned. Hudson and two other cops had guns drawn until I held up my hand to stay their fire. I didn't have that kind of power, but then Jed glared until the guns were lowered. Rayne came out of his hiding place and stood silently in the doorway, watching. No threats, no weapons, looking at us with half curiosity and half jealousy. Then he turned and walked back inside. At first, I assumed it was because we had the place surrounded, but no. It was something else. Maria, Jed, and I followed him.

I asked Maria, "How did you know he'd be here?"

"This distillery is important to him. I've told you before, it was run by someone special in his life, and it was the only safe place he ever mentioned. It was just a guess that this is where he has left."

"Good guess."

Rayne found himself defeated, kneeling on the floor inside a small building that had been used as a restaurant once upon a time. There had been parties here, and wine tastings. Empty chairs sat upside down on the counter tops. Rayne stayed on the floor.

His gaze was not directed towards me. He looked at Maria, and he did so with the kindest eyes I had ever seen. He reached up towards her face as she slowly walked towards him. Then he dropped his hands down together, as though shackled.

"Maria!" He smiled, then barely above a whisper said, "You look like her, you know."

I didn't know exactly who he meant, other than it must have been whoever ran this vineyard years prior. I wondered if Maria knew.

She knelt down, gingerly resting her body to sit on a short box. She pulled Rayne's shoulders towards her without fear and without a second thought. He was afraid to put his hands on her at first, his mouth hidden by her shoulder, his eyes wide, as if waiting for a knife to plunge into his back. He didn't look at me. He wasn't afraid of what I may think, but of what she might think. He was terrified that she would deem his movement too much and that she would run away or maybe disintegrate beneath his fingers.

Maria didn't move away. She faced him with a kind smile, and so he gently rested his hands on her waist, which meant most of her back as well. His hands were massive on her body.

A sinking feeling like something curdling within my intestines made me lean against a wall and grab a toothpick. I tried my best to keep my cool. I looked to Jed and found him with folded arms and a frown. Neither of us were happy about this. Hudson was in a similar position outside, ready to come running at my call.

Rayne closed his eyes tightly as she held him in her arms. "I'm not her though," said Maria.

"I know. I am sorry." He sniffed and eyed me angrily, gently but possessively digging his fingers around Maria's shoulder.

Rayne lifted his head with tears streaming down his cheeks as he said to me, "You want Candice? You can have her. I do not care. I do not care anymore. Give me something to write with, and I will tell you what you need." I handed him my notebook and a pen. Without hesitation, he gave us what we wanted. Black was somewhere closer to Cornsbrook, last he knew. He had the address where she was staying.

Maria gave me a nod to go on as she clung to his arm, which was about the same size as her entire everything. It didn't feel right leaving her like that, but she had the look of not giving me another choice.

I pulled Jed along behind me. We could hear Maria say softly, "Tell me your story. Please. Tell me about her and whatever happened to you." She pet his head and he slumped down even farther until his monumental head was in her lap.

Hudson eyed me as I walked toward the cars, "What happened? Everything okay?"

I tore out the paper with the address and handed it to him, "Rayne says this is where Black is. Let's send someone in there for Rayne's arrest, but do it gently. Don't have anybody rile him up. I think he'll go willingly. Meanwhile, we can go get Black."

Hudson pat me on the back, "I'm gonna go see if she's there. I've got people to come with me. You are going to go eat and sleep. You look like you're dying."

"Thanks. Look, this thing is almost done. Let's just go. I can do the stake out for Black."

"Kiddo, I've stuck my neck out for you every damn day for a year now. You can keep your damn foot elevated and wait for my call. I won't finish this without you. I owe you that much, but you need to take a damn break. You owe *me* that."

CHAPTER 30
Of Tying Up Loose Ends

The next day, Hudson texted an address to me with a fuzzy picture of a woman at a distance. It was enough to know that Rayne had told the truth.

"We got her," said the text.

Jed had never left my side, so we were quick to be ready to go.

"You need your gun," said Jed.

"Why? It's over. No more Old West shoot outs." I started to walk away, "We're just going with the real cops to see it end. That's all."

He grabbed my arm, turned me around, and placed the glock in my hand, "Just in case."

I was surprised to see such bright daylight given how late in the afternoon it was.

I had second and third thoughts in the car including, "They're booking her now, and it'll take a while for us to get there. Why even have us go? They'll be gone, right? She'll be shipped off to wherever already."

Jed said, "Nah. She's gonna put up a big fight. Takes a while to get a normal person booked anyway. Even if they already got her in the car, there'll be somebody there to tell us where she's being held. Hudson knows you want a goodbye-spit-in-her-face."

He wasn't wrong.

We pulled up behind Hudson's car, but no one was in that vehicle. No one was in any of the nearby police vehicles either. Jed tumbled over himself getting out of the car, and I followed in a slight panic myself.

I wished I had stronger eyesight, some way of zooming in as we scrutinized rooftops from afar, and glanced down streets. The air was wet and cold.

He heard the tussle first, and pointed to his ear before gesturing in the direction we'd need to move. I double checked that my gun was on me as we headed to the alleyway in question.

I peeked beyond a wall to find Candice with two police officers and Hudson himself. One officer, the woman I'd met twice, had a gun trained on Black. Another was on the ground, holding his bleeding stomach shut. A stab wound. Candice Black smiled with her hand around the hilt of a blade, holding that blade at Hudson's throat. He was on his knees on the ground, beaten. His head held up by her other hand entangled in his sparse hair.

The officer still standing started shouting commands, conveniently keeping Black's attention away from my direction. Hudson grimaced against the knife. I stopped thinking and ran. There was yelling, downright screaming. I didn't know if it was at me or her. I kept expecting gunshots, or for Black to spot me and react, but she was listening patiently to the shouting from now both police officers.

I kept to the wall as I dashed down and around, then hit her hard from the side, my shoulder cracked against ribs. Something broke. I could hear it. She dropped her hand away from Hudson's throat to swing the knife in my direction. He gasped. I used my forearm to deflect her wrist, then kicked out. She fell down with a thud and an audible exhale of pain.

I realized that my perception of the slow structure of those events was a trick of my adrenaline-soaked brain. What felt like minutes to me was probably only a couple of seconds, which explained the shocked expression on everyone else's faces. It took a moment before one came over to help Hudson to his feet. He had a nick on his chin, but he had probably done worse shaving. The knife lay on the ground. My eyes trailed from the blade to where Black had been. She was gone.

"Up there!" said Hudson, pointing to a ladder to the roof. I saw Black's foot disappear. The roof again? What was with this lady and heights?

We left the three officers as Jed and I made our ways up the ladder. Black wasn't moving particularly fast anymore. We watched her trip on a drainage hole before collapsing.

There she was. The monster that I had built up somehow looked so small in the flesh. Like a vicious dog who had gotten neutered a moment prior. Candice Black. She rolled onto her back with one leg bent, leaning on her elbows in order to prop herself up. The barrel of the gun glistened as I pointed it towards her smiling face. Would it be worse to let her rot in prison? Would she get out of the most secure penitentiary the way Rayne had?

"You little shit," she started, as though she were the one standing with the gun, "you are so meaningless. You know nothing. You are nothing. I've been following you. It's been years, hasn't it? I've seen it. You've busted your ass trying to finish this all, and I can't figure out why. No one even hired you for anything about my company."

"You killed my little sister."

She looked shocked. "I did what?" Then, roaring laughter splintered with, "I'm sorry... Haha! Did you think I'd remember that? Did you think she mattered too? Just like her big shot brother, right?" She sneered as she said, "Was this whole thing so you could stare me down like a big man and have me apologize before you final-"

The shot was not nearly as loud as I had imagined it would be. The act wasn't satisfying. I just wanted silence. Her voice was piercing and painful and I wanted her to shut up. It was too late to choose another path now. The back of her head resembled some kind of mushed up pizza.

Jed came over to me. I didn't even notice him there at first. I hadn't moved. He must've wondered if I had gone catatonic. He put a hand on my arm and forced me to lower

403

the weapon.

"It's over Gabe," he said quietly. I began to shake all over. Violently. I could feel my mouth turn into a horrible grimace. I thought everything in my head would explode. Jed took me into his arms and didn't say a word or even joke as he let me bawl like a damn child into his shoulder. I was hysterical. Completely fallen into god-knows-what. Was it really over? Could I have my sister back now? Where was Abby?

Jed and I kind of crumpled to the ground together. Out of the corner of my eye, I could see her blood-soaked hair stuck to the pavement, and it gave me quick bursts of comfort between the disgust. I imagined her getting back up, missing a chunk of her face. I kept imagining it, like a silent short film on a loop. And yet... And yet, I was so relieved that I could call it done. Jed noticed me looking in that direction and moved his arm to force my face into his armpit. I was thankful for that. If nothing else, I was embarrassed that Jed had seen me like this. I was sure he'd use it later, and I would have deserved that. In truth, he would never speak of it again.

Maria stopped by to visit with Rayne, and let him know what had happened. He was allowed such a thing after the officers were able to take him without a struggle. Then she met up with Jed and me at the station, with Liz. After all the paperwork had been filed, it was Liz who took me home. She didn't entirely understand what had happened until much later. She only knew that I needed someone, and that was enough of an explanation. The ride was silent, but she put a hand on my leg as we drove. My leg was so cold whenever she had to take it away to change gears.

Epilogue
Complete-Circuit

Home felt strange. I could barely feel the chair
beneath me as I sank into its purple upholstery. I decided
then was the time to call my parents to give them the news.
I faked an upbeat demeanor. It was better that way. It took a
few hours on the phone, with Maria on one side of me,
sitting on the arm of the chair, and Jed occasionally standing
to put a hand on my shoulder, but I told my parents
absolutely everything. On speaker, it was hard to tell if my
mom was sobbing out of grief, or crying for joy.

I heard her whisper, "I should have seen what was
happening."

I told her, "None of it was your fault."

My father said, "Listen, we're glad this whole story
is finally over, but next case you go on, you gotta tell me
when you get hurt. You were writing to me this whole time,
and you never said a damn thing about any of your injuries.
You okay now?" He was laughing, but I recognized it as a
flabbergasted kind of laugh.

He had a point, but I said, "If I told you every time I
busted my leg, or dislocated a shoulder or whatever, you'd
be flying down here once a week. I'd feel bad and want to
pay for your flight, and I'd be broke within a year." That got
a good laugh out of all of us.

"All right, all right," said Dad.

"Gabe, how are you feeling?" asked Mom. "I don't
mean physically. You've been through so much, Honey.
Are you okay?"

I took a breath, "It isn't better yet. I keep thinking
the other shoe is gonna drop, even though a whole damn
load of shoes has already fallen on top of me. I'm still
scared, but of nothing. Like some bit of adrenaline refuses
to go away. But, having said all that, I feel like it will be

okay, you know? I have hope for arguably the first time since childhood."

Jed piped in, "Maria and I take care of Gabe. Don't worry. We'll get him to therapy."

I didn't argue. My mom giggled and my father said, "Maria? She still puts up with you, huh? Well, thank God!"

Not exactly how it went down, but close enough. Yeah. Thanks Dad.

Liz smiled knowingly. I wished that my parents could've seen it. I could have had them on video chat, but then they would have seen my pitiful face as well.

Everyone cleared out, leaving me to my own thoughts. I opened my old black leather briefcase and took out the "Morning Meditation" CD from Jed. I sat on my living room floor on a pale green-cased pillow and listened to the first track on the CD.

My deep breaths followed the instructor on the disc. A peaceful, empty head followed, if only for a moment. I sat up as tall as I could, like a string was pulling the crown of my head upward, out through the ceiling. Started with breathing. In through the nose, deep, deep, deep, then slowly out. Raised my head and chest with each breath in, like the air was inflating, pushing and pulling my neck and face upward. Then I let go, like the lady on the recording told me, and slowly dropped my head, pacing myself when arching my back like a cat, to then do it all again. It worked for a moment. I used my journal to catalogue some easy breathing I could do on the road, sans recording, deciding I would actually do these exercises. I had such high hopes for myself. I wouldn't be able to say how long the recording was, but it was long enough to feel like I had taken a good nap.

I went back into the briefcase and found Maria's letter.

A week later was Abby's birthday. My parents decided to come down and make a big party of it for me, as a way to finally have that closure I had been begging for. It was my parents, Jed, his dad, Chloe, Maria, Liz, and me. My dad didn't think it was appropriate, but like my goofball mother before me had put a green and purple party hat on us at every birthday, I put one on my sister's urn.

Maria stepped up to be by me. We had performed our lives together and for once, everything was okay. I felt lighter.

I took her letter from my pocket, "I haven't read it yet. I thought you might want to be here when I did."

Maria took my hand and we went outside to the porch.

Most of the letter was about good times and wonderful memories. Some of it was about how proud she was of the work I did. The end was different. It read:

"Gabe, I wish you understood how you felt. I wish you could pin point it and not allow yourself to be consumed by fear. Loving you with everything I had left me with nothing for myself. You left me empty because you could not find the time to truly express how you said you felt. Still, I want you to know something very important. Yes, I am disappointed. I feel like I missed out on something for absolutely no reason. You assumed so much while I put you on a pedestal just in case you might one day live up to the image I had of you.

"...And I forgive you. I forgive you for not being who I thought you were. That wasn't your fault. It was mine. I put you there. I'm sorry I couldn't be whatever it was you needed me to be, and I'm glad that you know I deserve better. I'm still angry. I still love you. It may only be friendship now, but it is still a kind of love. Even if you never think of me again, I want to hold onto this. I want to keep this tiny love safe and sound, because it is so very precious and rare. I hope one day you can see how special

it is. Until then, this is all we are, and that's okay. I want
you to know that it is okay.

"I want you to know that I am not okay, but it isn't all
your fault. Part of it might be. I miss you. I will miss you,
I'm sure. But, while I am not okay, I know I will be. This is
not worth dying over. I have the want to save myself. I
wanted you to save me. Maybe, in a sense, you did. I hope
one day you do understand, even if it isn't for me. You
deserve real love. When you have it in front of you again, I
hope you let yourself experience it. Opening up to this will
make all the difference.

"-Maria"

I looked at Maria and tried to really see her.

I folded the letter up and stuck it in my pocket, "I'm
keeping this, because I want a reminder of what I could lose
if I screw this up for real. We are friends, and I love you."
We hugged for a while and wordlessly accepted each other.

Jed came outside and wrapped his arms around us
both.

Chloe and Liz got stuck listening to Jed tell his
version of the Rusty Clam story when Maria and I decided
to take a walk. We wandered down the road to a small
creek. A wise, old building stood nearby, prime for leaning
on as we watched the colors of the sunset. It was the kind of
scene you see in movies, not the kind that I'd ever
experienced and certainly not the kind that had ever been
real to me before then.

This period of our lives was a roller coaster. I hate
roller coasters. From a distance, they're very exciting, and
in theory very interesting… But my head starts to hurt, and
my neck has whiplash from the acceleration alone, and I
never fit right in the seat of the car. I can't even enjoy the
view while ascending because I'm sitting there in terrified
anticipation for that drop, on this ride I didn't even want to
go on in the first place. Floating nausea. But… This piece

of time was also the rest of the theme park. The cotton candy good moments, the whirling rides that made me thankful for a ticket, the beautiful sights, sounds, company- none of this was lost among that big drop.

I tried my hardest not to get sucked back into that line, waiting for that elevated curve. Before I knew it, the park was closing. It was time to go. I know I did absolutely everything I set out to do, and more. I know that.

Yet even after leaving, I'd hear the click, click, click inside my head like a cold, mechanical heartbeat that wasn't mine. Jed reminded me that we didn't have another ticket for that ride. Maria reminded me that I never needed to buy one.

We could go to other parks. We could have other adventures, and we would. I knew that. I also knew how hard it would be to move past that air time, and forget that feeling in my stomach when we crested over the hill-

The Drop.

My friends, my family, and I sat in that bench seat together, and I thought of what it was like to lose someone. Then, I remembered how nice it was to have someone. These particular someones.

And then? The ride slows down... Completes the circuit, and stops. We all leave the park together, headed for a better ride in the year ahead.

www.ingramcontent.com/pod-product-compliance
Lightning Source LLC
Chambersburg PA
CBHW072004110726
47910CB00005B/1656